ACROSS
THE
RIVER

ACROSS
THE
RIVER

A MYSTERY

C. SOLIMINI

This book is a work of fiction. Names, characters, places and incidents either are the product of the author's imagination or are used fictitiously, and any resemblance to any actual persons (living or dead), business establishments, events or locales is entirely coincidental and not intended by the author.

Published by
Deadly Ink Press
PO Box 6235, Parsippany, NJ 07054
www.deadlyink.com

ISBN: 9780978744229

Library of Congress Control Number: 2008926958

First Edition, June 2008

Book jacket photo by Chris Lupetti
Cover design concept by Rebecca A. Kandel
Cover design by Cheryl Bochniewicz

Excerpt from "God Bless the Child," written by Billie Holiday and Arthur Herzog, Jr., used by permission of Edward B. Marks Music Company.

Excerpt from "Whatever Gets You Through The Night" by Carson Whitsett, Dan Penn and Hoy Lindsey. (High Horse Music/BMI; Dan Penn Music/BMI; Hoy Lindsey Music/BMI). Used with permission.

FOR
STEVEN,
WHO CAN'T BE KILLED
BY ORDINARY WEAPONS,
AND
MERYL,
MY TEN-YEARS-YOUNGER TWIN

• *Chapter 1* •

*D*EEP BREATH, *R*INALDI. *Okay. Here goes.*

The double doors of The Rock Bottom swung closed behind me, shutting out the lazy light of a mid-June afternoon. Even in the gloom, the smoke-hazed saloon seemed smaller than I remembered. But then again, the last time I'd been in here I was in chaps, a holster and a ten-gallon hat.

It was Halloween, I was eleven and Mickey Giamonte had double-dared me to go inside the neighborhood tavern, promising me first dibs from his trick-or-treat bag if I did. So, with my courage fueled by a six-shooter loaded with blasting caps and a sugar high from two packs of SweeTarts, I'd made the play. I even scored some Slim Jims from Ted, the bartender with the scar on his cheek that spelled out his name. But Mickey hadn't delivered.

That was nearly twenty-five years ago. Maybe today we would settle the score.

I had taken only a few steps when I was lifted off my feet from behind by a pair of full-grown anacondas. Or so it felt. I looked up over a set of beefy forearms and into two chaffed, damp nostrils.

"Andie!" Then the watery sniffling started.

I recognized the sound before I placed the face. "Georgie?"

He released the hug, blushed to match his auburn hair, then swiped at his nose with callused knuckles.

"You remember me?" Excited as an Irish setter. "Mickey said you'd be coming, but I didn't believe it for shit! I would've known you anywhere."

"You too. I see your cold hasn't cleared up." I shifted my focus to the nearly life-size image of Saint Christopher around his neck.

It had always been hard for me to look Georgie in the face. He'd suffered from a seriously runny nose for the seven years we were in the same grade at Holy Mother Little Academy, known to its student body as "Holy Moly." The nuns had taken this personally, especially our principal, Sister Constance Patiens. (Never had a convent name suited a nun less.) "George Aloysius Mara," Sister Connie would scold him almost every morning, "are you the patron saint of Niagara Falls? Wipe your faucet!"

It must have been reflexive by this time because Georgie was now dabbing at his upper lip with the corner of his bartender's apron.

"So." My eyes stayed on St. Chris. "You work here."

"Nah! Well, yeah. Part time, when I'm not on the roster." He jerked a thumb in the direction of the firehouse across the street. "Need the extra money. Got two kids now. Plus I'm saving for a sinus operation."

"It'll change your life." I felt like I had entered *The Time Tunnel*, or worse, *The Twilight Zone*. "Where's Mickey?"

George tilted his head toward the back of the bar. "What can I bring ya? My treat."

"A Yoo-hoo."

He laughed. "Still your drink? Closest we got is crème de cacao."

"Yoo-hoo for grown-ups."

"I'll make you a Fudgsicle. Cacao, Kahlúa and milk."

As I headed toward the rear of the tavern, my brain returned to the past. I could still recite the names of all fifty-two of my grammar-school classmates, even though I'd moved away from this tiny riverside town after sixth grade. Though none of my friends could have been more than four-foot-ten when I saw them last, in my mind's eye I always pictured them as adult size, with adult personalities. Somehow, my preteen memory had transformed their faces into the celebrities of the day. Georgie became a redheaded Jethro from *The Beverly Hillbillies* (not far off the mark, I saw now). Brian Coffey was a pint-sized Jack Paar right down to the receding hairline. Mickey's buddy Jimmy O'Shea was a more fidgety Barney Fife of Mayberry. And poor Grace Kelly. Her parents must have had no idea what cruelty they had inflicted on their offspring at birth. Grace looked nothing like her glamorous blond namesake, but more like mousy, lantern-jawed Ruth Buzzi on *Laugh-In*.

I had somehow frozen them all in some kind of 1960s sitcom innocence. But now it was 1992. They must have changed, right? I sure knew I wasn't the same.

Michelangelo Giamonte proved me wrong. Rounding the corner of a curved booth, I found Mickey engrossed in a fan of playing cards he held in his left fist. Across from him, his much smaller opponent frowned at a similar splay, bit a lip, twirled a strand of hair around an index finger, then laid down the hand. She looked to be about five years old, with a nest of wiry red hair.

"Gin!" The cherub wasted no time scooping up the pile of wagered pretzel sticks in the center of the table.

So Mickey was still betting with little girls. And still losing.

He stifled a curse, then sighed noisily. "Well, that's enough humiliation for one day, Megan darlin'. Now, be a good girl and tell your Da to bring me something to drown me sorrows."

As Megan scooted around the table, Mickey turned and saw me.

We looked hard at each other. His hair was the same, curly

and full, but less of it covered his forehead. Its nearly white blondness was still startling against his swarthy skin and deep brown eyes. A Tony Curtis in negative. The struggle for genetic dominance, between his overbearing Italian father and his stubborn Irish mother, had ended in a draw. Bridget Giamonte even managed to stick an Old Sod nickname on her only son, to counteract the goombah tradition of naming the first-born male after the paternal grandfather.

I searched for the mischievous boy in this man's slightly fleshy features and found him easily. Neither of us moved or spoke. An old game.

After a good two minutes, I said, "Where's my Nestlé's Crunch?"

"Ha! I won! As always. And you, you still hold a grudge like it was your last breath on earth."

I sat without invitation. Georgie appeared, set down our drinks, patted me on the head, and loped off. Mickey watched me reach for my glass.

"No ring, Rinaldi." It was a statement not a question, and I automatically slid my left hand under the table and switched to my right. "Andrealisa, my love, you've waited for me." I nearly dislocated my eyeballs, rolling them as far up and around as they would go. "You're in luck. Only recently the second Mrs. Giamonte decided it was time to move on. I wish her well."

"So do I. I imagine she was long-suffering."

"Nice thing to say to the boy whose heart you broke." I might have thought he was blushing, but it was just the glow of the red exit sign behind me deflected off his cheekbones. "You know, I thought you'd at least write me or something."

"What? Was your writing hand crippled in a nose-picking accident?"

"After all we'd meant to each other—"

"You mean the name-calling, the hair-pulling—" It was just like old times.

"—the least you could've done was visit, even once."

4

"How? Steal my father's Barracuda? Besides, I didn't know how to drive."

"You still don't. I saw you trying to parallel-park. And what took you so long to come inside?" He narrowed his eyes, and his lips slid into a smirk. The familiarity of his expression jolted me. "Figures you'd have an old Beetle."

"His name is 'Ringo.' And you must be thrilled that the postal service just approved the young Elvis stamp. I take it the white Cadillac with the red leather seats in the parking lot is yours. Except for the 'Mickey G' plates, wasn't that the same car in *Love Me Tender*?"

"I like the classics. And you have a good memory."

"How could I forget? We saw that one together for a solid week when it was on *Million Dollar Movie*. Your parents thought Elvis was the devil, so my dad let you watch The Pelvis over at our house."

"Hey, you couldn't take your eyes off him." Mickey's smirk disappeared. "Sorry about your dad. He was a good guy. I heard Ma telling Jimmy O's mother about it at the time, but what do kids know about condolence cards?"

I shrugged. "Not your fault. Long time ago now."

Twenty-three years this December. My father moved us just ninety miles but a lifetime away from my hometown on July 13, 1968. A year and 171 days later he was dead. I knew the exact number because I mentally counted off the time during the funeral service, as if it were the answer to a math problem that would help me make sense of what happened. I'd forgotten that Mickey's parents had come to the Mass. Mom had only just learned to drive, and we hadn't done much traveling after that, certainly not to the old neighborhood. Still, over the years my mother stayed in touch with a few of her old friends.

"My mother's gone too," I said. "Last August."

"Jeez." Mickey looked stricken. "Ma said she hadn't gotten a card this past Christmas and wondered."

We both took a deep gulp from our glasses to get past the

moment. I nearly gagged on my Fudgsicle. Not enough like Yoo-hoo for my taste.

"And how is your Ma?" I hoped this was an easier topic.

"She and Pop just went into one of those over-55 communities down the shore, not far from where you moved."

"I hope their hearts can stand the excitement," I said. "Man, I hated it there. Nothing to do once the boardwalk closes down at the end of the summer. I can't believe Cat wanted to go back after college."

"And how *is* your Evil Twin?"

As happened whenever I thought of my sister, I smiled, even as my heart contracted. "Oh, she's fine. Doing something with computers now. It's all geek to me."

"That sounds too tame for Cat. I figured to see her one of these days on *America's Most Wanted.*"

"She's full of surprises." *Change the subject.* "And you should talk. I figured you'd be doing ten to twenty by now yourself."

Mickey didn't bother looking insulted. "As they say, it takes one to know one." He had learned at his father's knee that anything that wasn't nailed down was up for grabs. He never did tell me how he managed to steal an entire swing set from the Lincoln Elementary School playground. "When my life of petty crime didn't work out, I chose to use my knowledge for good instead of evil."

"You mean it takes a thief to catch a thief. That's where that TV show got its name. *It Takes a Thief.* Robert Wagner. Then there's the movie *To Catch a Thief.* Cary Grant." Now I was just babbling.

"Really? How fascinating." The smirk was back. "You oughta come down to the bar on trivia night. You'd clean up." He raised his hand and almost immediately Georgie dropped off another beer. Mickey took a swallow before fixing me with a gaze meant to pin me against the booth. "But you didn't just come down here to talk about old times or old flicks."

I kept my eyes on my nearly full drink and spoke in a rush.

"Listen, like I told you on the phone, I'm on assignment. My editor found out that I'd grown up with some of the principals in the Hartt case—Joel, of course, and you. So now, in addition to all the editing I do, I have to write a feature. Human interest, not an investigative piece. I'm no crime reporter. It's supposed to be an insider's point of view." I heard him snort. "Yeah, I thought that would make you laugh. Of course, I'm sure my editor is hoping I'll get something new, maybe an exclusive from you. So I thought I'd get that over with first."

I looked up then, at Mickey's clenched jaw. "Believe me, I don't want to be here, certainly not under these circumstances. Hardly the makings of a happy reunion."

Mickey slid his glass on its coaster, back and forth, hand to hand. Not a drop sloshed over, though his eyes didn't leave mine. "I used to see your name—whatchacallit, your byline?—in the city paper's health-and-science section. Then nothing. Who are you working for now?"

Deep breath, Rinaldi. "The *Moon.*"

His reaction wasn't surprising. "You gotta be kidding! How could you go from the Paper of Record to the Paper of Rectum?"

"They made me an offer I couldn't refuse. Plus free toilet paper."

"This does not make me eager to talk to you."

"We are mutually uneager, but the difference is that my rent is due. And I'm still a professional." *More or less.*

"So I should be your Deep Throat, for old times' sake, to be quoted in a rag I wouldn't use to line a birdcage. If I still had a bird. The second ex-Mrs. Giamonte took that too."

"Hey, you don't have to tell me a thing. I'll make it up—isn't that what you think we do anyway? Trust me, better it comes directly from you."

His eyes narrowed. Then he chuckled, without humor. "What am I being so touchy about? The whole world knows what I know. Reporters have camped out here on and off for the six months since it happened. My name's already been dragged through the shit and back again. How much more encrusted could it get?"

So COUNTY CHIEF of Detectives Michelangelo Giamonte sucked in a chestful of air and spoke as if reading these facts off a police-department press release for the thousandth time: "On New Year's, an hour after midnight, Emma Hartt, a well-known fashion model only ten years old, goes missing." He took another breath. "The father, Joel Hartt—widower, prominent local real-estate developer—allegedly searches the house and finds a ransom note, but no daughter. Note says to keep the cops out of it, so he does, for a few precious hours.

"Instead, he calls his best friend-slash-business partner, and they go over the house again, hoping to figure out what happened or who took her. Friend discovers a broken window in the basement, looks around some more and finds the little girl. Stuffed in the water-heater closet. Strangled with a length of heavy chain. Looks like a kidnapping attempt gone bad. Father finally calls in the locals at 6 a.m. By the time my boys get there, the crime scene is compromised and Hartt is only talking through his lawyer."

The recital seemed to drain him. "Nothing like starting a murder investigation with a holiday hangover."

So far, Mickey hadn't told me anything I couldn't have read in any paper in the country by now. "So why didn't Joel find his daughter's body when he was first looking?"

"Claims he wasn't looking for a body. Claims he'd found the ransom note on the hall table and never got down to the basement."

"Pretty strange that he lawyered up so soon."

"Joel's a strange guy—you must remember that much."

I thought of the boy I'd known, long-limbed, with a slender, pinched face and constant scowl—the dark side of Dick Van Dyke. You could have carved a full-size replica of Mount Rushmore from the chip on his shoulder. "Yeah, but not the kind of strange the media's been accusing him of. He was annoying, but not sick. I don't see him killing his own child. And molesting her? You know that for sure?" At least Mickey might be straight with me there.

"Nothing definite." Mickey sighed heavily. "He lost his wife two years ago and from what I'd heard, that nearly drove him nuts. Who knows what a guy goes through after that? Plus he'd had an Auld Lang Syne party in the house, lots of expensive booze. Champagne—Veuve Clicquot, by the way. Though I prefer Cristal, if you're thinking of getting me a present. Anyway, the guys who responded to the call that night said Hartt looked like he'd been run over by the Budweiser Clydesdales."

"But you have no evidence that he did it."

His anger flashed. "Do you think if we did, we'd suppress that? That his money could buy that kind of silence? You're like everyone else—thinking cops are animals!"

I leaned away from his disgust. "Not me, buddy. I'm just asking what the public wants to know. Consider this your chance to set the record straight. And you seem to have no other suspects."

He simmered. "No fingerprints, no *nothing*, except what you'd expect. Just those who lived in the house. The break-in looked staged. The shards of glass, most fell outside under the window, like it had been smashed from *inside* the room. That warm spell right before Christmas melted the little bit of snow we had the week before, then the cold snap right after froze the ground too hard to take a footprint. If there were any to be found."

"You're thinking it was an inside job?"

Mickey shrugged. "Someone had to have a pretty good idea of more than just the layout of the house. The so-called kidnapper hadn't come prepared—he wrote the ransom note with a pad and pencil from a kitchen drawer. How'd he even know where to find it? Didn't make sense then and it still doesn't."

"No handwriting match?"

"Nothing conclusive. But then, the note was all in block capitals—just like the nuns taught us in kindergarten penmanship."

"But Joel is Jewish. He went to Lincoln."

"Hey, thanks for reminding me, Rinaldi! That clears him absolutely." Mickey gave me a look. "The bottom line is, his story doesn't wash, but we can't shake him on it and can't turn up anyone or anything that contradicts it."

"You said he had a party that night. Maybe someone stayed behind in the house, then faked the break-in to divert suspicion."

"You don't think we thought of that? But it wasn't a crowd, just three couples." Mickey looked at me, as if expecting a question I didn't ask. He shrugged. "They all left around the same time. Joel saw each one out the door and they saw each other drive off. And don't say they were all in on it together. You may be hung up on old movies, but this isn't *Murder on the Orient Express*."

"I can't imagine a ten-year-old would have that many enemies."

"But her father does. Or at least people who might want to see his life effed up. He's into a lot of shit in this town, developing the waterfront. Many millions to be made if you have a piece of it. Some of those deals could have turned nasty and he's got more pending, once the economy turns around. There's a lot at stake for a lot of people. That's what's made this a nightmare to look into. But then again, it was New Year's Eve. The obvious contenders were toasting 1992 in full view of their nearest and dearest well into the morning."

"But if someone paid somebody else—"

"Man, you have a devious mind! Remind me not to double-cross you again." Mickey drained his glass while waving at Georgie again. He took a swig as soon as Georgie set down the new pilsner. "Yeah, there's that, and, sure, we've been working the underground pipeline. There may not be much honor among thieves, but a lot of them might have had second thoughts when they heard a kid died. Nobody likes that. Plus there are the usual suspects—lowlifes who think they can get rich quick kidnapping a millionaire's daughter, then something goes wrong. But no one's heard anything."

"Maybe just somebody passing through."

"Nah, it would have to be someone with more contact with Hartt. He'd just gotten some foreign financing for a mega shopping center on the South End. The ransom asked for the exact figure of the deal, one-point-two million. Who'd ever come up with that figure out of nowhere? It can't have been a coincidence and news of the signing didn't hit the papers until after the murder. Someone had to know beforehand."

"Then that narrows it." But my head was spinning

Now Mickey looked annoyed. "That narrows it to Joel Hartt, and we're right back where we started. Given the time frame, it's hard to see how someone from the outside could have done what he—or she—would have had to do, without Hartt knowing about it."

"What time frame?"

"Joel claims his kids were safe and asleep when he checked around twelve-thirty, and that a noise got him out of bed to look in on them again a few minutes before one. That leaves no more than a half-hour for someone to come in after being sure all his guests had left, make it from the basement to the second floor—stopping in the kitchen to write a ransom note, mind you—grab the girl, get her down to the basement, find a chain to strangle her with, dump her and flee. All without leaving a telltale sign. Not impossible, but not probable."

"The noise that woke Joel—was it the breaking window?"

"Couldn't have been, if that was the entry point. Hartt would have caught whoever in the act."

"So someone was already in the house and was breaking the glass to get out?"

"Why bother? You can open the window from inside. Or better yet, why not go out the front door? Forget it, Rinaldi. The broken window means nothing, a red herring. And you have to assume that what Hartt told us was the truth anyway. Which I doubt."

I was stuck on a killer in the house. "And no one else was

staying over?"

"Hartt says it was only him, his boy and the girl there that night. His housekeeper-slash-nanny doesn't live in."

"He has a housekeeper?" Someone else I should talk to.

He smiled then. "You don't know?"

"Know what? And why should I?"

His smile widened. "I think I'm going to leave that to you to find out. I gotta get some fun out of this." He checked his watch. "And I have to go back to the courthouse. I assume you know Joel still lives in his parents' place. So, you going over there now?"

"Yeah, but I thought it best not to call ahead."

"The element of surprise? If you make it past the dragon, *I'll* be surprised."

"Now you intrigue me."

"And *you* intrigue *me*." He took a last swallow of his beer, grabbed my still half-full glass and sniffed it. "What's this? Chocolate milk?"

I shrugged. "We maturing gals do need at least a thousand milligrams of calcium a day."

"So now I know you're not a drinker. Do you eat?"

"Whenever I can. I'd have thought that was obvious."

"Well, it seems to have settled in the right places." He stood up, and I saw that his own baby fat had disappeared. If he weren't careful, though, it would soon be replaced by a beer gut. "Next time, if I decide there's a next time, we meet inside the restaurant, The Stone's Throw. It's through that door," he pointed to the left of the bar, "where the grocery store used to be. Great steaks."

"I'm practically a vegetarian."

"One bite of the seventeen-ounce T-bone will cure that."

"Nice of you to promote local businesses."

"You think I'd bother? I own it. And this place." Mickey laughed at my expression. "Somebody's gotta be sure that Georgie keeps his snot out of the beer."

I HADN'T EXPECTED much from Mickey and I sure didn't get it. I'd

12

worked a few months on the police beat straight out of journalism school, enough to know that being suspicious of the press is in most cops' DNA. But I didn't care. Sure, I'd spent a good part of my preadolescence yearning to be karate-kicking Honey West, or cool Emma Peel of *The Avengers,* or maybe April Dancer, *The Girl from U.N.C.L.E.* Mainly I just wanted to look that good in a skin-tight leather jumpsuit someday.

My short stint covering the police log wasn't short enough. Dealing with the nasty side of human nature day in and day out made it hard to trust anybody, and I had enough problems in that area. So I transferred to the Features section, eventually covering health and medicine. Today, I'd do what my editor had asked me to do and then get back to pitching stories about celebrity face-lifts gone wrong.

I left my twenty-year-old burnt-orange Volkswagen Bug in front of The Rock Bottom to walk the two short blocks to my old street. I passed the heavy wood and brass outer doors of The Stone's Throw. It had once been K.C.'s Grocery, where the stock had been as old as the proprietor, who was at least seventy. You had to blow the dust off a box to see what you were buying. Since everything was twice the price of the supermarket in the next town, the mothers only sent us kids there if they were in desperate need of a vital ingredient for their tuna casserole or baked ziti.

I was relieved to see that the candy store was still on the corner. Except now, coyly renamed The Confectionery, it had been cuted up like a Fifties sweet shop—all chromed counters and red leatherette stools and booths, black-and-white checkered floor tile. Nothing like the dingy green space with the scarred-wood floor of my Sixties youth. Back then, the glass cases were so clouded by cigar smoke that we could barely make out the merchandise. Since the cigar-smoking counterman was K.C.'s father—ninety, if he were a day, and obviously the guy for whom Sour Balls were named—the stock was no fresher than the stuff in the grocery store. The Bazooka bubblegum was so rock hard that Johnny Gilpatrick once popped a piece in his mouth and chipped a tooth.

It seemed only right, in the interests of research, to see if new ownership had improved the quality of the confections. As I pushed through, the door jingled so merrily K.C.'s dad would have spit out his stogie in disgust.

The display cases gleamed to twinkling. Inside were neat rows of pure sugar in its various forms. There were the modern atrocities like Gummy Worms and Sour Patch Kids, which I was sure would never make it into the next decade, but the classics were well represented: streamers of multicolored Candy Buttons, Smarties necklaces, Pixy Stix straws full of fruit-flavored sugar, Necco Wafers.... No Bonomo's Turkish Taffy? I was getting a hypoglycemic buzz just by looking.

"Can I help you?"

Sucrose interruptus. The teenage counterboy was wearing a checkered paper hat tipped at just the right forward angle to make it seem studied cool with his two-tiered haircut and pierced left ear.

I tapped on the glass. "I'll take a Milky Way." That should hold me until Mickey produced the candy bar he owed me.

The kid passed me the candy bar and I handed over fifty cents for what used to cost me a nickel.

"Thanks." I looked around again. "Nice what they did to this place." The kid looked uncomprehending. "Um, I used to come around here all the time, before you were born." *Jeez*, I thought, *it's come to this. Talking like I grew up during the Depression.* "You're probably too young, but do you know what happened to the guy who used to own it?"

"Yeah, sure." He adjusted his paper hat as if it were a thinking cap. "I heard something about it from my mom. She's lived in town forever, like, thirty-five years." *Now I was officially old.* "Long time ago, maybe late seventies, he was busted for running numbers out the back."

Ha! I knew K.C. couldn't have made an honest buck from his

crummy businesses.

"They say he was, like, 103, but it still took two cops to get the handcuffs on him. His son came out of the grocery store and just watched him get dragged off, crying like a baby."

So K.C.'s dad, old Sour Balls, was the brains behind the operation? Who'd have guessed?

THE CHOCOLATE SUSTAINED me as I walked along River Drive, passing DeVries Lane, one of the uphill streets in this part of town that dead-ended into the cliffs. Each was lined with perfect parallel rows of two-family houses. When I'd lived in one of them, they were all brand-new, all built by Hartt Construction—the start of the creeping suburbia that would soon infest all of New Jersey. Each first floor was red brick; the second, wood shingle. Only the colors of the window trim and the garage door set them apart and helped us kids find our way home.

The homes in the North End looked a little more worn now, but otherwise hadn't changed much. My real shock had come driving up from the tunnel. The South End had been a grungy stretch of decaying freight piers, abandoned oil tanks, dying factories and noxious chemical plants. Now some of that had been razed to make way for condos and strip malls.

But the recent economic slowdown had obviously delayed much of the new construction. Wood and steel frames rose out of the landfill, the skeletons of some prehistoric Cubist beasts, with stacks of concrete slabs, each about the size of the monolith from *2001: A Space Odyssey*. Only one construction site I passed had been active.

I was more surprised that it had taken this long for someone to try to spin the sludge into gold. True to its name, Undercliff was shadowed by magnificent cliffs on the west and bounded along the east by iron-gray waters that reflected one of the most exciting and treacherous cities in the world. "Three miles long and three blocks wide," my dad used to say about my hometown, "caught between a rock and a hard place." With the bridge a half-mile north and the tunnel two miles south, and now a ferry in between, it was perfectly situated for commuting into New York City.

But few did back then. None of my friends' fathers worked there. The attitude was, *Why bother? We have everything we need on this side.* Besides, its residents paid the high rents to look at *us*, not the other way around. I'd never thought of crossing the river. The mythic skyline was just part of the scenery, the postcard view from our kitchen window.

At the foot of Clearview, my old block, I looked across River Drive. It was still there, the rustic wooden sign that marked the entrance to The Colony: *Private. Residents Only.*

There the land sloped down to the riverfront, with oak, maple, sycamore and sumac trees obscuring the homes beyond. I had no idea how many houses were down there. Our mothers had warned us never to go past that sign—not even on Halloween, when usually we were free to walk the whole length of town. We came up with our own reasons why we weren't allowed in The Colony. We imagined mobsters hiding out, fingers itching for an excuse to pump a few slugs into kids dressed up as hobos or ballerinas.

Jimmy O swore that a commune of midgets lived there too, that dwarves from the Barnum & Bailey Circus had built bungalows where everything, even the toilets, were half size. One summer, my sister, Caterina, loosely organized a scouting party to check out that rumor, but the rest of us all lost our nerve at the last minute. Only one of my Holy Moly classmates had lived in The Colony. She seemed to be normal height. But she'd never invited anyone home to meet her parents.

I turned up Clearview Terrace, narrower and steeper than in memory. Hard to imagine how I'd learned to ride a bike on this street. Because of the lane's pitch, each lot had to be terraced, leveled for the house foundations, with a drop-off wall separating the properties. My family had been one of the original settlers, all arriving within a year or two of each other. Most were new to the middle class. Upstairs tenants came and went, usually young couples who moved on once their fortunes improved or the first baby was brought home from St. Mary's Hospital a few towns away.

As I trudged past each house, I ticked off the names: Soriano, DiBoise, Anderson, Greenblatt, Gilpatrick, a couple whose name I never knew because they didn't have kids so who cared?, O'Shea, Jirusak, Giamonte, Rinaldi.

I stopped in front of number 10. The siding on my old house, now painted dark red, matched the lower floor's brick, with brown trim. The yard had somehow shrunk. My cousins, raised in a more urban setting, had thought I lived in a national park. Now the swatch of grass in front looked no bigger than the green felt of a pool table. More evidence of how kids' perspectives never match objective reality. What other tricks had my mind played on me?

My father had built a rock wall on the left, into the side of the hill, creating an elevated area for my mother's clothesline. This was now a platform garden, already flourishing so early in the season. My dad would have laughed at that. The only thing he could ever raise from the dirt was a blister, his shovel hitting stone with every thrust. Just plugs of grass between patches of bare, rocky earth, our lawn had looked like a bad hair transplant. But someone had taken the time over the years to layer on topsoil, to bring it up to suburban standards that my father never cared to meet.

The Hartts had lived above it all, off a long, nearly perpendicular driveway that looked down on us. Maybe because my dad never worried that we might mess up his landscaping, all the neighborhood kids had congregated in our yard. This had been a constant thorn to Joel Hartt, two years younger than Cat and me. He could see us playing and laughing, while he was confined to his mother's tight orbit.

The kid had no friends, thanks to Evelyn Hartt. She was so overprotective, Joel was practically a hostage in his own house.

She must have had him late in life, as she looked much older than the other moms. We'd catch glimpses of her when she pulled weeds from the slope below her front walk. Always dressed in a multicolored caftan, her head wrapped in a turban, she'd shoo us away if we dared step on their property. Which is why we tried every chance we got. We nicknamed her Endora, after Samantha Stephens' mother on *Bewitched*. And Joel knew it.

So Joel often stood on his own driveway, throwing down taunts as we played tag or hide-and-seek in my yard. No one paid much attention to him until the day he started hurling dirt bombs instead of insults. One, embedded with a rock, hit Patty Soriano's three-year-old brother Frankie in the eye. As Frankie ran home wailing and bleeding, we all stood around with our mouths open, except for my sister. Cat scrabbled straight up the driveway's embankment and started punching Joel with both fists. His mother swooped down, screeching, and tried to pull Cat off Joel, but my sister had gotten him in a headlock and wasn't about to let go. She only stopped after Patty's father, a wiry little guy who was quite speedy for a chain-smoker, sprinted from their house at the bottom of the street, threw down his cigarette and took over the job. That day we all learned quite a few new phrases that we would later be grounded for.

After that incident, my parents wouldn't let me go to Joel's. That pretty much cut off his contact with the outside, at least within our two-block world.

Until then, I'd been the only one his mother ever allowed to enter their domain. My visits there started when I was in kindergarten, after a spring shower, one of those first warm mornings that smell like clean laundry. On my way to the bus stop, I saw three-year-old Joel ripping up daffodils in the Giamontes' yard and waved. He had slipped out of the house without his mother knowing, but I didn't realize that. Catching up with Mickey and Jimmy O a half block along River Drive, I'd heard the screaming. Evelyn Hartt was on her knees on the Sorianos' front lawn, her usual caftan bunched up around her neck—like the scene in *The*

Wizard of Oz, when the Wicked Witch of the West melts beneath her clothes. Joel had followed me, running into the middle of River Drive when his mother tried to catch him. He laughed and threw daffodils as traffic skidded to a halt on the wet pavement. I dropped my Lassie lunchbox, ran up behind him, scooped him up by the underarms and dropped him in his mother's lap. It occurred to me now that she didn't even say thank you.

That day after school, Mrs. Hartt asked my mother if I could come up to play with Joel once in a while, when she was "indisposed." I guess my mother couldn't refuse, since my dad worked as business manager for Joel's father at Hartt Construction.

When Mom first delivered me to Joel's, I felt I was entering Brothers Grimm territory. The Hartts' house backed into the cliff, its steep front and side yards screened by gloomy evergreens and shrouded with close-packed shrubs. The balcony that ran the length of the middle floor had a million-dollar view (and that's in 1960s currency), but I rarely saw anyone enjoying it. The year before, our family had gone there to watch the Fourth of July fireworks, set off over the river courtesy of Palisades Amusement Park, above us on the cliff. Then Cat had knocked over a citronella lantern, setting fire to one of Mrs. Hartt's more colorful muumuus, and I expected that we wouldn't be on their guest list ever again. We weren't, but I think it had more to do with Joel's father moving out a few months after.

Instead, I went to those play dates, alone. Mrs. Hartt sweetened the pot by leaving bowls of Peanut M&Ms in every room. In those days, I could be had for the right sugar-delivery system (okay, maybe in these days too). There were other attractions, too. Joel always had every new toy before anyone else did: Etch-A-Sketch, a 102-piece Tinkertoy set, the latest Matchbox cars. And though he was whiny when he didn't win at Candy Land, he could be cute, hugging me tightly and telling me he loved me each time I left.

As he grew older, I was asked over less often, but I'd still felt protective of him and had tried to get the others to include him more. I'd overheard enough of his mother's ranting phone calls to her soon-to-be-ex-husband to feel more than a little sorry for him. But the dirt-bomb attack had been the last straw. Mickey had called a meeting in his basement, declared Joel to be the ultimate cootie and voted to shun him. I'd felt I had no choice but to go along.

So I didn't expect to be greeted with open arms now, showing up unannounced more than two decades later on the front stoop Joel had inherited. Maybe he wasn't even home yet. All I saw in the driveway was a rusting old Chevy Impala, butter yellow. Surely not his car. I would expect something more in the Mercedes family.

Before I could put my finger to the bell, the door jerked open and I was looking into the face of a brunette angel.

The boy was about twelve, with the greenest eyes I've ever seen, rimmed all around with long black lashes. It wouldn't have been wrong to call him beautiful.

"Evan, what did I tell you? You are *not* to go out the front door, do you hear me?" The woman's voice, hard with panic, came from behind him. I figured she had to be this boy's grandmother. Evelyn Hartt. She had probably come with the house as a package deal. Poor kid.

He hung his head and backed away as a hand gripped the door. It was ready to close when I planted my left foot on the sill and my right hip against the jamb, and peered around to see who was attached to the arm. The woman's face was balled up in anger like a fist and it didn't belong to Evelyn Hartt.

But I recognized it immediately. "Aren't you Doreen Josephs?"

• *Chapter 2* •

The woman startled. Like one of those hologram Jesuses, her expression shifted before my eyes, from rage to confusion and back again. Almost against her will, she grunted, "*Was*. Last name's Dougherty now. What's it to you?"

What *was* it to me? Mainly, an unpleasant surprise.

Despite what I'd told Mickey, I *had* come back to town, just once, on my own. It was April of 1980, on my way to my cousin Paula's wedding. Driving down from upstate New York, where I'd been living and working since college, I crossed the George Washington Bridge and impulsively took the first exit, and found myself cruising aimlessly through the familiar streets. I had wound up near Holy Mother R.C. Church. I sat in the car for a while, fighting the urge to go in. At that point, I hadn't voluntarily entered a house of worship since I was sixteen.

Then the red double doors of the simple brick building opened. Out walked a squat woman, one arm around an infant, the other hand grasping the wrist of a boy about four years old. As I started up my car, she crossed in front of me. She'd looked livid then too, pulling the wriggling boy along in her wake. I also saw that she was not fat, maybe pregnant, and unmistakably Doreen Josephs. Just twenty-four, already a mother of two with another on the way. We used to call her Do Jo. She hated the nickname, as she hated most everything and everyone else.

Bull-necked and always spoiling for a fight, she'd been Jimmy Cagney in a plaid jumper. Almost every day, she wanted to brawl, and she didn't care whom with. She'd walk up to her latest victim, punch him or her in the stomach and hiss, "Meet me in the church alley at 3:15."

I don't know why anyone even showed up, but they did, and then Doreen would cream them like spinach. She never tapped Cat, probably recognizing a kindred spirit. She picked on me once, though we'd always gotten along. But I had no reputation to protect.

"If I miss my bus home, Do Jo, my mother will kill me even if you don't," I'd protested. "Just say you won, okay? I won't tell anybody anything different." She'd looked almost as confused then as she did today, but she'd let me off.

Now she was Doreen Dougherty. Did she go by "Do Do"? The housekeeper-slash-nanny and Mickey's dragon. Well, she was certainly breathing fire, but intimidating? Not really. Though she'd once been much bigger than any of the girls, and even some of the boys in our class, she hadn't grown any since. She was downright short, maybe five-foot-two.

"Doreen! Great to see you!" I gushed. "Remember me from Holy Mother Little Academy? Andrealisa Rinaldi! I used to live next-door to Joel. You won't believe it, but I was just in the neighborhood. Can I come in?"

Doreen looked like she *didn't* believe it, but I'd caught her off-guard. "I don't know—Andie?" Startled again into stepping back, she left me just enough room to squeeze past her and close the door with my left foot.

"That's right!" I gave her a big grin, then a hug, which left her nearly catatonic. "How have you been?"

"Well, not so good since—hey!" She seemed to shake herself out of her daze and realize what had happened, but she couldn't very well throw me out. I now had six inches of height on her. Still, by the looks of her biceps, flexing in a tank top tucked into a pair of nylon running pants, she might still be boxing in her spare time. Better not risk getting within arm's reach. I sidled farther into the hallway.

Now she moved toward me. "We can't have you here! We've had, we can't—!"

What do you mean "we," kemo sabe? I wondered. Sounded like her connection to Joel went beyond employer-employee. Mickey said Joel was a widower now. Was Doreen in line to become the second Mrs. Hartt? And how had she come to know him, anyway? There had been very little mixing between the parochial and public school kids, and even less between South and North Enders.

Doreen seemed to suddenly remember the boy, who was staring at me. She turned abruptly and barked, "Evan, go up to your room. Now."

The boy hesitated for a second, then ran up the steps winding behind her. He paused once to give me one last look and to get one more scowl from Doreen. I gave him a smile before he disappeared.

Doreen faced me again, wary like an animal. "Andie, I don't know why you're here now and I don't want to be rude, but—"

"Doreen, Evan just ran past me. What's going on down there?" A voice, deep and strangely disembodied, came floating down the stairs the boy had fled up.

Doreen looked at me for the answer.

"A blast from the past!" I called up with a cheeriness that sounded as phony as it felt.

Doreen was back to anger and she moved toward me almost threateningly. "This isn't a good time..." She stopped as heavy footsteps hit the stairs.

I saw one well-polished wingtip, then another, then the cuffs on a pair of knife-creased charcoal pants. As white shirtsleeves came into view, I started to feel the same thudding in my chest that I felt watching *Attack of the 50-Foot Woman* on the Saturday afternoon Creature Feature.

He wasn't quite that tall, six-foot-four maybe, still long-limbed, his wavy reddish-brown hair tousled like a boy's. But Joel Hartt was definitely a man. And by the look of him, the saddest man in the world.

Tabloid stories—okay, the *Moon*'s, too—had implied that Joel Hartt was a cold, self-centered business mogul whose uncooperativeness with the police spelled out his guilt. But I saw no evidence even of the childhood chip on his shoulder. Instead he looked as if his every bone was broken, and he was holding himself up only through the sheer force of his will. I suddenly felt ashamed of why I was there and would have blushed if I could.

"Joel, I'm sorry." Without thinking, I reached toward him.

"Who are you?" His whole body stiffened and his face hardened. That was the look that made the front pages.

"Andrealisa Rinaldi."

Shock. Recognition. Curiosity. Then something like pleasure, then something like pain passed across his face. Then the mask fell back into place.

"I'm sorry, Joel. I didn't mean to intrude." Of course I meant to, but I wanted to get this out before he could recover too much. I was going to tell him the truth. "I just—"

"It's been a long time," he said as if from a long way off. "It's good to see you."

That stunned me. I had expected a reaction like Doreen's but clearly Joel didn't have it in him. Maybe he was resigned to being on display, like the sideshow freaks that came to the amusement park on the cliff. Like "Jo Jo, The Dog-Faced Boy." Do Jo and Jo Jo. I repressed what I was afraid would be a hysterical giggle.

"I just got home. If you'll give me a minute. You can wait in the study." He waved toward a doorway, then headed back upstairs passing his housekeeper, who was looking at him as if he had just sprouted a Bozo wig. "Doreen, would you mind getting Andie whatever she'd like to drink?"

Yes, Doreen would mind, her expression said, but his wish was obviously her command. Her eyes asked the question her lips couldn't form: *Are you out of your mind*? But he never looked back.

"Ice water, lemonade, whatever's easiest," I said helpfully.

Doreen glared at me, then stomped in the opposite direction, leaving me with the impression that, whatever beverage she brought me, it was sure to be poisoned.

NEVER LEAVE A writer alone in your library. It, pardon the pun, speaks volumes. I had heard that some well-heeled folks in the city pay book dealers to stock their shelves, from A to Z, with choice literature. A few first editions of the classics go a long way to establishing intellectual cachet, even if you're too busy making money to read them.

If I was any judge, Joel picked out his books himself. The floor-to-ceiling Mission Oak barrister bookcases, matching the rest of the room's Arts-and-Crafts-era decor, held mostly glossy books on art and architecture, biographies and autobiographies of statesmen, entrepreneurs and megalomaniacs rather than celebrities. *The Power Broker, Iacocca…* I pulled out Sun Tzu's *The Art of War* and opened the flyleaf. This one was a gift, not a personal choice, or so I guessed by the inscription: *Time to unsheathe your sword, young warrior! Fondly, Gordon.*

Then my glance fell on the spine of another volume on the shelf above. I knew this one all too well. It was *my* book, the only one I'd ever written. I felt the back of my neck tingle.

"Yes, I know you're a journalist." Joel had changed to khakis and a lime green polo shirt—the casual wear of the Forbes 500.

"That doesn't make me a bad person, does it?" I hoped that was true.

"No. People don't change," he said slowly, and I wasn't sure if he was even talking about me. "Thanks, Doreen."

She had snuck in on little cat feet and handed him a tall glass of something dark. Then she nearly threw a tumbler at me. Ice water.

Don't bother. It's the thought that counts.

Joel raised his glass to me, then to Doreen. "Time for you to go home, isn't it? We'll see you tomorrow."

For a minute, I thought Doreen was going to stay and, for a minute, she did too. But Joel just continued looking at her with a bemused expression until she huffed out.

"You know Doreen." He almost smiled.

"Another product of Holy Mother Little Academy."

"Ah, Holy Moly. Where you and Mickey Giamonte and so many others in our circle learned the fundamentals of Christian charity."

I blanched, then realized that this time he *was* smiling.

"No need to feel guilty," he said. "Believe it or not, I take full responsibility for my part in whatever hostility I evoked in those days. Or rather, like everyone else of our generation, I just blame it all on my mother."

Damn. I found myself liking the adult Joel. Would that be inconvenient if he turned out to be a murderer?

He waved me to sit on the leather-cushioned couch. I did, and he leaned his long frame against the Mission library table that seemed to serve as a desk. I recognized the power play: Always position yourself higher than your opponent. Something he learned from Sun Tzu probably.

I decided to charge forward. "Joel, I truly am sorry about your daughter. About Emma."

He stiffened at her name, the drawbridge going up and closing with a loud *thunk*. Maybe not the right military strategy, but I've never had a natural bent for anything but direct confrontation.

"I'd assumed you didn't suddenly get the urge to renew old ties." Whatever he was feeling he kept his voice low and even. "Considering your line of work, I should have expected a visit. But a little late, aren't you? The rest of the wolf pack has already picked these bones clean. Or are you your paper's secret weapon?"

I hoped he didn't know who my employer was now. Should I tell him? Well, he hadn't really asked. "I come in peace. Sort of."

"That's comforting. Sort of." He didn't look comforted.

"True, I'm here so I can write a story. But my perspective is that of an old—okay, former, maybe—friend."

He slowly put his drink down and crossed the room to lean against the wall next to where I sat. He didn't speak but stared straight ahead.

It would have been awkward for me to turn to look at him, but out of the corner of my eye I could see the angle of his head and realized what was holding his attention.

It was a painting of a woman. I'd noticed it as soon as I'd entered the room. Not one of those stiffly formal portraits meant to convince the viewer that this particular suburban matron is actually the matriarch of a long and distinguished clan. The woman—girl—in this picture seemed to have been painted on the wind. Wisps of color defined a full mouth, blond rays of hair, amused blue eyes, a delicate chin shyly tilted. She looked familiar. I couldn't see an artist's signature from where I sat, but it was skillful work. Joel's concentration on it seemed to be like a medium's effort to contact the dead.

"I don't think you knew Kristine," Joel said finally. "She was a few years behind you at Holy Moly. I met her at Midland High."

That made sense. Since Undercliff had no high school of its own, all its kids from the two small elementary schools and the even smaller Catholic academy were bused two towns away after eighth grade.

"We had the same art classes. It took me until junior year to ask her out." He moved away from the wall then, retrieved his drink and sat at the desk as if he needed to put something solid between us. "I wasn't much more popular as a teen than I was as a ten-year-old. But she didn't care." He nodded at the painting. "That was my senior project."

"Something tells me you got an A."

"And I got the girl." He stared into his drink. "We were married after I got my architecture degree. She started an art therapy program for chronically ill children at St. Mary's Hospital. She was a wonderful artist."

"So are you, I see." I gestured at the painting. "How come you didn't stick with it?"

"When my father had his first heart attack, I was conscripted into the family business. Ironically, I had a knack for picking real estate. I took the company more into property development and subcontracting the construction. I bought up some waterfront properties along the coast when it looked like the bottom was dropping out of condos. After this year's elections, I think we'll have a rebound, and we're ready." He raised his brow. "Much to the chagrin of the shortsighted guys who abandoned the gold mine."

That could earn a fellow a few enemies.

"Your father still alive?"

He shook his head. "He had a second attack, almost thirteen years ago."

"And your mom?"

"The cancer finally got her."

"Finally?"

"Your mother didn't tell you?"

"About what?"

"My mother had breast cancer most of my childhood. That's why she had you come over to play with me. On the days my mother had her chemo. That treatment wasn't really standard in the 1960s, but she was in one of the first research trials, at the city cancer center. She did have one radical mastectomy back then, and another in my freshman year in college. But by that time it was too late."

"No, I didn't know." I mentally slapped myself. Those loose caftans, the turban she wore—hiding the ravages of her illness. Now I remembered one day, in my search for a bathroom, I had opened a door and caught her without her usual head wrap; she had only a few thin wisps of reddish hair. I also recalled telling Mickey that Joel's mother was bald, and he told everybody else. Shame on me again. "I'm sorry."

"Not too many people were, I'm afraid. She wasn't an easy woman, as you probably remember." He rubbed the back of his neck. "The illness and the surgery pretty much drained off whatever interest my father had in her, too. The coward divorced her. Then he moved back into the house with me after she died."

I let that sit a bit, then nodded at the painting, "And the girl?"

"I got her. Then I lost her. She was pregnant with our third child, there were medical complications... "

I didn't know what to say to that except, again, "I'm sorry."

Joel leaned forward, elbows on the desk, stared at me. "I was sorry about your father when I heard back then. You know how people talk."

I sucked in my breath. "My mother's gone too now."

"So you know what it's like to lose someone you care about, way too young," he said. "Other people *think* they know, but they don't. And they think they know how you're supposed to behave. But they don't." He got up from the oak swivel chair, agitated now. His voice, though, remained flat. "There is no 'supposed to.' You handle it the only way you can, however that is. And then you do your best to protect those you have left. But sometimes..."

Was he trying to tell me something?

I had to tell him. "Joel, the paper I work for now. It's the *Moon*."

I expected anger. I expected to be thrown out. I didn't expect what he did next.

He turned his back, fingering a framed photograph from

among a group on a low credenza behind the desk. He picked it up, then turned to face me again.

"I won't talk to you about my daughter's death. But I *will* talk to you about her life." And he did.

THAT NIGHT I missed the ten-minute window of opportunity that would have allowed me to make it back to the city without losing my sanity. Traffic into the tunnel was a crawl, and it was an hour before I emerged from the other side. Good thing I'd stopped for another Milky Way before I'd gotten back in the car.

It took a half-hour more before I found a parking space near my apartment. That's why I drove a Bug—its compactness increased my chances. If I had less respect for my own life, I would have bought a motorcycle so that I could roll right into my lobby. A sensible city person eschewed auto ownership, but where I came from, not having a car was like not having a vital organ. Besides, I couldn't schedule emergencies around train and bus schedules. I needed to know I could take off any time I had to.

Though I'd moved to the city three years ago, I still wasn't quite used to New York's noise, dirt and indifference. But everything you could think of could be had within these few hundred blocks, and in varieties that boggled the mind. In the mood for, say, pad Thai at 2 a.m.? You could get it, takeout or delivery. It fascinated me that right around the corner from my place was a warehouse-size store that sold light bulbs. Just light bulbs. Another shop sold just lamp bases, and another, just shades. You'd think that eventually they'd get together, pool their expertise and their resources. But no.

That spirit of uncooperative entrepreneurship was another of the city's charms. Where else were there nightclubs and eateries whose sole business policy seemed to be to keeping out paying customers who wanted desperately to get in? And the history! No matter where you walked, you were never far from a seedy tavern where some major literary figure had drunk himself to death.

But the main attraction was that living where I did pretty much guaranteed no unannounced visits from my relatives. All of my unwieldy extended family—cousins, second-cousins, first-cousins-once removed, half-cousins, uncles, aunts, great-aunts and women I had always called "aunt" though we had no blood tie—lived on the other side of the river and believed strongly that all viable food, air and water stopped at its west bank. For propriety's sake, I occasionally invited a few relatives to my apartment, knowing that I would get the standard response, even from those for whom it would have been only a twenty-minute train ride: a hand clapped to the chest and a moaned, "Oh, that's so *far*." This from people who would endure three hours of bumper-to-bumper traffic to get to the beach, or would stand on line for an hour alongside chain-smoking felons to place a bet at the racetrack.

Not that I would have it any other way. My geographic isolation meant that no one had inside knowledge of my personal life. No one offered me unsolicited home-decorating tips. Of course, it also meant that no one dropped in with an extra pan of lasagna from time to time. But everything in life is a trade-off.

THE MUNICIPAL GODS were with me: I found a parking spot only half a block from my apartment. After stopping along the way for a double order of vegetable dumplings, I unlocked the street door, feeling, though not seeing, Mrs. Pemberton peering around the heavy brocade curtains on her ground-floor apartment window.

In the lobby, I released my mail from its box, clicked the metal door shut and shuffled through catalogs until I saw an envelope imprinted with the logo of my building's rental-management company. I tore it up without breaking stride toward the elevator. I hit the up button as I glanced through the other envelopes. Electric bill, gas bill, water bill, tax bill...and one with the return address of a suburban newspaper.

I ripped it open and pulled out the single sheet: *Thank you for your interest in employment opportunities at The Times Herald-Record, but the newspaper is not hiring at this time.*

"Not hiring"? But I'd answered a want ad in *Editor & Publisher,* fer chrissake!

Then I noticed that the elevator was out of order again. The perfect ending to this glorious day.

As I climbed the seven flights, I tried to look on the sunny side. Well, at least as long as I lived here I wouldn't need a gym membership. But that was all I could come up with.

I undid my deadbolt and knob lock, then entered my palatial domicile.

My apartment was the kind known as a railroad flat, spacious by some local standards, with a galley kitchenette that wouldn't have been out of place in a 747. A sink as wide as a dinner plate, a midget stove with a two-burner stovetop, one bank of cabinets above a counter that barely fit my toaster oven. The bathroom was worse. I watched my weight only to ensure that I could fit into the slender shower. The sink barely cleared the front of the toilet—which, as I discovered during a particularly vicious bout of food poisoning, was convenient if you had nausea and diarrhea at the same time.

I'd put a notice on the bulletin board at the nearby art college, and an interior-design major earned his thesis figuring out how to make my one room do the work of three. A double-bed frame was up on pilings just a few feet from the high ceiling to create a sleeping loft, reachable by ladder. A small sofa, bookshelves and bureau were tucked underneath. The adjacent dining table doubled as my desk: Computer and supplies nested in a separate cubby-holed console that could be raised and lowered on a soundless pulley system. The tabletop itself was hinged to the wall, so that, with the gate legs folded, it could drop down nearly flat if I needed more space, for, say, calypso dancing.

I'd paid another student fifty bucks to paint a mural around the walls, and she'd rendered some charming beach scenes, complete with a bustling boardwalk, blue sky and fluffy clouds overhead. It was a nifty space, worthy of a feature on *Lifestyles of the Poor and Obscure*. More important, the apartment's only window had a view of the river.

As the solid-steel door clanged behind me, I heard a noise by the wastebasket in the kitchen area. He came out then, a blur of gray heading straight toward me. I immediately reached for an infant-size diaper from a box in the closet next to the door, crouched down and waited for my welcome home.

ONE RAINY NIGHT not long after I'd moved in, I'd found him as I was leaving my garbage outside. At first I'd thought I'd have to smash him with the lid of the trashcan, but then I realized he was not a larger-than-average specimen of urban vermin. He was a dog, somewhat resembling a mastiff, only about one-fiftieth the size and shivering pathetically. It didn't help the rodent comparison that his bark was more of a squeak. No collar tag, and no one claimed him after I posted a notice on the telephone pole outside the building. (Well, only one poster and for only one week; I wasn't *that* anxious to find his owner.) I named him Ben, after the movie and the Michael Jackson song.

Ben was the perfect small-space pet. He slept a lot, he didn't shed, he barely pooped and he could last a good while alone with a bowlful of water and a handful of kibble. Not that I left him behind much; he was so quiet, and fit so easily into a coat pocket or purse that I could take him undetected onto most public transportation and into most public places. Ben has been to London and to *Les Miz*.

Now Ben zigzagged in short bursts in front of me. I palmed him and batted him back and forth on the hardwood floor. This delighted him. Almost anything delighted him. Unfortunately, such delight usually triggered the release of whatever was stored in his bladder. As he started to squat, I unfolded the diaper and shoved it under his butt. Pampers marks the spot, and it would save me from having to walk him after dinner.

I put Big Mama Thornton on the CD player (Ben and I both

preferred her grittier version of "Hound Dog" to Elvis's), then ate my takeout as I read a real newspaper. It seemed today our vice-president had incorrectly added an *e* to the end of the word "potato" at a spelling bee in Trenton. Too bad. He'd blown his chance to compete in the national championships.

I popped the last dumpling into my mouth and played back my phone messages. There was only one, from my boyfriend, Doug, saying he might be in the city Friday. Our long-distance relationship had seemed romantic the first two years after I'd relocated, but it was starting to show the strain. When I'd lost my job on the city paper, the main reason for my move, he'd thought I'd head back upstate. I'd thought better of it. We alternated weekends, when we could.

I looked at my watch. Nine. Not too late for a call. I hit number one on my speed dial.

"Hey, Kit Cat," I said, when the ringing stopped.

Caterina gave her ritual response. "Yo, Big Sister."

So I was, by nine minutes. I'd beaten Cat out of the womb first, making my premiere at 11:54 p.m. on November 30, without a backward glance. But my twin sister had bided her time, maybe knowing better than I did what the world had in store for us.

When it came time for our parents to enroll us at Holy Mother Little Academy, Sister Connie pointed out that Cat's December 1 birthday was past the cutoff date for that year's kindergarten class. My father wanted to fight it, but my mother thought it might be good for Cat to have an extra year at home. "The undivided attention will help her mature," I heard her tell my aunt Angela. The separation was good for me, forcing me to make my own connections. But for Cat, it only delayed the inevitable tough adjustment to a more disciplined environment.

From early on, I was both Cat's shadow and her guardian. Her seeming fearlessness amazed me and I followed her, entranced, into whatever breach she found. Once there, though, it was all I could do to keep her from hurting herself, starting a small fire or inciting a riot. Sometimes she managed to do all three.

Like the time she had climbed into a tree in the Gilpatricks' yard to get a better look at an old bird's nest, shimmying along the limb until it wouldn't hold her weight. She came down on top of Johnny, who had been using his magnifying glass on an anthill in an attempt to incinerate its occupants.

The fight that followed eventually involved me and five of the younger Gilpatricks. No one noticed that the magnifying glass was now focusing the bright autumn sun onto a pile of dead leaves. Luckily, the fire department was able to save the other trees in the yard.

See, her troublemaking was never malicious or deliberate. She never expected anything to end badly. It just always did. Yet, I preferred those times to the others, when she would retreat into herself so far I couldn't follow. She would sit for hours, arranging and rearranging the stuffed animals on her bed and wouldn't let me near her. Mom worried, while Dad reassured her that Cat would grow out of it, whatever it was. It often seemed like we traveled in the same circles, with my sister in an orbit all her own.

When we'd moved down the seashore, she barely left our new bedroom that whole summer. Then when Dad died, she took his death harder than any of us, which is saying something. We were fourteen by then, so it was easy to blame her withdrawal on teenage angst.

Somehow she made it through high school, even graduating with honors. I was already away at college, majoring in newspaper journalism. Cat, ambivalent about higher education, enrolled at the state university a few hours from home, with no plan in mind.

My senior year, her roommate called me, hysterical, in the middle of the night: Cat was hopping along the window ledge of their dormitory, eight flights up, yelling for me. After alerting the campus police, I drove six hours, without breathing, to bring her home.

The next decade was a farce of misdiagnoses, mismedications and misguided attempts at re-entry into society. The final label: bipolar with a touch of attention-deficit and a dash of a few other psychosocial disorders. "She's very complicated," her caseworker concluded. No kidding.

Sometimes it seemed that the doctors were only experimenting with new ways to make her into a zombie. But in the past two years they'd come up with a combination of drugs that seemed to bring her closer to reality. Slowly, Cat's old sense of humor began resurfacing, along with a new problem: OCD. Obsessive-compulsive disorder. In some ways, I guess it had always been there, but her life was now ruled by rituals that only she understood.

Still, her progress was steady enough that the county mental-health services had settled her into a group home, given her computer training and a job in data processing at the hospital.

Of course, the program's funding was in constant threat of drying up. If it did, I was sending Cat to live with George and Barbara in the White House. For now, though, she was within walking distance of an ocean beach, the only environment that could be counted on to soothe her.

But it was all too much and too late for my mother. She went to sleep one night last fall and decided not to wake up.

Yeah, a sad tale. But there are worse ones. Some days, I look into Cat's face, a mirror image of my own, and I think, *There but for the grace of...whom?*

Other days, I'm not sure what grace I've been given. Eventually even the unbearable becomes the everyday. Life is what it is. People are born, people die, the sun shines, the bills get paid, someone tells a funny story.

Tonight Cat was telling me one about her new roommate. "The chick's crazy," she said without irony. "Every five seconds she's looking to make sure she didn't put her hamster in the microwave. The thing is, she doesn't have a hamster."

"I didn't know you had a microwave."

"Yeah. I bought one that has an automatic 'Hamster' setting. Browns them up good." She exhaled noisily. She must have started smoking again. "And our counselor wants me to go to this support group for OCD." Her inhale was just as noisy. "But I don't think I can do it. I keep imagining a room filled with ovens and everybody jumping up every two seconds to check if they left the gas on."

Then, as often happened, she switched thoughts on a dime.

"I did not send you my birth certificate to get a passport so I can visit ancient Rome."

"No, Cat, you didn't." I heard the babble of the television in the background. Something must have set her brain cycling.

"Repeat it."

"You did *not* send me your birth certificate to get a passport so you can visit ancient Rome."

"I did not send you my birth certificate to get a passport so I can visit ancient Rome."

"You did not send me your birth certificate to get a passport so you can visit ancient Rome."

"Okay." The relief in her voice was immense. "Shit. I gotta stop watching these old movies. I'm *not* Spartacus, right?"

"Right, Cat."

"When you coming again?"

"I'll be down the Fourth of July weekend. And Cat?"

"Yeah?"

"In the meantime, try not to lead any slave revolts."

"I can't make any promises," said my sister.

• *Chapter 3* •

"Prostate cancer!" said Colin Eaton, editor-in-chief of the *National Moon*, jabbing his highly sharpened pencil in my direction.

"No, thanks," I muttered under my breath. I knew Colin wouldn't hear me. He was caught up in the sound of his own voice.

It was a typical Monday. My feature on Joel Hartt had run the Friday before last, and now it was business as usual. The rest of the tabloid's staff, who at that point in the weekly news meeting had nearly covered their notebook pages with hostile doodles, glanced in my direction then went back to their artwork.

Colin resumed his pacing. "Who in Hollywood's got it and why are they keeping it secret? I'll bet that Elizabeth Taylor's one. She gets *everything*."

"To the best of my knowledge, Colin," I began cautiously, "prostate cancer is an exclusively male disease."

"Who says?"

I hadn't the heart to argue with him. It would have been too cruel. "I'll check with my source in the records department at Cedars-Sinai in L.A.," I offered instead. "He's the one who gave me the heads up about that movie hunk who had an emergency... um, gerbil-ectomy."

"Brilliant."

Once upon a time, Colin Eaton had covered the Vietnam War, and every other Third World skirmish since, for a European publishing syndicate. He'd married the publisher's daughter and eventually been rewarded with a cushy editorship on the international desk at its London newspaper. Then the publisher acquired the *Moon* in the U.S. and pegged Colin to run it. He had no idea why he'd been picked for the job and even less of an idea how to perform it. He seemed genuinely baffled by the types of features that typically ran in American tabloids, though Britain certainly had a few publications that were even worse.

He brought up Elizabeth Taylor at nearly every meeting because she'd been born in London, and he'd seen her in *National Velvet* when he was eight. From his knowledge of celebrities, I concluded that he hadn't set foot in a theater in the nearly fifty years since, nor did he own a television set. I often doubted that Colin even read the *Moon*.

I hadn't either, before I started here a month ago. But 18.9 million others did, weekly. "The Earth Revolves Around The *Moon*" some advertising genius had plastered on highway billboards, bus kiosks and railway placards across the country, and sometimes it seemed like it did.

How I got here could be turned into one of the paper's headlines: *Scandal-Scarred Reporter Abducted by Aliens!*

After I'd gotten my journalism degree, I'd stayed in upstate New York to work on local papers, covering everything from the police blotter to school-board meetings. Eventually I'd landed in the features department at the capital paper. After a few years, when my predecessor left to make babies, I was made department editor.

By then, I'd realized that Baby Boomers, the generation who

swore never to trust anyone over thirty, were over thirty themselves. Now they trusted no one. They were their own doctors, their own lawyers and their own best friends. Where once they wanted to live fast, die young and leave a good-looking corpse, they now wanted to slow down, live to be a hundred and leave an even better-looking corpse. They turned to fad diets, high-tech exercise equipment, plastic surgery and liposuction. As consumerism replaced communes, they were fueling this obsession not just with their neuroses but also with their 1980s-size paychecks. Of course, I was one of them, bringing up the rear of my gen-gen-generation.

I fed on the self-help revolution, expanding the paper's health and medicine coverage. Through my reporting over the years, I'd hooked up with a cell biologist at the local university medical school who had some theories on reversing aging. I suggested he write a book. He suggested I help him. I took a year off to ghost-write it, spending almost as much time in the rumpled but cute Doctor Doug's bed as I did in his lab.

When *Forever Young* hit the best-seller list, it didn't seem to matter that it was a complicated discussion of free radicals, anti-oxidants and adrenal hormones. Boomers bought the book as if it gave the recipe for Eternal Youth, and they rushed out to buy vitamins in bulk. I didn't get a big cut of the royalties, but my skill at making the technical medical info readable did net me an offer for a job on the nation's biggest paper, housed in a skyscraper that looked out across the river to my old neighborhood.

My fall from that skyscraper last November was pure hubris. The year before, and two minutes before deadline, my editor had demanded that I spice up a routine story on potentially harmful drug interactions with a TLD—a "true-life drama." Like much of the mainstream media, the paper seemed to be getting away from health care into health scare, with headlines like "Is It a Mole—or Is It Cancer?" and variations on the theme: "Is It a Cough—or Is It Cancer?" "Is It Gas—or Is It Cancer?"

Piqued that two weeks of expert research wasn't enough,

I pulled out a nearly fatal case study from a medical journal and gave its unnamed patient a name—my cousin Paula's. Considering her past as a scam artist, I thought she'd get a kick out of it, and what was the harm? The facts were still the facts.

Paula could have cared less, but said she'd go along with it if anyone called to check. No one did. Not then.

What I didn't admit to myself at the time was that I'd really wanted to thumb my nose at Paula's mother, my aunt Angela. Paula was Aunt Angie's late-in-life baby. Since the day Paula was born, a few months after me and Cat, Aunt Angie had been holding her daughter up to us as the competition to beat. "Why can't you two be more like my Paula?" when we didn't run up to her with hugs and kisses like Paula did to suck up to the other relatives.

What Aunt Angie didn't know was that, since she was eleven, her darling was leading us behind the backyard hedge at family parties, telling Cat to lay chickie while she snuck puffs on a Virginia Slim. In high school, she "borrowed" some of my English papers and passed them off as her own. In her freshman year at an Ivy League college, she used Cat to smuggle a published term paper, stuffed down her pants, out of the graduate-school library. Naturally, Paula went on to get her MBA.

Such well-practiced life skills paid off big for Paula. Now she was the head of marketing at a major pharmaceutical firm, married to the chief executive officer and had produced the perfect Italian-American average of 2.46 kids. (She was now nearly five months pregnant.) CEO were the first letters of the alphabet Aunt Angela taught her grandchildren. So I thought Aunt Angie might be impressed to see my power to get her daughter's name into the most respected newspaper in the country. Silly me.

But of course, Aunt Angie read the article and knew her daughter hadn't nearly died from mixing the antidepressant Elavil with the ulcer drug Propulsid, as I'd claimed. Ever since, she never missed an opportunity to remind me of my lack of integrity, "not like my Paula." My cousin, at least, had the good grace to look embarrassed each time her mother said it.

But Paula had forgotten all about the article when a fact-checker called a year later. It was a fluke, really. Another major paper had been shamed when it was found that a star columnist had fictionalized a story, citing sources that didn't exist. Then the same situation turned up at a national newsmagazine. Our paper, to forestall any such investigation by an outsider, randomly pulled a few features and news pieces from the past eighteen months to scrutinize. My drug-interactions piece was caught in the dragnet.

When Paula failed to corroborate the TLD, I was called in. I gathered all my backup and was able to show them that it had been a legitimate, though anonymous, case from a respectable journal. I *had* talked to the doctor cited in the article, but he just wouldn't release the name of his patient. If it came up, the paper could claim it had changed the name to protect the patient's privacy. That saved me from a public flogging. But it didn't save me from getting fired.

Six months later, after sending out a ream of resumes, I ended up at the *Moon*. There, my "lack of integrity" was a selling point.

The weird thing was, I was relieved. No more pretense. Over the years, I'd realized I lacked a certain earnestness that was essential to keep from getting burned out, to keep you believing that you were presenting the truth, the whole truth and nothing but. Many of my college classmates had entered journalism in the wake of Watergate, and in the hope of bringing down a corrupt public figure or exploitative corporation. I had watched the trial hearings while making out with my high school boyfriend in front of the TV in his parents' rec room.

My former colleagues turned their noses up at the *Moon*. But their readers could afford the best doctors and tests. At least I was now giving accurate information on breast self-exams to those who probably couldn't swing even the HMO co-pay for a mammogram. So what if the story was illustrated by the bosomy babes of *Baywatch*? It got the job done. And okay, I admit it, the

Moon paid better. A lot better. I also admit to being a little star-struck myself, right from my *Million-Dollar Movie* days.

So here I was at the world's least respected tabloid, in a new skyscraper with a slightly different view of the river, rationalizing my mistakes in life like everyone else.

As a sign of dismissal, Colin Eaton had tucked his pencil behind his left ear. Before working for Colin, the only newspaper editor I'd ever actually seen do that was Walter Burns in *The Front Page.* Every time Colin repositioned his No. 2 Eberhard Faber, I thought he might accidentally give himself a lobotomy. But he never did. He knew his way around a pencil.

Unfortunately, that was about the level of his understanding of technology. Though management recently installed a new network to connect the newsroom to the printing plant, Colin refused to turn on his computer. Probably because he couldn't tuck the keyboard behind his ear. We had to print out our stories, then decipher the comments he hand-scratched in the margins.

As the staff filed out of Colin's office, Elise Kalember, the executive editor, sidled up to me. "We have to talk."

Inwardly I groaned. Nothing good ever came of a conversation that began with "We have to talk." And talking face to face with Elise was always an unnerving experience.

I followed her down the hall. But instead of leading me into her office, she kept going, down to the elevators, into a lift, through the lobby and out the revolving doors. I thought we'd reached our destination, but no. Down the block, a left, then a quick right into a tight alley between a dry cleaner and a falafel stand.

Before she said a word, she reached into the pocket of her full skirt, pulled out a Marlboro and a lighter, introduced the two to each other, then took a thirsty drag. I could see her body chemistry change right before my eyes.

"Ah," she coughed. "Sorry. I was dying." She glanced around curiously at our surroundings, as if she didn't know how we got there.

I knew *why* we were there. Colin hated smoking. The rumor was that a lit butt glowing in the dark had gotten him shot at in a rice paddy near Da Nang. Whatever the reason, he made everyone sign a nonsmoking agreement upon hiring, whether it was legal or not. I'd heard that Elise went through elaborate charades to cover up her habit. Yet she never caught on that they were pointless. Everyone else already knew. Hourly splashes of Obsession couldn't cover up that she smelled like a lightning strike in a Virginia tobacco field. Even Colin couldn't miss the stench.

"Don't tell anyone about this." Elise flicked ash. "It's weak, I know."

No one at the *Moon* thought she was weak. We all thought she was nuts.

Start with her hair. It was dyed the colors of a sunset—not one from nature, but a palette straight off a black-velvet painting sold out of a van parked under a highway overpass. It was nearly waist length, and she came up with new ways to arrange it that would have stumped a structural engineer. A Judy Jetson fountain out the top of her head one day, a Princess Leia set of earmuff braids the next.

Her wardrobe was the stuff of fiction too: High-heeled mules and little cocktail dresses that no one made anymore, with cross-over straps and flared skirts out of a 1950s movie starring Susan Hayward as a good-bad girl. But the outfits looked new, not vintage. Maybe she sewed them up herself. I liked to amuse myself by picturing her pumping the treadle of an old Singer, a cigarette clamped between her ruby-painted lips.

But though I'd never ask her for fashion advice, I was glad to have her vet my copy. She could plug a hole in a leaky story faster than that little Dutch boy at the dike and her quick-loading mental database would shame the National Center for Health Statistics. She came by this medical encyclopedia naturally—she was a world-class hypochondriac.

She also had a knack for knowing exactly what *Moon* readers wanted. Without her, Colin would be on the next plane to Heathrow.

"You know, we got an incredible response from your Hartt piece." Her breathy little-girl voice was, as always, disconcerting. "Sympathy was an angle we hadn't tried before. The stuff about his mother's cancer, his lonely childhood. It's getting attention from the TV networks, too. I got a few calls asking about you."

Great. I had tried to keep it from being too sensational; I had also described the tremendous changes in town and the greed that may have brought about a little girl's death. But Elise edited what I'd written to focus on Joel. I *had* been sympathetic to him, what I saw in him. Now interest was heating up in what had become a cold story.

I'd wondered how Joel would feel about that. I understood at the time that there was a chance, a good one, that he was using me to recast his image. It even worried me a little when he called and told me he liked the story, said he was glad he had talked to me. I mean, what if it backfired and pressure was back on to arrest a suspect soon—with him the only one handy?

"Colin didn't bring it up in the staff meeting, but we want another one," Elise was saying. "You can play up that 'a father's grief' stuff. *The Last Days of My Doomed Daughter.* Something like that. Talk to the people who were at his New Year's party too."

My insides curdled. "I've got a lot of assigning to do in the next few weeks before people go off on vacation and the editing will pile up, I don't think—"

She waved me off with the last inch of her Marlboro. "I'll give you until next Thursday's deadline. We can divide your other work around."

"Do I have a choice?"

The *Moon's* executive editor ground her cigarette butt on the pavement with the toe of her red stiletto. "Nope."

I spent the next day moving my files off my desk. Someone else would have to find out if Elizabeth Taylor had prostate cancer.

45

On Wednesday I left a message for Joel, asking for the names and numbers of his New Year's guests. While on the phone, I missed a call that bounced to my phone mail—a surprise offer from Mickey Giamonte to take me to dinner that night.

I left my own message to accept, but was having second thoughts, when Dovie dropped off a stack of clippings and print-outs she had gathered through LexisNexis, the news research service. Dovie Austin was my summer intern, from a small college in Tennessee. Smart, efficient and chatty as hell. She called me *ma'am*. Even worse, she was the reason I had the Hartt assignment. Two weeks ago I caught her reading about Emma Hartt in an old *Moon* issue, and offhandedly mentioned that I was once Joel Hartt's babysitter. That sure caught Dovie's interest, and also the attention of Elise, who was passing by at the time.

"You didn't ask me to, ma'am, but I pulled everything on anyone connected with the investigation." Her soft drawl wasn't even the most attractive thing about Dovie. Tall, thin, with fine mocha skin and cheekbones that could cut diamonds, she could have been a supermodel herself. What was she doing here?

"That poor child! That something so *horrible* could happen. Made me madder than a striped snake, I'll tell you." She pronounced "striped" as two syllables. "If there's anything else you need, ma'am, you just let me know."

Emma Hartt had made headlines while I was jobless, dealing with another Cat crisis and living at our old house down the shore. Now that I was expected to be an expert on the case, I had to catch up on the details.

I sighed and picked up the first clipping. When a kid dies, everyone's shocked. But, really, when the head counts are taken at the end of the day, the real surprise is that anyone survives childhood. You believe you can fly like Superman, you believe in Santa Claus, you believe all adults have only your best interests at heart. Until that moment when you stop believing, and childhood ends.

Maybe that's what killed Emma Hartt. Whom had she trusted

enough to allow herself to be lifted out of bed in the middle of the night?

It was six months later, with no new leads. I didn't understand why Elise wanted me to stay with it. Emma Hartt had already been knocked off the front page by a 17-year-old high-school girl, the 36-year-old auto mechanic who was her lover, and his wife, who the teenager had shot in the face. Like most of the tabloids, the *Moon* had taken their best muckrakers off the "Murdered Moppet Model" to get the latest on the "Long Island Lolita."

The page I held from the *Moon* was dominated by a full-color photo of Emma from about a year ago, stretched out on a chaise longue. The pose was gratuitously provocative, since the ad seemed to be selling the shoes that were kicked under the sofa. Most of the other papers and magazines reprinted this and the close-up of her made up like a 25-year-old.

Those images had stuck in my mind, and the public's mind as well. What kind of parents would allow their daughter to display herself in this way, rob her of her childhood? It made it easy to cast Joel in the role of villain.

It reminded me of all the public disapproval stirred up when Brooke Shields, the Ivory Snow Baby, played the *Pretty Baby* prostitute at twelve. Not long after, I'd stepped onto a New York elevator and there she was, a gorgeous teenager but still clinging shyly to her mom. Now a Princeton graduate, Brooke turned out to be pretty levelheaded—except for making that lousy *Brenda Starr* movie a few years ago.

Like Brooke, Emma had that startlingly sensual, almost adult beauty from an early age. It made some grown men think thoughts that they shouldn't. An advertiser's dream.

"Out of hundreds of innocent ads, those same two shots were printed over and over!" That was the only moment during our interview in his study ten days ago that Joel showed anything like genuine outrage. "Do people really think I'd let my daughter be exploited that way?"

The candid photos he then showed me could have come from any family album, starting with one of a joyfully pregnant Kristine showing off her swollen belly as one-year-old Evan clung to her leg. In the others, Emma looked like any other cute blonde munchkin blowing out the candles on her third-birthday cake, opening presents on Christmas morning, lighting the first Chanukah candle. (The Hartts seemed to give equal time to both religious holidays. Lucky kids.) Joel had lent me some of these snapshots to illustrate the *Moon* interview—which had sent my stock soaring with Elise.

My piece made it clear that Emma's career hadn't been her parents' idea. A photographer friend of Joel's had taken a family portrait of the Hartts and a few individual shots of the kids. Without asking permission, he had included one of Emma in his commercial portfolio. The art director at a boutique ad agency thought the sweet-faced toddler would be perfect for its new client, a former fashion icon hoping for a comeback with a line of upscale children's clothing.

The friend acted as go-between, but Joel was reluctant to let Emma model. Kristine, though, thought the experience might help Emma might get over her almost painful bashfulness. Neither had anticipated how their child would bloom under the camera's gaze. Emma's natural shyness evaporated whenever a lens was pointed in her direction. "She loved it," Joel had said in wonder. It was like playing dress-up, only this Barbie doll had an entourage of stylists.

When the ad campaign took off, more offers came rolling in. The Hartts tried to keep this sudden demand under control, allowing her to be booked only a few times a year.

When she was ready for kindergarten, they sent her to Holy Moly, along with Evan. Joel and Kristine figured parochial school discipline would help offset the influence of the wider world. Besides, you either learned from the nuns—or else. They wouldn't pass you just for occupying a classroom seat, or let fame—the Eighth Deadly Sin—go to your head.

As Emma grew older, her beauty matured too. Then came the Hollywood offers, small roles in big movies. Joel wouldn't let his daughter accept anything that would take her out of school for too long.

Kristine Hartt eventually quit her job at the hospital to manage her daughter's career rather than put her in the hands of someone whose only interest in Emma was a percentage of her earnings.

I'd noticed that, whatever Emma's public profile, Evan got equal time in the home picture gallery, which chronicled his own babyhood up to the present. He seemed just as photogenic. "No modeling?" I'd asked Joel.

Joel shook his head. "He tagged along on some shoots and was approached, but he was never interested. At least, not with that side of the camera. My boy has already decided he wants to be a photographer when he grows up." His eyes brightened, then lost what little light they'd had. "Emma had plans too. She was artistic, like her mother. She wanted to be a designer. She picked up a lot from those fashion people, asked a lot of questions. It held her interest more than school."

When Kristine died, Joel had wanted to cancel Emma's bookings. But just a few months after her mother's death, Emma was back in the studio, accompanied by Doreen or Kristine's sister. Joel had hoped this "routine" might help distract his grieving daughter.

But just before the holidays, Joel had decided to limit Emma's work, as he saw more and more ads heading in the prurient direction. Emma had been upset, and had even taken the usual commuter bus into the city on her own, to be at a photo shoot scheduled months before.

"We argued about it." Joel's gray eyes then locked onto my brown ones. "But she was my daughter and she was a good girl. It's not what you think."

"I wasn't thinking anything," I had lied.

After I'd left him that night, I still wasn't sure what to think.

As he'd shown me to the door, he'd placed a hand on my shoulder. "I know you'll do the right thing."

Now, almost two weeks later, I looked at the newspaper and magazine pages spread out on my desk and did think: What if this was my daughter? What if I was drunk and angry? Would I be capable of something that I could never take back?

I glanced at my watch. I had to leave in ten minutes if I was going to make my dinner date. As I shuffled the clippings together, another photo caught my eye. A couple walking out of a police station, heads bowed. I read the caption, then scanned the whole story.

Son of a bitch.

"SON OF A bitch," I said to Mickey, after we were seated in a back booth at the Stone's Throw. "When were you going to tell me that Juliet Rojas and Jesse Quindlen were Joel Hartt's guests New Year's Eve?"

"I assumed you'd done your homework."

I looked away to get my anger under control. The dark wood-paneled walls held framed photos of Mickey with his regulars, as well as some minor celebrities and state politicians sporting campaign buttons. I stared into the smug smile of a once-respected local newscaster who had gotten a national talk show that served up the usual daytime fare, like mothers who date their daughters' ex-boyfriends. With his puffy helmet of hair, he looked like a brown Q-Tip.

Mickey noticed my interest. "That's Ramon Santiago."

"You don't have to tell me. I had a teenage crush on him. He's why I joined the high school newspaper."

"He's got a place in The Colony now."

"Really? I'm surprised he hasn't featured any of the Barnum & Bailey midgets on that freak show of his." I turned away from the wall. "Don't change the subject. Who else do I know who's involved? Joel's lawyer, R. Taylor Fine—any relation to Gina?"

He looked at me with mock disappointment. "Jeez. Your best

friend from grammar school and you don't remember that her full name is Regina?"

"Gina's an attorney?"

"The best money can buy around here."

"This is too creepy."

"Yeah, like Old Home Week for you. Imagine what a kick it's been for me. Like we're all just back playing dodge ball on the Holy Moly blacktop. For some reason, they didn't treat me with the respect my authority deserves."

"I wonder why. Anyone else I should know about who was there?"

"Just Gordon de Porres, Joel's partner. Not a Holy Moly kid. He and Gina were together, mixing business with pleasure. That night, at least. Where's our food?" He turned to signal to our waiter, who shrugged. You'd think he'd have some influence here but the place was packed. "Oh, yeah, and the mayor. Kenneth Whalen. And his wife, Kathleen. She's a nurse."

"Whalen? Wasn't he mayor when we were kids?"

"If it ain't broke, don't fix it. It's not like we have term limits. And it's not like it's a full-time job here. Whalen teaches at the state university law school and still has his practice."

"Is he responsible for all the changes?"

"He's on board, for the most part. He pushed to get clearance for the old factory properties. But another rumor has it that next year's Election Day may be his last."

"If he's with the program, what's the problem?"

"Just that he'd like to see land set aside for a high school, with a football field and track. There's a chance the next new governor is going to approve some of the old dumpsites for development. Whalen wants to earmark a prime spot for the upper grades. He's asking for a few acres of waterfront—the old auto-parts plant—that would otherwise go to house a couple hundred new taxpayers."

"Nothing like kids frolicking over toxic waste during recess."

"It's better than having to catch a bus at 6:30 in the morning to commute for an hour to school. You missed that joy after eighth grade. Besides, they'll clean it up first. The law says they have to."

"I don't think they make a DustBuster powerful enough for that."

"They wouldn't let them build anything there if it weren't safe."

"That's what they said about Love Canal."

He dismissed me with a hand gesture. "Anyhow, the Borough Council seems to be split about whether to issue a bond to buy the property. Young families want the school, older folks don't want to pay for it. And the high-powered among us want more commercial properties, more revenue and their more 'progressive' candidate in office."

"Same old story. Risk versus benefits. Whoever winds up on the land will be suing the town when a cancer cluster pops up in twenty years." I took the hint from Mickey's exasperated look. "Alright. Back to the guest list. Did Joel have a date that night? Enough time had passed, right? It wouldn't have been so weird."

"Supposedly he'd invited Kaori Masako, if I'm saying her name right. She's the liaison in this country for the Japanese firm that's investing in his shopping plaza. But she got sick and begged off. Probably ate some bad sushi. Stuff'll kill you."

"My treat next time. I know a place in the city that serves excellent *fugu*."

"Excuse me?"

"A poisonous puffer fish. If it isn't prepared properly, it paralyzes your central nervous system and you stop breathing."

"Right now, I'm hungry enough to take the chance."

Luckily for him, our dinners arrived. The waiter rotated my plate so the bottom of the potato-crusted salmon lined up with the edge of the table. I hope he didn't expect a bigger tip for that.

"I thought you were a vegetarian." Mickey eyed my entree,

as he took a knife to his porterhouse. "Fish have faces too."

"It's not an animal-rights thing. It's a health thing. Mainly I try to stay away from red meat." I forked up a mouthful of my entree. "Salmon has omega-3 fatty acids. Good for the heart."

"Nothing wrong with my heart except that women keep breaking it."

"Why do I have such a hard time believing you're the injured party?"

"Because you're one of those feminazis, as my radio pal Rush Limbaugh says."

"Ugh. Change of topic. Why are you a cop?"

"Truth, justice and the American way."

"I didn't think you were brought up to believe in any of that."

"I wasn't," he agreed. "I had to rebel against my father somehow." He put down his fork. "I started law school but couldn't hack it. Too boring. I wanted to be where the action is. Not that there was a lot of action when I started on the force here. It's easy to keep tabs on everyone when half the town is related to the other half.

"It's changing, but you remember how it was. If you did something wrong, you were more worried your mom would find out than the cops. Anyhow, ten years ago I moved over to the County Prosecutor's Office, Criminal Investigations. Now I'm the youngest ever chief of detectives. And I have other ambitions." He lifted another hunk of meat to his lips.

Would I have to perform the Heimlich maneuver on him tonight?

"Now you." He chewed and swallowed almost simultaneously. "Why journalism?"

"Same reason. Truth, justice, et cetera. I liked to write, I was on the paper in high school. I thought I might go into broadcasting. Then came Watergate. I wanted to be Bernstein—Woodward was too WASPy—meeting unnamed sources in parking garages. Unfortunately, it wasn't until senior year that I realized I have a deathly fear of dark, underground spaces. I also am not that interested in politics. Even worse, I'm too polite to ask people the hard questions that win you Pulitzers. It must be the good-girl Catholic thing."

"Still a good girl?"

"Within reason."

"If it'll get you a juicy enough story?"

"What are you saying?"

With his next words Mickey cut his steak so violently I worried that he'd cut the plate in half. "I can't get two unscripted words out of Joel Hartt for six months, but now he's pouring his heart out to you."

"You've got to be kidding." I had my hand on my own knife now. "You think I slept with him for that?"

"It wouldn't be the first time a—"

"It *would* be for *me*." I didn't count my relationship with Doug. That started *after* a story. "Maybe he just wants his version out in the open. Everybody else has had their shot."

"The only version is the truth. That's the one *I'm* trying to get."

"So am I." I said it but I wasn't sure I believed it. "Listen, if he's willing to talk to me, maybe that can help you too. I already asked him about interviewing everyone who was there. Maybe talking to me instead of a cop, someone will remember something that would be helpful to your case. Work with me, okay?"

That only seemed to aggravate Mickey more. "Work with you? Let's see, what was the opening line of your story? 'When they were kids, Detective Michelangelo Giamonte accused Joel Hartt of having cooties. Now he's accusing his neighborhood nemesis of something much worse.' That was *very* helpful. Selling out your old friends."

"You can't sue me for the truth, Mickey."

"You made it seem like I've always had it in for the guy."

"Thomas Wolfe was right," I sighed. "You *can't* go home again."

"That writer? What do writers know?" He pointed his knife at me. "Don't *you* know when you're being used? C'mon!"

"Isn't that the way the game is played? You use me, I use you. We all get what we want."

"What *do* you want?"

"To keep my job. I just have to write one more piece here, and then that's it. I can go back to editing, go back to my other life."

"And what kind of life will that be, if you help someone get away with murder?"

He had me there.

• *Chapter 4* •

O N THURSDAY, I left the city and headed through the tunnel and north up River Drive, passing an elegant floating restaurant disingenuously named The Barge, then a shiny strip mall and a fuel-tank graveyard. The town's future, present and past side by side. At the sign for *Riverside Mews: Another Project of the Hartt Development Group,* I signaled right, steered through the gap in the chain-link fence onto a rutted dirt drive, past a metal trailer lettered *Quindlen & Sons,* and pulled into what seemed to be the parking lot.

Picking my way along the uneven ground, I ignored the group of hard-hatted workers on the scaffolding above me, eating sandwiches the size of their heads and throwing bread chunks at the pigeons strutting expectantly on the ground. But I knew I wouldn't get past them unremarked and steeled myself.

"Hey, babe! Want some lunch? I got a nice Italian sausage here!" one yelled down.

I blew him a kiss and kept walking. After a few years in the city, I stopped taking construction crews personally. I knew their notice had little to do with my looks, and my rapidly wrinkling linen pantsuit sure wasn't a come-on. I'd once walked past a work site in the dead of winter wearing a down parka, a ski hat pulled over my forehead and a scarf up to my eyeballs. A guy still whistled. It's a violation of union laws not to.

A smaller group huddled near the trailer. I assumed, by the hand gestures, that the fat guy holding the walkie-talkie was telling a dirty joke. He must have seen me coming because the gestures got more expansive and he raised his voice a bit. By the time I reached them, he hit the punch line. "So she sez to me, she sez, 'I like to do it chipmunk-style. How about you?' And I sez, 'I know about doggy-style, but I never heard of chipmunk-style.' And she sez, 'Chipmunk style—that's when I store your nuts in my cheeks.'"

As the others guffawed, Walkie-Talkie Guy made a great show of noticing me and feigning embarrassment. "Sorry, dear. Excuse my language."

"That's okay, cocksucker," I said pleasantly. "Can you tell me where to find Jesse Quindlen?"

He turned red and his finger slipped off the Talk button.

"Due north" came a staticky voice from the receiver.

I looked up. A figure gestured from the top of the five-story frame. One of the crew tossed me a hardhat and said, "Follow me."

I tried to, skipping over chunks of debris on the ground while buckling on the hardhat. When we came to a ladder-like section of scaffolding, the crewman pointed at it, twiddled his fingers skyward and left me to make the climb. I cursed them all under my breath.

When I reached the top, I had to walk the plank—a wide one, but that didn't make me any less nervous. I kept my eyes on my shoes, partly to make sure I didn't miss my footing and partly to avoid getting a good look at Jesse Quindlen too soon. I wouldn't have been able to handle it if he'd turned out to be prematurely balding with a pot belly and acne scars.

Jesse had arrived at Holy Moly in the third grade. A tough city kid, a pint-size Robert Mitchum, with the movie star's same heavy lids and lazy gaze and a worldliness that intimidated even Mickey at first. If a ten-year-old could have "bedroom eyes," Jesse did. Now those eyes were giving me the once-over.

I didn't mind. One day in sixth grade Jesse had looked down at my navy-blue fishnets, and said, "Nice legs." That memory *still* keeps me warm some winter nights.

"So, the Prodigal Daughter returns." His voice had the same rough-yet-soft quality and the rest of him could still make a girl's heart flutter. "If I'd known you were coming, I would have killed the fatted calf."

Damn. A flutter. "Ah, Sister Felicia would be happy to know you're keeping up with your Bible studies, James."

"James!" He laughed. "I'd forgotten about that."

Our third-grade teacher had refused to call him by his first name, as if that might confirm his outlaw status. "I have read God's Book from cover to cover and never have I come across a Saint Jesse," she'd said. "I will call you by your Christian middle name, James, and you will answer to it." He did, but not without correcting her every time. His stubbornness had earned him more than a few swats across the knuckles with her metal yardstick.

Now he ran his left hand—ringless, I noted—through slightly long, tawny hair, the exact color of his eyes.... *Snap out of it, Rinaldi!*

"A few years ago I read the Bible cover to cover too," he was saying, "and there *was* a Jesse. King David's father. Which means he was Jesus' great-great, about twenty-five more greats, grandfather."

"Still pre-Christianity and not a saint. The nuns always got us on a technicality."

"I never much counted on getting clearance into Heaven."

"There's still time to redeem yourself."

"Who wants to?" He looked at me as if extending an invitation to join him in whatever would ensure our mutual eternal damnation. I made a mental note to check my schedule. "So now," he gave me a half-grin, "what do you want from *me?*'

"You know what."

"Yeah...but I want to hear you say it."

"I want to get to ground level first."

"What's the matter?" He swung around and swept his arms out to take in the river. "You don't like the view from here?"

I'd closed my eyes as he turned and, when I opened them, they were on his butt. "Some of it," I admitted.

He turned back and grinned. "You know the owner. I'm sure you could get a deal. It's got to be better than what you're paying in the city. Since we started last fall, we've framed up four buildings. The plan is for 400 units with gourmet kitchens, nine-foot ceilings. At the rate we're going, the first ones should be ready for occupancy by the first of the year."

"Show me a prospectus. I'll look it over and, if I like what I see, who knows?" Actually, I was still thinking about his butt.

The trip down was much faster, on a telescoping platform that folded down on itself—a "scissor lift," Jesse called it. So, they'd set me up to make that climb just for fun. Macho crap. Charming.

Jesse opened the trailer door and waved me through. I stepped into the narrow space, packed with the usual office equipment but remarkably neat considering the chaos outside. Tacked to the walls were blueprints, work schedules, permits and other legal notices. Except for a blotter calendar, notes jotted down in neatly penned capital letters, the desk was clutter free. On the corner of it, a phone suddenly rang.

Reaching toward it, Jesse brushed against me ever so lightly.

"Hi, sweetheart." So, his ring finger didn't tell the whole story. "Yeah, I'll be home the regular time." He half-turned away. Was he self-conscious over this little domestic exchange? "Whatever you want to make." He stifled a laugh. "No, anything but that. Remember what happened last time. I don't want to have to repaint the kitchen." He put down the receiver as gently as if it were a baby.

"That the wife?" I had my back to him, pretending to study one of the blueprints. His prolonged silence forced me to turn around.

Jesse's eyelids were lowered to half-mast and the left corner of his mouth was curled up. "Never married, if that's what you're asking."

"Just curious."

"I guess that's why you're here. Just curious about a lot of things."

"I get paid to ask questions."

"I don't get paid to answer them, though. But Joel seems to think it's okay, so we'll see how it goes."

"You two close?"

He lifted a shoulder. "We've worked on projects over the years. We've gotten friendly. Yeah, I think he's a good guy. Wish I could say the same about his partner."

"Gordon de Porres, right? What's that about?"

Jesse seemed to pull himself back. "The usual business stuff. Nothing that concerns you. Or the readers of—what's that high-quality publication you work for?"

I let it pass. "You *must* be pals, to spend New Year's Eve together."

"I'm not much of a drinker, so it's not my favorite holiday. I go where I feel comfortable. Joel's parties are always sane."

"Really? He was pretty drunk that night, or so I heard."

"From who?" Jesse seemed genuinely puzzled.

"Well, the cops said he was still pretty well lit when they showed up the next morning."

"Then they got it wrong. Gordon's the drinker. It doesn't seem to affect him, though. Probably because he doesn't have a bloodstream." Jesse's jaw was tight. "Joel had maybe a glass or two of wine with dinner and a champagne toast at midnight. He wouldn't have gotten drunk with the kids there."

"The kids were part of the party?" I heard a boom, a yell and some shouting from outside, but Jesse didn't seem to notice. Probably all in a day's work.

"Sure. My niece was supposed to come—she's the same age as Joel's son and they're friends. But she got sick. Anyhow, it's a family night. We ate junk food and Sabrett hot dogs, played poker bingo. Very relaxed."

"Sounds like fun." I'd spent New Year's Eve in a hard plastic chair in a blue hospital room.

"It was. Joel's got money, but he's cool with it. Kris would never have married him if he was some high-end asshole."

"You knew her?"

"Sure, since she was a kid. A friend of my sister's. She was a sweetheart. A good person, a great mom."

"And Joel was a good person, a good dad?"

"Is." Under his work-site tan, Jesse's face flushed. "He would do anything for Emma and Evan. No doubt about that."

"No doubt?"

A knock. "Come in." Jesse didn't take his eyes off me.

I heard the trailer door open. I tore my eyes from Jesse's to glance at the guy who entered, hands behind his back, his head ducked down, his hardhat tipped over his forehead.

"Sorry to interrupt, Jess," the fellow almost whispered. "The crane dropped a load, and I had to jump out of the way, and the nail gun got away from me...."

"I'll be right with you."

The guy nodded, and his hardhat hit the floor. He reached for it, blushing to the roots of his black hair. His right hand was wrapped in a dirty rag. It was soaked with blood.

I gasped. Jesse swore. "Jesus, Ray, what happened?"

"Like I said, I had some trouble with the nail gun."

"Come on." Jesse grabbed some keys off a pegboard. "I've gotta get you to the hospital!"

"Gee, thanks, Jesse." Ray lifted his head almost shyly and I looked into the second most beautiful pair of green eyes I'd ever seen.

As Jesse's Jeep tore out of the lot, I checked my notebook for the names, numbers and addresses Joel had dictated to me over the phone that morning. I was just a few blocks north of my next destination, so I left Ringo parked where he was and sidestepped traffic to cross River Drive.

The next side street brought me to a parallel road hidden by the old canning factory. A few art galleries, a health-food store, a coffee bar and café were the clues that I'd entered the funky side of town. It took up all of two blocks.

The shop was easy to spot. Its facade was a psychedelic confusion of peace signs, smiley faces and flower bursts, with *Out of Time* flashing in purple neon above it all. In the window, a spindly mannequin, dressed in lime green hot pants and a red-leather fringed vest, frugged among a forest of pulsating Lava lamps.

I crossed the threshold into a warehouse of nostalgia: stacks of cartoon-character lunchboxes here, a pyramid of Etch-a-Sketches there. Shelves and glass counters displayed troll dolls, mood rings, jeweled cat's-eye glasses, Lucite bangle bracelets, Kennedy and Nixon campaign buttons and plastic wallets imprinted with the faces of the mop-topped Beatles. Clothing racks in the center of the room were jammed with polyester Huckapoos, rayon Hawaiian-print shirts, hiphuggers, Jordache jeans, even Nehru jackets. Re-creations or originals? I couldn't tell.

Stopping at a row of Magic 8 Balls, I picked up one of the black plastic spheres and turned it over. A message bobbed up from the inky blue liquid inside: "Reply Hazy. Try Again."

Toward the back, I saw a sleek head, hair like burnished mahogany, bent over an open cardboard box, one of many. I opened my mouth, curled my tongue, propped it up with the index and ring fingers of my left hand, closed my lips and blew.

At my whistle, the head popped up.

"Oh-oh-oh!" Juliet Rojas jumped up and down, chapping her hands—no kidding—then ran toward me. "Sis, is it really you?" As her arms wrapped around my neck, I melted into her warmth, just I had on my first day of kindergarten when she rescued me at recess.

I'd been standing alone, at a loss without Cat by my side. Mickey had abandoned me, pretending he was too cool to hang out with a girl. Then Juliet had stepped up, thrown her arms around me and said, "You're my sister!"

I found out later that she had five brothers, and her parents had promised her a sister if she'd stop crying and get on the school bus that morning. Our coloring was enough alike that she thought *I* was her parents' reward. Until my last day at Holy Moly, she still called me "Sis."

She later taught me that two-finger whistle, which still comes in handy hailing taxis. And she also taught me about reverse psychology: When boys on the playground teased us, I would threaten them with a fist, as Cat would have. That didn't stop them. Juliet offered to kiss them instead. From then on, the boys left us alone.

Eventually the two of us drifted into different crowds, hers infinitely hipper than mine. Holy Moly hadn't required school uniforms, and Juliet had been the first to show up on the playground in the latest styles from "mod" London—white patent-leather go-go boots, fake-fur vest, culottes, even a paper dress, imprinted with a giant Op Art eye in black and white.

Now here she was holding me at arm's length. I waited for her evaluation. I guessed by the crease in Juliet's upturned nose that she didn't quite approve. Then she tried to tug the wrinkles out of my suit.

"Give it up," I said. "I'm still a *Glamour* 'Don't.'"

She laughed. "You're not so bad. You should go for more tailoring, though. Show off what you got."

"I'd rather keep it my little secret." I nodded at the boxes. "Go on with what you were doing."

"It's vintage, honey. It'll keep. The older it gets, the more I can sell it for. Now, come. Get comfy."

The shop had a sitting area in a corner. I flopped into a beanbag chair, she stretched out on a chenille-covered chaise longue.

"Great place." My butt sank farther into the shifting pellets.

"Thanks." She looked around critically. "It's finally coming together. I had a smaller place in the city, but I wanted to increase my range of retro. Couldn't afford the extra square footage there."

"Why here?"

"Why not?"

"A little off the beaten path for the Greenwich Villagers."

"I send out catalogs to my old customers." Juliet shrugged. "I get a lot of high school and college kids, nostalgic for the past they never had. Plus we do have some artsy types around. And once the condo market picks up again and the city exiles move in, I'll be in Boomer Heaven."

"Always ahead of the trend."

"Just as long as I'm not too far behind."

"Maybe I'd get a clearer picture of the future if I bought one of your Magic 8 Balls."

She sat up and leaned toward me. "And what question would you ask it?"

It didn't take me a minute. "Who killed Emma Hartt?"

Juliet looked away. "Reply hazy. Try again."

"That's all I ever get."

"The 8 Ball only works for 'yes' or 'no' questions anyway," she reminded me. "That poor little girl. But if my vote counts, her father didn't do it."

"How well do you know him?"

"Not very. I've been away myself. After high school, I went to California, UC-Davis, for textile design, came home for a short while, then spent nearly ten years in Berkeley. Missed the family, so I moved to the city so I could be close by and opened my first place, way downtown. It did great. But when it came time to expand, I saw what was happening on this block and figured I'd give it a shot."

"You aren't living in town?"

"Honey, I'm in a rent-controlled illegal sublet. You don't just give that up." A dreamy smile. "I'm also seeing this guy Jean-Claude, a chef at this hot new bistro in my neighborhood. I have to make sure he can get to me at any hour of the night."

"Then how do you know the Hartts?"

"I opened up last summer. Emma came in with Doreen. You know about Doreen Josephs, that she works for Joel, right?"

"Right. Now *that* girl needs a makeover."

"She wouldn't look half bad if she got that scowl off her face." Juliet looked sympathetic. "We got to talking, and she's had it hard. Two kids, a disabled mother, a husband in prison."

"Why doesn't that last item surprise me?"

"She's not so bad really. Just no sense of style." To Juliet, that was the greatest sin. "But Emma! She knew her stuff. I've got a kids' rack, but she'd pull out all sorts of things and work them in combinations—wear an oversize flowered shirt as a mini dress with a macramé belt and patchwork vest. She fell in love with a tie-dyed scarf that I'd found in a storeroom in Haight-Ashbury. Mint condition, still sealed in its plastic bag. I put a high price tag on it."

"She could afford it."

"She did bring her father in here to see it, but he wouldn't buy it. I think he was afraid of spoiling her. She got so much attention everywhere she went." Her smile held a tinge of guilt. "I gave her the scarf on New Year's Eve. I figured, who knows? Maybe she'd wear it in a *Vogue* photo shoot and I'd get an on-page credit. Drum up more business. But nothing was better than the look on her face. She couldn't have been sweeter."

"How did you wind up getting invited for New Year's?"

"I didn't. Jesse Quindlen took me." She sounded casual and I wondered if casual is what it was. "Until then I hadn't seen Joel since that one time. Never even met the mother, Kristine. Though of course I remembered Katie."

"Katie?"

"McCarrick. You know, 'Saint Kathleen.'" Jules laughed. "I almost confessed when I walked in and saw her that night. After what we did to her!"

I raised my eyebrows. "You mean, what *you* did."

After seeing *The Song of Bernadette* in sixth grade, Kathleen "Katie" McCarrick devoted herself to becoming worthy of a Lourdes-like Visitation. While the rest of us jumped rope after lunch, she would slip next door into church to pray to the Virgin. One day Juliet and I followed her, slipping into the church's side exit, near the Mary statue.

Then Juliet hissed, "Kathleeeeeen..." sounding like Glinda the Good Witch.

From around the flickering bank of novena candles, I could see Katie's head snap up.

"Yes, Kathleen McCarrick, it's me, the Holy Mother."

Katie shrieked and doubled over, moaning with such intensity I nearly bolted. Then she stood up. A dark stain was spreading on the back of her skirt. Terrified we ran back to Holy Moly and returned with Sister Simon Peter, the school nurse. Katie was still standing, whispering, "The Virgin Mary, she came..."

"What's come is your menstrual cycle, dear," Sister Simon said. "Now let's get you to the infirmary for some pads."

Juliet laughed now at the memory. "I still feel bad about that. Katie was actually pretty nice. Still is."

"Did she ever take her vows?"

Juliet shook her head. "She wound up marrying old Ken Whalen, the mayor. Do you believe that? Now there's an April-December romance for you."

"Mickey Giamonte didn't tell me Kathleen Whalen was Katie McCarrick."

"Mickey wouldn't tell you if your shoelaces were on fire, if it didn't help him."

"I was hoping he'd changed."

"Some things you can still count on."

"Like Jesse Quindlen?"

"Ah, you've seen Jesse." She gave me a sly look. "Yeah, he still acts like God's gift, doesn't he? But don't be fooled. He's a serial monogamist. He was in between soul mates that New Year's Eve, so I filled in. You in the market?"

"Could be." My conscience twinged as Doug's face suddenly floated to mind. "Actually, I've been with someone for a while, but he's upstate and... Maybe we're just suffering from travel fatigue."

"Say no more. It's hard enough maintaining a relationship when you're just around the corner. Next time your man is in the city, give me a call. We'll double-date."

"Why didn't you get anything going with Jesse?"

Juliet wrinkled her nose again. "Not that there's anything wrong with Jesse. But he likes commitment. I'd already been bound and gagged, for two years, and I didn't handle it well. But serves me right. I should have known better than to marry a cop."

Her father had been a local patrolman, sometimes coming to Holy Moly to give safety talks. Look both ways before crossing the street, ride your bike in the direction of traffic, that sort of thing. He'd been stabbed trying to stop a robbery.

His was the first funeral I ever went to. Sister Giuseppina had trooped our fifth-grade class into the church. I watched Juliet walk up the aisle, her arms around the waist of her older brother, her face buried in his wool jacket. For once, a roomful of eleven-year-olds was as still as the marble saints around them. Until Father Behan started waving the incense around the altar, and Debbie Boyle passed out in our pew.

"Really? You married a cop in California? One of those CHiPs?"

Juliet suddenly stood up from her squatting position. "Wanna go get some lunch? My treat. I'm starving. The café down the street is pretty good. We can catch up."

"Sure." Was she avoiding my question? I picked up my

shoulder bag and followed her to the door. "But what happened with your cop?"

"Looks like there's something else Mickey didn't tell you, Sis. Figures." She sighed. "I'm the first ex-Mrs. Giamonte."

• *Chapter 5* •

THE LATE-AFTERNOON traffic was picking up and the stream of impatient cars made crossing River Drive again a lethal game of dodgeball. After I sprinted across the last lane and onto the dirt driveway of the construction site, I noticed that all the workers seemed to have left. A little early for quitting time.

Jesse's Jeep was in front of the trailer, loud voices coming from inside. One was his, punctuated by what sounded like pounding. Then silence. I was making my way stealthily toward the stairs—it would be natural for me to stop by to say good-bye to Jesse before I drove off, wouldn't it?—when the door was flung open. Two tasseled black loafers backed down the steps, their wearer shielded by the open door.

"You're making something out of nothing." The lightly accented voice sounded amused, not in the least ruffled.

That only seemed to raise Jesse's volume. *"Nothing?* That's what *you'll* be if you don't take care of this!"

I considered ducking behind the trailer, but Mr. Loafers was now fully in view, dressed in a silky black-and-cream shirt and black dress slacks. It took him only a second to register that they had an audience. He gave me a show of gleaming white teeth set in a seamlessly tanned face before turning back to Jesse, whose own steel-tipped work boots were starting down the stairs after him.

"Now be careful what you say in front of witnesses." All playfulness, he wagged a finger in front of Jesse's nose, now barely six inches from his own.

At the sight of me, Jesse tried hard to twist his face into something less than pure hate. Loafers swept his right arm, weighed down by a massive Rolex, in my direction. "And who is this lovely young lady, my friend?"

Jesse's look gave lie to the man's assumption of friendship, but he grudgingly introduced us. "Andrealisa Rinaldi. Gordon de Porres."

So this was Joel's business partner and Gina's New Year's Eve date. I wondered if he paid his stylist a little extra to put the perfect patches of silver at the temples of his thick, slicked-back black hair.

"Ah, Joel's friend, the reporter! At last we meet!" He linked his left arm through my right with the ease of a ballroom dancer, then waltzed me away from Jesse as if he were steering me clear of a mud puddle. But I had already figured out I'd better watch my step with this guy. I looked over my shoulder at Jesse, but he was stomping back up the stairs, and soon the door slammed behind him.

"Like you, I have known Joel since he was a boy. I worked for his father. Nathan recruited me right out of graduate school to be his business manager. Columbia, by the way." He said this as if confiding in me. As if I cared. "I was class of '68."

Now I cared. It was in 1968 that we'd moved away. So this was the guy who took my father's place at Hartt Construction. My eyes narrowed. Did Nathan Hartt fire my father to bring in this cheeseball?

"He even suggested I change my name to Gordon. 'Godofredo' was a mouthful to spit out, he said. I was indebted

to Nathan. To take a chance on a poor young man—very generous! He enabled me to stay in this country."

In my memory, "generous" was not one of the words Joel's
mother ever used to describe her ex-husband, especially during
their fights over child support. During those times, I would hustle
Joel up to his bedroom, distract him with a game of *Trouble*. No,
Nathan Hartt probably wasn't an equal-opportunity employer;
he just figured he could get a "poor young man" cheap.

But de Porres was still enthralled with himself. "Then to
become a partner to Joel years later—what opportunities I have
had in America! To think, I wasn't sure in my youth what industry
I would pursue. But land development, well, it has so many pos-
sibilities, doesn't it? Really molding the future of a community."

"Then you live here?" I was getting tired of this. He had all
the passion and sincerity of a soap-opera star.

"Oh, no!" De Porres tried not to look appalled. "Not that I
would not love to. The views! But I have so many business and
social contacts in the city, and our offices are just across the
bridge, so it is just as convenient to zip over when I need to.
Which is not often, since Joel takes care of so much on this side
of the river."

"So it's unusual, for you to come down to a site?"

"Well, yes, but I am not a silent partner. I'm involved behind
the scenes every step of the way. There was a concern that needed
my personal attention."

"Something Joel couldn't handle?"

"Not at all! But contracts are my purview, whereas Joel"—he
bent closer as if we were sharing a secret—"prefers the more cre-
ative end, the 'vision thing,' to quote our President Bush. I am
all business, sad to say. But someone has to make it happen and
work out the kinks."

"Is Jesse kinky?"

We had reached my car by then and Gordon had finally
released my arm. He faced me to give me the full effect of his
appreciative chuckle. "Kinky—ha! Not that I would know, but

that could be the key to his appeal to the ladies. So watch out!"

"I've heard you have your charms too."

His smile this time seemed genuine. "I nearly forgot you know my Gina!"

"She didn't share all the details when I called her this morning. But I'm going to her office now. Who knows what I'll find out." I don't know why, but I wanted that to sound like a threat.

"She's an incredible woman." Again, I glimpsed something like real feeling behind the bigger-than-life facade. "And what she has done for Joel..."

"Acting as his mouthpiece with the police."

"Of course! He needed her! How could he protect himself from their insinuations?"

"What were they insinuating?"

"It doesn't matter. What happened that night was the work of a madman, pure and simple. To lose a precious child and be accused of an unspeakable crime..." His sigh said he could not bear to think of it.

"You and Gina were there that night and saw nothing out of the ordinary?"

"It was a delightful party, as Joel's always are. It would be even too much to call it a party. More like a night with close family. The children were there. They showed us whatever toys and gadgets Santa had brought. We played games, we even danced. Emma wanted me to teach her the tango. She knew I had been in competitions." I was startled when Gordon's voice broke and his eyes filled. "My God, I tucked her into bed that night. That was the last time I held her in my arms." He was quiet for a moment, then laughed. "She kept waving around that outrageous scarf Juliet Rojas gave her and tripped us both up!"

"Joel told me Emma had a flair for drama."

"Yes, I always said that she inherited that from me. I was her godfather, you know."

"No, I didn't know."

"Kristine had asked me, along with her sister, to be Emma's

guardian almost from the moment she knew she was pregnant. I was quite touched."

"And who are Evan's godparents?"

"I don't really know." Gordon looked nonplussed for the first time. "I wasn't in the country when Evan was born. Not long after Nathan died, I took a leave of absence, to look after some family business in South America for a year or so. When I came back, I offered to buy into a partnership with Joel, to expand our interests on the other side of the river. He accepted." He now made a show of squinting at his Rolex. "Speaking of which, I have to get back to the city by five."

Before I could stop him, he swept me up in a full-body hug, kissed me on both cheeks and released me. I had to lean against my car to recover my balance.

"We'll be seeing each other again soon. Give Gina my love." He strode to a shimmering black Mercedes 500SL convertible, folded himself into the front seat, and screeched away, honking and waving.

"Well, Ringo," I said as turned on the ignition, "let's see you beat *that*."

"Jeez, you look exactly the same. Except now you have breasts."

"Thank you, Gina. I was waiting for someone to state the obvious. Leave it to you."

I sat across from my childhood pal, a stainless-steel desk between us. I was enjoying the buttery taupe leather of her client chair and the dizzying fifteen-story view that took in both the smog-smudged city skyline and the treetops of the town where we grew up.

Gina lived in one of the luxury high-rises that now soared from the site of the old amusement park. On the phone that morning, she'd told me she owned not only the condo that housed her law office, but also the two-bedroom next-door, with a door cut in between. Which, considering the real-estates prices in this area, meant her practice was doing very well. She was, too, judging by her silk suit that probably cost more than my month's rent.

I was glad for her. Her father had worked in the auto-parts factory, and she had to share a bedroom with her three sisters in a small split-level in the South End. I'd only been there once, in all those years of our friendship. As with most of my school-mates who lived on the other side of town, we'd seen each other only from 8:00 to 3:15 Monday to Friday, September to June.

I tapped the nameplate on her desk. "R. Taylor Fine? What's that about?"

She shrugged. "Hide the sex. Muddle the ethnicity. Most peo-ple never pronounce my last name right anyway, with the final *eh*. They think I'm Jewish."

"Hide. Muddle. That sounds like a lawyer to me. Is that the advice you give Joel?"

"Whew! I thought we'd go through the niceties first, *How's the folks* and crap like that, but you're getting right down to it. I like that."

I knew she would. That's what I'd always liked about her, too. No punches pulled. Maureen O'Hara in *The Quiet Man* or just about any other Maureen O'Hara movie. Gina's thick, still-long hair was sandy, not red, her eyes hazel, not green, but she had Maureen's same strong no-nonsense carriage, tall and confi-dent, smart and funny. She'd been my staunchest ally, as well as my severest critic when I wouldn't stand up for myself.

I hadn't seen her since our first summer living at the shore. Cat and I were so miserable that my mother suggested we each invite a friend to stay for a week. Cat would have none of it, some-how thinking we might move back if she held out. I asked Gina to come. The three of us went to the beach every day, crabbed off the dock, hung out at the boardwalk. Gina had a blast and even Cat seemed to enjoy herself. I, on the other hand, felt thoroughly uncomfortable, and couldn't put my finger on the cause. Perhaps she reminded me too much of what we had left behind. I hadn't invited her back the next summer, and then, after my father's death, well...it was unthinkable.

We did write to each other on and off, though, through high school and into a year of college. Then even that petered out. Now, watching the familiar gestures of her slender but strong hands, I realized how much I missed her. "Well, R. Taylor, what kind of advice *did* you give Joel?"

Her answer was, as always, direct. "The $450-an-hour kind. He called me right after he phoned the police. It was my idea to be there when they arrived and for him to limit his direct communication. Local law enforcement tends to peg whoever's in the room for the deed, and I didn't want Joel to get railroaded. He was too distraught to deal with this with a cool head. That's where I came in."

"So you're saying he isn't guilty?"

Gina narrowed her eyes. "It's not a question of guilt or innocence. He has never been charged with anything. My job right now is to protect him and his family from intimidation and harassment.

"And I'm protecting his business. The police have been looking into all of his dealings, to see if there is a connection, if someone had planned to kidnap Emma as a bargaining chip. Reasonable, under the circumstances. But that line of questioning can scare off investors, create problems with upcoming projects if word gets out. And word always gets out. Some beat cop or low-level bureaucrat is always willing to leak to the press to make himself seem more important."

Nice move. She was putting me on the defensive. But without malice. It was simply the best strategy. We'd always had arguments, but we always resolved our differences like adults, with no hard feelings, no repercussions. I missed that, too, in the friendships I'd had since. So I just smiled. "Do you remember what we use to argue about?"

"Probably something really important, like, who was cooler, Dr. Kildare or Ben Casey."

"Kildare," I said.

"Casey."

"Kildare."

"Casey."

We both grinned.

"Well, I just met Gordon and I see you still like them tall, dark and handsome." I didn't think it would be diplomatic to add that I thought her boyfriend was a creep. "Did he introduce you to Joel Hartt?"

"No, Ken Whalen did, years ago. Ken was one of my law professors, and recommended me to Joel when he was looking for someone to represent him in a partnership agreement. With Gordon, as a matter of fact."

"Then isn't dating Gordon a conflict of interest?"

"Not anymore. Affair over."

I was relieved. "He acted like you were still together."

"And he probably believes it. He just hasn't figured out a way yet to get me around to his way of thinking. That's Gordon."

An intercom on the desk buzzed sharply twice, and Gina gave a long buzz in return. The connecting door opened immediately and a young woman entered. Her short hair, blonde tipped with brown, was punked out, her lobes sported four earrings apiece and a barbed-wire tattoo encircled one upper arm. But her freckled, snub-nosed face looked friendly enough and she was carrying a child, somewhere between baby and toddler.

"Here's the precious cargo." Her voice lilted Irish. "She ate hearty, she did, though she's still not fond of her peas. Clean nappy on and ready for the Land o' Nod." The infant tucked her head under the girl's chin sleepily as if in confirmation.

Gina came around her desk to take the child in her arms, stroke her head, brush her lips against one plump rosy cheek and whisper, "To your bedchamber, princess." She handed the baby back to the girl. "Thanks, Sinéad. I'll be in to read her a story soon."

When they left, I said, "What a cutie," and meant it. "What's her name?"

"Artemis."

"You always did like *The Wild Wild West*. I get it! Ross Martin played Artemus Gordon. So I guess that means Gordon's the father?"

"Good God, no! I hadn't been seeing him that long. We didn't start dating until after Missy was born. Not that I would have minded mingling our DNA at the time." She gave it more thought. "Though he can be ruthless and I wouldn't want to dump an extra dose of that in with my gene pool."

I never thought of Gina as ruthless. Perhaps she knew herself better than I did now. "So do I know the father?"

"I sure don't, at least not his name." She laughed at my expression. "A few years ago, I realized I didn't want to be the oldest mother on the playground, but no other suitable partner presented himself. It made more sense to make a withdrawal from the sperm bank."

"How romantic."

Gina shrugged. "At least you get your choice of swimmers. I bought my little girl a blond, blue-eyed Nobel Prize winner. You try to give them the best of everything, and that isn't enough to protect them."

"No shots to immunize them to real life."

"Funny you should say that." Gina looked at me as if I were her prize pupil. "We were talking about that on New Year's Eve. Jesse Quindlen's niece was supposed to come but had gotten sick. The girl's mother had never had her vaccinated, and Jesse was worried she had the mumps. That can be dangerous after puberty."

"I know." I'd written a story on how the number of young adults infected with mumps had been rising in the past decade. "Swollen pancreas, inflamed ovaries or testicles, possibility of encephalitis or meningitis..."

"Enough, Dr. Kildare. Anyway, Ken Whalen said he didn't catch mumps until he was in his forties, and had a bad time. So we made a game of coming up with things we wanted to be inoculated against as adults: bad credit, lousy lovers, stuff like that. Then we decided that what we all really needed was a vaccine against the Seven Deadly Sins." She shook her head. "That's when Gordon changed the subject and wanted to play Monopoly. *His* favorite game."

"Which sin do you think killed Emma? Anger? Greed? Lust—"

"I'm not playing *that* game with you, Andie. Though I think it's safe to leave out Gluttony and Sloth." Gina seemed uncomfortable now. "Safe. That's all I want for my little girl."

"Artemis is lucky to have you for a mom." I meant that too. "Though Sister Felicia might have something to say to you for not giving your daughter a saint's name."

"I don't have to answer to nuns anymore. I'm with the Unitarians now. They're much more tolerant."

"Heaven help us!"

"They could care less that I named her for the Greek goddess of the hunt."

"Preparing her for her future, I see."

"Better to be the hunter than the hunted."

As I LEFT Gina's, the sun was making its slow summer descent behind the cliff and the commuters were making their even slower descent down River Drive. Like me, most people probably had the next day off for the start of the July Fourth weekend, and so were all heading for the nearest exit out of the city and the suburbs. I was just glad that, with no stories to file, I didn't have to go back to the office to meet the *Moon's* usual Thursday night deadline.

Passing The Rock Bottom at a snail's pace, I saw Mickey coming out. I honked. He trotted up, reached into the open passenger-side window, yanked up the lock, opened the door and got in before I had come to a complete stop.

"Thanks for the lift, Rinaldi."

"What happened to the Elvis-mobile?"

"In the shop. Dropped it off and hitched here."

"Do you ever go to work?" I said as I merged into the rush hour traffic.

"My day off. I'm on call for the holiday weekend." He played with the levers on my dashboard. "Where's the air-conditioning?"

"That's not standard on a '72 Beetle."

"Oh, God, no air in this tin can? What are you, a masochist?"

"Must be, if I'm giving you a ride. Where to?"

"Drop me off at my grandmother's."

"She still in town?"

"Yeah, she wouldn't move to the retirement village with the folks, though my father made the offer. Said she didn't want to hang around with a bunch of old people waiting to die. Remember where she lives?"

I nodded. Though it was quite a walk, we'd always hit Grandma G's on Halloween. Instead of bags of candy corn, she gave out homemade cannoli.

As I turned right at what used to be the town's only traffic light, up Center Street, Mickey looked at me out of the corner of his eye, pushing the fly window as wide as it would go. "Crack the Hartt case yet?"

"No. You?" I put my blinker on to turn onto Cliff Way.

"I'm on to other things. Not all of our crimes make the national tabloids, but the local citizens do try to uphold our standing as the most ornery county in the state."

We rode in silence until I stopped the car in front of a two-story rowhouse dressed in bright green aluminum siding, one of the South End's best. "How's my memory?"

"Fine. But you can't parallel park for shit." Mickey got out, closed the car door, then leaned back into the open window. "Come on in and say hello. Nonna would get kick out of seeing you."

I couldn't pass up that invitation. She might have a plate of pastries out.

I followed him up the steep porch steps and through the screened front door. He led me through the living room and past the brocade sofa—the same one she had when we were kids. It still looked brand-new. I guess encasing it in heavy plastic had preserved it for a quarter of a century.

Next to it, the dark-wood étagère held two shelves of photographs. Weddings, grandchildren, great-grandchildren, including Mickey in a wide-collared shirt, his curly blonde hair to his shoulders—the Peter Frampton look. I could imagine the fights he had with his father over that. Another shelf lined up a set of Readers' Digest Condensed Books. Below that, Tom Clancy, John Grisham, Stephen King...and a copy of *Jonathan Livingston Seagull*? Nonna's taste was a little more eclectic than I would have thought.

Mickey's grandmother was at the kitchen counter, her back to us. I could see that her straight, fine hair, pulled into a tight bun, was still mostly black. But she seemed to have shrunk to the size of a garden gnome.

"Nonna! I brought you a surprise. You remember Andrealisa, the ugly girl, *la faccia brutta*, who used to live across the street from us?"

She looked over her shoulder, distressed. "Michelangelo! What are you bringing a guest in here for? I'm not dressed!" She was, of course—in a flowered shift that looked like it had just come off the ironing board.

"You look fine." Mickey had to bend over to kiss the top of her head.

"Sweetheart, you hungry?" she said to me. "You want something to eat? I've got some chopped meat here, just made into patties." To prove it, she turned and held out two rounds of hamburger, the size of salad plates, on her open palms. "I can fry them up right now. Only take a minute."

I shook my head and tried not to laugh. "No, that's very sweet but I'm meeting someone for dinner." No one but my dog, but I thought that would be an easier out than saying I was trying to abstain from red meat. Most Italians, and grandmothers in particular, do not understand the elimination of any food group.

She brandished the patties at Mickey. "*You* want to eat, right?"

Mickey's head was already in the fridge. "Sure."

"You want one hamburger or two?"

"Just one. I had a big lunch."

Grandma G looked at the meat on her palms, stymied for a moment. Then she nodded, as if coming to some Solomon-like decision, and brought her hands together, kneading the two patties into one.

McDonald's would be out of business in a year if Nonna made the Big Macs.

Once she dropped the meat in the skillet and washed her hands, she gave me a hug.

"Look at you, all grown up! Your mamma and poppa must be proud. They're well?"

I shifted my eyes from hers. "Unfortunately, they've both passed."

Her face fell and she threw up her hands. "Too young! That's not right!" She brightened a little. "But you have your husband to comfort you."

I knew Italian grandmothers, and what this one was fishing for. "I'm not married."

"Ah! Well..." And she glanced pointedly at Mickey, who was circling us.

"Nonna, you trying to get rid of me again? Remember what happened last time?" He hugged her from behind.

Nonna spat, dryly. "She had the *mal occhio*. Evil eye."

"She had two, and they were blue." Mickey winked at me over the top of his grandmother's head. "But isn't this better, me living with you? You're the only woman I need." He kissed her bun and she pushed him away with her elbows. To me, he said, "It's just until my ex sells the condo and we split the proceeds. Very amicable."

Nonna spat again, then faced the stove, flipped the burger and slapped it with the spatula as if it were the second ex-Mrs. Giamonte. I made a mental note never to get on Grandma G's bad side.

• *Chapter 6* •

DURING THE SUMMER, traffic to the seashore was horrendous, but leaving late at night was always better, especially on a Fourth of July weekend. I had no patience for crawling for four hours alongside cars full of blitzed college students in their high-school graduation-gift convertibles or vacation-bound families packed into their minivan along with the entire contents of their rec room. Life is too short as it is.

It was after 1 a.m. when I arrived at the house—the house that had been my parents', and now was mine and Cat's. In the garage, I flipped the switches to start the hum of electricity and the water pump. Suitcase in one hand, paper bag in the other, I walked through the connecting door, passed through the living room and into the kitchen.

I reached into my shoulder bag for Ben, already asleep, and set him in the doggy bed in the corner. He lifted his head, squeaked once, and was out again. Then I opened the fridge, turned the temperature gauge from off to five and transferred the eggs, juice and milk I'd bought at the 7-Eleven. Tomorrow morning, after I picked up Cat from her group home, we would shop for more weekend provisions, maybe even a lobster from Captain Ahab's Fishnet.

I poured myself a glass of juice, and carried it with me outside, pulling a lounge chair off the porch and onto the small, smooth golden stones that made up our backyard. My father hadn't even entertained the idea of cultivating a lawn from this sandy soil. He'd laid down sheets of plastic to keep weeds from poking through, then we shoveled and raked the pebbles to cover every inch of ground except the driveway.

Cat and I had to learn how to walk barefoot over the always shifting, sometimes scorching surface without wincing. Eventually, our calluses built up and it had seemed as effortless as skipping on linoleum. My sister said that if we were ever captured by slave traders and forced to walk across a pit of burning coals to win our freedom, we had the training. Cat was always ready with a worst-case scenario.

Tonight the stars were in full sparkle mode, no competition here from street lamps or floodlights. The house was built on a lagoon, one of a series of man-made waterways that led to the bay and, eventually, the ocean. Across the bay, on the narrow peninsula of beaches, bungalows and hotels, I could see the glow of the boardwalk and the shape of the illuminated Ferris wheel, still turning at this time of night. I tried to concentrate on the bright rotating ring. Maybe I could hypnotize myself into not worrying.

I didn't know how much longer we could keep this house. It had been paid for—my father had taken care of that, only because it had been so much cheaper than the one we'd moved from. But when Cat was first hospitalized, my mother had taken out a mortgage to cover the rapidly mounting medical bills, counseling, medication. The payments plus taxes and insurance cost me an extra $1,200 a month. The utilities were shut off most of the year, but this past winter and spring, I had lived here full time, and the furnace had blown. Nearly twenty-five years old, the roof would have to be replaced soon too.

I had hoped I'd be able to hold on to it until Cat was ready to move back. That's what she wanted, she'd told me after Mom died last August. And I'd promised her. But then a month later she was off her meds. The next month I lost my job. A manic-depressive episode had landed my sister in the psych ward at Shore Medical, and I'd spent the holidays by her bedside.

Whatever money I'd saved from my book royalties was nearly depleted by Cat's hospital bills and my own expenses that unemployment couldn't cover. The only blessing was that the mental-health center agreed to take Cat back once she'd stabilized. Ariel, her social worker, had gotten her on state disability and Medicaid, which she was always in danger of losing. In some ways, it didn't pay for her to get well.

I stayed for those first few months to be sure I'd be close by in an emergency. I almost considered applying for a job on the local paper, but then *I* would have had to be sedated. The thought of sticking myself down here forever would have been a sign of defeat for both of us. It wasn't that hopeless. Yet.

CAT WAS IN a good mood when we came back the next day laden with groceries—plus a five-pound lobster, a burlap bag full of scallops and two dozen littlenecks.

We had arrived at Captain Ahab's to find the shack-like fish store closed—an illness in the family, the hand-lettered sign said. A pickup loaded with buckets and wire traps pulled into the gravel driveway after us. The driver cursed when he saw the sign, then turned to us. "You ladies want anything? I gotta get rid of it anyway and can't haul it all over the place in this heat. I'll charge you what I woulda charged him." So that was how we netted a seafood extravaganza for twenty-five bucks.

Maybe too much for us to eat even over the whole weekend, but we'd share our good fortune with the Martells next door. Both retired schoolteachers, Don and Betty kept an eye on the house when we weren't there and let me use their phone when our service was cut off. I also suspected that Betty, who still had the key my mother had given her, came in once in a while to vacuum. Fine with me.

Later from my lounge chair, I watched Cat dive off the edge of the bulkhead, cutting cleanly through the green-gray water. We were mirror images in more ways than one. She swam like a fish; I floundered whenever I was in over my head. I sighed and went back to reading *The Joy Luck Club* in paperback.

She pulled herself up on the narrow dock, then stood and shook herself out like a wet cocker spaniel. Her shoulder-length hair, longer than mine now, spun out, sending spray like a lawn sprinkler in my direction.

"Hey!" I dropped my book under the chair to protect it and startled Ben, who'd crawled there to escape the sun.

"Sorry. But it wouldn't kill you to get wet for once." She grabbed a beach towel, wrapped it around her waist and tucked in a corner to secure it.

I pretended to read again, but I was checking her out from behind my sunglasses. She looked only a little heavier. The medications she was on tend to slow down metabolism, but her natural nervous energy—and her reclaimed cigarette habit—probably compensated. She knew better than to smoke around me, though.

"Put sunscreen on," I said automatically, as she flopped down on the chair next to me.

"Okay, mom. Jeez." She did slather on some lotion, then stretched out on her stomach.

After realizing that I had reread the same paragraph three times, I looked over at Cat again. I wanted to tell her everything: about the murder, meeting up again with Mickey and Joel, seeing our old house. I couldn't talk about all this over the phone; it had to be in person, so I could gauge her reaction. I always hesitated bringing up anything that might start her thinking about the past. I was never sure if it would be welcome or would just agitate her.

Gradually, I started the story. She asked a few questions—"Is

Mickey still full of himself?" "Does Joel still have a stick up his ass?" "Is Jesse still hot?"—so I knew she was listening. But as she responded less and less, I let the conversation drift away. After a few minutes, she said, "I'm on the web."

Oh, crap. What did I say to start her on that? I tried not to seem disturbed.

"Really. You're on a web."

"Not *a* web. *The* Web."

"Did you take your morning meds?"

"Yes." Annoyed. "Stop it." She turned over, sat up. "The World Wide Web. It's a networking system between computers all around the world. As the name implies."

"Sorry. I thought you were starting to have fantasies about Spiderman."

"I'm not saying I *don't*—you know I can't resist a man in leotards—but that's not what I was talking about." She flashed me a grin to let me know she had no hard feelings.

"So tell me." I'd read a little about it, but wanted her to feel good about knowing something I didn't.

"You connect through the telephone line to something called a browser, which lets you *browse* through thousands, maybe millions of documents.. Then you type in a URL—it's like an address where a file lives. The computer knocks on the door, and pulls up all kinds of information that maybe is not readily available to the public. Or it would be if everyone could get connected. You have to know the exact address where the stuff is stored, or else you can't get to the information."

"Sounds like an obsessive-compulsive's dream."

"It's pretty cool, actually." She lay back down, smiling to herself. "The Web's not regulated, so anyone with the know-how can set up a site and do what they want. So there are all sorts of weird things. There's this one university in England where a video camera is pointed at a coffeepot in the faculty lounge. The picture is updated every minute, so everyone in the world can see what's happening."

"To a coffeepot? That sounds riveting. Do they have one where you can watch paint dry?"

"Not yet." Cat was warming to her subject. "It's really mainly used by research labs, colleges and the government. When I'm tracking information at the hospital, I can go into the state medical system's database to see if someone has been a patient somewhere else. Helps to see if someone is trying to scam us for meds, things like that, or if they have some other condition they're too messed up to remember that could interfere with treatment. They gave me a password so I can get in and out."

"That sounds great." And it did. I felt relief that she was interested in something new.

THAT NIGHT WE steamed the clams, some corn on the cob and the still wriggling lobster, layered with rinsed seaweed in between. With typical Italian overkill, Cat also sautéed the shucked scallops in garlic, oil and lemon juice, then tossed them into a vat of linguine. "What we don't finish, we'll have for breakfast tomorrow," she said. Cat was even a better cook than me, when she wasn't having odd thoughts about kitchen implements.

We heard the crunch of stones as Don and Betty Martell made their way across from their backyard to ours, and Ben squeaked a greeting. Betty, big and blowsy with her long iron-gray hair held back by a bandanna, bounded in through the sliding screen door, holding out a bakery box.

"You shouldn't have." I lifted the lid to see a huge marble cheesecake smiling up at me. "Is this enough for four people? Next time, bring two."

Don, compact and wiry and a full head shorter than Betty, came out from behind her, offering a bottle of Chardonnay and a hug to Cat and me. "I know neither of you ladies will indulge, but at least get me a corkscrew."

Over dinner, I watched these two seventy-somethings. They seemed always to be touching—a hand on a forearm, a check, a thigh, brushing against each other whenever they could. I guessed they still had a lot of catching up to do. Don had been a monsignor and Betty a nun when they met in their late forties. Followers of the Sixties activist priests Daniel and Philip Berrigan, they had marched shoulder to shoulder in antiwar protests, raided Selective Service offices and burned draft files. "I held 'em, she lit 'em," Don had told us.

They hadn't been allowed to share a jail cell, though, and a year's separation had convinced them never to be apart again. They left the Church, took up teaching and continued fighting for peace in quieter ways. Somewhere in there, they had adopted two preteen African-American boys, brothers in fact. One had mild cerebral palsy; the other had endured several operations for a heart defect as a child. Peter was now a civil-liberties lawyer and David, a CPA. Cat knew them better than I did, as I had met them only a few times in the twelve years the Martells had lived next door to my mother.

"Peter was asking after you, Cat," Don said with a wink, as he passed her a slice of cheesecake.

"I don't need a lawyer yet, unless my roommate keeps giving me reasons to snuff her."

"Don't worry. Peter could get you off." Betty's laugh left no doubt that she meant the double-entendre.

For once, my blunt sister was embarrassed. "How crude! Were you ever really a nun?"

"Darling, nobody appreciates a dirty joke more than an ex-nun." Betty placed a hand over her husband's resting on the table.

HOURS LATER, CAT was snoring lightly from the other room, but I couldn't sleep. My brain was buzzing, as it usually did after a full day with Cat.

I could see improvements. She had taken the initiative in cooking dinner and seemed able to focus on the talk around her. But I knew that, in those moments when she was quiet, she was straining not to ask repeatedly for reassurance that everything was okay, or not to act on whatever random whim was filling her head. Those whims could be anything—from thinking she'd left her shoes in the car to being concerned she'd somehow hurt someone. A split-second scene on TV or a scrap of overheard conversation could trigger them. Her mind would grab the trailing thread of a sentence and tie it to her worst nightmare. This is what she lived with every day, and I couldn't help her. And I missed her—the old Cat who had seemed so sure of herself, to whom I had turned when I was unsure of myself.

I got up, closed my bedroom door, then lay back down. I propped myself upright with pillows, then snapped on the nightstand light and reached for the manila envelope I had brought down with me. More clippings from Dovie the intern's dogged research on Emma Hartt's background, more familiar images and hysterical press coverage of the murder. One newspaper had snapped Doreen Dougherty, her face rabid, as she was coming out of the front door of the Hartt home. I could see she was clutching a kid—Evan?—to her side with one arm, the hand of the other held up to shield his face from the camera.

As I picked up the folded page to look closer at the photo, another smaller clipping—actually, what seemed to be a photocopy from a library microfiche machine—fell out from behind it. On it was a paragraph of white print on a black background.

Carpenter Sentenced to 12 Years

UNDERCLIFF, N.J.—A local construction worker was sentenced today to 12 years at a federal prison camp in Yankton, S.D. Raymond Dougherty, 27, of 364 Cliff Way had been found guilty last month by a federal jury of felony drug possession with intent to distribute.

Dougherty was first arrested near a fuel-storage facility in August after borough police officer Michelangelo Giamonte stopped a car Dougherty was driving for a broken taillight. After a routine radio check indicated that the 15-year-old Ford Mustang was stolen, Officer Giamonte searched the vehicle, discovering in the trunk five kilos of cocaine and a crossbow.

Later, U.S. Drug Enforcement agents tied the seized goods to an ongoing investigation of drug trafficking they had been conducting in the area.

The piece seemed to be from the Metro section of the city newspaper, December 12, 1979. Twelve years. He'd be out by now.

I had asked Dovie to run the name "Dougherty" through the system, to see if Doreen's jailbird husband, whom Juliet had mentioned, might pop up. Dovie confirmed this in red marker at the top of the page: "The housekeeper's husband!!!!!!" I assumed she'd crosschecked the address, which seemed familiar.

Something else did too. The small head shot, rendered as a negative on the photocopy, was none too clear. But it sure looked like the Ray I had met in Jesse Quindlen's office.

THE SLAM OF car doors woke Cat and me up the next morning. We were being invaded. So much for not locking up.

By the time we shuffled into the kitchen, Aunt Angela was already deep in the fridge, pulling out eggs, milk, juice with the energy usually reserved for her thrice-weekly Jazzercise classes. Our cousin Paula, her belly barely swollen yet by her pregnancy, was arranging bagels on a plate with one hand while she talked on a mobile phone that nearly obscured her profile. She'd been the first in the family to go cellular, while I had only recently replaced my rotary dial Princess with a push button.

Uncle Lou had commandeered the porch, Sunday papers strewn as he scanned, then discarded each section. His jet-black toupee, though expensive, seemed to have a mind of its own. It was slightly askew, the nape creased and folding up from his polo shirt collar, showing a patch of pink skin between it and his remaining fringe of hair.

Ben was running (more like sliding) back and forth on the kitchen linoleum, hoping someone would drop something edible. Alexis and Samantha—a.k.a. Alex and Sam—sat at the dining table, confused by their grandmother's advice to "Go outside and play or something." Paula's two daughters had their date-books filled in at birth and rarely knew an unscheduled moment. Actually, I liked the girls, especially when they weren't around their parents. They had a sense of irony that was sure to have their grandmother pulling out her permed, highlighted hair when they reached their teens. I couldn't wait.

Aunt Angie had found the frying pan and was at the stove. "How do the girls want their eggs?" she called over her shoulder to Paula.

"You can ask *us*. We're right here, Gram," sighed eight-year-old Sam.

"No, Sam, remember? We activated our invisibility shields." Alex was eleven and perfecting her sarcasm.

"Oh, right. Then she won't see me taking this bagel."

"Put that down, young lady! We'll all eat together!"

Cat led the girls to the sliding door. "Let's go catch some crabs for breakfast. Come on—you too, Ben." She snatched two pop-py-seed bagels on their way out. "Crustaceans only eat kosher."

I hadn't told anyone we'd be here, but no one could slip under Aunt Angie's radar. Paula and her husband, Marcus, had bought a beachfront bungalow on the ocean side a few years ago, and whenever she was staying at her daughter's, Aunt Angie had never thought twice about dropping in on my mom unan-nounced. My mother hadn't minded. I did.

Still, I let my aunt do her thing. It was dangerous not to. She was always jumping in to "help" where you didn't want her to, and acted hurt if you didn't accept her "generosity." You paid for it later. Cat told her to bug off once, and Aunt Angie waited three years to explain to a roomful of Christmas guests that Cat had been such a handful as a baby that my mother decided not to have any more children. If the psychotherapy handbook had been illustrated, my Aunt Angie's picture would be under "con-trol freak."

I had to give my mother's older sister some credit, though.

She sure knew how to brew a dark roast. I poured myself a cup, the color of crude oil, and brought one to Paula. She was staring out at Cat and the girls leaning over the water, and looked poised to start CPR if necessary. I sat across the table from her and waved to get her attention.

"Where's Marcus?" I asked more out of politeness than interest. Her husband was not just a CEO but also a WASP, and always seemed overwhelmed when more than two of our family members were in a room at one time.

"He's working at the cottage. He just got one of those laptops and wanted to test the spreadsheet program. We thought we'd give him some peace and quiet this morning."

And take away ours. *Thank you.*

"And how's the drug trafficking?" I almost wish I hadn't said that.

"The pharmaceutical industry is healthy, thanks for asking." Paula didn't take offense easily, a trait she probably had to develop to cope with her mother. "You know, we're always looking for writers for our brochures and package inserts."

"You mean the ones that say this medication will cure your allergy symptoms but you might go blind?"

She ignored me. "The work pays pretty well. You have the background, and it's got to be a better way to get back into the real world."

"What? And give up show biz?"

"I hear the *Moon* is being sued again. Doesn't anyone there corroborate a story?"

"We do. We just can't compete with celebrity hush money. The gardener and nanny blab about what really goes on behind closed Beverly Hills doors, then get paid off to deny everything. Or the stars get their own publicity machines going to discredit our sources."

"Don't you think famous people are entitled to a private life?"

"Which one? The one we report or the one they manufac-

ture? They hire a team of handlers to make sure we get pictures of them visiting sick kids in the hospital. They can't have it
both ways. Besides, it's human nature to create gods and human
nature to destroy them."

"When did you get so cynical?"

"When did you start caring?"

I had gone too far. But Paula always had more self-control
than me. She shrugged good-naturedly. "Better late than never."

"WHAT DO YOU think this means, Cat?" I'd just shown her the clipping about Ray Dougherty's criminal past.

Our early-morning invaders long gone, we were sitting on
the edge of the bulkhead, our lazily swinging feet just skimming
the water. In the fading light, rainbows streaked the surface,
from the film of gasoline and oil left in the wake of cabin cruisers
coming in for the night. While we made a smorgasbord of whatever was leftover in the fridge, I finished telling my sister about
the hometown cast of characters, including meeting Doreen's
husband, the meek man with the gorgeous green eyes. Just like
Evan's.

"It seems pretty obvious that this Ray was sticking it to
Kristine Hartt," Cat snorted.

I shook my head. Ben, who was dozing in my lap, lifted his
head and shook it too. "Joel would have figured something out
before now. He wouldn't need a DNA test to confirm whom Evan
got his looks from."

"You said Doreen didn't start working for them until Evan
was born, so why would he know Dougherty before then? They
wouldn't travel in the same circles. He's just a guy on Jesse's crew.
Kristine might have hooked up with him somehow twelve years
ago without Joel's knowing. She gets pregnant, then Ray goes to
prison in godforsaken South Dakota. Kristine could keep her little secret back home."

"Hmmm...and Ray would have been behind bars until just
before Christmas."

"Yeah!" Cat suddenly straightened up, swinging her legs faster in her excitement. "Sure, Ray gets a job with Jesse, and Joel runs into Ray at the construction site, see? So Joel's slapped in the face with the evidence that Evan isn't his, figures everyone at his New Year's Eve party knew before him, works himself up into a drunken fury and—"

"Strangles his daughter? Why not Evan? Or better yet, Ray?"

"The guy is paranoid now. Trust me—this is my area of expertise. Neither kid looks like Joel, right? He starts thinking, not only isn't he Evan's father, but Emma isn't his daughter. Maybe over dinner that night he'd figured out who is. Kills the girl as revenge against the man who cuckolded him."

I joined in her soap opera. "I'd put my money on Gordon. A sleazeball if ever there was one."

"Ah, but the little girl is blonde, right? And from what you told me, Gordon is the dark Latin-lover type."

"Her mother was light."

"Please. You can't mix vanilla with chocolate and get vanilla."

"That's not how it works," I said. "Did you fall asleep in freshman biology and miss the part about Mendel's peas?"

"You're talking vegetables. I'm talking dessert."

"Which reminds me. Do we have any cheesecake left?"

"I'm thinking Jesse," Cat mused.

"I said cheesecake, not beefcake."

"No, for the surrogate papa."

"Him and Kristine? No way." Or was that just jealousy talking?

"How about the mayor? Wasn't he a blond before he got old and gray?"

"What, did this woman have a 900 number? You've got Kristine Hartt sleeping with every guy in town."

"Mickey's blond. You think Mickey had her?"

"Now you're grossing me out."

Cat was quiet for a while, and I thought maybe her mind had

wandered off the planet, until she said, "I'd look into this Ray some more."

"Because he may be Evan's father?"

"Because he's got a record. What's to stop him from attempted kidnapping?"

"Very different crime from drug running. Plus, he didn't really look the type. Too jumpy."

"Exactly. When things started to go wrong, he panicked."

"Unless the ransom was a ploy. Joel has Ray's son, so Ray takes Joel's daughter. Just desserts."

"What *is* for dessert?" She jumped up, then stopped on her way toward the house. "Or did I already have it?"

Later, as I was sliding into sleep, Cat called out from her room, "Doreen did it!" It was the last thing I remembered.

• *Chapter 7* •

The Monday morning news meeting was fairly uneventful. But as everyone else scuttled out of Colin's office, he waved me back.

"What do you make of this?" He began unbuttoning his shirt.

"Of what?" I stayed in the doorway, poised to make a run for it if I had to.

"This bloody thing." He pointed at the back of his neck. I came closer and peered past his shirt collar and his index finger at a raised brown lump that looked like Alfred Hitchcock in profile. Thankfully, it wasn't actually bloody. "My, er, wife" — I suspected Colin really meant Elise — "noticed it the other night."

"It seems to be a mole."

"Yes, but do you think it's cancer?"

"I'd have someone take look at it."

"That's why I called you in here."

"I mean, someone with a medical degree."

"Doctors are all gits. They scrape off a piece of you, then say you'll be dead in a week. Two years later you're still alive and owe them a thousand quid, don't you? When they tell you it's nothing, that's time to ring up the undertaker."

I squinted at the mole again. "Did it always look like that?"

"How should I know? Don't have eyes in the back of my head, do I?"

"Well, it *is* an irregular shape. That's often a sign of melanoma." I figured if I scared him enough, he'd make a doctor's appointment.

"Bloody bleeding hell. I knew it."

So much for a second opinion.

At my desk I played back a phone message from Kathleen Whalen. She apologized for not being available sooner, but she and her husband had been on holiday the week before. She suggested I come over for lunch at one and offered directions to her house in The Colony. I left a confirmation on her answering machine. Maybe our machines could just talk to each other.

I started typing up my notes from last week, but the prospect of interviewing yet another ex-schoolmate made me feel too jumpy to sit. I decided get on the road before Colin asked me to perform his biopsy.

I still had an hour before meeting with the Whalens, so I drove aimlessly through town and again, as I had many years before, found myself in front of Holy Mother R.C. Church. Maybe it was a sign. Maybe a Dead End sign. Well, it couldn't hurt to go in.

I pulled into a parking spot down the street. Walking toward the church, I realized I was passing 364 Cliff Way, the address listed for Ray Dougherty in that police-blotter clipping of thirteen years ago.

It was a beige brick rowhouse, with a rickety but freshly painted green wrought-iron fence boxing in the tiny front yard. The curtains were drawn against the heat, and I didn't see any air-conditioning units in the windows, unlike the other houses on the block. Two flags—one American, the other Irish—flanked the screened storm door, which might have been the house's only source of ventilation.

Cat thought I needed to find out more about Ray. Should I? It had nothing to do with my assignment. But almost against my will, I pushed through the gate, took the few strides to the front door and knocked. I could hear fans whirring inside, loudly, so I knocked harder, but couldn't see much in the darkened hallway. Then a gray shape moved toward the door.

"Is this the Dougherty residence?" I asked the shadow.

"Sure, come on in!" A surprisingly warm welcome.

The door swung inward and the speaker stepped back into the gloom. "I gotta go to work, but my grandma's here."

I stepped inside and squinted to take in a checkered paper hat, fade haircut and a teenage grin. "Hey, you're the kid in the candy store."

"Yeah, right. I'm R.J. Do I know you?" He squinted back at me, looked thoughtful, then snapped his fingers. "Milky Way!"

I laughed.

"Yeah, I never forget a candy bar." He jerked a thumb behind his back. "Go on in." He shouted over his shoulder, "Hey, Gram! Someone's here. Be sure to tell her how bad your arthritis is acting up today!" A wink, a wave and he was gone.

I stepped into the dim hallway. Framed photos jockeyed for position along the walls, chronicling the milestones of a girl and a boy, obviously R.J., from birth, through birthdays, communions, confirmations. Something nagged at my memory. Hadn't Doreen looked pregnant when I'd nearly run over her with her two kids? Perhaps the baby hadn't survived. That might further explain her charming disposition.

Not sure of where to go next, I figured I'd start with the first doorway on my right. That seemed to be the room with the loudest fan noises.

"Hello! Over here!"

It took me a second to focus in on where the voice was coming from, as the wind whipped my hair across my eyes.

She was seated on a rattan peacock chair almost in the center of the room, electric fans aimed at her from each corner, a ceiling unit twirling above. As if they weren't enough, she was waving at herself with an unfurled Chinese paper fan. "This heat is gonna kill me. I'm just gonna turn into a puddle of sweat, I swear!"

That might take some time, as she was enormous. She was Sydney Greenstreet as Senor Ferrari in *Casablanca*, except for her flowered housedress and tightly curled gray perm. The sagging skin of her fleshy upper arm flapped along with the fan.

"Mrs. Dougherty?" I yelled through the gale.

"What, dear? Oh, no. I'm Ella Josephs."

"Doreen's mom?"

She nodded cheerily. "You looking for my girl?"

"Mmmm..." I wasn't sure what I was looking for.

"Up at the Hartt place, as usual. Spends more time there than she does at home. I thought you were that nice nurse. She checks up on me, brings me my medicine. Can't move around much with this arthritis. Some people, heat helps. I gotta tell you, it lays me out."

Mrs. Josephs pulled up a set of eyeglasses from her chest, where they'd been dangling on a bright blue cord around her neck. She squinted through them at me without bringing them to her nose. "You look familiar."

I recognized her, too. Though she had been heavy when I was a kid, she was twice that size now. Her weight had made her seem old then, but she'd probably only been in her late thirties. She was the organist at the church, accompanying us at school recitals and choral practice. She'd been chirpy and bouncy despite her heft, and easy to make fun of. I suspected that had been at least part of the reason Doreen was so ready to punch out her classmates. It didn't help that we all knew the church owned their house, and the Josephs were living in it practically rent-free. A charity case, I'd heard my mother say. If there'd ever been a Mr. Josephs, he'd been long gone from the scene.

But his family was in the same house after all these years? It looked as if marrying Ray Dougherty hadn't moved Doreen any higher up in the world.

I told Ella Josephs my name. "I used to go to Holy Mother Little Academy with Do Jo...Doreen. And I have a sister, Caterina—"

That made her drop her glasses and clap her hands to her face. "The twins! Yes! The two of you were like seeing double of Annette Funchinella, the curly-haired girl from the Mickey Mouse Club!" She brought her glasses back up. "You know, you still look like her. Cute as a button."

She meant Annette Funicello. I tried not to cringe. I had hoped my days of being mistaken for a Mouseketeer were over. "Thanks," I said anyway.

"Yep, before I got a good look at you, I thought you might be that McCarrick girl. But you're too dark and too tall. Oh, but I forget she's a Whalen now. You must know her. She was in Doreen's class like you. Nice girl. She helps me with my insulin shots too. Got diabetes, you know. Doctor says I should change my diet, get some exercise, and maybe I won't need the shots, but this arthritis! And he expects me to take up jogging at my age?"

We both heard the screen door bang open. I turned to see a blur pass.

"Amanda, is that you?" Ella called over the fans.

The sound of running stopped. "Yes, Grandma!"

"Come in here this second!"

A face nearly obscured by a waterfall of dirty-blond hair peeped around the doorframe. "What?"

"Young lady, what are you wearing? Show me."

Amanda's brown eyes looked at me almost pleadingly before she dragged herself into her grandmother's view. Ella's vision couldn't have been that bad. She managed to glimpse in a split-second dash that her grandchild wasn't dressed to her liking. The denim shorts, barely covering her butt, would have made Daisy Mae blush. A swathe of a colorful print fabric was wound and tied across her breasts, providing as much coverage as a Band-

Aid. She was short for her age—about fourteen, I guessed—but already lush.

"What did you do to your shorts, and where did you get that?" Ella waved disgustedly at the girl's bandeau top.

"From mom's closet."

"Well, go put something else on, a tee shirt, anything. You're not leaving this house again looking like that."

Amanda's body drooped. "But Gram, it's so damn hot!"

"What! What did you just say to me?" I thought Ella might actually rise from her chair.

Amanda hung her head.

"Amanda Louise Dougherty, get that off your body now!" But the command came from behind me this time.

The girl whirled around. None of us had heard the door open again, but Doreen was standing in the parlor doorway looking at her daughter, horrified. She grabbed her by her upper arm and pulled her from the room toward the hallway stairs. "Get changed now!"

Amanda was so stunned by her mother's reaction that she offered no protest. As she ran upstairs, I heard a sob.

"Ma, how could you let her go out looking like—" Doreen had finally noticed me. And was not pleased. "What the hell are you doing here?"

"I was just in the neighborhood—"

"Not that shit again!"

"Doreen, watch your language!" Ella Josephs piped up. "If you don't want Amanda talking that way—"

"Shut up, Ma!"

Ella looked as if she had been slapped.

Doreen stared me down. "Get out."

"I just wanted to ask you a question."

"Joel Hartt can talk to you all he wants, but I've got nothing to say to you."

"When did Ray get out of jail? Before Emma Hartt was murdered?"

Now it was Doreen's turn to look slapped. "What?"

"Is he Evan's father? Did he have an affair with Kristine?"

"Doreen, what's she talking about?" Ella pumped her paper fan even faster.

I found out Do Jo was still strong. She pulled me out of the room, then opened the front door and shoved me onto the stoop in one fluid motion, like a shot-putter. Before I could turn to get in the last word, she had slammed and locked both the screen and the wooden doors behind her.

I was starting to feel that Doreen didn't like me.

Now THAT I had brightened Do Jo's day, I returned to my original plan, and walked up to the church. I pulled on the left handle of the double door. No give. I grabbed the right one and yanked. Locked. Well, if this was my sign from God, I could take a hint.

However, gaining entrance was now a matter of principle. Churches were supposed to be open. Always. What if I had really needed sanctuary? I went down the side steps to the alley and tried the rectory door, then the church hall, which faced the street behind the main entrance of the church.

"Is everyone on vacation?" I asked the statue of the Virgin Mary encased in her plaster capsule on the small, ivy-covered lawn. With her arms outstretched, palms up, she seemed to shrug, *What do I know? Nobody tells me anything.*

Next-door was the long, single-story brick building that was Holy Mother Little Academy. I expected that to be closed over the summer break, but surely a nun or two would be holding down the fort. Unless the Sisters had a time-share down the shore. The Church always secured the best oceanfront property for its retreat centers.

The left-hand wing of the school housed the sleeping quarters for the nuns who taught there; the kindergarten, eighth grade and cafeteria anchored the other side. In the center section, one through seven lined up, just one classroom per grade, each with a bank of casement windows and a door opening onto the blacktop playground that sloped down to the sidewalk.

Three times a day, during recess and bus arrivals and departures, the street was blocked off to traffic. Every morning, the bell would ring, the first warning to summon us to stand perfectly still and shoulder to shoulder in front of our respective doors, ready to recite the Lord's Prayer and the Pledge of Allegiance to the flagpole next to the basketball hoop. On the second ring, you had better be in place or Sister Connie would grab you by the ear, pinch a lobe between her chalky fingers and lead you there.

I walked up to one of the classrooms and looked into a window, cupping my hands around my eyes to shield against the midday glare. The blackboard was wiped clean, bulletin boards stripped, textbooks stacked rigidly on low shelves. I hoped that they had updated the teaching materials. My geography book had suggested, "Maybe one day the territories of Alaska and Hawaii would be added to the Union," years after their statehood had been achieved.

The wood-and-metal pedestal desks were still in impossibly straight rows. Unlike other friends my age, my schoolmates and I had never been subjected to the nuclear-attack drills common in the Fifties and Sixties. No diving under initials-scarred desktops to protect us from being instantly vaporized. I guess the nuns thought, if we were to implode in a mushroom cloud, that was God's will. Or maybe they had a better grasp of physics than I had given them credit for. Scientific research has since proven that standard school desks are ineffective shields against nuclear annihilation.

I walked the length of the school, giving each doorknob a twist. When I had reached the double doors leading into the kindergarten wing, they flew open, missing my nose by not much.

"Yes? Can I help you?"

I looked down, way down, at Sister Constance Patiens. It was a shock. The woman who had terrorized me and legions of other Holy Moly students was about as tall as the actual penguin she resembled in her long black tunic, white wimple and crisp biblike guimpe. Nuns had started dressing in street clothes by the time I left Holy Moly, but obviously Sister Connie hadn't given up the habit.

Despite the heat, there wasn't even a bead of sweat on her sharp-featured face. In fact, it was barely lined. It would have been possible to believe she had not aged at all, if her thick eyebrows hadn't grayed. But they were still drawn into a frown, which she seemed to be taking some effort to smooth out.

"If you've come to register your child with us for September," she continued in what I'm sure she thought of as a pleasant tone, "we have a few openings left in the upper grades."

Was I old enough to have kids that age? Jeez. Doreen did. I was. "No, sister, I don't have a child to register. I used to be a student here, almost twenty-five years ago."

She let the frown return. "What's your name?"

"Andrealisa Rinaldi."

"I don't remember you. Are you sure you were enrolled here?" As if my memory, not hers, could be at fault.

"I'm sure. Would you mind if I had a look around, for old times' sake?"

Sister Connie shrugged, waved me inside and led me briskly down the hallway.

I asked her back, "Is Father Behan still at Holy Mother?"

Sister Connie stopped at a door that had her name plaque on it, and turned, looking pained. "He left us about ten years ago."

"I'm sorry to hear that."

"Why? He's not dead, child," she snorted. "He accepted a teaching post at a seminary in Miami. He took up snorkeling at age eighty-five. We should *all* have his life."

Suddenly, the nun snapped her head back to look up at me, then pushed her half-glasses higher up her nose. "Did you have a twin sister?"

"Yes. I still do. Caterina."

"I had you both for kindergarten. That was an interesting situation. We'd never had twins in different years. Were you the one who released the guinea pigs into the cafeteria?"

"No, that would be Cat."

She adjusted her glasses again, as if to bring me into better focus. "Then you were the quiet one."

"I guess." I had never understood adults. If you acted up, you were a brat. If you kept to yourself, you were a mute. A kid couldn't win.

"Your sister was quite a handful. I enjoyed her." Sister Connie actually smiled. "Once, she wouldn't settle down during nap-time. Kept banging the toes of her shoes on the floor. I finally told her to get up, stand in the corner and keep still. She could barely manage that and had such a black look on her face! After five minutes, I called her over and asked if she was mad at me. 'Yes, sister,' she said. 'You're such a pain.' That child could not tell a lie to save her life. Well, I asked the question, so I couldn't fault her for obeying the Ninth Commandment, could I?"

"I guess not, Sister." I was a little stunned that Sister Connie was turning out to be such a Chatty Cathy.

"You both took the lessons you learned at Holy Mother to heart, I hope? Kept on the straight and narrow, have you?"

"I'm not sure you might think so, Sister. I'm a member of the press."

"Whom do you work for?"

I steeled myself. "The *Moon*." I was sure it wasn't on the Church's approved reading list.

The scowl returned at double strength. "Oh, you're the one, are you, who's writing all this nonsense about the Hartts?"

"Only the most recent one, Sister—I mean, no, mine wasn't, I didn't..." I squirmed, just as I had when she criticized my backward *S*'s in kindergarten. "I talked to Joel Hartt, and he said it was okay—"

"Well, it's hogwash! You people should be ashamed, making a circus of this tragedy! Joel Hartt had nothing to do with his daughter's death."

"Do you know who did?" Somehow, that didn't seem outside the scope of her powers.

"Of course."

At last, all would be revealed!

"Who?"

She looked straight at me, not blinking. "Satan."

"Er, *the* Satan? The Prince of Darkness?"

"Only someone possessed by The Devil himself could do such a thing."

"And Joel isn't possessed?"

"I would know if he was." The tiny nun pursed her lips. "I saw him with his family and talked with him at parent-teacher conferences. Emma was a student here. As was her mother, Kristine—O'Leary, back then. Kristine was very devout. Even after she graduated, she would stop by to see me. When she became an art therapist, I saw her at St. Mary's Hospital during my weekly visits to the children's ward. Joel would come by to take her to lunch."

Sister Connie seemed somewhat embarrassed. "I admit that when she told me she was marrying Joel and he wasn't Catholic, I tried to talk her out of it, but you can't tell young people anything. However, I saw that he adored her—and his daughter when she came along. Emma was a happy child, a precious gift to them. She was their miracle baby."

"A miracle baby?" Sister Connie was sounding a tad overdramatic and *Moon*-like herself.

"Kristine had almost given up hope of having a child. But I told her not to despair, not like her sister."

"Her sister?"

"Kathleen." Sister Connie's brow knit again, with what seemed like concentration not annoyance, this time. "You must know her. You were in the same class, I believe."

I squeezed my brain. "I don't remember a Kathleen O'Leary."

"Oh, they were half sisters. The mother was widowed not long after Kathleen was born, then she married that no-good

Sean O'Leary, with his women on the side." Sister Connie was a regular gossip pipeline. "Kathleen went by *her* father's last name, McCarrick. Now, of course, she's a Whalen."

Another connection Mickey had failed to mention. So that's why the mayor and his wife were at Joel's on New Year's Eve. Part of the family. "Kristine couldn't have children?"

"Oh, those girls had so much trouble with their menses. Every month they'd be in the infirmary, groaning and moaning. I'm sorry to say it now, but I thought it was all hogwash. But of course, when they were older, a doctor finally diagnosed severe endometriosis."

"Oh." I said. "But having it doesn't always affect fertility." I learned this last month, after a major soap opera actress had become a fund-raising spokesperson for endometriosis research and admitted she was sufferer. I'd assigned that piece, outlining some treatments—laparoscopic surgery, hormone therapy, new drugs such as Lupron and Synarel, herbal remedies, with hysterectomy as a last resort. Of course, the *Moon* had run this helpful information alongside a picture of the daytime-TV star dressed in the leather dominatrix outfit her character frequently wears on *Days of Our Hope.*

"Conception can be difficult, and Kathleen had tried for years without success. As Kristine suffered from this as well, she assumed she had little chance."

Something still didn't fit.

"Sister," I asked, "why was Emma the miracle? She already had a brother." But suddenly I knew the answer. No pictures of Kristine pregnant with her first child on Joel's bookshelf. No pictures of Doreen's third child in her hallway gallery.

"Oh, Evan, yes," Sister Connie said as if she had forgotten the boy. "He's adopted."

SISTER CONNIE TALKED nearly nonstop while showing me around my old school, and made me nearly fifteen minutes late finding the Whalens in the labyrinth of streets that made up The Colony.

Houses were packed closely together, with narrow lanes shooting off and twisting up and down along the steep incline to the waterfront. It was as if each property were jockeying for a better view of the river. The mishmash of architecture was jarring, with log cabins tucked next to Italianate monstrosities swathed in stucco with faux colonnades and marble statuary. More proof that the town was at odds with itself between the old and the new, the white collar and the blue.

I finally stumbled upon Maple Drive and the Whalens' mailbox. The only part of the house visible from the road was the roof, which was at eye level. The thick holly bushes along the front of the property almost hid the wooden stairs that wound down to an unpretentious white clapboard on the embankment.

The steps brought me to a carved wood door with only a cast-iron knocker shaped like a lifesaver to announce guests. I lifted the ring, let it drop and was startled when a ship's bell started clanging somewhere in the house. Seconds later, the door opened, and Kathleen McCarrick Whalen was outlined in a halo of sunlight.

Her hair was still sleek and gold, cut into a chin-length bob. She smiled at me almost shyly and in that instant I saw the resemblance to her sister, Kristine, or at least to the portrait in Joel's library.

I started to introduce myself and apologize, but she laughed, "Andie, of course! Come in, come in!"

She led me through to a bright, efficient-looking kitchen, and called out, "Kenny, come meet Andie Rinaldi!"

I heard a glass door slide open and Kenneth Whalen walked through the parted curtains, from an outdoor deck. My first thought: It's Brian Keith from *Family Affair*. He was at least thirty years older than his wife, a big bear of a man, now white-haired. I remembered him from when he had first been elected, athletic and charismatic, like a dark-blond Kennedy brother. Which, I gathered from listening to my parents and their friends, had been part of his political appeal at the time. Already a prominent attorney in the county, he then became the youngest mayor the town had ever had. About the age I was now.

"Delighted!" His handshake was still a younger man's.

"Ken, ask Andie what she'd like to drink and charm her while I finish in here." She looked apologetically at me. "I just got back from seeing a patient, and it took me longer than I thought it would."

"I can help." I offered.

"No. It's ready. I just have to get everything together and I'll be right out. But let Kenny show off his view first."

Once I stepped out behind him onto the cantilevered deck, I could see why he'd want to. The wide water, and the bridge crossing it upriver, stretched out in silvery bands under the strong sunlight. A few pleasure boats, a barge and a sightseeing cruiser were passing by, against the ever-present backdrop of spires, skyscrapers and high-rises reaching up from the forested park on the opposite bank. I leaned over the deck railing. Below us, a short stretch of very green lawn ran to the dock. Moored to it was an America's Cup-worthy sailboat, with gleaming blond woodwork, a bright blue hull and gold script on the stern spelling out *Bonny Kate*.

"Amazing." I pointed to the boat. "And she's a beauty."

"Yes, she is," Ken's chest puffed out proudly. "Do you sail? Katie said you moved down the shore."

"Rowboats are more my speed. I was once a passenger on a Sunfish captained by my twin sister. A voyage in terror I've never repeated."

Ken laughed. "Those bathtub toys are not for the faint of heart. One big puff and you're over the side."

"Try six times in fifteen minutes. As I was spitting out a seawater, I wondered where the sailing part came in."

"Don't give up on it. The big boys are easier going, like you're gliding on air." He gave me a childlike grin. "You're welcome aboard anytime." He gestured toward the rolling bar cart next to the sliding doors. "Now what'll you have?"

As he poured club soda for us both, Ken asked me my impressions of the changes in town, as if my opinions counted, then offered his own. He was all for opening the waterfront to developers, commercial and residential, but wanted growth to be slow, so he could gauge its impact on quality of life. And he wanted prime riverside land set aside for a new high school, with a sailing program for the kids. "Might even retire and teach them myself."

If he were campaigning for something, I'd vote for him.

His deep voice was soothing and his gaze attentive as we sat across from each other at the redwood patio table, already set for lunch. Trees shaded the deck and a breeze whipped up off the water, taking the sting out of the heat. I felt surprisingly relaxed by the time Kathleen appeared at the glass door, a tray in hand. Ken jumped up to help her.

The conversation, over a dilled shrimp-and-pasta salad and homemade cole slaw, continued so companionably that I'd almost forgotten my mission. As Ken poured coffee and Kathleen set out a plate of lemon squares, I finally roused myself. Luckily, Ken had just asked how I decided on a career in journalism, so I figured I could get just as personal with my own questions.

"So how come you never got thee to a nunnery?" I asked Kathleen. "I thought that was your life's ambition."

She blushed. Ken laughed. "She got a better offer about fifteen years ago," he said.

Kathleen took a sip of the second glass of Chardonnay Ken had poured for her. "I guess 'Saint Kathleen' flunked out. I was a novitiate, going for my nursing degree and training at the hospital—"

"—where she ministered to the first of my many ills," Ken picked up. "I woke up from my angioplasty to see this golden angel hovering over me. Nearly had another heart attack from surprise. I'd always assumed I'd end up in the Other Place."

"Who says you won't?" his wife shot back. "You still have to atone for the sins you committed before you met me."

I smiled at their light mood, almost reluctant to darken it. "Kids?" I asked not so innocently.

Kathleen's face clouded, and Ken jumped in. "No luck there," he said with a small sigh. "But Katie has her hands plenty full with me."

Kathleen hesitated, then said, "I guess it wasn't meant to be." She smiled ruefully. "But I got a heavy dose of reality working in obstetrics and pediatrics. To be a parent, worrying all the time—I don't know if I could ever really handle that."

"You got to see that firsthand too, with Kristine and her kids," I prompted.

"Yes, yes, I did." She looked more alert. I guess she'd suddenly remembered why I was there.

"Katie loved Emma, and Evan, too, of course," Ken said softly, his eyes on his wife.

"Kristine was very sweet about that." Kathleen's smile now was achingly sad. "We spoke nearly every day during her pregnancy, and each day after. She made me feel a part of Emma's life, more than just her aunt. She shared her daughter with me. Totally unselfish. But that was Kris."

This seemed to call for a moment of silence. "If you don't mind my asking," I said finally, not waiting to find out if she did mind, "why didn't you adopt, like Joel and Kristine did Evan?"

The couple exchanged startled looks. Evidently Evan's adoption wasn't common knowledge, but they now seemed to assume Joel told me. Ken shifted in his chair.

Kathleen flushed. "I was the selfish one, I guess. Everyone assumed I'd be happy to have any child. But I knew I would only be satisfied with a baby of my own, our own." She glanced at her husband, who had turned slightly to look out at the water. "You know how it is, when you see a family and someone says, 'Oh, she has her mother's eyes' or 'his big toe is crooked, just like his grandfather's'...silly things like that?"

I nodded.

"That was part of my fantasy." She sighed. "Funny, that's how it was in that last moment I saw Emma on New Year's, wearing her new scarf. After she'd hugged us all goodnight, she stopped in the doorway of the living room, looked back and winked at us. She was the spitting image of my little sister."

"It's okay, honey." Ken came around to embrace his wife from behind.

"I'm okay, Kenny. Sorry, Andie." Kathleen roughly brushed away her tears, then swatted her husband's arms away. He started clearing the table. When he left to take the tray into the kitchen, she turned back to me. "It's just that I think I needed that family connection. I don't know that motherhood would come naturally to me with someone else's baby."

"But Kristine didn't feel that way?"

Kathleen shook her head. "Kris was more open to it. I guess she had seen me struggling for a few years and thought it was probably hereditary. When the opportunity came up, she didn't hesitate."

"And Doreen was the opportunity."

Ken had come back through the sliding door and said firmly. "This has to be off the record. Will you promise that? Joel said we could trust you. We're only talking to you about any of this to help him, to let you see he wasn't responsible, that no one close to them could be."

I could always cross my fingers under the table.

As if she sensed my thought, Kathleen grabbed my hand resting on my knee, squeezing a little harder than I thought necessary. "It's just that Evan doesn't know that he's adopted. Doreen insisted that he never be told—she made it a condition. It would be devastating for too many people if this were made public."

"But won't Evan find out eventually? Somebody in Doreen's family—his grandmother, his biological father, Ray—will slip up sometime." I was thinking the real danger was Sister Connie's loose lips.

"They don't know."

I blinked. "How could they not? I met Ray and I saw the

resemblance in a split second. They had to know Doreen was pregnant. Wouldn't they wonder where the baby went after nine months?"

"They didn't know that either," Ken said.

I looked at them in disbelief.

Kathleen nodded. "Doreen found out just after Ray was sent to prison. She only visited him in South Dakota after the birth. Her mother got sick around that time, too—her diabetes was always way out of control—so Doreen had that excuse. When Ella got out of the hospital, Doreen sent her to recover at her aunt's in Florida. And Doreen was a bit heavier then. Anyone else who noticed, well, she told them she'd lost the baby. You know how people are. No one ever brought it up again."

"But surely now that Ray is back, he must have seen Evan."

Ken rolled his eyes. "Heaven help me—Ray is my sister's kid—but he's never been the sharpest pencil in the box. If Doreen kept it from him, he wouldn't suspect a thing."

"But see?" Kathleen seemed to be looking for my approval. "Our brother-in-law adopted our nephew's son. It's all still in the family."

Mickey had said it: Half of town was related to the other half.

"Doreen was out of her mind with worry, two young children, a disabled mother, her husband gone. She had scheduled an abortion." Kathleen pursed her lips. "But then Sister Connie found out."

I'd always suspected the little nun was omniscient.

"She thought she could talk Doreen into carrying the baby to term if she could find someone to adopt. She approached me first at the hospital, then I told my sister. When Kris and Joel agreed to it, Doreen gave birth in another county hospital. Sister Connie arranged everything, somehow pulled some strings with the Catholic agency to make it alright for them to take Evan without the father's consent and the usual red tape."

So Sister Connie felt the ends justified the means? "And then

Kristine became pregnant with Emma," I offered.

"Some women do seem to conceive once the pressure's off." Kathleen's hands swept some imaginary crumbs off the table. "But Kris had a hard time through the pregnancy. Gestational diabetes, just like our mom. It was worse with her second one. When she died..." Ken looked like he was going to come to her rescue again, but Kathleen waved him off. "After that, I quit working obstetrics. I'm a visiting nurse with the home health-care program now. Check on the old folks who can't get around. At least you *expect* them to get sick."

I remembered what Ella Josephs had said. "You saw Doreen's mother today."

"Just before you came actually. Mondays and Thursdays." Kathleen laughed. "Ella is stubborn, though. I keep telling her if she had a healthier diet and walked more, she could get off most of her medicines, especially the insulin. But no one ever wants to hear that. They all want a magic pill."

"So you take care of Doreen's mother and Doreen takes care of Joel's—*her* son, really. Still all in the family, huh?"

Ken and Kathleen seemed pleased that I was getting the idea.

But I wasn't. "Pardon me, but I think it's weird that Joel and Kristine would have Doreen come work for them."

Kathleen leaned closer. "You didn't know my sister. She thought that was the perfect resolution. Until then, Doreen had a factory job, night shift. This way she could still see Evan almost every day and know he was in good hands." Kathleen's voice faltered. "Everybody called me Saint Kathleen, but Kris was the real saint."

"And Joel too," Ken added. "He got Ray construction work as soon as he was out of the federal prison."

"The first Jewish saint?"

He laughed. "Well, the Pope has already beatified Sister Teresia Benedicta, who was born Edith Stein. Joel could be next."

I shook my head. "This seems too wild. How could you expect everyone involved to keep this a secret?"

Kathleen found both my hands and held them tight. Her strength surprised me. "No one who cares about them would ever tell."

• *Chapter 8* •

I HAD TO tell Mickey.

No, I didn't. He wouldn't tell *me* anything.

But what if the Whalen-Dougherty-Hartt family secret had something to do with Emma's death? Evan was adopted without Ray knowing—but maybe he did find out, and planned to kidnap Emma as a way of forcing Joel to give back his son. See how it feels to not have your child. The cops should be investigating that angle.

No, that made no sense. Wouldn't he kidnap Evan?

Unless Ray became confused in an unfamiliar house, walked into Emma's bedroom by mistake, strangled the girl to keep her quiet and then staged the ransom demand.

Why was I even getting involved in this? I had vowed to get in and get out, write the piece assigned to me and move on.

But if I broke this story...

But I promised the Whalens it was off the record.

But the *Moon* doesn't care about journalistic ethics...

But *I* do.

The *buts* alone were gonna kill me. That's the problem with being a Catholic, even a recovering one. It's always a choice between good and evil, right and wrong, heaven and hell, black and white. There's no gray area. Even Purgatory...limbo...that's worse than Hell, not knowing what's going to happen next or if there *is* a Next.

Add to that an ethnic heritage known for extremes, turning on a dime from hysterical joy to inconsolable sadness. Never mind Cat. All Italian-Catholics are manic-depressives.

By the time I'd finished debating with myself, I was in front of The Rock Bottom. Maybe I wouldn't *tell* Mickey, but I could ask a few questions, see if he'd even looked into the possibility of Ray, the ex-con, as a murder suspect.

But surprise. Mickey wasn't there.

"He's working," Georgie said, as if he couldn't believe it either. He handed me the telephone from behind the bar and recited Mickey's beeper number while I dialed. A minute later, Mickey called back.

"I'll come by about 4:30. Tell Georgie to run a tab for you until then." He laughed insanely, as if he'd said the funniest thing in the world, and hung up.

No way could I sit and breathe in stale cigarette smoke for the next hour, so I pushed back out the double doors. The temperature had dropped, but not much, and nearly forced me back into the air-conditioned bar. Then I remembered the woods, a shady refuge on the hottest days of my childhood. I wondered if the path was still at the top of DeVries Lane.

To GET TO the woods, every kid on our block used to cut through Mickey's backyard to DeVries, climbing over the Giamontes' chicken-wire fence and hopping a low cinderblock wall. We did this so often that the fence bent almost to the ground. Mickey's mother hollered at us every time we did it.

Kids from Clearview risked Mrs. G's wrath to get to the path that ran above the property line of the last house on DeVries. Like several other trails in the woods around town, it led up the cliff to a break in the wooden fence that surrounded the amusement park on the heights. Though none of us were officially allowed to take that route, the boys in the neighborhood went all summer long. This let them skip on the admission fee, though they still had to lay down their dimes for rides on the Ferris wheel, rollercoaster and other stomach-churning attractions.

The first and last time I'd taken that route, my parents had to call the cops.

One summer afternoon, while Cat was still recovering from a bout of chicken pox I had passed on to her, I'd seen Mickey and Jimmy O'Shea heading up that way and followed. I thought I saw them ahead of me on the path and gave them the two-fingered whistle Juliet taught me. But the boys coming toward me weren't Mickey and Jimmy.

I recognized one of them from school—Gary, my classmate Eileen's brother. Gary's friend, Dooley, a public-school kid I'd seen around, was scrawny, scab-kneed and wouldn't have had a chance in life on his own. I asked Gary if he'd seen Mickey pass by.

Gary frowned, then turned to his friend. "Hey, Dooley, don't you think she should lift up her shirt?"

"What?" I was nine, and couldn't imagine why that would be interesting. By the blank look on his face, neither could Dooley

"If we tell you, you have to lift up your shirt." Gary nodded, pleased with his negotiating skills.

I edged past them. "No thanks, then. I'll find him on my own."

But Gary had grabbed the hem of my sleeveless blouse.

I smacked his hand away. "Leave me alone!" I really wished Cat were there. She would have done something crazy to distract them. So I did the only thing I knew how to do. I screamed.

Mickey and Jimmy charged out from behind a stand of pines ten yards away, with Mickey tugging at his fly. They must have stepped off the path to pee. I wondered if they had actually been watching the whole time.

Gary included them in the festivities. "Don't you want to see what's under her shirt?"

Jimmy O gave it some thought. "Yeah, okay," he said.

I glared at him.

"Don't touch her." Mickey was in Gary's face. Mickey had two younger sisters, which was probably the only reason why his chivalry kicked in.

Gary shoved at his shoulder, and Mickey jumped back. The scrawny Dooley let go of me and pushed down Jimmy, who was pretty scrawny himself. When Mickey turned to help Jimmy, I saw Gary pick up a glass Coke bottle from the ground.

Without thinking, I ran up to him, grabbed his arm and cracked it over my knee. A judo move I'd just seen on *Honey West*.

"Aw, shit!" Gary dropped the bottle and cradled his forearm with his other hand. "I think she broke my wrist!"

"And I'm gonna break your head!" Mickey had Gary by the hair now.

Soon they were so busy punching and shouting and shoving each other, they forgot about me. So I ran home.

By the time I had hopped the chicken wire, I was bawling, though I wasn't sure why. In her backyard, Mrs. Giamonte was pinning laundry to the clothesline and was about to scold me when she saw my face. "What happened, Andie?" She was at my side in seconds. "Andrealisa, *what happened*?"

"The woods...two boys...I got to go home..."

By the time I walked through my front door, Mrs. G had already called my mother and my mother was on the phone to my father. He came home and called the cops.

I was embarrassed when they rang our doorbell. Mickey, hanging around outside, had already filled them in. Cat and I could hear him through our open bedroom window, giving the details and calling the two thirteen-year-olds "the perpetrators." So maybe he had been training for a career in law enforcement even then.

That night Dooley's father brought him to our house to apologize, but Gary never showed. Two years later, I came face to face with Gary again, at the summer recreation program at the Lincoln Elementary. He was a junior counselor. When he realized who I was, he finally apologized. He even became buddies with Cat and taught her to play tennis. So you never can tell how people will turn out.

THE PATH CLIMBED, then leveled off, then climbed, then leveled. It was no longer a much-traveled route—the amusement park had closed twenty years before—but it still seemed a favorite byway, littered with fresh candy wrappers, cigarette butts and soda and beer cans. A few more lightly traveled trails broke off in various directions. It was cooler here, just as I'd thought, under the green-leaved canopy and stony outcroppings.

Walking around a heavier thicket of pines, I stepped onto gravel, which I realized was a section of driveway. Farther up the cliff, through the trees, I could make out the outlines of a cabin that I didn't remember being there

But, close up, it was more like an elf hut, complete with turret, walls of smooth river stone with a slate roof, thick rough wood beams framed the windows and door. It seemed to have been formed by whatever had tumbled down the cliff.

I walked through an ivy-covered arbor onto a slate patio that led to a flourishing vegetable patch. I walked around it and nearly tripped over a girl, kneeling in the dirt. Her fine blond hair was pulled back into a flyaway ponytail. Perhaps she was a woodland sprite. One with huge pale blue eyes, a wide smile, and gardening gloves about two sizes too big.

She stood up and shook off the gloves. "Hi," she said, as if she had been expecting me. "My uncle's not home yet, but you can wait inside. I made lemonade. Want some?"

I was charmed. I hadn't had her poise at that age. Actually, I didn't have it *now*. "Sure. That sounds great."

Who her uncle was, I hadn't a clue, but I felt like staying.

"What's your name?" I said as she led me through the rough-hewn front door.

"Beth," she said, and floated over the stone threshold.

I tripped over it, into the living room, which also seemed to be the dining room and kitchen. Cool in here too, even without air-conditioning. Wide-board oak floors, a fieldstone fireplace, overstuffed sofa and side chairs that looked like they'd swallow you whole if you dared sit. I wanted nothing more. Had Beth sprinkled me with fairy dust?

The lemonade was fine, not too sweet, and Beth was gracious, even setting a plate of sugar wafers at the small barnwood coffee table.

"So, Beth, you're visiting your uncle...?" hoping she would fill in a name.

But she didn't. She shook her head and a few more strands came loose from her ponytail. "I'm living here now."

I nodded as if I knew what that was all about, hoping again that she'd supply the details. But again she didn't.

"I was out staking my tomato plants, is it okay if I...?" Her high forehead creased with concern that she might be derelict in her hostess duties.

"No, please, do go on, Beth," I said as if mouthing lines I hadn't rehearsed enough. "Nothing worse than top-heavy tomatoes." I had no idea what I was talking about, but was glad that she'd be leaving me alone to poke around this enchanted cottage.

A few small, dreamy watercolors of river scenes, seascapes and a lake view scattered on the barn-wood walls. What looked like antique wooden fishing poles and a creel hung over the fireplace. No photos on display to give a clue to the homeowner's identity. Floor-to-ceiling shelves on both sides of the hearth, books perfectly alphabetized, from James Agee to Thomas Wolfe. But no Tom Wolfe, few modern novels at all, from what I could see. A narrow, nearly perpendicular staircase to the right—leading to a garret bedroom? And a latched barn-wood door in the center of the wall—the gateway to the turret chamber?

The strange atmosphere made me lose track of time and I checked my watch. Oops. Almost late for Mickey.

I took my glass and the cookie plate over to the tiny sink to wash. As I turned to place them in the mini dish drain, I saw a slightly blurry photo thumbtacked onto the wood cabinet and moved in closer.

"That's me and Uncle Jesse." Beth had appeared behind me, noiseless as a wood nymph. "My friend Evan took that picture. His father gave him this great camera for Christmas last year. A Leica. Am I saying that right? He's just learning how to develop from negatives himself." She wrinkled her nose at the photo. "That one's not so good."

"Evan? Evan Hartt?"

"Uh-huh." She seemed pleased that I knew her friend.

So this was Jesse Quindlen's house. He must have a rich fantasy life. I'd like to find out more about that some other time. But if Jesse found me here now, he'd probably think I was stalking him.

"Well, Beth, I really want to thank you for your hospitality, but I have another appointment. Do you know how to get to The Rock Bottom from here? I came from along the cliff path from DeVries and I'm not sure how far I am."

"I take that path all the time to visit Evan. It's, like, five minutes. But you're closer to The Rock now. Once you're at the bottom of the driveway, you're on Cliff Way near Runyon, and it's right down on the corner."

"Great." I had a foot out the door. "Do tell your uncle that I called on him," I said under my breath, hoping it wouldn't register until I was down the driveway.

But no. "Okay. Wait—what did you say your name is?"

Oh, well. I thought of the bookshelves. "Amy Carleton," I said, then hit the gravel at a run.

MICKEY WAS ALREADY in the back booth, a half-full beer glass in hand and a Fudgsicle across the table. As I slid onto the bench, I made my decision: Purgatory.

"So Juliet Rojas was the first ex-Mrs. Giamonte."

"Ah, this is what is so important that we talk about? You jealous?"

I bristled. "I'm concerned about your lack of candor."

"Gee, then I guess I'll have to stock up on candor the next time I'm at the candor store."

"You also failed to mention that Doreen's husband has a record."

"So?"

"And he was released from federal prison around the time Emma Hartt was killed."

"I know when he got out. I arrested him. I keep track of such things."

"Don't you think he might have been involved?"

"Why?"

Mickey was enjoying this, and I wanted to slap him silly. "Maybe he tried to kidnap the girl to get something from Joel."

"You mean money?"

"Could be." It was killing me not to say more, so I raised my glass to my lips.

"Or do you mean Evan?"

I choked on my drink, spattering my blouse with brownish milk that would never come out at the dry cleaners. "You know about Evan?"

"That he's Ray's son, not Joel's? Sure."

"How — ?"

"I must be smarter than I look. Or maybe my kid sister works at Catholic Adoption Services." He raised an eyebrow. "But I'm still not clear on how this makes Ray a killer. Maybe you could fill me in."

I had gone over my theory in my own head so many times I thought I could wrap it all up for him neatly. "Ray must have found out that Evan was his and demanded his son back. Joel wouldn't play ball, so Ray decided to kidnap Emma to show him how it felt to lose a child.

"Maybe Doreen had changed her mind by then too and helped him get in, gave him her key. Maybe they were going for ransom money, too, huh? They'd need cash if they were going to leave town. But they screwed something up and the girl died."

I was gratified to see Mickey listening attentively. Now he raised both eyebrows. "Wow." He waved his empty beer glass in the air.

"Why couldn't it be him? He's got a record. The family is obviously broke. Doreen could have overheard how much Joel was getting in his shopping-center deal and written the ransom note."

"Yes, all those things are true. Or could be true. But you don't have any idea where he was that night. What if he had an alibi?"

"I'd look into it more closely if I were you."

"I have." Mickey tilted his head. "Two friends swear he was playing pool and darts with them until the wee hours."

"So you know these lowlifes?"

"Hey, Georgie." Mickey grinned as the burly bartender slid another beer in front of him. "Andie thinks you and I are lowlifes."

"Maybe *you*, Mickey," Georgie laughed and walked off.

"You guys are his alibis?"

"'Fraid so."

"All night?"

He nodded. "We throw a big New Year's party here every year. You might want to put that on your calendar for next December 31."

"But what about Doreen? Maybe she did it herself, knowing Ray would be the obvious suspect and you'd vouch for him. Damn, she could lift a ten-year-old girl and strangle her with one hand." I was still feeling her forceful grip on my upper arm.

"She was here too. Sitting right where you are now." Mickey looked as if he felt sorry for me. "She'd have had to pass us on her way out."

I wasn't going to accept his pity. "Ray has to be connected somehow. Even if he didn't do it himself, he could have passed Doreen's key on to someone else and—"

"Ray is harmless." Mickey took a long swig from his glass.

"Harmless? The guy had a trunkful of cocaine. And a crossbow! Or was he off to play one of the Merry Men in a community theater production of *Robin Hood*?"

"It wasn't his. Neither was the cocaine."

"*You're* his character witness now? The guy who arrested him?"

"That was my job. One of my last jobs as a patrol cop here in town, as a matter of fact. I figured Ray would get off, but we couldn't find the guy who set him up, and he took the fall. It was the DEA's case by then and none of the locals could convince the Feds that he wasn't part of it somehow. They lost their big fish and had to fry up *someone*. Ray cooperated as much as he could, though, and he got less time than he would have under the circumstances."

"How do you know he was set up?"

"Did you actually talk to Ray?" He rolled his eyes when I shook my head. "If you did, you'd know too. Everybody else knows he's a real sweet guy, and a damn good pool player, but he's always been a few deuces short of a full deck. Cocaine? Crossbow? He wouldn't know one from the other. He'd more likely snort an arrow up his nose."

"Well, he knows how to steal a car."

"He didn't know it was stolen. Or what was in the trunk. He thought he was meeting up with some classic-car buff." Mickey slumped back, as if tired. "The vehicle was a decoy. Whoever planned this knew the Feds were watching as the shipment moved up the coast. They had dropped off the car at the docks, loaded with ten kilos, while the rest of it went where intended. Ray was just a mook hired to take the car from Point A to Point B, where someone was supposed to meet him, but the guy never showed."

I shot him some skepticism.

"Look. Ray had two young kids, needed the money, and heard about the job from a guy who knew a guy who knew a guy... You get it. I'm sure it was always meant to be Ray who was picked up. Like I said, everyone in town knows he would be the last one to catch on if something underhanded was going on. His is a trusting nature."

"That's very poetic of you." I was running out of things to say.

"I'm a very poetic guy, which you'd find out if you took the time to get to know me." He leaned forward again.

"You forget. I *do* know you."

"Not really. You knew a boy, once upon a time."

"Sounds like the start of a very unhappy fairy tale. Something from the Brothers Grimm."

He closed his eyes and sang, "Fairy tales can come true..."

Young at Heart. We used to sit around the stereo—my dad had bought the first one on the block—and listen to my parents' record albums, mostly Sinatra. Mickey remembered this was my favorite song.

"...they can happen to..."

He was just trying to distract me. Maybe he had another reason he didn't want me to look at Ray too closely. I stood up abruptly, bumping the table, and sending Mickey's half-full glass into his lap.

"...*yooooouuu—ewwww*!" The song ended on a very un-Sinatra-like howl.

I LEFT MICKEY to mop his crotch, and phoned in to the office for messages. Dovie said Joel had called. Now I could kill two birds with one stone, so to speak. Mickey might not take my suspicions seriously, but Joel would.

His silver Volvo was in the driveway, but so was the yellow Chevy. Doreen's car. I didn't want to deal with her twice in one day. I checked my watch. Nearly five. She would be going home soon. I'd just hide behind a bush until then.

I bypassed the porch steps and followed the slate walkway to the left. Casement windows were set into the foundation, level with the ground. The putty around one of them seemed lighter, newer. Was this where the "kidnapper" got in, near the front? What if he had already been hiding in the basement, let in by Doreen before Joel's guests had shown up? But why break the glass later, from the inside? Why not undo the latch, crawl out and then smash the window?

Maybe it was simple panic, or plain stupidity. Again, that seemed to point to Ray Dougherty, who didn't seem capable of complicated thought. But Ray had an alibi. Or so Mickey insisted.

The walkway brought me down around the corner and into a field of flowers.

Gardening had been Evelyn Hartt's only consuming interest besides Joel, and someone had kept it up. But instead of the formal-looking roses and bedding plants that I remembered, this was a wild but wonderful mix of black-eyed Susans, daisies, tiger lilies, lavender and other blooming things I had no names for, some taller than me.

Wood-chip trails ran around and through it, and I followed, drawn in by the fragrance. In the center of it all was a twig bench, and I took that as an invitation to sit. Much better than hiding under a bush.

"Hi."

I think I may have screamed.

Evan Hartt was squatting above me on a ledge cut into the cliff, overlooking the garden. "Sorry I scared you."

"No, Evan, I just saw a spider." And my life flashing before my eyes. "Hi, I'm Andie, a friend of your father's." I thought that was the truth.

"I remember you." If he was troubled by the memory of Doreen's reaction to me, his face didn't show it. "Wanna come up?"

"Sure. How?"

He pointed out a set of stairs also chiseled from the stone. At the top was a slate-paved patio, which hadn't been there when I was a kid. Brass tiki torches, smelling strongly of citronella, were planted in terra-cotta pots around the perimeter.

Evan was now seated at a wrought-iron table covered with loose photos and spiral-bound books. "I'm organizing my albums," he explained.

"You dad said you liked to take pictures." I picked up one. It was of Emma, in a very long blonde wig, leaning out of a turret window—obviously taken at Jesse's cottage.

"That's Rapunzel." Evan said. "Aunt Katie gave Emma that fake hair."

"These are great!" They were. "I really like that one." His sister's face was half in shadow, turned serenely into the pillow.

Evan nodded proudly. "Sleeping Beauty. I'm putting together a fairy-tale book. It was my sister's idea. She posed for them before she died." He said this very matter-of-factly.

"Evan!"

Doreen's voice made us both jump.

Oh, God, no. A back door behind the house opened. But she couldn't see me.

"Evan, come in and wash up. Dinner's ready, and your father's on his way downstairs."

Evan shrugged. "Sorry, maybe you can look at them some other time," and gathered up his photos and albums. I figured I'd wait until he was inside before sneaking back down into the garden, wait until the coast was clear and ring the front doorbell.

Unfortunately, the boy had impeccable manners.

"Shouldn't we invite Dad's friend for dinner?" I heard him ask as he jumped up the last step.

"What? Who?" Doreen stuck her head out.

My teeth started to ache.

"Andie. She's on the patio. I was showing her my pictures."

I left the patio and slowly came up behind Evan.

I expected a repeat of our encounter earlier today, but instead Doreen said evenly, "I'm sure she has other plans."

"As a matter of fact, I don't," I said brightly. "But I don't want to impose on Joel. Though he did want to speak to me. That's why I'm here." I gave Doreen my sweetest smile.

"I'll go ask Dad." Evan ducked past Doreen.

She and I eyed each other.

"I know about the adoption," I said.

Doreen jumped, looked behind her to be sure Evan had gone, then came out and shut the door behind her.

"If you print one word about that..." She didn't need to finish the sentence. I got it.

I held up two fingers of my right hand. "I won't. Scout's honor."

"As I remember it, you were a lousy Scout."

"Okay, so I never earned my Hospitality Badge. You were worse. You dunked Grace Kelly's head in the campground toilet when we went on that overnight."

"She deserved it. She put a frog in my sleeping bag."

"Tit for tat. Does revenge run in the family?"

"What do you mean?"

"Ray. Joel has his son, so Ray takes his daughter."

"Ray doesn't know anything about Evan."

"C'mon, Do Jo—"

"Don't call me that!"

"Sure Ray has an alibi, and a good one. A police detective no less. Ray makes a copy of your key to get one of his jailhouse buddies to go kidnap the girl—"

"That's insane! Ray isn't like that, he would never—"

"But something goes wrong. Emma wakes up maybe, starts to scream—"

"Stop it! Why can't you mind your own business?" she hissed. "We were finally being left alone."

"Don't you care who killed Emma?"

Her face froze.

"The police still do."

"The police?" Doreen snorted. "You mean your pal Mickey? Ask him what happened to the drugs they found in the car Ray was driving."

"What do you mean?"

"Ask him how five kilos of coke disappeared right out from under his nose, huh?"

That triggered something in my memory. Mickey had said he found ten kilos in the car. But the newspaper clipping said Ray had been convicted on five keys. Half had gone missing between the arrest and the sentencing?

Doreen was still talking. "Then ask him how he could afford to buy that tavern a year later."

Yep. Those were two good questions.

They led me to another one: Did Mickey have some other motive for giving Ray Dougherty an alibi?

EVAN WAS TALKING about F-stops and fixing baths, and I was still feeling disoriented, seated in the Hartt dining room eating roast chicken and mashed potatoes. Joel was asking Evan questions that kept him on his favorite subject.

When Evan asked what kind of camera I had, I admitted I favored disposables. "I had a 35-millimeter or two, but I kept breaking the rewind. It didn't matter what kind of camera I had anyway. Everyone I ever shot wound up with glowing red eyes, like in *Rosemary's Baby*."

Evan looked concerned. "That means the flash is too close to the lens. The camera picks up the flash's reflection off the blood vessels at the back of the eyeballs."

"Ick. That sounds even more gruesome than *Rosemary's Baby*. Is there a cure?"

"Either don't focus straight on at someone, or turn on more lights so your subject's pupils aren't so big."

"Thanks for the tip."

Two years ago, this boy had lost his mother—or rather, the

woman he *thought* was his mother. Eighteen months later, his sister's gone too. Yet Evan seemed very self-possessed for his age, and certainly not scarred by tragedy. Other adults would reassure themselves with the "kids are resilient" line, but I knew better. The effects wouldn't show until much later. Kids take their cues from the adults and fill in where needed—good or bad. Some act out to distract the grieving parent, give them an outlet for their anger at loss. Others take over emotional responsibilities, or work double-time to cheer up everyone, win approval. It seemed like Evan had assigned himself the caregiver role, asking his father about his day, even asking me about mine.

I told him I'd visited his aunt and uncle.

"They're cool." High praise. "Aunt Katie took me to a photography exhibit in the city last month. And I go with Uncle Ken on his boat sometimes."

Okay, at least Evan had his family, loving and supportive, if unconventional. That would help later on.

When Joel asked, I said no to dessert and yes to coffee, and explained I had to get back soon to feed my rat-dog. As Evan started in on his wedge of blueberry pie, I told him about Ben.

Evan laughed, showing his purple-stained tongue. "Could you bring him around sometime so I can take his picture?"

I thought Ben would like that and said so.

Joel stood up. "Do you have a few more minutes before you go? There's something I want to show you."

I followed him into the library with my mug, expecting this to be his excuse to interrogate me about my day's interviews, out of Evan's earshot. Instead he walked over to a wall cabinet and opened the doors. "What do you think of my collection?"

Inside was a glass case fitted with tiny compartments, each holding a miniature vehicle labeled by make and year.

"Oh my God. Your Matchbox cars."

He pointed. "Remember this one? You gave it to me on my sixth birthday.'

I read the label. "The '64 Mustang."

"I slept with it for a week afterward. Until I woke up one morning with tiny tire tracks on my cheek. Then my mother checked my bed every night."

"Probably afraid it was an early sign of auto eroticism."

He laughed. "She couldn't save me from that forever." Closing the cabinet doors, he said casually, or so it seemed. "Everything okay with the interviews? Friends and family being cooperative?"

"Yes, rather. Which naturally makes me suspicious." I kept my tone light. "I may have found out a few things you didn't want me to know."

Did he stand a little straighter? "Such as?"

"Such as, that Evan is adopted."

Joel seemed to relax. "He is my son. I don't make the distinction. And you shouldn't either." His tone was firm but not unfriendly. "I don't want that information made public. I hope you understand that."

"I do. Still, the circumstances are unusual."

"To you maybe. But it has worked out to everyone's advantage, and no one was hurt by it."

"What about Ray? Don't you think he would be hurt if he knew?"

"There is a saying that what you don't know can't hurt you." Joel winced at himself. "I'm sorry. That was flippant." He ran a hand over his face. "The decision that Doreen made was based on the circumstances at the time, what she thought was best. I continue to abide by her wishes. If at any time she felt that Ray, or Evan, should be told, I would honor that too."

"It was nice that you found Doreen's husband a job when he came back."

"Nothing nice about it. Everybody knows he's a good worker and a good guy."

Who is this Everybody everybody keeps talking about? It just reminded me that, no matter how much it seemed like old times, I was an outsider now. Not one of the Everybodys.

"Have you thought that maybe he's not so good? That maybe he learned a few bad things out there in South Dakota?"

He turned from me, went to his line up of family photos, spoke to them. "If you're thinking what I think you're thinking, don't think it."

"Why not?"

"It will get you nowhere."

"If you're so sure—"

"I'm sure."

"Then you must know how that sounds, that it must mean you know—"

"All I know is what I'm sure of. That neither Ray nor Doreen could be involved." He faced me again. "Is there anyone else you wanted to talk to?"

"I'll let you know." Joel seemed to be about to say something more, but didn't. So I asked the obvious, "Not to look a gift horse in the mouth, but why are you helping me?"

"Payback for the Mustang. It's a collector's item nowadays."

"No. Seriously."

He took a minute. "A lot has been written that wasn't true, especially about my daughter. Your paper reaches a large audience. And I knew you would be..." He searched for a word.

I supplied one. "Sympathetic?"

He shook his head. "Not necessarily." He paused again. "Fair. I knew you would be fair."

"How could you be so sure, after all these years?"

"I'm sure about a lot of things, aren't I?" He smiled. "People are who they are. Circumstances bring out their best and their worst, but they don't change. You always gave me the benefit of the doubt. Until the one day that I did something indisputably mean. Can't say I blame you. Now, your sister," he smiled, "she always reacted to the moment, regardless of the consequences. Not one to step back and see the big picture, like you. So, how is Cat?"

"She's had her ups and downs but seems to be finding her

way." That's all I felt like saying for now.

"Tell her I remember her. And her right hook." He was quiet for a moment. "But this will be your last article, right?"

"Scout's honor."

I sure was stretching the limits of my long-expired GSA membership today.

• *Chapter 9* •

Thursday morning Elise walked by my desk, crooked a finger. "Follow me."

Dovie, who was sitting there as I edited her first feature, arched one eyebrow at me. I raised both of mine, but went.

Where would my executive editor lead me this time? Down a manhole? Nah. In her flowered chiffon number, she wasn't dressed for it. So it was anticlimactic when she turned into her own office and shut the door after me.

She shuffled through papers at her cluttered desk. "Now, where is that? I printed it out last night to read at home, but I know I left it right here on top this morning. That intern always moves things. Give me a minute."

It was more like ten. "Okay, here it is. Your piece on Emma's last hours." She took ten more minutes scanning the pages. I used the time to pick imaginary lint off my slacks. "Yeah, well, it seems to be missing something," she said finally, not looking up.

The offices were kept at the temperature of a meat locker, but sweat formed under my collar nonetheless. "Look, I was hired as an editor," I said defensively. "I might need to work more on writing in the *Moon* style—"

"You see, at the end here, you quote the nun," Elise continued as if I hadn't spoken. "You ask her who she thinks is behind this girl's murder, and she says Satan."

"Uh-huh," I said warily. "That's what she said."

Elise finally raised her head but gazed to the left of me. "Have you looked into that?"

"Into what?"

"Evil. The possibility of the occult."

"You mean, like the Children of Satan?"

"Or the Devil's Spawn, one of those groups."

I kept my face straight. "I can honestly say the thought never crossed my mind."

Elise dropped the pages back on her desk. "Well, we have to be objective. Get me a quote from a devil worshipper and we can wrap this up."

When I got back to my desk, Dovie was still there, staring at my phone, then at me. Her mouth opened, but nothing came out. My intern, struck dumb?

"Is something wrong, Dovie?"

"You just had a call." More silence.

My first thought was that something had happened to Cat, or that Cat had happened to something. Those were always my first thoughts. So I said too impatiently, "You'll either have to tell me who it was or fetch me my Ouija Board because I'm not good at guessing games."

"It was Clothilde."

"Who?"

"*Clothilde.*"

I almost said *Who?* again, but then a brain synapse fired. "The fashion photographer?"

Dovie nodded. "She wants to talk to you about Emma Hartt and her father, at her studio. Actually, it was her assistant who called. She gave me the address."

"Now?"

"She said she'd be there all day for a shoot." Dovie suddenly was in my face. "Pu-leeze, ma'am, can I come? She does all the top models in my magazines." Dovie was playing her Tennessee twang like a banjo. "I promise I'll be as quiet as a church mouse with laryngitis on Whitsunday."

I had no idea what that meant, but I didn't mind her tagging along.

The cab dropped us curbside on a dingy side street. On our left, guys in bloody once-white overalls loaded slabs of cow into once-white refrigerator trucks. On our right, guys wearing Salvation Army handouts lounged full length on the sidewalk, coddling their beer cans or pint bottles in paper bags. Both groups soon let Dovie and I know just how desirable we were. And single women complain that there are no eligible men in this city.

"You sure you got the address right?" I asked Dovie.

"Sure as a chubby boll weevil loves a cotton field."

I must remember to get a Southern-to-English dictionary.

After a few passes, we found a sliver of an entryway with the right number fading above it, and rang the buzzer marked "Studio C," as Dovie had been instructed.

A metallic voice said, "Who?" and we answered. The reply click-and-buzz got us through the foot-thick steel door and into an elevator the depth of a No. 10 envelope. Maybe it was a warning: *If you're not thin enough, you don't belong here.* Luckily, Dovie didn't take up much room and I managed to keep the door from closing on my 34Cs.

The catsup-slow lift finally opened onto an ochre hallway with identical doors. Each was distinguished only by a taped-on index card printed with what seemed to be a password to outer space: "Omega," "Ion," Zardoz." Probably the names of businesses too cool to be called "John Doe & Co." Another warning: *If you're not hip enough, you don't belong here either.*

The door to "Studio C" was slightly open. I pushed through,

and was nearly blinded. The space was huge and flooded with light, from the floor-to-ceiling windows as well as the freestanding kliegs. We were probably in a former slaughterhouse. Ironic, since none of its current occupants had any meat on their bones.

They reminded me of the squadron of skeletons that popped out of the dusty ground in *Jason and the Argonauts*, a cheesy epic Cat and I saw at the drive-in long ago. Only these creatures weren't wielding swords.

One skeleton was having makeup applied by another. A third held up a round aluminum ring covered with shiny white paper, whose purpose seemed to be to reflect light onto the face of a fourth skeleton dressed in plastic wrap.

Looking at them made me hungry. I eyed the catering table laid out with a salad of exotic greens, bay scallops, the skinniest green beans I'd ever seen, tabbouleh, baguettes, miniature pastries—a typical expense-account spread that would be charged to the client. All seemed untouched.

As I was about to snare a tiny Napoleon, the skeleton leader—in black bicycle shorts, black guinea T, black Doc Martens, black crewcut—pivoted toward us, abandoning the camera tripod whose legs where thicker than her own.

"That's *her,*" Dovie whispered.

"Too bad," I whispered back.

The human pencil spoke. "I was not expecting warge-size modews today."

"Excuse me?" Now I was riveted.

"Miss Clothilde, ma'am, we're not large-size models," Dovie interpreted. "This is Andrealisa Rinaldi from the *Moon,* and I'm her assistant, Dovie Austin."

"Widicuwous!"

"Excuse me?" It wasn't that I hadn't understood her the first time, I just wanted her to do her Elmer Fudd impersonation again. "Clothilde," my widicuwous ass. She had one of those generic European/Slavic/Asian accents, but I'd bet a week's salary that she was Sophie Smith from Pittston, P.A. This city was full of Sophies. And I loved them all. Theater, without the overpriced ticket. Who were they, really, when the curtain went down?

"Your awticle—widicuwous!"

"Are you a subscriber or do you pick up your *Moon* at the checkout?" I had to know.

"What?" She blinked like a camera shutter. "What you say is not twue!"

"How so?" I could listen to her forever.

"Joew a good father? He is a tywant!"

"A tywant?" I couldn't help myself.

"A ty-rrrrrrrant." She trilled at me.

"Really?" I had to fight not to say "Weawwy?" That always happens to me—picking up the accent of whomever I'm with. It's unconscious, but some have thought I was making fun of them. I've had to be careful all summer not to imitate Dovie. "That's not what I've heard."

"I shoot Emma a hundwed times. Just before Chwistmas, he comes *bang!* into my studio, scweaming I cannot take pictures of Emma."

"Why didn't he want you to take photographs of Emma anymore?"

"He says they are *suggestif.* I say they are *art.* Who knows better?"

"This was his daughter. He was looking out for her." I was defending Joel against a walking pool cue?

"Wook out for him! Emma calls me, but he takes the phone away, scweam at me, scweam at her. Bang!"

"He hit her?" I couldn't believe that.

"He swam down phone."

He swam down...? Oh. *Slam.* "Did he hit her?"

She answered me with a sly look. "She calls me again. She leaves me a message New Year's, just after midnight. She wants to come to the studio again, not tell her father."

"And Joel Hartt found out?"

Clothilde suddenly spoke perfect English. "Tell the truth. No more lies." Then she grabbed my intern's cheeks. "Fabuwous face! Wose a few pounds, I take your picture."

I pulled Dovie out the door by her skinny wrist. "Come on. I buy you wunch."

"RIDICULOUS!" SAID JOEL. "That woman is ridiculous."

"*Did* Emma call Clothilde that night?"

Silence on his end of the line. Then, "Yes. A few minutes after she went up to bed. I was still downstairs and she probably thought I wouldn't catch her. I saw the number and time on my phone bill later in the month. "

"Does Mickey know?"

"The police eventually subpoenaed my phone records. He questioned me about it, but Gina pointed out that it wouldn't prove anything, even if I had known about the call. Just because my daughter was planning to defy me again doesn't mean I would want to harm her."

Maybe not intentionally. But if he had overheard the call and he'd been drinking.... It was New Year's Eve after all. Which reminded me: "This was more than six months ago. Why would Clothilde wait until now to bring this up to the press?"

Joel laughed humorlessly. "At the time, I threatened to have her arrested if she used Emma again without my permission. Now she's got troubles of her own, and probably wants to divert attention before the news hits."

"What news?"

"My photographer friend heard that Clothilde is under investigation for supplying her underage models with diet pills."

That would make an even more interesting story, and I passed the tip along to one of my *Moon* colleagues to make up for the extra work he had to do on my account. He was able to get enough confirmation to pound out a short piece before deadline: "Famous Fashion Fotog Feeds Fat-Fighting Pills to Preteens." Ironically, it ran alongside Dovie's first story, "Biggest Sitcom Stars Share Their Slimming Secrets."

When that issue hit the newsstands the next day, it also included my last piece on the Hartt family.

That night my boyfriend Doug surprised me at my apartment, passing through on his way to DC to deliver a paper to the National Society of Cell Biologists that weekend. I propped myself up on the bed pillows and tried to pay attention as he talked excitedly about "Re-expression of senescent markers in de-induced reversibly immortalized cells." But instead of Doug's bearded face, I kept seeing Evan Hartt's smooth-cheeked one. Their obsession with their favorite subjects was no different. They seemed oblivious to all other occupations in the world.

I didn't bother to show Doug my latest story. Why spoil the mood?

After he left early Saturday morning, I tossed a bag and Ben into Ringo's backseat and drove down to pick up Cat at her group home, a former boarding house close enough to the beach that most of its shell-pink paint had been scrubbed off by the blowing sand.

I stopped first to check in with the live-in counselor, a perky social worker named Ariel. Tiny and fresh from grad school, she was convinced that Cat was making progress, assuring me that my sister was doing well at her job and with her fellow residents. I hoped Ariel wouldn't be here ten years from now, her pretty face ravaged by the unending fight for better services and low-cost medications for her charges. For Ariel I wished marriage to a nice pharmacist and a houseful of real toddlers someday.

Cat knew I was coming, but wasn't waiting in the lounge as usual. I found her sitting on her bed, sliding sheets of paper into a very creased manila envelope.

"Hi! I'm Daisy!" My sister's new roommate was aptly named. Short platinum-blond hair radiated around her yellowish moon-shaped face.

"Hi, Daisy, nice to meet you. I'm Andie." I offered my hand, but Daisy shook her head.

"Germs, you know."

"Smart girl."

Cat rolled her eyes, then grabbed her duffel bag and the stuffed envelope. "Let's go."

"What's that?" I said, lifting my chin at the packet.

Cat glanced at Daisy, who had returned to rearranging a collection of ceramic frogs on her dresser. Whispered, "Not here." Louder, "See you on Monday morning, Daisy."

"Will you be here for breakfast?" The younger woman suddenly seemed panicky.

"Sure." I was surprised to hear Cat speak gently, kindly. "It's okay, Daisy."

The young woman seemed reassured. "See you, then."

Once at our house, Cat immediately dumped her duffel on the kitchen floor and pulled papers out of the envelope and onto the table. Ben, tail twitching to some doggy beat only he could hear, lay on top of her feet.

I snagged two sodas out of the fridge and handed one to Cat. On the manila envelope was the logo for the hospital where she did data entry and retrieval. I raised my eyebrows. "Homework?"

"No, this is for you. For your story."

I looked closer at the top sheet. "But this is from St. Mary's, not Shore Medical." I felt slightly sick to my stomach. "Cat, where did you get this?"

"I told you, I can get all kinds of stuff off the Web."

I took the first page and read:

AUTOPSY REPORT

Name: Hartt, Emma

DOB: 02/06/81

then skipped down to:

CLINICOPATHOLOGIC CORRELATION: *Cause of death of this ten-year-old female is asphyxia by ligature strangulation.*

I put the paper down. "Cat, did you read this?"

"Some of it. When it started getting into all the organs, I lost interest."

I looked into her eyes, trying to see more than that. "This didn't upset you?"

She shrugged. "I didn't know her."

I gathered it all back into the envelope. "I'll look at them later."

"No, it's okay," she said. "This might help you."

I tried to smile. "Thanks for that. It probably will help. But right now"—I pulled her up—"I don't want to think about work. Instead, what if you try to teach me the backstroke and I try not to drown?"

THAT NIGHT THE Martells invited us to dinner next door. Their sons were visiting and manning the barbecue. Peter, the civil-liberties lawyer built like a linebacker, was flipping hamburgers with one hand while the other steadied himself on one of his crutches.

"I hear you don't eat red meat, Andie." He said it like a hostile cross-examination. I wouldn't want to meet him in the courtroom.

"Barbecue burgers don't count. Make mine rare."

David, a much slighter version of his older brother, carried out a bowl of potato salad and a platter of corn on the cob, and set them both in front of Cat.

"Thanks, Dave," Cat said. "Now, what's everyone else gonna have?"

David's dark skin turned darker. He seemed intimidated by my sister, though not in a bad way. He flushed again, but probably not for the same reason, when his brother came around and set a burger before her, then placed his free hand on her shoulder and squeezed.

"Saw you in the water today, Caterina," Peter said. "You're Olympic material."

David slid onto the other bench across from Cat and ladled some potato salad on her plate, though Cat, gazing up at Peter, didn't notice.

"I'm a little long in the tooth for competition." Her manner was almost shy. Another surprise.

"Hey, look at Mark Spitz. He was over forty when he tried out for this year's Games in Barcelona." Peter squeezed again. "You've got a few good years left."

"Notice that he didn't qualify. Another Boomer trying to recapture his youth." Cat made a face. "And I think I have a few more handicaps than just age."

"Nonsense!" Betty had come up behind us to deliver a wooden trough filled with salad greens. "You could do whatever you set your mind to, I know it."

Cat sighed. "Except that these days, my mind is set to obsess over whether that barbecue is going to burst into flames and charbroil us all."

Peter laughed, but hopped over to close the grill lid. Don, setting a pitcher of lemonade and a bottle of wine on the table, leaned in close and whispered, "Give yourself a chance, Cat."

As we ate, Cat brought up the Hartt murder telling the Martells about my interviews for the *Moon* and the cast of characters from our hometown. I was pleased to see her take the lead in a conversation for a change, but wasn't sure I wanted to follow. Peter, of course, knew about the case, and even had a passing acquaintance with Gina through the state bar association.

"She's tough," he said. "If I were guilty, I'd hire her."

I squirmed. "There's no evidence that Joel did it."

"Keeping your reporter's objectivity?" Don teased. "That must be a first at the *Moon*."

"Now, don't make me have to defend my employer too."

Betty put down her ear of corn. "All I know is, if Peter or David had been killed, I'd be moving Heaven and Earth to find out who did it. The guy has more money than God, he could buy a team of Sherlock Holmeses if he wanted to, but he sits on his hands waiting for the cops to solve it?"

I squirmed again. "He did offer a million-dollar reward for information leading to an arrest."

Betty lifted her gray eyebrows high. "Please."

"I think it's Doreen," Cat offered.

"From what you say about her, she has plenty to hide," Peter agreed. "But why would Hartt protect her over his own child?"

"Or is she trying to protect *him*?" Don pointed at his son with a chicken drumstick. "After all, he's her bread and butter."

"Maybe they are protecting each other. But, from what?" Betty stopped to think. "Do you think they might be lovers?"

I laughed. "Not unless Joel is a masochist. After all, as you said, he has enough money to buy whatever he wants, even that."

David had been taking it all in quietly, but he finally cleared his throat. "Statistically, murders are more likely to be committed by a family member than a stranger."

Cat nodded. "I have a few relatives on my hit list."

Hours later, I waited until I heard Cat's snore before I flicked on my bedroom light again and opened the packet she'd brought me. I took a deep breath and started reading the autopsy report, ten pages of excruciating detail on the physical remains of a young life.

The findings were what I would have expected of a strangulation death. The rough neck wounds matched up with the width of thick chain still wound twice around Emma's throat. The heavy-duty lock was still fastened in the last link, a dragging weight that made the metal bite deeper on the left side. Pinpoint ruptures had reddened the surface of her eyes and the inside of her lids from sudden pressure on blue-green capillaries. The hyoid bone—the small v-shaped support for the tongue—had fractured. Not usual in such an attack on a child that age, the ME had noted. Young bones are usually pliable. It would take a lot of force to account for it.

But what seemed to be missing were the marks of a struggle. The medical examiner noted a few contusions and abrasions, but not fresh ones—bruises and scrapes on her arms and legs that any little girl could pick up riding a sled or skating on a pond during her winter break. No obvious scrapings from an assailant's skin under her fingernails. No signs of a sedative or other drugs in the toxicology study. Had she been so thoroughly asleep? Or had she just trusted whoever had lifted her from her bed in those early hours? No wonder the investigators didn't seem to take the outsider theory seriously.

No abrasions around the genitals, though. No signs of sexual penetration or the attempt. Where had those rumors of abuse come from, the fodder for several issues of the *Moon* and other tabs last winter? And why hadn't Mickey refuted that when I brought it up at our first meeting? Maybe he wanted me, and the rest of the world, to think the worst of Joel.

The rest was a clinical inventory of body parts: "The chest is symmetrical. Breasts are prepubescent. The abdomen is flat and contains no scars." Organs were removed and weighed and deemed normal, healthy, "unremarkable." "Pink-tan" thymus, "tan-pink" myocardium. Who made up that color chart?

And what had Emma been spared? Liver unsullied by alcohol. Aorta and vena cava free of atherosclerosis. Lungs not yet marred by first- or second-hand cigarette smoke. Heart not yet broken by love.

I went back to the page describing her body still whole, dressed in black-spotted white cotton-blend pajamas with red ribbed collar and cuffs. On the lower right sleeve was "a dried brown-tan stain measuring 2.5 x 1.5 inches, consistent with mucous from the nose or mouth." Maybe she had a slight cold when she died, wiped her runny nose on her Dalmatian PJs, like any kid would. "Around the right wrist is a yellow metal identification bracelet with the name 'Emma' on one side and the date '12/25/91' on the other side." Her last Christmas gift.

These words wrinkled under drops of wetness and I realized that I was crying.

THE NEXT MORNING, David invited Cat to play tennis at the town courts and did little to hide his annoyance when Don and Peter proposed doubles. After the four of them had driven off in David's BMW, I settled into one lounge chair and Betty took the other, with a drinks-filled cooler between us. The brim of Betty's straw hat was nearly as wide as she was, and Ben took advantage of the generous shade by jumping up on her belly, circling once and camping in her lap. While Betty worked the Sunday crossword, I gave the medical papers another look in the light of day.

Analysis from the forensics lab followed the autopsy report. Stray hairs on Emma's body and clothing had been tested and traced to their sources. Nothing that raised a red flag. Quite a few of Joel's reddish strands had been found, but so were Gina's. From what they'd told me, everyone at the party that night had given the little girl a bedtime hug—the hairs could even have rubbed off from their own clothing. None seemed to have been ripped out, scalp tissue clinging to roots, as might be expected if Emma had tried to reach out and grab. None caught between the small, slender fingers bagged at the scene. Still, the body had been moved before the police had arrived. What may have been lost in the trample, carried out and away on a rubber-soled cop shoe? Only Emma's own gold strands were snagged in the metal links that had encircled her throat.

Man-made fibers had been matched to the carpet, her bed linens, a pink nylon scarf and white bunny slippers in her bedroom. No surprises. Toward the bottom of the page was the heading *Unidentified*. Deep in one of the neck wounds, someone had found a fiber of "cellulose-based material, measuring three-sixteenths of an inch." The thread was revealed to be dyed bluish green, coated with "a mix of esters, cerotic acid and saturated hydrocarbons, with an alkane-like..."

The sentence seemed to continue but no pages followed. I turned the sheet over. Nothing there that translated the tech-speak. With the red editor's pencil I had pulled from my canvas shoulder bag, I underlined the words I didn't understand.

Had Cat missed a page? Maybe she'd been interrupted

while printing it out. Could I ask her to look for the rest without making her feel that she'd messed up somehow? No. More importantly, I couldn't risk her spending any more time amid the gruesome details.

"Unidentified." That probably meant it matched nothing in the house, nothing collected from possible suspects. Had it come off the unidentified clothing of an unidentified killer? Maybe he'd brought a gag. I flipped back through the autopsy report, but saw no note of injury to the corners of her mouth, of an abrasion left by some bluish-green cloth tied tightly enough to silence a terrified child.

I stared out beyond the lagoon, beyond the spit of land, beyond the bay. The Ferris wheel had stopped. For an impossible second I imagined I saw a girl, thick blond hair whipped upward by the breezes off the ocean, wave from the gondola swaying at the top. Impossible because it was too far, too far...

"Do you feel what she feels?"

I jumped at Betty's voice. "What? I'm sorry."

She peered at me over her outsized sunglasses. "Your sister. Do you ever pick up when she's in trouble?"

"You mean, like when she broke her arm doing an Evel Knievel on roller skates over a drainage ditch near the public school, did I yelp in pain three blocks away, as I sat reading a Nancy Drew in my room?" I grinned and shook my head. "Sorry. No Psychic Twin Network. But then, we're mirror twins, so technically I should feel the opposite of whatever she feels."

"Except for your hair length, you look identical to me."

I pulled down the neckline of my tank top to show the beauty mark above my right breast. "Cat's is on the left." I raised the pencil in my left hand. "And she's a righty. Our printing looks the same, but our handwriting slants differently. And my left cuffs were usually stained with fountain-pen ink, from having to drag my arm back across my schoolwork. Always a dead giveaway when we tried to switch classes at Holy Moly."

"Did you do that a lot?"

"Not much after we were caught the first time, when I was in the second grade. The nuns were no fools. They'd been waiting for us to try something. Got away with it a few times in high school. If it hadn't been for Cat, I would never had passed those President's Physical Fitness tests. She had to hold back a little, though, not to make it too obvious. She put me into the eightieth percentile."

Betty chuckled. "I envy you. I always wanted to be a twin."

"Pluses and minuses. We fought as kids, natural competition. But we always knew that we'd have each other, a built-in best friend. Almost as if it didn't matter if we had anyone else. We'd never be alone."

Betty touched my hand briefly.

"But other people compared us constantly. And the obvious stuff from strangers: 'Who's the oldest? Oh, it must be you, you look a little taller. I bet I can tell which is which.' That drove Cat nuts. But my father told us, whenever someone started in, we should excuse ourselves to go to the bathroom. That worked most of the time."

"Could your parents tell you apart?"

"Most of the time." I waited a beat, then stood up. "Excuse me, I have to go to the bathroom."

Betty's booming laugh followed me as I slid the screen door behind me.

AT THE STAFF meeting Monday morning, Colin said nothing about my last Hartt piece, for which I was grateful. My reporting days over, my colleagues felt free to dump work back on my desk. I tried to edit a feature on "Liposuction Gone Wrong," but couldn't focus. I picked up the blurry telephoto of an aging pop star in a thong bikini that would fill out the page.

The truth was, I was bored. This week's issue would be especially slim, so I only had this piece and a few sidebars to worry about. In the media biz, summer is notoriously nonproductive. Even Elise was away, probably visiting relatives in Transylvania.

I hadn't worked there long enough to earn vacation time.

My thoughts kept going back to Emma's autopsy and the unidentified fiber. Just to satisfy my own curiosity, I bit the bullet and dialed. What I was about to do would obligate me to the grave.

My cousin's assistant, who sounded as though she hadn't had her caffeine yet, put me through after the full Muzak version of The Captain and Tennille's "Muskrat Love."

"Paula, I need a favor."

"Great! Let me call the Publications Director first and I'll tell her I told you to contact her for an interview, then—"

I tried to keep the grit out of my voice. "No, Paula, I'm not looking for a job right now."

"Why wait until the last minute? You can still get a resume on file and—"

She was her mother's daughter after all, certain she knew what was best for everyone.

"Sure. I'll do that." Anything to shut her up. "In the meantime, cuz, I have a technical question. How tight are you with your lab guys?"

"I'm married to the man who signs their paychecks, so that's as tight as you can get."

"Okay, then. If I fax you a chemical analysis, can you find someone who can translate it into English for me?"

"I guess so...wait. This isn't something sordid, is it? Like you need to find out what was in the stomach of some celebrity who overdosed?"

"Sorry. Nothing like that."

"How soon do you want this?"

Within a half hour, Paula called me back. "Beeswax."

"Are you telling me to mind my own business?"

"You're always so touchy. No. The words you underlined— esters, cerotic acid, saturated hydrocarbons. That's the chemical composition of beeswax. It seems that your fiber"—she stopped and I heard paper rustling—"your cellulose-based fiber bears minute traces of waxes and resins. The reference to 'alkane,' that's paraffin. The most prevalent compound is a greenish blue fiber-reactive dye, most likely Procion. Or so my chem majors tell me. You want me to fax this to you?"

I barely heard her. "Wax? So somebody dripped a candle on this thread?"

"Listen, Miss Marple, this is all I can tell you. Draw your own conclusions. Are you coming to Sam's birthday party Saturday at the bungalow? You never RSVP'd."

"I guess."

"And of course, bring Cat."

Of course.

WITH ELISE ON vacation, no one else would notice if I were gone the rest of the day. I told Dovie I was going to a luncheon press conference at the Sheraton, sponsored by the Society of Obesity-Clinic Physicians, and probably wouldn't be back until late afternoon, if at all.

She frowned at her desk calendar. "I don't have you down for that."

"Emergency meeting. Someone just found out that Oprah gained another pound."

I left her to guess if I was serious.

I picked up Ringo and headed through the tunnel. Traffic, too, was midsummer light, and within twenty minutes, I was in front of Juliet Rojas's shop. I opened the door onto The Turtles' "Happy Together" blaring from a boombox behind the sales counter.

Two adolescent girls were by the shelves filled with novelty items. One was trying on a fake-nose-and-eyeglasses combo and the other, X-Ray Specs. Their giggles were as innocent as their Madonna-wannabe bustieres were not. Juliet Rojas wasn't in sight, so I made my way around the clothes racks to the lounge area.

Someone was lounging alright, but it wasn't Jules. Stretched out on one of the chaises, watching the preteens and sucking from the neck of a Coke bottle, was Jesse. He barely moved his head toward me when he swallowed and murmured, "So, if it isn't my old friend Amy Carleton."

"Not today." I felt my whole body flush, but not from embarrassment. "How'd you know that was me?"

"Beth gave a pretty good description. Interesting choice of pseudonym. Now, what was it that Wolfe wrote about Amy Carleton? Something like, 'She had slept with everybody, but she had never been promiscuous.' Is that right?"

"About me or Amy?"

"Take your pick."

What would be the answer he would want to hear? "If I remember correctly, she had also tried everything in life—except living."

"Now that would be truly sad." Jesse swung his legs around. "Miss Carleton doesn't know what she's missing."

"Who's Miss Carleton?" Juliet appeared, swinging a plastic bag.

"Andie's alter ego," Jesse said.

I cut in quickly. "A character from *You Can't Go Home Again,* by Thomas Wolfe."

"Oh, I think I've read him. *Vampire of the Vanities.*"

"*Bonfire,* not *Vampire.*" Jesse looked fondly at Juliet. "And that's Tom Wolfe, not Thomas. A little difference of about half a century."

"Hey, I was a textiles-arts major. We weren't required to read, just sew, weave and macramé. But I'm almost finished with *Heartbeat,* by Danielle Steel. Yay for me." She reached into the bag, tossed Jesse a white butcher paper-wrapped bundle. She pulled out another one and waved it under my nose. "You eat? Wanna split a tuna sub?"

The three of us sat next to each other on the sofa, trading pickles, potato chips and insults as if we were back in the Holy Moly cafeteria. Every once in a while Jesse's knee would touch mine and I felt a jolt that was almost more painful than pleasant.

"So what did you think of my place?" Jesse pointed his pickle spear at me.

"Lovely, as was the fairy princess you keep locked in your turret."

"Oh, you met Beth!" Juliet seemed delighted. "Isn't she the coolest thing? Amazing she's so together after all she's been through."

Jesse shot her a glance, then seemed to decide it was okay. "I have custody of her while my sister's in rehab." He responded to my concerned look. "No, Jody's doing okay. We expect her to be out by the time Beth goes back to school."

I remembered his sister, Jody, a few years younger than us. Thick, rusty hair shorn in a pixie cut. Freckled nose. The nuns, of course, had called her by her middle name, Frances. She was a damsel in distress even then, shadowing her older brother during recess or begging him to defend her from some imagined slight on the merry-go-round. Jesse never acted like he minded.

"Beth has a little brother, Brandon. He's three," he continued. "My mom takes care of him during the day. Beth can be on her own. She's with Evan most of the time anyway. Doreen keeps an eye on both of them."

"It's nice that Evan has Beth for a friend," I said. "He strikes me as kind of...isolated."

Jesse cocked his head. "Just his personality, I guess. He gets into things and loses himself. Now it's his camera, a year or two ago it was model planes. He had so many hanging from the ceiling of his bedroom, it looked like a stackup over Newark airport."

"They're both great kids. They're gonna be fine," Juliet decided.

We balled up our sandwich wrappings and tossed them in the plastic bag. Jesse grabbed it and headed toward the door, but first gave Juliet a quick kiss on the cheek. Then he turned to me, bent me back, planted his lips firmly on mine and was gone.

I couldn't move for a while. Finally I flopped back down on the chaise. "Whew!"

"The effect will wear off after a few hours," said Juliet. "In the meantime, don't operate any heavy machinery."

"Does this count?" I pulled a Slinky off one of the shelves, and bounced the metal coil up and down like a yo-yo. "I have to get Cat one of these. It'll annoy her roommate for hours."

"On the house."

I watched Juliet pull out a handful of ridiculously wide ties from a small box and arrange them behind the glass counter. "Textiles-arts major, huh? Actually, that's why I came by today."

"Four-point-oh average. Just ask me how they make seersucker."

"Too easy. You get a bunch of fortunetellers together in a room and give them straws. No, what if I said, 'Procion'?"

"Too easy." She laughed. "That's the brand name of a fiber-reactive dye that's been around as long as we have, since the late Fifties. Fiber reactive—that means a dye that bonds with the cloth and won't wash off. It becomes one with the fabric."

"How magical mystical."

"Probably was to the company that invented it—ICI, Ltd. of the UK. Made a fortune off it for industrial use, but it was sure in demand during the Sixties. All that tie-dyeing!"

"That's what it was used for?"

"That and solid dyeing of everything else woven of natural materials. Before then, you couldn't get those saturated, brilliant colors on cottons and rayons with a nonreactive dye."

Something started gnawing at the back of my brain. "Does beeswax mean anything to you?"

"Probably the same thing it means to you. Wax made by bees."

"I mean, as an artsy fabric person. Paraffin, too."

"Same era most likely, though it's an ancient technique. Batik, that is. You stamp on a mix of waxes to areas you don't want dyed, or where you want the first dye to show through, if you'll be using a couple of different dyes."

The gnawing stopped. "But you don't really use it for tie-dye?"

"You could, but more likely it's batik. Why?"

"I was thinking of that tie-dye scarf you gave Emma."

"Oh, that was unusual. Tie dye with a batiked border."

I stiffened. "Would it still have wax on it after all these years?"

"You do remove it after dyeing, but you usually can't get it all off. And that rayon scarf was still in its original bag. Probably never got another cleaning."

"Is rayon cellulose-based?"

She nodded. "Extruded wood pulp. Doesn't sound very attractive, but it feels great. Rayon was originally called 'artificial silk,' though it's not synthetic." Juliet was warming to her subject. "That's what is so great about Procion—it sets with tap water instead of simmering or steaming. Less stress on the fabric."

I held my breath. "What color was the scarf border?"

"Now that's interesting. There's another major fiber-reactive dye series, Cibacron, but only Procion made turquoise in that era."

"Turquoise? You mean, greenish blue?"

Juliet looked amused. "That says turquoise to me. What's all this about?"

I tried to seem casual. "I guess if that scarf was so special it must be nice to have it back."

She looked puzzled, then horrified. "You mean, after...? Oh, no way! Ask for it back? I couldn't do that. That's just too..." She couldn't finish.

"I just thought, considering you only just gave it to Emma that night, Joel might have returned it."

"I can't imagine him even thinking about that! From what Jesse has told me, Joel can't bear to go into her bedroom. They haven't touched a thing in there since—"

I raised my hand so she didn't have to go on. "Sorry, to bring it up. I just thought you might have it. I would have loved to see what it looked like."

"The border was turquoise and black, but the tie-dye was deep blue and gold. It was so wonderful with Emma's hair and eyes." She brightened. "You can see it. I have a picture."

"Really?"

"I take Polaroids of some of the more unusual stock, for insurance records—God forbid, there's a fire or something."

"That's smart."

"Let me go look in the safe."

She was back in two minutes with a folder. She opened it up on the glass counter, tapped her finger. "Look at this. Beautiful!"

I looked over her shoulder at the print. The scarf was beautiful alright. But I knew the colors were even more vivid in person. I'd seen that fabric myself, just a week ago. Wrapped around the breasts of Amanda Dougherty, Doreen's daughter.

• *Chapter 10* •

I DON'T KNOW how long I stood hanging over the railing. The river rolled out a few hundred feet below me, like corrugated iron. Gradually, I realized that the rumble of traffic along the bridge was getting louder, more frantic, horns honking, tires screeching. Must be rush hour—

"Hey, lady, don't jump!"

I did jump, nearly out of my skin, when a hand grabbed my shoulder.

"Whatever it is, it can't be this bad!" A man, a boy really, gangly in a brown jumpsuit with "Bobby" stitched neatly in tan over his heart. A stream of swerving commuters was enthusiastically cursing his delivery truck, stopped dead in the right-hand lane.

I gave Bobby the cheeriest smile I could fake. "It's okay. I used to come up here a lot as a kid. A good place to come and think. I'm not checking out just yet."

"You sure?" He seemed reluctant to believe me.

"Sure. Hey, I have tickets for Springsteen at the Meadowlands next month."

That convinced him. A big grin. "Where're ya sittin'?"

"First tier. In the end zone." He whistled and I impulsively gave his pockmarked cheek a kiss. "You're a doll. Really. Don't worry. Now move your truck before we're both thrown off this bridge. The natives are getting restless."

I watched him drive away, then stepped back up on the bottom rail and looked over again.

My father had brought Cat and I up here for the first time one autumn Saturday before we turned five. We walked clear across the bridge and back. "That's three thousand five hundred feet one way," my dad said, "nearly a mile and a half round-trip, if you want to brag about it."

He'd told us about the Dutch who had settled along the banks, the Revolutionary War generals who had unsuccessfully fought off the British from both sides. He'd pointed downstream, explaining how this river started as a trickle hundreds of miles north, how it emptied into the bay, then the ocean. "Small things always lead to something bigger," he'd said.

It became an annual pilgrimage and lecture, with one of us always interrupting him with "Yeah, Dad, we know. You told us that already." Which was part of the ritual.

Only once had Cat and I come alone, hiked the half mile uphill along River Drive, then across the river while my parents waited for the moving truck to show up. That was July 13, 1968. Twenty-four years ago today.

Now the car fumes hung in the heavy air around me. Yet, the acrid smell was clearing my head.

At first I couldn't figure out what it all meant.

A pink nylon scarf, not a turquoise rayon one, had been found near the body, according to the autopsy. If a turquoise fiber was listed as unidentified, forensics couldn't have found the tie-dye scarf in her bedroom, or anywhere else in the house either.

Instead, Amanda had found it in Doreen's closet. That's what the girl had said that day I'd been at the Dougherty's. But supposedly Doreen wasn't at the Hartts' on New Year's. She wouldn't have seen Juliet give the scarf to Emma, wouldn't even have known the scarf existed, since it disappeared that same night.

Kathleen Whalen had mentioned Emma had been wearing the scarf as she left the living room that night. So what happened between the time she went to bed and when the cops viewed the body? They would have sealed off Emma's bedroom, the whole house then. Yet the scarf had to be gone by then, or they'd have matched the fiber.

Unless someone else hid it and gave it to Doreen later. Joel? And would she really cover for a murderer and still leave her son, her biological child, in the care of such a man? Still, why hide the scarf?

My thoughts went in a circle that always came back to Doreen and Ray. The scarf had been in their home, so this proved they knew something about Emma's death. Sure, everyone said Ray was a nice guy, but he had done hard time. Prison had to have changed him. A $1.2 million ransom could give him and Doreen a new start, somewhere else. Maybe take Evan with them, finally.

But they had alibis, from a cop no less.

Then I remembered what Mickey had said: "She was here too. Sitting right where you are now." Sitting in the back booth that Mickey and I always met in. Sitting right under the glowing red exit sign.

Why *couldn't* Doreen have snuck out that way? Who would notice, in a bar full of New Year's revelers? From there, it would have been easier to take the path by Jesse's, through the woods. Five minutes there, five minutes back. In the dark? Maybe it was a full moon that night. I could check. Maybe she had one of those purse flashlights. She definitely had a key.

She would know where to find pen and paper in the kitchen, write a ransom note in the well-formed capitals that Sister Connie taught us in kindergarten. She was strong enough to lift a little girl not much more than four and a half feet tall, barely sixty pounds. If Emma had woken up, she wouldn't have been alarmed to see Doreen, she wouldn't have struggled. But maybe she did, once Doreen had taken her down to the basement, maybe she started to scream. Doreen was also strong enough to wrap a heavy chain around a little girl's neck and snap it tight enough to fracture the hyoid.

The scarf? Maybe she'd found it the bedroom, took it along in case she needed to send proof that she had the girl, something unique. Isn't that what kidnappers in old movies always did? No wonder Doreen had freaked when she saw her daughter, Amanda, wearing it as a bandeau top.

How long would all that have taken? Fifteen, twenty minutes? It could look like she'd just stepped into the ladies' room. Mickey couldn't have had his eyes on her the entire night.

That's what was eating me up now. If I told Mickey what I knew, where would it get me? Would he just laugh at me again? Or worse, take the credit to cover his own failings and leave me to beg for the details like every other hack journalist? Any other reporter would kill for this lead. Crack the case, be part of the story, make headlines not just in the *Moon* but every news outlet in the country. But is that what I wanted for me? I would be linked forever with the tabloids. As Mickey had asked me once: *What kind of life would that be?*

The cars whizzed by, shaking the web of wire cable and steel rods that were all that came between me and a high-dive. Then I knew what I had to do.

I STOPPED FIRST in front of the Rock Bottom. I didn't see Mickey's Caddy in the lot. I could have asked Georgie where he was, but I was looking for an excuse not to talk to him before I went to Joel.

Maybe I was making a mistake, but I thought I owed him a warning before I brought my suspicions to Mickey. It seemed like the right thing to do. After all, he'd given me access to his life and his friends, made my job easier. And how could I let Evan spend another minute in the care of a murderer, even if she was his real mother? I'd go to Joel, tell him about the scarf, tell him about Doreen.

But I still wrestled with the thought that something didn't quite fit. Why hadn't Joel noticed the scarf was missing? Emma had loved it, made a big show of it that night. Why wouldn't he mention that to the police? Maybe he had, but forensics couldn't positively I.D. the turquoise thread without the scarf. Yeah, that must be it.

So I left Ringo parked by the tavern, in case things went wrong. If I went missing, Mickey would see the car and figure out where to look for me. At least I hoped so. Maybe I'd put a note for him on the front seat. Maybe I'd leave my last will and testament too.

Just thinking like that made my stomach lurch. A Milky Way or two or maybe a KitKat bar would calm it down. Luckily, R.J. wasn't working the counter at The Confectionery, so I didn't have to trade pleasantries with Doreen's son right before I accused her of murder. I settled on a Milky Way, a KitKat and a Snickers, as this might very well be my last meal.

By the time I reached the top of the lane, I had finished two of my three courses. Doreen's Chevy wasn't in the driveway. She must be gone for the day, which is what I was counting on. But Joel's car wasn't there either. Nobody home? Now what?

I still had the KitKat bar for dessert. Might as well sit down and enjoy it. I went around the corner to the garden and started up the stone patio stairs.

"Oh, hi!"

Evan greeted me like an old friend. He was perched on the edge of his wrought-iron chair and held up one of the two spiral-bound books that had been in front of him on the table. "I'm starting a new album. Dad took me to the beach this weekend and I got some great pictures. Did you bring Ben the rat-dog?"

I hid my anxiety behind a smile. "Sorry, Evan. I didn't know I'd be stopping by. Next time, I promise."

I guess I'd have to share the KitKat now. I snapped off a stick of the chocolate-covered wafer and held it out. "Want some?"

Evan eyed it uneasily. "Dad's not home yet and we're supposed to go to Aunt Katie's for dinner."

"I can keep a secret."

"Me too." He took the chocolate, taking care not to drop crumbs on the pages now open before him. In between bites, he rearranged his photos in the plastic sleeves: a view of the boardwalk from the top of the Ferris wheel, a little girl at an arcade holding a stuffed dog as big as she was, an elderly woman eating a fluff of cotton candy that matched her own puffy bouffant. His photos had a child's sense of wonder—and humor.

I picked up the other album and read the hand-lettered label on the cover: *Once Upon a Time*. "Can I finish looking through this?"

He nodded proudly.

The first page made me laugh. Emma, with what looked like a Christmas tablecloth draped over her head, was holding a fruit-filled basket. Little Red Riding Hood. The story itself was printed carefully on the next two pages.

Another shot caught Emma, hand to her mouth, looking horrified at "The Big Bad Wolf"—a German Shepherd puppy tucked into a doll's bed.

Evan glanced over. "That's my friend Beth's dog. She let us borrow Rolf for the picture."

"I know Beth. I didn't meet Rolf, though."

His bright green eyes darkened. "He got run over a month ago."

Jeez, did no one here live out a natural life span?

On the next page, a peasant dress and a dark wig topped with a red bow turned Emma into Snow White, followed by seven dwarf-size stuffed animals wearing paper party hats. After that came Cinderella trailing a black velvet cape thrown over a white nightgown, posed outside on the snow-dusted stone steps, a silvery high heel in her wake. (Its mate was still on her right foot and about five sizes too big. No wonder she'd lost it.) There was her Rapunzel again, leaning out of the turret at Jesse's house.

These tableaux were adorable. When I wrote about Doreen's

arrest for the *Moon*, maybe Joel would let me use one of these to go along with the story.

I turned the page to Sleeping Beauty.

"That's the last one I took." Evan's face was somber. "I only got the camera at Christmas, and then Emma died. We didn't have time to finish."

"I'm sorry," I said.

"That's okay," he said. "It's not your fault."

A chill ran through me. I remember my mother looking horrified when I said the same thing to a neighbor who offered condolences after our father died. But Emma's death *was* someone's fault. And I thought I knew whose.

"That's not right," Evan was saying to me. He had walked around my side of the table and pointed to the Sleeping Beauty picture. "I didn't like that scarf with all the colors. It wasn't a princess scarf. She had this other pink one. It had sparkly things on it."

I looked closer at the photo and stopped breathing. "A sparkly one."

"Yeah. I was going to change it."

"You were?" There was a pink scarf on the floor, the night Emma died.

"Uh, huh. I tried to get the other one off without waking her up."

"Did you?"

"It got stuck."

"When, Evan? When did you try to change the scarves?"

His green eyes opened wider at my harsh tone. "New Year's."

"And the turquoise scarf was stuck?"

"Yeah, I pulled it really hard but it wouldn't come off, then—"

"Evan." Doreen spoke almost in a whisper as she came up behind us. I'd been so focused on the boy, I hadn't heard her approach. "Your father's on his way. Why don't you go put those in your room?"

He obediently gathered up the albums, as I stood up.

Doreen's hands were behind her back. When she turned to watch him go, I saw that one hand held a very long, very pointy knife.

"It was Evan, wasn't it?" I thought about running, but I suddenly forgot how.

At my words, Doreen stepped closer to me.

It seemed so obvious now. Why else would Joel give up so easily in finding his child's killer? He was protecting the only child he had left. He would do what he had to do to make it look like a crime only an adult could commit. And Doreen would help. With Evan's future at stake, Doreen was capable of anything, too.

She was between me and the stone stairs. I could try to make it to the back door of the house, but I'd have to leap across the table first. Not a chance for someone who never passed the President's Physical Fitness Test on her own. My only other exits were straight up the cliff face on my right or straight down the cliff face on my left. Damn. Why hadn't I taken up rock-climbing?

I saw my purse on the chair. What was in there? Pepper spray? A police whistle? Crap. I never carried that stuff. What kind of city dweller was I?

"You had to interfere, didn't you?"

"Doreen, I can see why you might be upset."

"If you had just minded your own business."

"I understand. He's your son. You don't want anyone to think badly of him."

"You can't even begin to know!" she screamed, then lunged toward me.

On reflex I half-shut my eyes and thrust my arms out.

Doreen ran straight into them, threw herself around my neck and began sobbing.

"It was an accident!" she choked out. "Can't you see that? He didn't know what he did! He just wanted to take her picture!"

"There, there," I said.

Where, where was that knife?

I heard it clatter to the slate. I kicked it over the side of the patio before I brought up my own arms and awkwardly patted Doreen on the back. Her tears were running uncomfortably down my cleavage.

"You can't write about this! You can't!" Doreen wailed.

Oh, god almighty. Once upon a time, *I* wanted to be a cowboy. The leather vest, the cool hat, the tooled boots with silver spurs. Why didn't I pursue *that* as a career? I'd be riding the range right now, far, far away, maybe in Montana. Cows weren't complicated. They just moseyed along over the grasslands until you herded them to the slaughterhouse.

Stop. This line of thinking wasn't helpful.

"Doreen." I tried to be gentle. "Why don't you tell me what happened that night? I won't know what to do if I don't have all the facts."

Doreen sat down at the patio table and I handed her a tissue from my bag. She honked like she was heading south for the winter. "It's all been too much, too much," she sniffled. "Holding this in. I told Joel you might find out. But he trusted you. He said you would be fair. You wouldn't tell if it meant hurting Evan."

Nope, not Montana. The cattle drive would start in Texas, then head along the Chisholm Trail to Missouri. Wasn't that John Wayne's plan in *Red River*?

"I just wanted to see Evan, you know, the first day of the year. They were going off on a ski trip the next day, and I wasn't going to be with him for a few days. I don't regret letting Joel and Kristine adopt him. I really don't. But sometimes, on special occasions, I just need to see him. Joel understands. Ray didn't even notice that I left the bar."

But John Wayne's trip took 14 years, and they only got as far as Abilene. Stick with Montana.

"I took the path to the house, went through the back door to the kitchen, so I wouldn't run into any of Joel's guests. Everyone was already leaving out the front. Joel said Kathleen hadn't been feeling well, and the party had broken up right after midnight. I went up to Evan's room, but he wasn't there."

Of course, I'd have to learn to ride too. Cat and I went horseback riding once, when we were sixteen. She started to gallop and my horse wanted to follow hers, but my foot slipped out of the stirrup on a turn, and I was thrown off by centrifugal force. As Cat helped me back in the saddle, her horse sneezed on my leg.

"I found Evan in Emma's bedroom. On top of her. He wanted to switch the scarves, he said. I told him to go back to bed. At first, I didn't think Evan had hurt her. But her face wasn't right. So pale. I unwound the scarf from her throat. Joel really should have checked that she had taken it off before she went to bed.

"Joel told me he'd take care of it so no one would suspect Evan. He had me write the ransom note, while he poured himself a whiskey. I'd never seen him drink anything hard before. He told me to go back to The Rock, like I'd never been here. I didn't even realize I had put the other scarf in my coat pocket until I got home."

Who was I kidding? No home on the range for me.

"Are you even *listening*?" Doreen snapped. Her tears released, she was back to her irritable self.

I was already missing the sagebrush and the wide-open spaces. "Doreen, what do you want me to do?"

"Nothing! Do nothing! Forget this!" She was close to screaming again.

"But you've both committed crimes—you've removed evidence, Joel has manufactured evidence. Justice has been obstructed big time."

"But we were just protecting Evan."

"If it was an accident, nothing would have happened to Evan."

"*Nothing*? He would have had to talk to the police. His name

167

would be all over the papers. Don't you think someone would uncover that he was adopted? The cops might have thought he was jealous of Emma, of her being famous, maybe think he did it on purpose..."

"I don't think—"

"Even if it didn't get that far, Ray might find out what I'd done, giving Evan up."

"Yeah, but—"

"And Evan. He's a sensitive boy. How could he deal with knowing that he killed his sister and knowing that everyone else knows? What would his future be worth? Do you see how many lives you could ruin?"

I saw. And I had told Evan that I could keep a secret. All cowboys could.

My NEXT FEW days would have made Hell seem like Club Med. Bad enough that Doreen pleaded with me not to tell Mickey. I couldn't give my Scout's Honor pledge this time, I told her, but I'd sleep on it. That was too optimistic. By Thursday I'd given up all hope of ever sleeping again.

I had left without talking to Joel; I couldn't face him. He had risked everything to shield the boy, and now I had the power to expose it all. And I couldn't promise I wouldn't. But I had to weigh the consequences. Who would that help? Who would that hurt? Joel had said he thought I would be fair. What was fair about this?

I was only grateful that Elise was still away as I stumbled around at work, bleary eyed. Dovie seemed to think my nodding off at my desk was due to some wild nightlife we big-city editors and other sophisticates enjoyed as a matter of course.

"Did you see anyone famous last night?" Dovie asked as I struggled to get the plastic lid off my deli coffee cup.

"Like who?"

"M.C. Hammer, Paula Abdul, maybe Roseanne Arnold?"

I didn't have the energy to shake my head. "No, they all left just before I got there." Wherever "there" was. "I think they had to get to a birthday party at David Hasselhoff's."

I made a mental note to pass along to Dovie any press invites for club openings or movie premieres that came my way. Celebrities supposedly hated the *Moon*, but their publicists didn't.

The last thing I needed that morning was a phone call from Mickey. But I got one anyway. "So, you suck me dry and now that you don't need me anymore, you don't call, you don't write—"

"Suck you dry? You gave me dust from the beginning. Anything I came up with was on my own."

"Ungrateful wench. The least you can do is make me dinner."

"Mickey, this is really not a great—"

"I've got to work a little late. I'll be there at 8:30."

"I don't think I can—"

But he had already hung up.

Ten hours and a few doses of aspirin later, I heard a knock, peeped through the peephole, then opened the door.

"Mickey, how'd you get in without ringing up first?"

"That lovely woman on the ground floor."

"Mrs. Pemberton? She won't even let *me* in when I forget my key."

"You lack my charm. And my badge. She seemed quite taken with both. Found it very interesting that you might be wanted for questioning in a mail-order porn ring."

"If you really told her that, I'll ring your neck."

"What's the problem? She looked like a potential customer." His eyes took in my apartment in one sweep, which wasn't hard to do. "Nice shoebox."

In a few strides he was at the nearly floor-to-ceiling window, my small air-conditioner wedged under the bottom sash. "Nice view of your hometown, though. So you've had an eye on us all this time and never stopped in?"

"Some things are better kept at a distance."

"That seems to be your motto." He turned to the wall unit holding my CD player and music library. "Wow. Compact discs. I'm still on vinyl."

He leaned in to read the labels. "Billie Holiday, Etta James, Big Mama Thornton . . . lady, you've got the blues and you got 'em bad." He hit a button and Billie sang, *Them that's got shall get/ Them that's not shall lose/So the Bible said and it still is news....*

God Bless the Child. How appropriate.

"What do you know about music? As I recall, you thought the Monkees were groovier than the Beatles."

"The century is not over yet. History will prove me right. Have you ever really listened to *Pleasant Valley Sunday*? If you play it backward, you can hear very clearly, 'Davey Jones...is... dead—"

We both heard the frantic scrabbling of toenails on the hardwood floor.

"What the...?!" Mickey yelped, as a gray streak shot across the room. "What is that?"

"Ben," I said.

"Not *who*. *What*." He picked up the quavering creature squeaking at his feet. Ben looked even tinier than usual in Mickey's hands. "Does the health department know about your rodent problem?"

"He's a guard rat, fully bonded. Don't worry. He's had all his shots."

"What he needs is growth hormone."

"Glad you like him. The feeling seems to be mutual, so watch where you step."

Mickey winced at the puddle near his shoes. "Why does everyone react that way to cops? We're public servants. We're the good guys." He set Ben down. "Don't suppose you serve alcoholic beverages in this establishment?"

"Somebody accidentally gave me Galliano one Christmas ten years ago. So it's nicely aged. Would a before-dinner after-dinner drink do?"

"It'll have to."

I handed him the bottle, then mopped up the puddle and washed my hands. As Mickey poured the liqueur into a juice glass, I pulled a pie plate out of the oven. "Where did you park?" That was always the most important question I asked visitors. Some of the local lots had valet service—where they drove your car directly onto a freighter bound for Brazil.

"I didn't. It's a nice night so I walked from Nonna's and took the ferry." Mickey looked at what I put on my little table. "Quiche. What are you, like, stuck somewhere around 1979?"

"It took me that long to perfect the recipe. It's made with crab Cat and I caught in our backyard."

"Cat is somehow involved in this? I should test it for poison." He broke off a piece of piecrust and popped it in his mouth. "Isn't quiche made with eggs? I thought they were high in cholesterol. Shellfish too. Is that how you're trying to get rid of me?"

"Saturated fats, like in steak and butter, are what raise blood cholesterol. High-cholesterol foods are only bad if you already have a cholesterol problem. Actually, eggs and shellfish are good sources of protein."

"Thanks. I hope there won't be a test."

"Wait'll you see what I have for dessert."

"Oh, God, no. I hope it's not your famous chocolate cake. What came out of your Easy-Bake Oven could have been classified a lethal weapon. Made a decent puck for street hockey, though."

Over salad, French bread and the quiche, which Mickey actually seemed to like, we avoided talking about the Hartt case. We tried politics, with Mickey doing an impersonation of Ross Perot's speech withdrawing from the presidential race that day—except his version ended with Perot claiming he'd been anally probed by aliens. "That's why I talk like this."

But when Mickey praised George Bush with "Any guy who doesn't like broccoli is okay by me," the conversation deteriorated into me defending a cruciferous vegetable.

"It's tough enough getting people, especially kids, to eat healthfully without the President of the United States putting down one of the best foods for you. A report just came out that it has sulforaphane, too. It reduces the risk of all kinds of cancers."

"You have to die of something," Mickey countered.

I threw a hunk of bread at his head.

Mickey switched to filling me in on the whereabouts of former classmates.

"Stan Zimeski and Billy Birdsey are on the town PD. Stan's in line for lieutenant," Mickey said, rinsing a plate. He'd shocked me by clearing the table and offering to wash the dishes. "Oh, and you'll never guess about Brian Coffey."

"You mean 'Brain,' I said, reaching into my tiny freezer. "In first grade Sister Mary Magdalene had to correct him all the time for spelling his own first name wrong. He kept reversing the letters."

"Right. In high school, they figured out he was dyslexic. It turned out he *was* a brain. Went on to medical school. Does research now at the biotech lab in the South End."

I handed Mickey a Fudgsicle, which made him laugh. "Remember," I said between licks, "that time you bought Jimmy O one of these because he didn't have the money for the Good Humor man?"

Mickey plopped on my sofa. "And Maureen started screaming out the window for him to come home for supper—"

I plopped next to him. "She was a real pill. More like his mother than his kid sister."

"Well, she was the oldest girl. With ten kids, Mrs. O always had one on her and one in her, so Maureen had to take over."

"So Jimmy sticks the fudge pop in his pocket—" I prompted.

"It was a hundred degrees out and by the time he walks in the door, it's melting through his shorts and he has a big hole in his pocket, so chunks of it fall out the leg. His father thought he'd shit in his pants, and sent him to bed without his supper. Or the Fudgsicle."

"Man, Jimmy O was such a sorry case." I tossed the wooden ice-cream stick across the room into the sink, and asked, "Whatever happened to *him*?"

Mickey threw his own stick after mine before answering. "Killed in the fall of Saigon."

I stopped laughing. "How could that be? The draft was over by the end of high school."

"He had been left back, so he was a year older than us, remember? He wasn't the brightest Crayola in the box. Never had much interest in school anyway. After he turned seventeen, he enlisted. I tried to talk him out of it, but he didn't listen. Said the war would be over soon, maybe he could get trade school paid for by the GI Bill and be a plumber like his Dad. That family, with all those kids. It was the only way he could afford to go."

"Oh, God. I didn't know." I let my breath out. "He never had any luck."

"Yeah. Last day of the war, and he gets in a jeep accident, transporting evacuees. They gave him a Silver Star anyway." He was quiet a minute. "Maureen took it hard. Left home as soon as she could. Became a stewardess. After a few years of that, she went to college down south and came back here to teach at the public school."

"So she turned out okay."

"Sort of. Then she married me." He shrugged. "Yeah, well, as the second ex-Mrs. Giamonte likes to say, I do all the wrong things for all the right reasons."

For the first time I could remember, I saw sadness and regret in Mickey's eyes. "That sounds like my sister," I said.

I told him about Cat then, not all the details, but enough. When I finished, he said only, "That must have been rough."

"Worse for Cat than me." I looked away. "You know, sometimes I wonder how things would have been different if we'd never left town, if my father hadn't...." No point in continuing with that thought. "Clearview Terrace was the last place that felt like home. Who would have believed it? As a kid, you never think, *Now is as happy as I'll ever be.*"

Mickey cupped my chin and turned my face toward him, then gently ran an index finger over my left eyebrow, as if trying to smooth it.

I pulled his hand away and held it. "You can't fix it. I have a scar there. Can't see it, really, but the hairs never grew back right."

"What happened?" His voice was husky.

"You don't remember?"

"What?"

"You hit me with a baseball bat. Split my head open."

He grabbed my other hand, maybe to keep me from swinging at him. "Now, wait a minute. I didn't hit you. You were too close to the plate."

"Yeah, because I was the catcher and I was just getting into position. You didn't check behind you."

"I figured Cat was winding up because you were ready, so I cocked the bat."

"But you know Cat, you should've—"

He pulled me to his chest. Obviously the only way he could think of to shut me up was to cover my mouth with his. He did, hard.

After a while I said, "What took you so long?"

"Maybe if I'd hit puberty before you'd left."

The phone rang. I let the machine take it, listened to me saying I wasn't home right now.

Beep. "Sorry, honey." Doug's voice sounded sleepy. "It looks like I'm not going to be able to get away after this conference. A buddy talked me into checking out some research he's doing in Seattle. I'm heading there from here. I promise I'll get down there next week." *Beep.*

Mickey got to his feet abruptly, disturbing Ben who'd fallen asleep on the arm of the sofa. "Well, I guess I should have asked first if there was at least a potential future ex-Mr. Rinaldi. But I'm a detective, damn it. I should have dusted you for fingerprints."

"Well, it's not quite that serious." I felt a twinge of guilt. This was the second time in two weeks that I had made light of my relationship with Doug. Would I deny him thrice?

"It is to me." Mickey walked over the window.

I made up my mind. I would tell him about Evan. Maybe I felt I had to make it up to him somehow, for his disappointment...in life? In me? He'd be able to figure out a way to handle it quietly so that what happened wouldn't be made public. And I wouldn't make it public either.

"Mickey, I have to tell you something."

"Never mind." He said sharply. "Where's your car?"

"Around the corner, but listen—"

"Come on. You're driving me back."

"Okay, fine, if that's how you're going to be about it. But first can I tell you—"

He pulled me roughly over to the window and pointed. He was right. This wasn't the time to talk. My hometown was on fire.

MICKEY DROVE—OR, rather, *careened*. He flashed Ringo's hazard lights, honked, changed lanes, in direct violation of all the tunnel warnings posted. It must be fun to be a cop, I thought just before I closed my eyes and prayed for my soon-to-be-departed soul.

We somehow made it through alive, and sped along River Drive toward the South End, now clouded by thick, black smoke. Ash floated past the car windows. We barely made it to the edge of town before we were stopped by police cars blocking the street and patrolmen directing other drivers to turn around. Mickey pulled up on the sidewalk and jumped out. I apologized to Ringo, promising the car an oil change and deluxe waxing, then followed Mickey. He called out, "Billy, what happened?"

A cop turned. Billy Birdsey's baby face hadn't changed since kindergarten. He still looked like Beaver Cleaver. "Jeez, Mickey. The whole complex went up like a box of matchsticks. Someone reported it about 8:30 and it just got out of hand. Wind blew the flames across the street, jumped a block, then up the cliff. Burning debris dropping everywhere. Some houses are already gone."

Mickey sprinted away before Billy finished. I knew I'd never be able to keep up with him, so I moved slowly through knots of rubberneckers that grew thicker as I went north. It was mostly the old industrial area, though there were homes behind it along the cliff. I tried to think if anybody I knew lived on this side of town now.

Mrs. Giamonte.

No wonder Mickey was running.

A crowd had gathered in the parking lot of The Barge restaurant to watch fireboats sending streams of river water toward the source of the blaze, now more smolder than flames. It was almost 10 o'clock and the sky should have been nearly dark, but the glow made the hour seem like sunset.

It was The Mews, Joel's apartment project.

I went up a side street and spied Juliet standing on a retaining wall, her hands to her face. I reached up to tug on her paisley culottes. Trust her to look great in an inferno.

"Jules, the store! Don't tell me—"

"Andie!" She jumped down. "No, it looks like it didn't make it that far south. It went west, almost in a perfect straight line. I saw Jesse. He said they have the fire contained." She managed a rueful grin. "Some of the houses, the vinyl siding is dripping off like melted Velveeta. Can you imagine all my plastic, nylon and polyester boiling into one giant lava lamp?"

I suddenly felt a fine mist on my forearms and looked up to see a row of firefighters high up on the cliff, spraying the roofs of the houses below.

"There've been small brush fires," Juliet said. "The guys have been trying to keep them from spreading. And they're wetting down the neighborhood so the embers don't catch. I swear, every engine company in the state is here."

I saw that many of the bystanders were not just gawkers. There were kids in summer pajamas, folks gripping duffel bags, others with cats and even houseplants cradled in their arms. What do you save when you think you might lose it all?

I stood there for a while, then started walking blindly forward. A block away, an older woman was clutching a photo album in one hand, a small jewelry box in the other. Tears had sketched rough paths through the soot on her cheeks.

"Mrs. Giamonte, are you alright? Did Mickey see you?"

Mickey's grandmother looked at me confused and frightened for an instant. "Oh, Andrealisa! Yes, he found me." She pulled the album and box tighter to her chest, her knuckles turning white. "The fireman came knocking on my door and told me I had to leave. This was all I had time to take. The kids' pictures and my wedding rings."

She cried out as an explosion boomed and echoed against the cliff. A man at my elbow muttered, "Christ. I hope that's not the tank farm. That old oil storage field — it's on the other side of the warehouse. If that goes, we all go." He wore only a muscle tee and boxer shorts.

Across the street I saw Georgie Mara, wearing a helmet, but no other firefighting gear. The worst must be over. I pushed my way through the crowd. "Georgie. That explosion. The tanks. Shouldn't you tell these people to get out of here?"

He turned to me, but his eyes were unseeing. "Nah, it's okay. It's contained. They told me those are just propane canisters from the construction site." He pointed at his own freckled legs poking out from his shorts. "Look at that. I've been up and down the blocks around the fire. All the hair's gone. I had to take off my Saint Christopher medal, it was branding me. All that, just from the heat." But for once, his nose wasn't running.

"Any casualties?"

Relief softened his worried face. "Nah, thank God. We started evacuating people first thing. It's friggin' amazing that everybody got out in time. A couple of guys with heat exhaustion, but nothing serious. And everything's under control, so we should be alright."

The walkie-talkie squawked and George brought it up to his ear.

"What?" Georgie yelled into it. "What! You gotta be kiddin' me! Who is it? Is he alive?" He listened. "Oh, Jesus Christ."

I grabbed his arm. "Did somebody get hurt?" I thought of that idiot Mickey, always doing the wrong things for the right reasons.

"Somebody's dead." He looked dumbfounded, as if, in all his years answering alarms, it had never occurred to him that someone could die on his watch. "They found a body under a slab of fireboard at the site."

"Who, George?" I nearly shook the walkie-talkie out of his hand. "Who did they find?"

"They're pretty sure it's the guy who owned the lot."

My heart went cold. "Joel Hartt?

He took off his helmet. His red hair was soaked with sweat and he swiped it back off at his brow. "No, the other guy. Gordon de Porres."

• *Chapter 11* •

SOMETIMES IT'S NICE to be a card-carrying member of the media. By flashing a laminated white square imprinted with big red letters that spelled PRESS, I could skirt the outer edge of the burn zone and work my way around what seemed to be a few hundred firefighters. My estimate might not be far off—the ladder trucks I passed bore the names of towns from three counties.

The blaze was out. Many of the men, and a few women, were standing around talking, or moving back and forth returning equipment to the trucks. Some were hauling hose to resoak hot spots where smaller fires had broken out.

I had to cover my mouth and much of my nose with one hand, as the smell was almost unbearable, a blend of sodden smoldering rubber, molten metal, singed plastic, charred wood. The westerly wind coming off the river and the almost solid force of the blaze had tossed burning rubble onto parked cars, trees, backyard kiddie pools and swing sets. Everything was wet, as if soaked by a summer thunderstorm.

Down one side street, near Mrs. Giamonte's house, I passed a no-longer-white white Cadillac, its tires collapsed and melted to the street, smoke rising up through what was left of its convertible top, soggy scarlet upholstery blackened with ash. Mickey's Elvis-mobile.

On River Drive, near the construction site, an ambulance was idling, its back doors open. Suddenly two uniformed cops and two white-jumpsuited EMTs ran up, pushing a gurney. Before I could get closer, the EMTs hopped in the cab and the van took off down the street, red lights flashing. But no sirens. No rush. Obviously, their black-bagged cargo was beyond getting the express ride to the hospital.

I couldn't claim to be the first reporter on the scene. Across the street, someone in a fire chief's hat—my guess, the fire chief—was squinting into a backlit television camera shouldered awkwardly by a skinny, shorts-clad techie and talking into a mike held by...oh, no. Ramon Santiago? Mickey had said that the ex-newscaster-turned-talk-show host lived in The Colony. Nice to see, though, that despite his national status, Ramon couldn't resist covering a local five-alarmer himself.

Other reporters were also huddled around, some leaning in with their own mikes and cameramen, others holding cassette recorders or scribbling into steno notebooks. As I reached their perimeter, I heard Santiago ask, "Fire Chief Nuzzo, I understand a body has just been recovered from the flames. Who is the unfortunate victim?"

The camera light perfectly illuminated the chief's exhausted face. "The victim has not been positively identified at this time."

"Isn't it the developer of this construction project? Joel Hartt? The father of the young girl murdered here last New Year's?" Santiago shoved the mike into the chief's face.

"Now, you know I can't tell you anything until the victim's family has been notified, Ramon." He pronounced Santiago's first name as if it were one "d" short of "Raymond," then walked away.

Joel? I felt sick to my stomach. Had Georgie gotten it wrong?

The small group started to disperse, and Santiago gestured to his cameraman, who took a slow panning shot of the smoking ruins with the city as backdrop.

We all turned as a police car, light-bar flashing, pulled up farther down the street. A shout from Santiago, and he ran toward the snowy-haired man who emerged from the black-and-white. Kenneth Whalen. I guess now that the real danger had passed, it was time for the mayor to step up to the front line and rally the troops. The other reporters also noticed his arrival and trotted in his direction.

I was about to join them when I spotted a lone figure sitting on the stoop of a three-story brick apartment house that, except for a smear of soot across its facade, looked miraculously untouched by the fire. His head was down on arms crossed over his knees, as if he trying to catch a nap. A car alarm went off somewhere and he looked up.

It was Jesse.

He didn't seem surprised to see me. He half smiled, but not in his usual lazily flirtatious way. He looked like he'd had the bravado knocked out of him. His eyes were red, his heavy lids swollen. Probably irritated by the fumes.

"Months of work gone in minutes." He said as if to himself. "Well, at least the folks on the Cliff Way will get their river view back." His laugh was hollow.

"I heard it was Gordon de Porres in there."

His eyes flashed. "Better him than one of my guys."

"Why would *anyone* have been there at night?"

He didn't seem to hear me. "I hope he's burning in Hell right now. Out of the fire and into the frying pan."

From what Jesse had once said about Gordon, I didn't expect a glowing eulogy, but this seemed a little extreme. "What's going on around here, Jess?"

"It could have been one of us." He whacked his fist against the iron guardrail. "I told him, if something happened and my guys weren't covered, I'd fucking kill him."

I was taken aback, to say the least. "You confessing to murder?"

This seemed to slap him out of it, whatever "it" was. "Huh?"

"You seem to be saying Gordon got what he deserved."

"That's true enough."

"So, did you give it to him?"

"Jeez!" He jumped up and started pacing in front of me, like he didn't know whether to run away or stay. "He probably set the fire himself and got caught in it. The guy was a major asshole, I'm telling you. He hadn't insured my people, like he was supposed to. I found out when I took Ray Dougherty to the hospital. Had to pay from my own pocket. That's not all that scumbag de Porres was up to."

"Did Joel know?"

"I told him this morning. I gave de Porres time to straighten it out, but then I checked again and sure enough—"

"Where is Joel? Shouldn't he be here?"

"The cops have been looking for him, but so far no one's been able to find him."

Jesse suddenly grabbed my shoulders and pulled me in toward him so close that I had to put my head back to see his eyes. Though his grip wasn't tight, I felt electricity shoot through me. I wasn't sure if that was a good thing.

"First Emma Hartt's death, now this," he said. "Whatever's going on here, it's not over. I want you to be careful."

Was this concern or a threat? His look was so fierce I wasn't sure of that either. Whether it was the smoke in the air or something else, I had to blink a few times and clear my throat before I could speak. "You don't know that these deaths are connected. This could have been an accident."

"It wasn't."

We looked at each other. Neither of us saw Mickey until he had shouldered his way in between us.

"Rinaldi, I have to talk to you."

Jesse let his hands drop.

Mickey glanced back at Jesse. "We want to ask you a few questions, too, Quindlen. About who was working today and what was going on at the site before everyone left." He waved up the hill. "Go up there. Talk to Stan Zim."

"Yes, sir." Jesse leaned around Mickey to plant a kiss on my forehead, then headed up the street.

Mickey frowned. "What's that about?"

I frowned back. "What's *this* about?"

"I was going to ask you to drive my grandmother to my sister's, the next town over. Nonna's with Juliet at her store right now. But it's late and I want her out of here. She'll give you directions."

"You're kidding me, right?"

"Hey, the power was knocked out too. I can't get through to my sister to come pick her up, so I'm asking you a favor."

"What do you give me in return?"

"What do you want?"

"A quote." I don't know exactly when I decided I had to write all this up for the *Moon*, but I had.

"I've got a suitcase full of them: 'The investigation is inconclusive at this time.' 'We are doing everything in our power to bring the perpetrator to justice.' And my personal favorite, 'No comment.'"

"Just confirm that it was Gordon de Porres you found."

"The investigation is inconclusive at this time."

"Bullshit, Mickey."

"We are doing everything in our power to bring the perpetrator to justice."

"Do you treat all the reporters with such contempt or just me?"

"No comment."

"Have it your way."

"Are you gonna drive Nonna or what?"

"Why didn't you ask Juliet?"

"You're going in that direction anyway. Thanks." He left without waiting for me to agree.

So I was being dismissed. I didn't mind doing the favor. But being brushed off by Mickey, that I did mind.

Nearly blind with fury, I walked straight into a group of cops.

One of them dropped a large Ziploc. "Jesus, lady! Watch where you're going!"

I apologized and picked up the plastic bag. Inside was a black loafer, its tassel nearly singed off. It was all the confirmation I needed.

REGARDLESS OF MY own conflicts, a fire and another death linked to Joel Hartt was newsworthy and I had to report it. By the time I pulled up outside the *Moon* offices and stuck my press pass on my dashboard, I had written my eyewitness account in my head.

That's how I usually worked. Before I ever sat down to a keyboard, I had the opening paragraph and the piece's structure set in my brain. As I typed, all the details would drop into place, like oversized pieces in a kid's jigsaw puzzle. Often, I couldn't sit down to work at all until I was sure I had all the elements. I always knew something was missing if my unconscious hadn't started to organize the story automatically. Often the process felt as if I were channeling someone else. And I rarely went past two drafts of any story.

Tonight would be a test. It isn't often the presses are stopped for breaking news in medical research, so my years on the features desk rarely required top speed. It was nearly midnight, and the paper would be put to bed by 2 a.m. for its weekly Friday morning distribution.

I had called Colin from Mickey's sister's, waking him up from his *Nightline*-induced sleep. I could hear anchorman Ted Koppel in the background after Colin's groggy "Who's this?" So at least I was wrong to think he didn't own a television.

Now I watched him, shirt untucked and hair standing on end, barking orders over the phone to the printing plant, to remake the cover with the headline he'd written: *Murdered*

Moppet-Model's Godfather Goes Up in Smoke. I'd never seen him this excited or engaged in the three months I'd worked there. It suited him.

To make room for my story, Colin decided to drop our coverage of the shoplifting conviction of a former child star from a 1970s sitcom. I wasn't worried that we were doing a disservice to our readers. It was a sure bet we'd have something similar, and with a better set of mugshots, for next week's issue.

I pounded out the ten inches of type needed. Our readers don't have the attention span for more words than that. Most of the two-page spread would go to the pictures anyway. The photo editor, tracked down at his boyfriend's apartment, had pulled aerial photos of the fire off the news service wires, and even managed to dig up a local photo of de Porres attending a high-society fund-raiser with some unidentified redhead on his arm. It wasn't Gina.

Colin handed me a faxed typeset proof of my own immortal words within an hour after I'd written them. I'd dutifully reported that neither Mickey nor the fire chief would confirm the identity of the fire's only victim, but I also went with Georgie's unguarded statement that the dead guy was Gordon. It was a risk, but a calculated one. I threw in my observation of the tasseled loafer found at the scene, and my own firsthand knowledge that "it was of a shoe type favored by the alleged victim, Godofredo 'Gordon' de Porres." I had inserted myself into the story, *Moon* style. Part of me cringed. Another part of me didn't. When I returned to my apartment and a disgruntled Ben at 2:30, I fell quickly into the sleep of the innocent.

The alarm woke me early so I could channel-surf the morning news shows. Plenty of footage of the fire and local officials refusing to speculate on what had started it, though they did confirm that a body had been found in the rubble and Joel Hartt was still missing. Around 8:30, as Ben crunched his puppy chow and I ate my oat bran flakes, I happened upon "special correspondent" Ramon Santiago. "My sources have positively identified the victim as Joel Hartt, father of model Emma Hartt, brutally murdered on New Year's Day."

Those words had barely passed Ramon's lips when a piece of paper slid across the news desk from someone off-camera. He glanced down and, for a millisecond, his eyes narrowed, but barely losing breath, he continued. "Let me repeat that. The victim has been positively identified as Joel Hartt's partner, Gordon de Porres, also the godfather of murdered model Emma Hartt." Nice save, Ramon.

On the way to the office, I picked up all the local morning papers and scanned the stories on the fire. Not one mentioned Gordon de Porres. The *Moon* had scooped them all.

Colin noticed, too. When he shuffled in at 11, looking barely more kempt than he had eight hours before, he waved a sheaf of newsprint at me and mumbled something like, "Brilliant." So I was golden for the moment.

I spent the rest of the day following up. The official statement from the mayor's office—delivered by a trembly voiced clerk—confirmed that de Porres was the corpse, the cause of death pending an autopsy. The fire was now being investigated not only by the county prosecutor's office, but also by the Bureau of Alcohol, Tobacco and Firearms.

Routine, said the crisp spokeswoman for the federal agency, whom I called next. When a fire causes this much damage, the town becomes eligible for federal relief funds. Some displaced residents had found shelter at the community center, with help from the Red Cross.

Along with the four hundred apartments under construction, twelve one- and two-family homes had gone up in smoke, and the intense heat had scorched maybe twenty other homes, two smaller apartment complexes and an untold number of cars parked in the vicinity. It might take weeks, even months to sift through it all to find out what had actually happened that night.

By now Joel was no longer missing in action, but wasn't available for a phone conversation, at home or at his office. To every question, his administrative assistant monotoned that "Mr. Hartt is cooperating with the authorities on these tragic matters and has promised to compensate townspeople reasonably for losses not covered by insurance or federal assistance." Obviously, that was the script she had been given.

I also tried to reach Gina. Her relationship with Gordon may have been over, but it certainly warranted an expression of condolence. I had to be satisfied with leaving her a message, including my home and work numbers, "if you want to talk." I didn't expect to hear from her. I had already been having a hard time with the dividing line between friend and reporter, and I can't imagine that it was any easier for her.

Mickey, as an old pal or as a county investigator, didn't return any of my calls. I guessed he'd read the *Moon*.

Around four, when it became apparent that nothing more would be disclosed for a few days, I dragged myself back to my apartment. Ben was delighted to see me home early and expressed it in his usual way. We treated ourselves to Jiffy Pop and the last few minutes of Oprah, whose thought-provoking question of the day was "Are You Too Attached to Your Pet?" Ben and I agreed that the answer was "No" and switched channels until we came upon *Arsenic and Old Lace*. Long before Cary Grant said, "I'm the son of a sea cook," the pet and I were asleep.

SATURDAY AFTERNOON, CAT was in Ringo's passenger seat, a red toolbox plastered with Barbie stickers on her lap. The stickers were my idea; the toolbox and what was inside was Cat's.

We were expected at my cousin Paula's for her daughter's birthday party and we were already late. I had picked Cat up that morning to shop for Sam's present. Cruising the aisles of a mega toy store, Cat had dismissed the board games, electronic gadgets, crafts projects. "They all come with instructions," she scoffed. "What fun is that?"

I followed her into the hardware store next door. Almost immediately, Cat picked up the toolbox and started filling it—a small hammer, set of screwdrivers, hand drill, nails, hinges and other hardware. "Sam will figure out what to do with them," Cat said. "I wish someone had given me something like this instead of that stupid Betsy Wetsy."

Over lunch, I filled Cat in on my week solving murders and attending fires. She was glad I hadn't told Mickey about Evan's role in Emma's death.

"He wouldn't understand what that kid would have to live with." Cat's face was flushed, her eyes bright. Had I stirred up yet another disturbing image for my sister to dwell on?

But then Cat laughed, "I can't believe you assumed Doreen took the tie-dye scarf to prove she had the girl."

"Why not? I think that was in an episode of *Mod Squad*."

"I read the autopsy report. Emma got an I.D. bracelet for Christmas. That's easier to drop in an envelope than a scarf."

"Okay, fine. Next time I'll leave the deductive reasoning to you." But I grinned at her. However much she battled her churning thoughts, her essential intelligence was intact. It gave me hope.

But her social skills still left a lot to be desired. When we went into Paula's bungalow, Cat dropped the toolbox among the perfectly wrapped presents on the dining-room table and smiled at the clunk it made. Then barely glancing at the guests milling around on the back deck, she headed straight for the kids' volleyball game in progress on the beach. My twin could get away with not interacting with our relatives, and sometimes took advantage of it. I couldn't.

So I made the rounds, hugging the host and hostess, greeting family from our side and Marcus's. Aunt Angela managed to get in an "It's about time" before I was pulled aside by Marcus's mother, June.

"So what about that fire on the cliffs?" she asked breathlessly. "And the little girl's godfather found dead! Do you think it's connected to her murder?"

I was nearly struck dumb. This streaked-blonde matron,

wearing pearls with her tennis shorts, took the *Moon* to the checkout?

"Yeah, what about that?" Uncle Lou had grabbed my other arm, coughing cigar smoke into my face. "Maybe it was a gangland hit. Maybe those guys've been dealing with loan sharks and they couldn't make the vig. A little rough stuff, light a match, *poof!*" Uncle Lou liked to talk like a Mafia chieftain but was way too disorganized for organized crime.

As more closet *Moon* readers joined the conversation and offered their own theories, it took all my willpower not to scream, "Shut up! Let me tell you what *really* happened!"

I slipped away finally to sit on the last of the weathered wooden steps that led from the deck to the beach. I watched Cat leap up, spike the volleyball, then collapse in the sand to the cheers of her pint-size teammates. Alex yelled, "Victory sandwich!" and dove on top of Cat, followed by Sam, her other cousins and friends. Cat retaliated with a tickle attack and soon everyone was giggling, including me.

A pair of strong hands kneaded my shoulders. I didn't need to look up. "Hey, Sal," I said. "When'd you get here?"

"A minute ago. I had to go look in on a job on the way first."

My cousin Sal was the contractor of choice on several housing developments around the state. Very respectable, too. Somehow he managed to conduct business without the "help" of some of the industry's shadier connections. He had that kind of gift, my mother's oldest brother's oldest son. That title carries a lot of weight in an Italian family, and Sal lived up to it. He was the only one who'd come to visit Cat in the hospital last winter. That carried a lot of weight with me.

Sitting on the step behind me, he leaned his chin on the top of my head. "She's getting better, right?"

"Sure." It was more important to Sal that I agree than it was to me to tell the truth. And who knew what the truth was? Each day I just hoped her foundation would weather whatever it had to.

"I called her last month. She said she was working with computers. That's a good field. Good future there."

"That was nice of you, Sal." I reached back and patted his cheek.

"No problem." His raspy voice softened. "What's tough is what she went through." He paused and I assumed he was watching the action on the beach. "You know, when I see her, I just think of the little brat who used to follow me around all the time."

"You were her first crush, kiddo, didn't you know that?" Sal was a decade older than us, and, at eighteen, had looked like trouble. His wavy brown hair was close-cropped and thinning now, and he had the start of a successful man's paunch. "You were so cool with your Beatle's shag and bitchin' motorcycle. You were Paul McCartney on a Hog. What eight-year-old wouldn't fall for you?"

"Now I'm just a hog. The wife's got me on a diet. Some no-starch crap. If I didn't sneak over to Ma's for the macaroni, I'd go crazy." He squeezed my shoulders once more. "Hey, I saw your story about the fire. That was some marshmallow roast."

"I'll say. They claim the whole thing went up in ten minutes."

"Not surprising. At some point in construction, you've got to leave the framework exposed for a while to dry out. Someone's got good timing. One spark, then oxygen flows through and fans the flames like Gypsy Rose Lee. *Buon' anima.* God rest her soul."

"You mean, someone wouldn't need to help it along?"

"Not necessarily. But hey, if you have a cash flow problem and your insurance is paid up, a splash of gasoline couldn't hurt. Though that's not the way I'd do it."

"No?"

"Nah. The arson guys would sniff it out. There's plenty of stuff already on a site like that to do the trick. Propane for welding. Start a campfire next to one of those tanks, and bang! It's on its way. Who could prove it wasn't an accident?"

AT WORK MONDAY afternoon I finally got a call from Mickey. But not directly. And not what I expected.

"Hey, Andie," said the eager-puppy voice at the other end. "It's me, Billy Birdsey. We were paired up in the Thanksgiving Day pageant at Holy Moly. Fourth grade."

I'd recognized Billy, the *Leave It to Beaver* look-alike, at the fire scene, but otherwise couldn't recall much about him. I guess we'd run with different packs. I'd completely forgotten our walk down the church aisle. We'd been chosen by Mrs. Sukarnoputri, our first "lay" teacher, a former Catholic Missionaries volunteer and native of Jakarta.

"Oh, yeah. Little Mr. and Miss Indonesia offering food gifts of their nation," I said. "Mrs. Sukarnoputri gave me one of her daughters' saris or whatever you call 'em to wear. I had to stick a plastic gardenia in my hair and carry a basket of bananas to the altar. You had to bring a can of tuna fish."

"That's right!" Billy was pleased I remembered. "Of course, what StarKist had to do with Indonesia I still don't know." His voice grew serious. "Anyway, Andie. Mickey Giamonte gave me your number and told me to call. I'm a town cop now and I'm sorry to bother you, but Mickey asked me to ask you, could you come down to the station for some questioning? Like, right now?"

"What?" I'd thought *I'd* be doing the questioning.

"Andie, I'm just following orders. He's taken over the captain's office to talk to people about the fire. And stuff." I assumed the "and stuff" was Gordon.

"Billy, Mickey knows I only got there after it was all over. I can't see why he'd need to talk to me."

"Andie, like I said, Mickey told me—" His voice had gone up an octave.

"Okay, okay. I'll come down as soon as I can." I could always turn the tables once Mickey and I were face to face in the interview room.

"Great! Thanks!"

I was disturbed by this turn of events, but at least I'd made Billy happy.

It wasn't easy getting there. The South End looked like a war zone. River Drive was still blocked off entering town, and so were parts of Cliff Way. Traffic was diverted up and down side streets. I was stuck a few times behind dump trucks hauling away debris and tow trucks hooking up scorched cars. One detour brought me past Juliet's shop. She was outside washing its soot-smeared window. I honked and she came over.

"Sightseeing? Or are you here for the fire sale?"

"Nah, your ex-husband summoned me. I'm on my way to get grilled." I grimaced at myself. "Sorry for the horrible, insensitive pun."

"You can make up for it. Come back when he's done with you, tell me everything and help me pack up some clothes I'm donating. The American Legion is taking up a collection for the folks who lost everything. "

"Now I really feel guilty. It's the least I can do."

When I finally presented myself to the desk sergeant, he picked up the phone, then waved me toward a straight-backed bench against the wall. "Detective Giamonte is in Captain Fagen's office. You'll have to wait until he's ready for you."

The scarred and unyielding wooden seat made it harder to sit still. Why was I here? Was Mickey just yanking my chain?

I had been squirming for twenty minutes when Gina pushed through the front door, wearing a cobalt blue suit, the skirt a little shorter than might be legal. She exchanged her own few words with the sergeant, then spotted me.

I found myself smiling at her with what felt like pride. "I don't think I need a lawyer." I gave her a hug.

"Everyone does." Close up, I saw her eyes were underlined by gray patches that her concealer couldn't conceal. "Thanks for the call about Gordon, by the way."

I held her hand as we sat down. "Are you alright?"

She tried to control the tremble in her sigh. "It was a shock. I usually wish bad things on all my ex-boyfriends, but this…"

"Nasty breakup?"

"No worse than some of the others." Her eyes narrowed. "But that doesn't have anything to do with this."

Some instinct made me ask, "What *does*?"

Gina opened her mouth, hesitated, then surprised me with a full-out laugh. "Okay, so who are you now? Friend or foe?"

I shrugged. "Honestly? I won't know until I know the whole story. And this town seems to be full of secrets. So I'm not sure who you are either."

"That's honest." She let go of my hand and pulled a little away from me. "You know, I wasn't too happy when Joel started talking to you. I'm still not sure what he was trying to prove. There was never any evidence linking him to his daughter's death. There never will be." She looked at me hard. "Things were starting to calm down. But now this. Is it a coincidence that someone else has died since your stories ran?"

I was stung. "No one seems to know yet how Gordon died, whether it was an accident or...something else. You can't think that what I wrote had anything to do with his death."

"I don't know what to think." Gina rubbed her forehead with her fingertips. "All I know is that however all this winds up, whether anyone learns the 'whole story' or not, it affects the future of this town. I still have family here, and friends."

I wasn't sure what she was getting at. "You think this is going to put an end to the riverside development?"

"Someone may not have wanted Joel to seem sympathetic. A lot of the old-timers see him and Gordon as carpetbaggers, buying up the best land for cheap and selling out to the yuppies. In a lot of ways, this is still a blue-collar town and the locals don't like change."

"But that's happening everywhere. You can't stop it just by targeting two developers."

"You can stop it here if you scare away the others. Me, I think the growth will be good for everyone in the long run. More businesses, more residents to pay taxes. Cleans up the waterfront. Maybe they'll finally get that high school built. But the shopping centers and condos are not going to fill up if people think the town harbors murderers. And what was that wacko group you quoted? Satan's Spawn? What you write has consequences no matter how innocent you think it is."

A phone rang. We both jumped. The desk sergeant put the receiver down, jerked his left thumb behind him. "Andrealisa Rinaldi. Down the hall, make a right. Third door on the left."

The office wasn't hard to find, since Billy Birdsey was standing outside it, at attention. He gave me a lopsided grin as he opened the door.

I entered talking. "Okay, Mickey, I'm sorry I didn't tell you right off the bat that I have a boyfriend. Sort of." Three strikes, you're out, Doug. "But that's no excuse for this macho guinea bull—"

Mickey, hunched over a cluttered wooden desk that looked like it had been kicked hard and often, pretended to consult a piece of paper in front of him. He waited until the door closed before saying, "Please have a seat, Miss Rinaldi. It is *Miss* Rinaldi, isn't it?"

"Ms. to you, Detective Giamonte." I dropped onto another rump-busting chair. Good God, don't cops believe in cushions?

"*Ms.* Rinaldi." Mickey was still not looking up. "I'm sorry to have to interrupt your workday"—*right*—"but we are investigating a suspicious fire and possible homicide"—he got my attention with that. Was he giving me something?—"and need to ask you where were you at about 8 p.m. last Thursday evening." A shuffle of paper. "That would be July 15, 1992."

"Jesus, Mickey, you know where—okay, I'll play." With Mickey, I'd only make it worse for myself if I gave him a hard time. I swallowed, "I was at home, in my apartment, preparing dinner for an old friend of mine. A *very* old friend. In fact, he reminds me a lot of you. Though much more attractive, if you like the swarthy blond type."

The corners of his mouth twitched, but I wasn't going to get a smile. "Thank you for your cooperation."

"You're welcome. Hey, shouldn't there be a female officer in here? You know, as a witness in case I charge you with sexual harassment or, more likely, police brutality." I wasn't going to be *that* cooperative.

His left hand came up from underneath the desk. It was holding a Polaroid snapshot. "Ms. Rinaldi, have you ever seen this item before?"

I leaned in for a closer look, and jerked back. "What the hell, Mickey. Where did that come from?" The muscles in my thighs tightened. My fight-or-flight response must be kicking in. "Was that at the crime scene?"

"Please answer the question."

"Yes, I might have." Something made me chose my words carefully, as if I were already on a witness stand. "It appears to be a miniature model of a Mustang." It had been photographed next to a coffee mug, for scale. In fact, the coffee mug at Mickey's right elbow.

"A 1964 Ford Mustang, as a matter of fact. Of a type commonly known as a Matchbox car." Mickey seemed to be waiting for me to say something more, but I didn't. "When did you last see it?"

"I don't know that it's the same one."

"If it isn't, why would your fingerprints be on it?" Mickey said it so casually I almost forgot to listen.

"How did—?" *Oh, right.* My prints were on file. That had been a requirement of my orientation at the stationhouse upstate when I'd briefly covered the police beat. My managing editor had said it amused the cops to see the new reporters get their fingers dirty. I'd ruined my favorite blouse when I'd nervously brushed my cuff against the ink pad. Now my whorls had betrayed me. "I must have picked it up from the glass case." Did I say that out loud?

"And where and when was that?"

My thoughts scurried and doubled back like a rat trying to find its way out of a maze. Who would I be implicating with my answer? "Mmmm, let me think..."

"Ms. Rinaldi" — he was really laying the *Ms.* on thick — "this shouldn't be so hard to recall."

I could always take the Fifth. "What difference does it make? You know I was nowhere near the fire when it started."

"Please answer the question. Unless you have something to hide."

"Two." I cleared my throat, which suddenly felt as if I were sucking sand. "Two weeks ago, Joel Hartt showed me his Matchbox collection. I gave him—I had given him a similar miniature car on his sixth birthday."

"Thank you, Ms. Rinaldi. That will be all."

"What? That's it?"

"Do you need help finding your way out?"

I stood up. As I opened the door, a wave of nausea hit me. "Wait a second. You didn't actually say my fingerprints were on it." Gina was right. I *did* need a lawyer. Someone who would tell me when to shut up. "You know I had nothing to do with this."

Mickey still didn't look up.

I walked in a daze back down the hall. So much for turning the tables. I'd been too flustered to interrogate him. Not that it would have gotten me anywhere. I guess I did learn that the police were treating Gordon's death as a homicide. And that the little car was somehow a clue.

As I rounded the corner, I saw Gina. Maybe I should retain her, or at least tell her what happened. When she hurried out the door, I followed.

I had assumed she'd come to be questioned about her relationship with Gordon. For some reason, it hadn't occurred to me that she might be here in her official capacity.

"Watch out, or I'll have you up on charges!" she yelled at the two uniformed cops bent over the open rear door of a patrol car.

Each had taken a forearm of the backseat passenger and roughly pulled him to his feet on the sidewalk. With his wrists handcuffed behind his back, he couldn't have gotten out by himself.

I didn't need him to straighten to his full six-foot-plus height to know it was Joel.

• *Chapter 12* •

A CLUTCH OF reporters and a TV cameraman surrounded the patrol car, shouting questions. Someone must have tipped them off. Over their heads, Joel gave me a look before tucking his chin into his chest. The cops hustled him up the brick steps.

Obviously, Mickey knew the Matchbox car was Joel's before I sat down to confirm it. Had he called me in just to witness the spectacle of Joel being brought into custody? And he hadn't given me any information that the whole world wouldn't know from the six o'clock news.

Ringo was blocked in by a line of traffic honking at a dump truck trying to make a K turn on the side street. So I walked to Juliet's shop, hoping that the exercise might release some of the calming endorphins I'd heard so much about. Instead, I worked myself into a sweat and felt a whole lot worse. What had Joel gotten himself into?

"How did a nice girl like you wind up with a prick like Mickey?" I asked Juliet after we had packed two boxes with T-shirts, jeans, shorts and even some games for the kids made homeless by the fire.

She was now arranging boxes of "Mystery Date" on a waist-high shelf. "As my father used to say, 'It was New Year's Eve and it seemed like a good idea at the time.'"

"New Year's. That seems to be when all the trouble starts."

"Look at these." She held up one of the games. "Found them through a dealer I know in Japan. You can't find the originals in the States." She dropped it back on the shelf. "Actually, Mickey wasn't so bad as a husband. Mmmm.... In some ways, he was very good." She winked at me. "Is this just your way of asking my advice on how to win his heart? Because I think you already did, a long time ago."

"What? That's ridiculous. We did nothing but rag on each other as kids. And that hasn't changed."

"Well, you know how boys are. They can't admit that they actually like you. That doesn't change with age either. Mickey's mom told me that, in second grade, when Sister Thomasina told us to bring in St. Valentine's cards for our friends, he swore to his mother he was not giving any to any of the girls in class. Then she saw him making one out for you, so she says, 'I thought you weren't giving a card to any girls,' and he says, 'She's not a girl.'"

"That was just Mickey changing the rules so he would always be right."

"All I know is that whenever Mickey and I were in bed sharing childhood stories, you were in practically all of his."

"For God's sake, we lived across from each for nearly thirteen years. In fact, we even fought over *that*—who owned the street between us. Drew imaginary property lines on the asphalt with the toes of our Keds and threatened to pound whoever crossed it."

"Sounds like true love to me. That's what all marriage is about anyway. Drawing battle lines."

"Well, he's crossed the line with me this time." I told her what had happened at the police station. Yes, I even told her about our kiss in my apartment. "So what line did Mickey cross with *you*?"

"It wasn't like that. The first year was great, actually. Mickey had just moved over to Criminal Investigations. He already had the bar, but then he bought the grocery store and turned it into a restaurant. That started eating up our time together. Then one day he got a phone call and started obsessing about this one case, even though it had been closed years ago. Mickey was convinced the guy was innocent. So he started spending whatever down time he had looking into it. After a while, we started forgetting what each other looked like. Finally, I decided to move back to California. It just wasn't the right time for us."

"Well, after I go back to my desk job where I belong, he'll forget what I look like too."

"What if he's really your Dreamboat?" She started singing the old TV commercial jingle, "Mystery Date. Are you ready for your Mystery Date? Just open the door..."

I gagged. "Pul-eeze. I've seen too many old movies. Cary Grant and Katharine Hepburn, or Rosalind Russell, are at each other's throats for two hours and then, ah! We find out they're really meant for each other all along. But can you ever really imagine them together after the credits roll?"

"I give up." Juliet sighed. "You'll be going to the prom with Poindexter then. The Dud."

The door's bells tinkled and Jesse's voice rang out. "Hey, Jules, get a move on if you want me to help you take those boxes over to the community center."

"Speaking of dreamboats," I muttered. "Hi," I said cleverly when Jesse rounded the corner.

He nodded curtly, turned his back to me and lifted the two cartons. "I'll bring these out to the Jeep." The door jangled closed.

I stared at Juliet. "Whoa. Check me for frostbite. Man, did he just give me the deep-freeze?"

Juliet looked embarrassed. "I think he's upset with you because you ran that picture of his sister."

"What are you talking about?"

"The one in the *Moon*. With Gordon."

"The redhead was Jody?"

She nodded. "He told me Jody dated Gordon for a while, two years ago."

"Oh, jeez. How could I know that was his sister? I haven't seen her since she was, like, eight. I wouldn't have recognized her. She grew up to be a knockout."

"Unfortunately, she didn't really grow up. So needy! The father of her kids, one of the Culligan boys, finally left her. Then her thing with Gordon ended badly. Jesse blames Gordon for her drug problem. The photo just brought it all back."

"Well, I didn't do it on purpose. Put in a good word for me, will you?"

She looked out the front window. "Where's your car?"

"At the police station."

"Then we'll give you a lift and you can put in a good word for yourself." She pushed me out the door. As she locked it behind us, Juliet hummed, "Mystery Date. Are you ready for your Mystery Date...?"

By the time we pulled up alongside my car, Jesse seemed more willing to accept my apology. He even gave me a peck on the cheek before I hopped out. Not a lip lock, but it would have to hold me for now.

But as I put my key in the ignition, I realized I was letting my hormones get in the way of facing a chilling possibility. During the ride, Jesse had told me Jody's story, of de Porres taking her to parties in the city where lines of cocaine had been set out like hors d'oeuvres. Supposedly, Gordon himself hadn't indulged, but he didn't stop Jody from joining in. After a few months, he had found out she'd been trying to score on her own, using his friends as contacts. That had ended the relationship. And started two years of hell for Jody, with Jesse and his family trying to get her help.

I remembered Jesse's threat when I first—and last—saw Gordon. I rewound the tape in my head, of de Porres saying Jesse was making a big deal out of nothing and Jesse's reply: "Nothing?! That's what you'll be if you don't take care of this!"

Had that really been about de Porres not insuring the workers? Or driving Jody to addiction? It looked like Jesse had a few reasons for wanting this guy dead too.

But if Mickey could have his pick of suspects, what had led him to bring Joel in?

I shut off the Beetle's engine. Mickey owed me an answer.

The desk sergeant said he'd gone for the day, but it wouldn't take a boardwalk psychic to know where he went.

The Rock Bottom was packed with the after-work crowd, a democratic mix of business suits and blue jeans, and couples waiting for a table to open up in the restaurant next door, a few regulars hogging the pool table. Lively chatter hung above them like the gray-blue swirls of cigarette smoke. I'd never quite understood the bar scene, even in college. Usually, a few drinks turned most strangers into best friends, but all alcohol ever did for me was make me want to crawl under a stool and take a nap.

Mickey was in his usual booth, but it took me a few seconds to recognize his tablemate. They were leaning in, their foreheads nearly touching, Mickey doing all the talking.

I stuck a palm in.

"Hi, I don't think we've ever been introduced. I'm Andrealisa Rinaldi. You're Ray, aren't you? Doreen's husband?"

Mickey slapped his hand over a Polaroid that had been between them, then slid it into his shirt pocket. But not before I saw it. I'd thought it might be the Mustang photo, but it was a picture of a dark man with a heavy mustache. Like Gordon, only younger.

Ray raised that guileless face, and those green eyes lit up. "Oh, hey, hi! Doreen told me about you. She was really excited to see you again."

I'll bet. Something told me Ray seldom heard a discouraging word. But considering what it must be like being married to Doreen, twelve years in federal prison would have been a day at the circus. "It's been a treat for me too."

"Excuse me for interrupting this lovely moment." Mickey was not hiding his annoyance. "But what do you want?"

"I have a few bones to pick with you. A whole carcass, in fact."

"It's okay, Mickey. I've got to get home anyway. Doreen doesn't like it if I'm late for dinner." Ray stood up. "I'll think about what you said and see if I remember anything else."

Mickey patted his arm. "Whatever, Ray."

I slid into the vacated bench. "Interrogating another suspect at headquarters?"

"We have all the suspects we need at present, thank you. Unless you've come to confess."

"Has Joel really been arrested? Or was that for my benefit?"

"A little self-centered, aren't we? Do you think I have nothing better to do than arrange entertainment for you?"

"Because I'm sure he didn't have anything to do with this."

"Really? You have some information you'd like to share?"

"I just know, that's all."

"I can't believe after all these years, you're still protecting him!" He was close to anger. "Listen, just because you saved his life once doesn't mean that you're responsible for him forever. That's just an old Chinese saying. And you're not an old Chinese."

"That has nothing to do with this," I said hotly. "You're the one stuck in the past, Mickey. You're the one still hanging out in the old neighborhood, marrying hometown girls and nursing old grudges."

"And you? Not at home anywhere, never married, with a job you're ashamed of. What are you doing but running away from the present?"

"No fair, Mickey." I was coldly furious. "*No fair.*"

"Then be fair to me. Do you really think I'm such a creep

I'd put someone away just because I could never stand him? I'm also a better judge of people than you seem to think."

"Then why do you think he killed his own daughter?"

"I don't."

My mouth flapped a few times before words came out. "You don't?"

"Rinaldi, you're getting on my nerves. Did you think I got my detective's badge out of a box of Cracker Jacks?"

"No. I figured you sent in a few cereal box tops to Battle Creek, Michigan."

"Give me a break. Stevie Wonder could see that kidnap scene was a set up. There was no sign that anyone else had entered the house after the party guests left. Yeah, it all pointed to Hartt. Or he was covering up for someone else."

"You know?" I said.

"Nothing else fit. After all this time, why would a parent subject himself to all the tabloid crap, do almost nothing to help find his child's killer?"

"You know," I said.

"To protect the only child he had left."

"You know," I said for the last time.

He nodded.

"Why didn't you do something about it then?"

"I couldn't prove it. Once Hartt brought Gina in, she made it impossible for us to question the kid. I as much as told Hartt that I knew. We would have made it easy on Evan, but Joel wouldn't budge."

"So you leaked that it might have been sexual abuse."

"Okay, *that* I'm not proud of. But I thought at the time it might embarrass him into telling the truth. We could have gone easy on him for tampering with evidence. But we can't look the other way on a child's death. The community has to believe their children are safe, and cops have enough PR problems these days. Your little piece in the *Moon* didn't help my credibility any. I'd been waiting for the media attention to die down, to give Hartt another chance to bring Evan in before we got a court order to question the kid, with as little publicity as possible. Then this happened. After *you* happened."

I ignored his implication. "I don't get it. If you know Joel's not the murderer, why are you so sure he killed de Porres? Or do you think he's protecting Evan on that too." I let my sarcasm drip.

"No, this one's all Joel. He was at the construction site with Gordon that night."

"He told you that?"

"He didn't have to. I saw them together. On my way to catch the ferry to your place."

Before I could react, Mickey added, "Oh, yeah. What I just told you? It's off the record."

As THE STEEL door banged behind me, my apartment had never seemed tinier. Could it have shrunk in the heat? I'd swear the walls were closing in. Even Ben was suffering from claustrophobia. After peeing on his diaper, he began running around and around in smaller and smaller circles, sure that if he was just fast enough, he'd catch that hairy worm waving from the end of his butt. *Note to Self:* Pick Ben up a new chew toy.

More bills, another job application rejection, another letter from the super. I dropped the rest of my mail on the kitchen table and re-read the notice from the management company: *As you have failed repeatedly to respond to our request for an inspection appointment time convenient for you we are informing you that there will be an inspection of the premises on Thursday July 23 1992 9 am.*

Great. I was about to be evicted by people who had absolutely no clue about comma usage. If I no longer had a job by Thursday morning, where I lived wouldn't be an issue. At least I could always get work as a copy editor.

I pushed aside the cold sesame noodles I'd picked up from the Chinese takeout, and rifled through my shoulder bag for the Nestlé's Crunch I'd bought at The Confectionery after I left

Mickey. Chocolate was good for nausea. Chocolate was good for everything. It triggers the release of endorphins, those natural painkillers, and you don't even have to exercise. Scientists had just found out chocolate also contains phenyl ethylamine, the same brain chemical that giddily shoots through your system when you're in love. The only surprise is that a university had squandered its grant money to research what any nursery-school class could have told them: The stuff makes you happy.

But tonight it wasn't working.

Instead, Mickey's words were eating at me.

Okay, so I'd never been married. Never been in love really, not in a chocolate kind of way. Lust, yes. Lust, often. Though there was that one guy in college... No, not really.

But I also hadn't been divorced twice or even once. Hadn't even regretted those I had lusted and lost. Who needed the emotional roller coaster of a 'til-death-do-us-part relationship?

And the job... No, I wasn't ashamed of it. The truth? I was ashamed of myself. Ashamed I'd blown my career through some childish game of one-upmanship that I played with myself. If the *Moon* was my penance, my Act of Contrition, then so be it. After I said my five Our Fathers, the slate would be wiped clean and I could start over.

I was ashamed, too, that I didn't have the guts, or the stomach, to be an investigative reporter. I had a private life and I didn't feel right prying into someone else's. I could write about medical breakthroughs or cancer symptoms, stories where it was easy to separate the good guys from the bad germs, and nobody got hurt. Even at the *Moon*, I thought I was doing Cher a favor by pointing out the dangers of too many collagen implants.

Until now, I hadn't had to badger grieving fathers, second-guess cops. What Mickey had told me was off the record, and much as he aggravated me, I'd been brought up to respect authority, be it in a blue uniform or a black-and-white habit. Always the good girl, that's me. Mickey knew it. That's why he was sure I wouldn't print what I knew. That's why he double-dared *me*, not

Cat, to go into the Rock Bottom that Halloween when we were eleven. He knew Cat would have gone in, without hesitation. But me...

But I had surprised him that day. I took the challenge, I took the risk. That taught me I could do it, if the stakes were high enough.

Slim Jims versus...what? What good would it do to tell this story? If Mickey had enough on Joel to put him away for Gordon's murder, Joel might confess to killing Emma, just to close that book. And what would happen to Evan then? Who would get custody? Doreen? I shuddered. Maybe Kathleen and Ken Whalen would take him in.

What good would *I* get out of it? Mickey had given me an even more sensational story, a cop covering for a twelve-year-old killer. For all I knew, everyone in town was in on that cover-up, a twist on *Murder on the Orient Express*. But I couldn't write it, didn't want to write it. It would drag me down to *Moon* level, and then I could never crawl out.

Yep, I'd go in tomorrow and tell Elise that my Lois Lane days were over, that from now on I intended to stick to assigning others the dirty work. And she would fire me. That was the one thing I was sure of.

So I'd have to move back to the shore house. Big deal. As Mickey had reminded me, I didn't feel at home anyplace anyway, so what difference would it make where I lived? I'd see if they needed an editor at the Seaside Pennysaver. People need pennysavers. They needed to save pennies. I would help them get a good deal on a used living room set, "retail price $4,000, asking $1,500 or best offer." I would make sure there were no typos, because don't you hate it when an ad says $150 and it turns out to be $1,500? It would be a nice life—me, my rat-dog and my nut-case sister. Anyone else would kill for such a life.

My obsessive thoughts were depressing me. I had to share them with someone who could relate.

"What are you doing?" I asked Cat when she answered.

"Thinking too much," she said. "What about you?"

"Thinking too much."

"You're starting to sound like me, and I don't like it. What's going on up there?"

I told her about my day, wondering, not for the first time, if somehow they had put the wrong sister on medication. Some Paxil with a Luvox chaser might do me good right now.

After I'd finished, Cat didn't respond for a while. But I could hear her breathing. Finally, "So Mickey knew all along it was Evan?"

"So he says."

"He's just like his dad—a sneaky mother-effer."

"I'm surprised by your restraint."

"I'm trying to watch my fucking language. Daisy is a Born-Again." I heard the click of what was probably a cigarette lighter.

"Are you smoking?"

"No, I'm just lighting Daisy's hash pipe."

"She is not!" came a plaintive wail in the background. "She's smoking and she's not supposed to do that in the room! She has to go outside."

Cat's sigh was thick, but I heard the cap of the lighter snap shut. A year ago she might have thrown it at Daisy, still lit.

More silence. "Are you still there?"

More hard breathing. "What was all that about the Matchbox car?"

"You mean the one I gave Joel for his sixth birthday?"

"That's funny. It's the same year and model Ray Dougherty was driving when he got busted twelve years ago. But his was life-size, I assume."

"What are you talking about?"

"You showed me that newspaper clipping that you brought down to the house Fourth of July. Ray was driving a '64 Mustang when Mickey caught him with the coke."

"How did you remember that?"

"I've got to fill up my head with new crap to squeeze out the old crap, don't I?"

BUT NOW THE new crap in my head wouldn't let me sleep. Cat's observation added a new puzzle. I kept telling myself that I didn't have to deal with this. I could quit, not even wait for Elise to fire me. I didn't have to care about what happened to Joel or Mickey or any of them.

But it bothered me that I'd missed the Mustang connection. Was Cat right? Did the Matchbox car tie Gordon's death to that long-ago drug deal? Why else had Mickey been talking to Ray at the bar? Whose picture had he shown him? It couldn't have been Gordon—Ray would know who de Porres was from the job. Or would he? De Porres had said he rarely came to the construction site.

I started replaying the day's conversations, then climbed down from the loft bed and pawed through my purse. I found Juliet's home number in the bottom. It was nearly midnight, but I picked up the phone anyway.

"Juliet, I'm sorry to bother you so late. But something got stuck in my head and I won't sleep until I get it out."

"No bother. It's just me and Cary Grant on cable. Ever see *I Was a Male War Bride?*"

"For a week straight on *Million Dollar Movie*. How come he's a French lieutenant but has a British accent? My favorite part is when the army clerk asks him the question from the war bride application, 'Have you ever had any female trouble?' and Cary says, 'Nothing *but,* sergeant.'"

"Mine too. So what's troubling *you?*"

"Mickey. You said he was hung up on an old case while you were married. Do you remember which one?" I felt funny bringing this up, questioning her about her ex-husband. But I couldn't ask him myself. I didn't think it would get me anywhere.

Juliet didn't sound put out. "Some drug bust. He'd spotted the guy driving around by the old fuel tanks and pulled him over. The guy had coke in his trunk."

"You mean Ray Dougherty."

"Doreen's husband? I don't think Mickey ever mentioned his name. The arrest was when I was in California. That would have been two years before we got married, and, jeez, it's been eight since we were together."

"Why wouldn't he let the case go?"

"He didn't talk to me much about it—like I said, we were two ships in the night by then. But one thing I remember. It started when someone called him about the car. It had been sitting in impound all that time, while the Feds made their case. He went off to look at it and when he came back, he said he noticed something funny."

"Like what?"

"The tail light was out."

"I thought he knew that. That's why he stopped Ray."

"I mean *gone*—not burned out or broken. The bulb was missing. He couldn't understand why a classic in otherwise good condition would be without a tail light."

Unless someone wanted to give a cop a good excuse to stop a car driving around a restricted area in the middle of the night. Someone who wanted ten kilos of cocaine to fall into the hands of the police.

• *Chapter 13* •

I PACED IN front of Elise's office. I was going to quit. I wasn't going to quit. I was going to quit. I wasn't going to quit. I was going to pace until I had a massive heart attack and died on the spot.

She waved me in without turning from her computer screen. She always seemed oblivious to her surroundings, yet she had 360-degree peripheral vision like some small but cunning creature that must fight for its survival in a mist-shrouded bayou. A swamp lizard. A swamp lizard that today was wearing a sarong.

I waited for her to give me her full attention. When I realized that wasn't going to happen, I said, "So, how was your vacation?"

"Hmm? Fine."

"Weather not so good?

"It was fine."

"Oh. You don't seem to have a tan." If possible, she was paler than when she left.

"SPF 50. You can't be too careful."

"Right." She must have slapped that sunscreen on with a trowel. "Elise, I wanted to talk to you about the Hartt features."

"Colin told me what went on while I was gone. Hot stuff."
She didn't seem aware of her pun. "Good thing you were at the
scene."

"Well, actually, that's what I wanted to talk you ab—"

"And I want you to stay on the scene. Camp out on those
cliffs if you have to. They have the dad in custody, right?"

"He hasn't been formally char—"

"Did he do it?"

"I don't thi—"

"Talk to Hartt again. 'Accused Killer Talks Only to The *Moon*!'
That sort of thing. He's your friend. He trusts you."

"That's the prob—"

"A problem?" The lizard finally swiveled to face me. The
eyes behind the harlequin glasses—today's affectation, as Elise's
vision was better than 20/20—were blue lasers.

I felt the rational part of my brain vaporize. "No. No
problem."

"Good." The fog rolled back in. "It's been a slow week."

Maybe for *her*.

I CALLED GINA's office, then the beeper number her answering
machine gave out. Within minutes, my phone rang.

"I'm at the police station. I would have ignored your call, but
Joel does want to speak to you. Against my advice. Again."

"Thanks for the vote of confidence. I'm on your side,
remember?"

"That's what I'm worried about. Well, hurry up and get down
here. They want to transfer him to the county courthouse."

"They're charging him?"

"Jerking him around is more like it. They can only hold
him for forty-eight hours and Mickey wants to play it for all it's
worth."

"Don't let him take Joel away until I get there."

"Why do you think I get the big bucks?"

"I owe you one."

"More than one."

I was headed out when my phone rang again.

"Hey."

"Jesse?"

"Dinner."

"When?"

"Tonight."

"When?"

"Seven."

"Where?"

"The Barge."

"Why?"

"Because."

"Okay."

He hung up. Hands down, that was the most satisfying conversation I'd ever had with a man.

THIRTY MINUTES, TWO near-collisions and a labyrinth of detours later, I walked through the precinct door. No one was at the front desk. But a small figure was hunched on the wooden bench against the wall. Her legs were swinging under a long Indian-print skirt and she was gnawing on a thumbnail as if it might be her last meal. Amanda Dougherty, Doreen's daughter. But no Doreen in sight.

I slipped next to her. "Hi, Amanda."

She looked up only long enough for me to see her wet lashes.

"What's the matter?"

"Nothing." More gnawing.

"You here with your mom?"

"She's in the toilet."

That didn't give me much time. "What happened?" I didn't know that anything had, but it was a good bet.

The tears spilled over and the legs swung faster. "We were just fooling around! Jerry Gleason said no one would see us down there, and it was just cigarettes and some weed! My mother is acting like I'm a freakin' crackhead. And the fire was an accident! We were just smoking and dropped our ciggies and ran when we heard those guys fighting. That wasn't my fault, jeez!" She cocked her head at me. "Who are *you*, anyway?"

I hoped Amanda wasn't planning on a career in the CIA. It didn't take much squeezing to empty her toothpaste tube.

"Andrealisa Rinaldi."

I didn't say that. It was Doreen, hovering above us more like a dyspeptic vulture than a mother hen. "And where she goes, trouble follows."

"Check your train schedule. Trouble arrived before I got here."

"So you say." For Doreen, that passed as repartee.

I couldn't help myself. "So Amanda started the fire that cremated Gordon de Porres?"

Doreen's face turned white, then an unattractive maroon. She was like a human mood ring. Except that she had only two moods: pissed off and furious.

"Stay away from my kids!"

"All of them?" Oh, shit. Bringing up Evan was a low blow, even coming from me. But Doreen seemed to bring out the worst in me.

She yanked Amanda off the bench and out the door before I got to my feet.

"How to win friends and influence people." Gina was behind me, hands on her hips.

"Just call me Dale Carnegie."

"Okay, Dale. The prisoner will see you now. And behave yourself or I'll sic Doreen on you."

Gina led me into a small windowless room outfitted with nothing more than a folding table and chairs. Officer Billy Birdsey had been posted by the door again, I guess to discourage us from stealing the lavish furnishings. But he also nervously checked my shoulder bag for concealed weapons, or maybe a file with cake in it, stammering an apology when a tampon escaped and rolled across the floor. Luckily, it wasn't loaded.

When he saw me, Joel shifted on his metal chair. His long legs were folded under the shabby table, his arms on top of it, his fingers clasped together. Except for the handcuffs, he looked like a grown-up trying to squeeze into a first-grader's desk on Parent-Teacher Night.

I sat down across from him. "We have to stop meeting like this," I said as Billy closed the door behind us.

One corner of his mouth went up. "That's what I was thinking." Then he looked past me and said firmly, "Gina."

"I'm not leaving this room." Gina noisily dragged out a chair and sat down.

Joel shrugged. "Suit yourself. You always do. But don't interfere." Back to me, "What would you like to know? Ask me anything."

Gina groaned.

I leaned toward Joel. "Why were you at the construction site that night?"

"I didn't intend to be. I was driving to meet Kaori for dinner. Kaori Masako. Her firm is a partner in the Asian shopping plaza we're planning for the South End."

"Okay. I know about her. How'd you meet up with Gordon?"

"I saw his Mercedes in the lot by the site. I'd been trying to reach him all day. I had...something to go over with him."

"I know about that too. Jesse came to see you that morning about the workers' insurance. Or rather the lack of it."

"Yes." Joel looked surprised but relieved. Interesting since he hadn't been willing to share that information himself. Was he protecting Jesse now? "I thought Gordon would have a reasonable explanation. I parked and saw a light on in the trailer. When I knocked, Gordon came out, acted like he had been expecting me. Before I could say anything, he said he wanted to show me something on the site. He took me up on the scissor lift overlooking the river, and he started this song and dance, waving his arms around and saying how we were going to own the water-front, rent out the skyline. Then I realized this was about what *he* wanted, not the company, not me. He was trying to dazzle me with bullshit so I wouldn't confront him. "

"So you fought."

Joel lowered his head. "I yelled at him. And he kept smiling. Then I lost it. I had him by the throat—"

"Joel!" That was Gina.

Joel shot her a warning look. "—but he kept smiling. Then it hit me."

"He hit you?"

"No, no. The *thought* hit me: He was just like my father."

"What do you mean?"

"The charm, the bullshit. Just like my father. I felt so stupid. How did I fall for that crap again for all these years?"

I shrugged. "It's like a woman who goes from an abusive home to an abusive marriage. You don't always choose what's good for you. You choose what's familiar." Suddenly I was Dear Abby.

"I guess." He took a deep breath.

"What happened next?"

"I left. I let go of him and climbed down on my own. And he was still calling after me."

"Why was he there to begin with?" I asked.

Joel frowned. "I don't know."

"Could there have been someone else in the trailer when you got there?" Out of the corner of my eye, I saw Gina bend forward on her chair. Maybe I was giving her a line of defense.

"I hadn't thought about it. There could have been. I never went inside. But the crew was gone. And I didn't see another car in the lot. "

"What about the Matchbox car they found at the scene. Did you bring it?"

"Whatever for? Mickey has been asking about that. I'm assuming Gordon had it. Why, who knows? But he's seen my collection. He could have taken it anytime."

"Not anytime. You showed it to me, in its case, just last week."

"Then that narrows it down." He thought a minute. "Actually, it could have been the same day. I'd been trying to reach him, and left messages. Doreen said he finally came by the house around five, and she took him into the study to wait. But he left a few minutes later, saying he'd try to catch me at the office."

"Okay, after you left him, where did you go?"

He began twisting his fingers together. "To meet Kaori at The Barge. But I was late and they'd given away our reservation. Besides, I was still upset. Instead we went to her hotel near the airport and ordered room service."

I tried not to raise my eyebrows. "What time did you get home that night?"

He hesitated. "I didn't. I stayed." He tensed up then. "Listen, I don't want that in the papers."

Gina snorted. "Then you shouldn't have told her."

Joel ignored her. "You have to understand. Our relationship could compromise Kaori with her bosses and mess up the deal. They might think she's favoring my side."

I sighed. "Do you really think no one else will find out about you two?"

"More importantly, I don't want Evan to find out. Not yet, and certainly not this way."

"Then you'd better tell him yourself and soon. The tabloids will have a field day with this. 'Killer Caught in Asian Love Nest.' Sorry." I'd forgotten that I *was* the tabloids.

I thought a minute. "So you didn't know about the fire or Gordon's death until the next morning."

"Saw it on the room TV after Kaori left. I contacted the police right away. I cooperated. I didn't deny I was there."

"Have the cops talked to Kaori to check out your story?"

"She was stopping off at different sites in Europe on the way back to Japan. She'll be out of touch for a week at least."

Gina jumped in, exasperated. "But that doesn't matter anyway. She can't account for what happened before he joined her at the restaurant. Whatever she says can only make it worse."

"You left Evan alone that night?"

Joel looked affronted. "Of course not. I dropped him off at Kathleen's for a sleepover. Ken promised to take him for a sail."

I looked sideways at Gina, then asked, "Doreen told you I knew about Evan, didn't she?"

He nodded.

"Did Gordon know? "

"What about Evan?" Gina's voice was tight.

Joel put a hand up. "Yes."

"Did that come up in your...argument?"

Head down. "No. Why would it?"

"Did he threaten to tell?"

More finger-twisting. "No, that wasn't the issue. He was undermining the business, our projects."

"Why?"

I was surprised when Gina answered. "Gordon wanted to do his own deals, without Joel." She sighed heavily. "Sorry, Joel, I didn't think he'd go that far."

"I was beginning to suspect that he was channeling money into a separate account. I'd just hired an independent auditor to look into it. I didn't know about the insurance."

"Then why *wouldn't* you want to kill him?"

Joel laughed. "That would have let him off too easy. Suing him, ruining his reputation—that would've hurt him more."

One last question. "So, by telling me all this you think I'll do—what?"

He looked surprised. "I don't care what you do with it. I just wanted you to know the truth." A small smile. "Isn't it the truth that sets you free?"

"No. If you're lucky, it's a jury of your peers." Mickey had come into the room, a uniformed officer at each elbow. "Okay, kids, recess is over."

He nodded at the two cops, who hauled Joel to his feet and led him out. Gina followed.

I started up from the chair.

Mickey put a hand on my shoulder to keep me down. "What did he tell you?"

I shook my head. "Like you weren't listening at the door."

He looked impatient. "Listen, this isn't a game. If I didn't have probable cause, I wouldn't have brought him in."

"So Amanda placed him at the scene?"

Mickey's eyes narrowed.

"But she ran away while they were still arguing, so she didn't see Joel actually attack Gordon."

His eyes got narrower.

"So that and a Matchbox car is your case," I said.

"The investigation is ongoing."

"You don't really have anything, do you? The fire was an accident, not a deliberate attempt to cover up a murder. What really killed Gordon will decide who you can pin this on—Joel or Amanda and friends."

Was it my imagination, or did I see a little admiration in his eyes. "No comment." His robot tone softened, his thumb smoothed the collar on my silk blouse. "What are you doing for dinner tonight?"

I ignored him. "Did Gordon die by violence, or from smoke inhalation?"

"The coroner's report will be released Friday. You can find out then, like everyone else." He leaned in closer, and I got a whiff of aftershave. Was that Polo? I liked Polo. "Dinner?"

"I've got a date." I liked the look that brought to Mickey's face.

His hand dropped from my shoulder. "Anyone I know?"

I only smirked.

"Whoever it is, I hope he's been vaccinated for cooties."

I was dying for a salami-and-capocollo sub, but I didn't need the meat or the nitrites. So I by-passed the Number 2 and settled for the Number 12, mozzarella-and-tomato, at The Fill Yer Belly Deli down the street from the stationhouse.

As I chewed, I made notes on my conversation with Joel. What could I trust in his story? On some level, he seemed to need my approval. Leftover sentiment from our childhood relationship? Or just an act? Short of hooking him up to a lie detector, I had no way of knowing. He'd gone to great lengths to protect Evan. Gordon had been in on his secret, and that would be a powerful bargaining chip if Joel had threatened to end the partnership. Joel would have had every reason to shut down the partnership permanently.

But why speak to me? What was my part in this? To plant doubt in the mind of the public? Or if it wound up that he *did* kill Gordon, was he playing on my sympathy to be sure the real reason for the murder never came out? In any case, how could I write a story that wouldn't make me look like a complete fool if it fell apart later? I had to protect myself.

"Hey, Andie." Officer Billy Birdsey sat down at the tiny table next to me, with a bag of potato chips and a sub sandwich the size of an actual submarine. He flushed. "I'm really sorry about that…what happened when, er, I was searching your bag. I had to do that."

"Of course, you did. Don't worry about it."

Billy's face turned sunny again, making me smile.

"Do you like being a cop?" I asked as he ripped open the chip bag.

"Sure. I like helping people, keeping the peace—though it's usually pretty quiet anyway. Mostly I chase kids hanging out by the liquor store, trying to con someone into buying them beer. That's gotten worse since the state raised the drinking age to twenty-one." He took a chomp out of his overstuffed sub. "But then that little girl getting killed, and the fire and the other homi—the alleged homicide sure shook things up."

I gave some attention to sucking up the last of my Diet

Pepsi. Here we were, just two old classmates chatting about the weather. And there's too much ice in my drink.

"Are you getting close to finding out exactly what happened with all that?" I hoped the "you" made Billy feel good about being part of this crack team of investigators, good enough to share some of his pride with me.

Billy did puff up a little. "I wouldn't know much. The county detectives like Mickey are handling the real investigation. They had to bring the city guys into it, to get a warrant and go over to that guy de Porres' apartment."

"Oh, right. He lived in the city. Probably not in my neighborhood, though."

Billy laughed. "Yeah, he had some ritzy place. Gold faucets and velvet wallpaper in the bathroom even."

"You saw it?"

"Nah, I overheard the guys talking. They just came back to report to Mickey."

I helped myself to one of his chips. "Did they say if they found anything that's helping with the, er, *alleged* murder?"

Billy frowned. "Can't say for sure. Mickey made me shut the door." He brightened. "But after they left, Mickey looked awfully excited and headed out. Told the desk sergeant he was going to the mayor's." Billy crammed the remainder of his sandwich into his mouth, rubbed his hands together. "Gotta go. Mickey told me to go pick up Ray Dougherty and bring him back to the house around two. You can finish my chips if you want."

My second-most satisfying conversation of the day.

RAY DOUGHERTY AGAIN. It couldn't be a coincidence. Cat was right. Somehow he was linked to de Porres. But I didn't know enough about his case to see the connection. But maybe my first love, the public library, would help me out.

I found the T-shaped brick building after a few wrong turns. I parked down the street, leaving the windows open to keep the VW from turning into a convection oven.

Once through the red double doors, I stopped first at the circulation desk. No librarian, but I did see a nameplate.

"Grace Kelly?" I read out loud.

"Yes?" A head poked around a nearby bookshelf, eyes squinting through black-framed glasses. Grace still more closely resembled Ruth Buzzi. Her dark hair was slicked behind her ears, and I could see her jawline hadn't shortened over the years.

I smiled, went through my by-now routine: "You probably don't remember me but—"

"Of course, Andrealisa!" She had been schoolmarmish even in kindergarten and had never called me Andie. "I knew you were around—you can't keep secrets in this town. We subscribe to the *Moon* here, you know. We stopped it for a while, but got complaints. I even read that book of yours when it came in a few years ago, before I logged it in and filed it in the 613s."

Grace emerged from behind the stacks—and I saw *she* was stacked. Little Grace now had a killer body. "Oh, I've thought about writing a book myself," she continued. "I have all these great ideas! But I'm so busy. Well, one of these days."

How come you never hear anyone say to a brain surgeon, *Someday, when I have the time, I'm going to perform a frontal lobotomy?* But who was I to kill Grace's dream? I said instead, "With this job, it would be like a busman's holiday."

"Oh, this is just what I do in the daytime. Actually, I'm a singer."

"Really? Do you have a gig around here? Maybe I can come by and hear you."

Her face lit up. "Every Thursday night I'm at The Rock Bottom. Come on down!"

"Sure. Thursday."

"Great! So, what can I do you for today?"

"I'm looking for back issues of the *Record* from 1979, August to December." Those were the dates of Ray's arrest and later sentencing in the clipping, as I remembered.

"Those will all be on microfiche. You go sit by the viewer and

I'll bring them over." She gave me a conspiratorial look. "Is this for a story you're working on?"

"Could be."

"How exciting!" She skipped off and soon returned with a cardboard box with about ten small boxes of reels. "Usually we don't give out more than five at a time, so no one hogs the viewer," she whispered. "But it doesn't get much use in the summer, with school out and all."

It was slow going, cranking through the microfiche page by page, looking for details on Ray Dougherty's arrest and trial in white on black. I would have worked up a sweat, but luckily the taxpayers had sprung for air-conditioning since I was last in the library.

After August, when the arrest and investigation had made the front page for a few days, there was little follow-up coverage until the Federal trial three months later. I didn't learn much new, except that the Mustang had been registered to and reported stolen by one Ruben Baracas, who had never reclaimed the car and was himself reported missing. Two surprises, though: Ray had been represented by Kenneth Whalen, mayor and, it seemed, pro bono attorney. And somehow Doreen had come up with $250,000 to post Ray's bail after his initial arrest.

Then I found an item buried in the back of the news section, a week before Ray's sentencing in December.

Someone at the DEA had the cocaine retested and discovered that five of the ten bags seized contained only milk sugar, which is usually used to cut the pure drug for street sale. There seemed to be some disagreement among local and federal officials over whether all the bags had been tested the first time, or the same five had been tested twice. One DEA agent suggested that half the coke might have been substituted for the sugar while it was in custody. But no one seemed to know when in that five months a switch could have taken place.

In a bizarre twist, a police property-room clerk had been brought in for questioning—and had a heart attack right in the county prosecutor's office. His death had not been ruled suspicious. The sergeant's poor health had been one of the reasons he'd had that desk job in his last months before retirement.

Now I knew what Doreen's accusation against Mickey was based on. I didn't want to believe it. But where else *would* a cop get the kind of money needed to buy The Rock and convert the old grocery store into an upscale steakhouse? Maybe Mickey's obsession with that old case was really his fear that the original dealer would be found, and admit that the other five bags had been filled with coke until Mickey got his hands on them. Maybe the switch had been made before he'd even turned them in.

Maybe Mickey was the guy Ray was supposed to meet in the first place. His dad had taught him that whatever wasn't nailed down was up for grabs. What did my grandmother used to say? Something about the apple not falling far from the tree?

I dropped quarters into the viewer's coin slot to print out the articles about Ray. As the glossy negative images slid out of the machine, I looked them over again. They raised more questions than they answered, and I still didn't know if this had any connection to Gordon's murder.

Until I figured that out, I had to come up with a new angle for this week's *Moon*. Okay, Amanda had accidentally set the fire. But every other reporter would know that by tomorrow and it would be old news by my Thursday night deadline. The real story would be what had killed Gordon—the fire or whatever had prevented him from escaping it. Bullet to the heart, piano wire around the throat, a dent in the skull?

Mickey said the coroner's report wouldn't be released until Friday, too late for the *Moon*. So no matter how I played it up, the only thing I had for our readers was a self-serving interview with Joel saying he didn't do it. Not exactly the keg of dynamite Elise expected.

I returned the microfiche to Grace, who waved a good-bye. After tossing the photocopies through the open back window, I got in the car and steered toward The Barge. Once I turned onto

River Drive, I gave the gas pedal an extra nudge. I didn't want to cut it too close in meeting Jesse.

Right. Tonight I had a date. Or something like it. Checking my face in the rear-view mirror, I saw one of the microfiche copies rise up from the back seat. It swam in the air for a second or two, then floated out the passenger's side window and skipped down the street.

A swerve to the curb, a slam on the brakes, and a grope under a parked car for the now smudged paper. Not that it had been so readable before. In this fabulous age of computer technology, you'd think there'd be a more efficient way to retrieve archived material—

Holy Moly.

Now I knew who could supply the dynamite.

I spotted a pay phone and ransacked my purse, but I had used all my silver to make the photocopies. The deli was down the block. A minute later, I walked out with a fistful of quarters. And another Diet Pepsi. The counter guy wouldn't give me change unless I bought something.

"Cat, I need your help," I said after the operator had told me to please deposit $2.75 for the first three minutes. I took a deep slurp through the soda straw. Too much ice again. I set the drink on top of the phone kiosk.

"*You* need *my* help?" She sounded puzzled but pleased.

"I don't know if it would even be filed yet, but do you think you can go on your Web and find the autopsy report on Gordon de Porres—you know, the guy who died in the fire last week? That is, if it won't get you into trouble."

I'd said the magic words. "I can do it. No problem."

"Okay, I'll call you after work tomorrow to see if you got it and come pick it up. Then I'll buy you a lobster dinner at The Beachcomber, and tell you about my date tonight with Jesse."

"You're going out with Mr. Smooth? And when did you break up with Doug?"

"I didn't, um, not really, we haven't been..." Catholic guilt was making me stammer. "This isn't really a date anyway, I mean...." My throat closed up. I reached up for the soda and knocked it over instead, dumping brown liquid and crushed ice down the front of my blouse. "Ewwww! Shit, shit, shit, shit, shit!"

"I didn't realize this was such a touchy subject," Cat said.

I DIDN'T HAVE time to drive home for a new wardrobe but I knew where to go for one. Juliet looked like she'd won the Publisher's Clearinghouse Sweepstakes when I walked into her shop, begged for a makeover and told her why.

"Honey, I have just the thing!" She pulled out a swathe of magenta dangling from a hanger by two skinny straps. "It's a surplice wrap dress, from the Sixties. A tie at the waist, a snap at the cleavage. Easy on. Easy off."

I came out of the dressing room feeling as self-conscious as when Cat and I would try on Easter outfits for our mother. "I don't know. Were women smaller in the Sixties? I have to wrap this pretty tight to keep it closed."

"Oh, Sis, you look great!" She insisted sky-high platform sandals were the finishing touch. She also re-did my makeup in a way I'd never be able to reproduce at home. I knew I'd never look this good again, ever.

Ten minutes later I wobbled up the ramp to The Barge. I didn't see any visible drool, but Jesse did open his eyes wider than I would have thought possible and breathed a whistle. Otherwise, he didn't say a word, but took my hand, tucked it into the crook of his arm and led me inside the floating restaurant.

The evening was a surprise. I had expected more of the same flirty banter that seemed to be Jesse's stock in trade. But instead, he asked questions, lots of them, about my job, about living in the city, about those years after I'd left town. I found myself talking about Cat, her struggles, and mine, in a way I hadn't been able to with anyone else in a long time. Maybe because Jesse had been open about his own problems with his sister, I figured he'd understand.

But would this be all that we had in common? Would we just turn into a two-member support group? I'd had that before—relationships with guys who felt they had to "rescue" me or whose hang-ups were worse than mine. That became all it was, dueling dysfunctions. Doug had been okay, though, caring and concerned in an offhand way, never making me feel guilty for taking off when my mother needed help with Cat. But until recently, I hadn't had sole responsibility. What right had I to involve anyone in that?

And what was I doing now? Already thinking about Doug in the past tense. Already obsessing over my future with Jesse after just an hour of pleasant conversation and a plate of shrimp scampi?

And I conveniently kept forgetting one other detail: Jesse may look really good in a khaki blazer, but I couldn't eliminate him as a suspect in Gordon's death.

Still, the flickering candlelight, the gentle rocking of the dining room in rhythm with the river, and my one glass of wine were lulling me into feeling mighty cozy with a possible murderer. It seemed perfectly natural that we should share a Mississippi Mudpie for dessert and fight over the last chocolate-mousse mouthful.

The sky was still rosy over the cliffs when Jesse steered me outside the restaurant onto the pier. We stood for a while watching the city lights compete with the stars. A full-sailed sloop glided toward us, pushed by a steady breeze off the water. Then the wind shifted suddenly, hitting me with an acrid smell that made me cringe.

Jesse stepped in front of me as if to block it. "Sorry. Stinks like it's still burning, doesn't it?" He looked upriver. "Except for the foundation, you can't even see were the site was anymore. Amazing. I never thought it would all go up that fast. I'd called it in right away. "

"You reported the fire?"

"Yeah."

"What were you doing there?"

"I had gone back to the trailer for some paperwork on our insurance problem. I saw the flames and even tried to go after it with a fire extinguisher from the trailer. But then one of the propane tanks blew."

"So you were on the site when the fire started."

"Yeah. I told Giamonte that. Hey, look." He squatted down, pointing at a spot on the piling, below the dock. "The first time I played hooky from Holy Moly, I carved that, lying on my stomach. An early display of self-confidence."

It took me a minute to find my voice. "It's too dark. I can't read what it says."

He stood up, stepped closer and slowly unsheathed a smile. "Jesse Quindlen the Greatest."

"And are you?" All I could smell was him now. Was he wearing Polo? I love Polo.

"*You* tell *me*." He leaned in.

I closed my eyes.

Lights pulsed behind my lids. I felt my whole body vibrating. It was like sirens went off, as if from far away, then closer, closer…

Wow.

Then I realized they were real sirens. I opened my eyes. Both black-and-whites and blue-and-whites screeched into the parking lot. A Klaxon blared off the river. I heard shouting from all directions.

A Coast Guard cruiser was roaring up to the sailboat, now drifting as if rudderless in front of us. With the next breeze, it turned, showing us the gold script on its stern: *Bonny Kate.*

• *Chapter 14* •

IN THE CHAOS that followed, Jesse and I were largely ignored, so we had a front-row seat on the action. Suddenly I would have given my right arm to work for a daily paper again. Though without a right arm, I might have trouble typing up the story.

Someone from the river patrol had boarded the sailboat to guide it into a slip, while a uniformed cop sprinted down the pier, did a long-jump onto the deck and crept toward the cabin, gun drawn. A second later, he called out for someone to radio for an ambulance.

Into the middle of it all strode Mickey. He did a double take when he saw me, his eyes taking me in from platform sandals to spaghetti straps. He nearly grinned, then saw Jesse behind me, his hands on my shoulders.

I pulled away from Jesse. "Mickey, that's the mayor's boat, isn't it? What happened?"

It was clear he didn't want to answer, but just then the ambulance rolled up to the end of the pier, two attendants jumped out with a gurney and raced toward us. "Just a distress call."

"Oh, yeah? That's why these guys have their weapons out? Is that usual in a medical emergency?"

Mickey turned to another cop nearby. "Get everybody out of here who's not authorized." Then he grabbed for the mooring line tossed to him by the river patrol, pulled the sailboat in close to the dock and secured it to a cleat.

The cop was Billy Birdsey, who looked apologetically past me to Jesse. "Sorry. You heard him. We have to clear the area."

"No problem, Billy." Jesse took my arm firmly and headed me down the pier.

"Walk slow, Jess. I want to see who they carry off that boat."

"Give it a rest, Brenda Starr. I think we'd better get out of here."

I stopped abruptly, nearly losing my balance on those damned heels. "I can't." And I couldn't. "I have to find out what's going on." And I had to. "You know, that's my job."

Something—I hoped disappointment—flashed on Jesse's face, but he nodded. "Do you want me to stay with you?"

Yes.

No.

Maybe so.

"I don't know how long it's going to take."

He nodded again. "We'll have to do this again sometime." He ran a finger slowly along a spaghetti strap. "And you can wear this again." Then he smoothed back my bangs and brushed his lips against my forehead. As he walked away, "Give me a call when this is over."

When *what's* over? This night? This story? This truly unpredictable life that now seemed to be mine?

I heard clattering behind me. Flanked by EMTs, the gurney was bumping down the last stretch of the pier. Its white-haired cargo was unmistakable, even though an oxygen mask was covering the lower half of Ken Whalen's face.

SOMEWHERE AROUND MIDNIGHT I drove to my apartment to

change, feed a groggy Ben and check messages, but I was back at the hospital within ninety minutes. If I were going to learn anything new, it would be at Saint Mary's.

Of course, I wasn't the only one with that idea. The word had gotten out of this latest turn in the events surrounding Joel Hartt, and TV news crews, local reporters, even another tabloid hack were hunkered down across from the entrance, ambushing anyone who might offer information. We weren't allowed inside the building, but bits and pieces filtered out: The police had merely been trying to bring Ken Whalen in for "questioning" on the de Porres case, when the distress call had come. No explanation on why this would require a whole police squadron and the Coast Guard. An officer found Mr. Whalen onboard his sailboat, collapsed from a heart attack. The mayor was now in critical but stable condition.

Soon after I'd arrived, Kathleen Whalen had been brought to the emergency entrance by a cop car and hustled inside. As the other newshounds rushed forward, my mind jumped to Evan. If his aunt was here and his father was in jail, who was watching the boy overnight? Maybe Gina had been able to get Joel out that afternoon. For some reason, that thought comforted me.

As the night wore on, I was surprised at how pumped I felt. Of course, it could have been the ten cups of caffeine and three bags of Peanut M&Ms. An enterprising local had come by with his lunch-wagon, so we buzzards were amply supplied with snack foods, stale bagels and coffee. I brought a cup and a Hostess Twinkie to Billy Birdsey, who was guarding the hospital doors.

An instant camaraderie sprang up among the newsies that stayed on the scene. I was the only woman there, but once I told them this was my first stakeout and they'd gotten the usual *Moon* jokes out of their systems, they'd offered me NoDoz and a seat at their low-stakes poker game. Sitting cross-legged in the back of a TV van, I checked my hand and raised them three Cheez-Its.

As the sky lightened, we kidded about staging a coup, if only to gain access to the hospital bathroom. Feeno Heath, the other tabloid reporter, a raw-boned Australian I was starting to take a liking to, said that too bad he didn't have his lab coat with him. He'd bought it years ago to get inside a hospital morgue in Los Angeles and photograph a heavy-metal rocker who had OD'd. "Caught him in his cooler drawer," Heath said. "'*Stab on a Slab*' made my career."

I held in a laugh, because, in my case, the bladder issue was getting serious. It was getting on to 9 a.m. I couldn't hold out much longer. "Cover me, boys! I'm going in!"

They cheered me on as I trotted up the stone steps. But Billy Birdsey held up a hand.

"Billy, there's a ladies' room right by the admissions desk. I can see it from here. If I'm not out one-two-three, you can come in after me."

He hesitated, but then must have remembered the Twinkie. "Okay, Andie, but be quick. I could get in trouble."

"I wouldn't want that. Thanks."

Pushing through the bathroom door, I nearly knocked over an elderly man and his very full water bucket. The three white hairs remaining on his head stood up.

"Sorry, please! You no want go in there!"

One look and I knew he was right. I gestured to the other stall. "How about—?"

He shook his head. "That one very worse."

I grimaced. "I'll take your word for it."

As I left the rest room, Billy turned and lifted his chin. I walked toward him to ask permission to find another ladies' facility. Then I heard the shouts. Even the blasé crew at the admissions desk turned to look.

Through the glass doors I saw a county car pull up to the curb. Mickey jumped from the front passenger seat to open the rear door for a very tall, very thin, nearly bald guy in a gray suit—his boss, I guessed, since I couldn't imagine Mickey extending that courtesy to anyone else. Within seconds, they were surrounded by my stakeout pals as well as a few new faces. A shoving match started. Billy Birdsey quickly pushed his way out the door, either to offer crowd control or to watch the fight.

Good, I thought. Now I'll sneak off and find another... Then it hit me that I was inside the hospital and nobody was paying any attention to me. *Where, oh where, did Ken Whalen go? Oh, where, oh, where could he be?* I hummed to myself.

Following the signs to the ICU seemed my best bet. Okay, up one of the elevators to the fourth floor. I stepped out, and looked around. A nurse's station was to my left and I knew I wasn't going to get past it without a visitor's pass. Far down the hall I saw a cop stretch his arms overhead, yawn, then check his watch. The night shift was over, probably. Maybe I could claim to be his replacement. But I knew I wasn't going to get past him without a badge or a gun.

Now what was I going to do?

Better yet, what would Cat do? Probably start a fire in a linen closet to distract them all. That nearly made me laugh out loud, but wasn't an option.

Yet.

An elevator dinged behind me. The doors opened on Sister Connie struggling with two stuffed shopping bags. One fell over and, as she bent to pick up the Raggedy Ann that had tumbled out, I grabbed the other bag and shoved the elevator door back as it started to close.

"Sister, can I help you with those?"

"Thank you, child."

Both bags in hand, I followed the nun down the hall.

"Good morning, Sister," the two nurses at the desk called out nearly in unison.

"God bless you, girls," she replied.

She had gotten me past the first checkpoint. Maybe I could figure a way to hide out until the changing of the police guard, and sneak in somehow. I almost regretted not having a camera on me. Okay, maybe I couldn't stomach taking a deathbed shot of Kenneth Whalen for the *Moon*, but it would make a nice souvenir for Feeno.

"Nice haul you have here, Sister," I said as I matched her elderly penguin pace. She didn't seem to recognize me, which was just as well.

"Used toys for the children's ward. We put a donation box out last Sunday and these are the last of them."

"Some look brand-new."

She *tsk-tsked* loudly. "Youngsters today are spoiled brats. They play with something once and forget all about it the next day and then scream for the next mindless time-waster they see on TV. And the idiot parents buy it for them." She fingered the rosary at her waist as if saying a silent prayer for their greedy souls.

"Sister, the sign says the children's ward is this way.' I gestured down a corridor to our right.

She kept going straight. "I need to call on an old friend first."

I nearly stopped breathing when she walked up to the cop leaning against the wall.

"This is Kenneth Whalen's room, isn't it, Officer?"

"Yes, Sister." He glanced at me.

I kept my eyes down, trying to look meek and mournful. Maybe he'd think I was a nun-in-training.

"I'm here at the request of the family. May we go in?"

Another glance at me, but I guessed by the O'FENNESSEY squeezed onto his nametag that he wouldn't dare question anyone in a habit. "Yes, Sister."

The door closed behind us. The room held two beds, one empty. Around the other, a curtain was drawn, and on the far side all I could see was a chair back and an elbow.

I heard a stifled sob, and stepped back into the corner, quietly setting the bags down.

"Sweetheart, don't try to talk. Don't." Kathleen's voice was hoarse and full of tears.

I felt my own eyes fill and closed them.

"*You're* sorry, Kenny? Oh, my God. Oh, my God."

The nun moved forward. "Kathleen, dear. It's Sister Constance."

The chair scraped back and I moved farther into the shadows.

"Has he seen a priest, Kathleen?"

"What, Sister? No, no. He doesn't want one. I hoped you could convince him. That's why I called you."

"Kenneth Francis Xavier Whalen, now you to listen to me. Whatever you've done, you must make your peace with God. If not for your own sake, then for Kathleen's."

Sister Connie was in full Mother Superior mode. It had the same chilling effect on me now as it had when I was a kid. I peeked behind the half-open door on my right. A closet. Khaki slacks, bright green polo shirt and navy blue windbreaker hung up, a pair of boating shoes on the floor.

"Kenny, yes, for my sake." Kathleen's voice cracked.

I moved along the wall to a second door. A winner. I carefully closed it behind me. I couldn't risk snapping on the light, so I groped my way into the bathroom, guided by the handicap rail.

Voices out in the hall. A door opening. More noise.

"Okay, O'Fennessey, take a break." *Mickey.* "Could you please give us a moment here, Mrs. Whalen? Sister?"

"Aren't you the Giamonte boy?" Sister Connie sounded irritated.

"Yes, Sister." Mickey's voice was almost contrite.

"Are you staying out of trouble?"

"More or less, Sister. I'm a cop now, remember?"

"Hmmm, yes. Isn't *that* a surprise for the Ages," she said.

BEFORE THE DOOR closed again, I had composed myself. I didn't hear anything more, so I slowly turned the knob, opened the door a crack and nearly slammed it shut again.

The tall, thin guy I'd seen outside was leaning against the foot of the empty bed, barely five feet away.

Mickey was on the other side of him, parting the other bed's curtain. "Looks like he's asleep," he said.

"Better he should sleep forever than to face this. Poor sorry bastard." The Thin Man had a soft but remarkably high-pitched voice. "He didn't want to talk to a lawyer?"

Mickey turned. I jumped back from the door.

"We made him aware of the charges. Read him his rights. He waived them." Mickey sighed. "I even brought in Gina Fine for him."

Gina was here? I must have missed her when I went home to change.

"He talked to her. But then reminded me he *is* a lawyer and he was advising himself to confess." Mickey snorted. "The guy's still a piece of work."

"You're sure he knew what he was saying? He's under an oxygen tent, fer chrissake."

I heard springs creak, twice. They must be sitting on the unused bed now. Getting nice and comfortable.

"He knew. I told him what we found at de Porres' place, the papers and the stuff off his computer. Whalen offered up that de Porres was trying to use an old drug deal to blackmail the mayor into giving up that property lined up for the high school."

"Did Ken admit to his part in the cocaine switch?"

What? Did I hear that right? I nearly called out to them to speak up.

"Yeah. Damnedest thing, how all that tied in. Last week Hartt calls de Porres' family in South America. A cousin flies up to claim the body for burial. Who does it turn out to be but Ruben Baracas—the guy who reported the Mustang missing, the one I caught Ray Dougherty driving. What, this guy thought I'd forget his name after only thirteen years?"

"You told me Baracas didn't know about the drug-running de Porres was doing back then."

"Of course he says no. But he's scared shitless and more than willing to tell us what he does know. De Porres had him sign some papers for the car and later say it was stolen. Then he goes back home to Venezuela or wherever. Yesterday Ray ID'd Baracas as the guy who hired him to drive the Mustang around—"

"Because they already knew the Feds were on to them."

"Yeah, they knew they were being watched. That's why de Porres brought the mayor in, though Whalen didn't know de Porres was behind it. Back then they shared the same bookmaker, the old guy, K.C.'s father, who used to run the candy store. De Porres knew Whalen always owed a bundle to some loan shark or another. He filed that info away, and went off to do his deals in South America. Then when de Porres needed him, he had one of the local sharks contact the mayor and offer him this fabulous opportunity to cancel his debt by switching the coke."

"It's hard to think Kathleen finally got him to stop gambling, and now it comes back to haunt him." The Thin Man sighed big. "Poor sorry bastard."

"Since he's Ray's uncle, Whalen knew he could take his case pro bono and no one would think it was funny. He could snatch the coke while it was in custody, without the dealers having to expose their own couriers. They only lost half the load. Of course, that one was just a dummy drop for another shipment unloaded farther up the river."

"Ken had to know how bad this was."

"I don't think he knew at first that the Feds were involved," Mickey said. "Probably he thought he could make the switch and still get Ray off. But once the DEA took over, they wouldn't let Ray go. I think that was eating Ken up. He got him the best deal he could. I found out Ken raised the bail bond for Ray's wife and funneled the family money over the years. Kathleen even takes care of Doreen Dougherty's mother, gratis." Mickey was quiet for a minute. "And I helped those assholes run their game. Spotting that missing taillight. I gave them a police escort."

"Don't beat yourself up, Mickey. That doofus Ray would have driven in circles for days. The security guys at the tanks would have caught him eventually."

"Worse thing is I wouldn't have even looked into this angle if it hadn't been for that tabloid reporter."

The Thin Man chuckled. "Your girlfriend at the *Moon*."

My ears perked so far up I almost hurt myself.

"Rinaldi? My girlfriend? Nah." For some irrational reason, that miffed me. "But I owe her one. If her story hadn't mentioned that de Porres' real first name was 'Godofredo,' I wouldn't have made the connection. I remembered that was who the Feds were looking for, the only name they had. Ray heard Baracas say it that night."

"And that whole time de Porres wasn't even in the country."

"Nope, but he was pulling the strings. Then he comes back a year later and suddenly has the cash to buy into a partnership with Joel Hartt."

"Then wants to get out of it ten years later."

"Yeah. Hartt told us this morning that de Porres was finagling with joint funds, pocketing money that should have gone into insurance, higher-quality building materials and other things. Instead, it was going toward a stake for his own development deals."

"I guess de Porres figured that was less risky than trying to be the next Pablo Escobar. Times have changed."

"But not for greed. The way Whalen tells it, he blocked de Porres' bid for the land, and convinced the town council to float a bond for a new high school. But de Porres had this ace in the hole and he played it. Phone records show that someone called the Whalen house from the construction site trailer that night. Who else but de Porres, to get Whalen there?"

"But did anyone see Ken at the site?" The Thin Man seemed desperate to find a loophole in the story, even though the mayor seemed to have already confessed to the crime.

"We had reports of his boat on the river. He even waved to a busboy sneaking a cigarette on The Barge pier. Easy to dock near the site and meet de Porres, who does his song-and-dance about ceding the property, then threatens to tell the council about Whalen's past. Cute touch, bringing that Matchbox car as a little reminder of what a fine, upstanding citizen the mayor wasn't. The guy had *cojones*. But the mayor had a two-by-four and creases his skull with it, knocks him three stories into the basement and breaks his neck. He thought he cut a break himself when the fire started. But unlucky for him, the falling body knocked over some fireboard, which covers the corpse and preserves the evidence."

"Poor sorry bastard." I was beginning to see that The Boss lacked originality of expression. "Good work on this one, though, Mickey."

"Good work? Feels more like dumb luck." Was that Mickey being modest? "Man, I have to pee. Been drinking sludge all night."

I don't know how long I'd been holding my breath, but without thinking I let it out in a gush that sounded like a death rattle. Which it would be if Mickey found me.

"What was that?" Mickey said.

"Katie...?" Whalen already sounded like a ghost.

"Jeez, is that him?" said Mickey. "Maybe we'd better get the doctor."

Their footsteps moved them away from me. "Kenny? Kenny, it's me, Tom Wainwright, buddy. You want Kathleen? I'll get her for you." Under his breath, "Poor sorry bastard. Jesus, Mickey, what are we gonna do? Take him out of here in handcuffs? We're lucky, he makes it to lunchtime. We write up a statement, get him to sign it. That's all we can do."

"Right." More footsteps. "What are these kids' toys doing here?"

A door opened. I got into sprint position.

A few minutes passed. Softer footsteps entered the room.

"Katie...?"

"Here I am, Kenny."

Heavier shoes and rustling skirts. "Kenneth, I've called for Father to come in to you." I almost didn't recognize Sister

Connie's voice, it was so gentle. "Otherwise, I'd be missing your company in Heaven, wouldn't I? And you never did finish telling me that joke about the priest, the rabbi and the Jehovah's Witness."

As I slipped out of the bathroom, I snagged the shopping bags and tiptoed through the open door. Luckily, O'Fennessey wasn't back at his post. He, the Thin Man and Mickey were by the nurses' station, their backs to me. I ducked back in the doorway. Funny, how easily "The Hail Mary" came into my head, without even trying to remember the words, especially the last part.

Holy Mary, Mother of God, pray for us sinners.

How many would I need to say to wipe my slate clean?

Now and at the hour of our death.

I was hoping that wouldn't be soon.

Amen.

Amen.

I had recited the prayer to myself five times before Sister Connie came out, frowned at me and led me back down the hall. Said three more before we reached the intersection and made the left toward the children's ward. When I was sure we were out of Mickey's sight, I said another one, for good measure.

Maybe it would also count as an act of penance that I helped Sister distribute some of the toys and games to the kids in their hospital beds.

They greeted her like an old friend. She let them pick out their own, chatting nonstop. "Richard, you look just like that Captain Picard on *Star Trek*" to one boy who chose a plastic model of the Starship Enterprise and whose hair had been lost to chemotherapy. "Elizabeth, didn't I tell you not to chew on your fingernails? I said it would give you a pain in your tummy, didn't I?" to an appendectomy patient who pulled out the Raggedy Ann and hugged it close.

We took the few remaining toys to the common playroom and set them on the shelves. I held out the folded shopping bags and asked Sister Connie if she needed help with anything else.

"That's it for now. God bless you, Andrealisa."

I nearly dropped the bags. She'd said my name.

"And give my blessings to Caterina when next you talk to her." She tucked the bags under her arm and waddled away.

THE CLOSEST STAIRWELL led me to an exit door behind the hospital. I skirted back around to the parking lot, trying to blend in with the rest of the reporters. Only Feeno Heath had noticed how long I was missing.

He pulled me aside. "Whaddya do, Rinaldi? Fall in?" But his eyes crinkled. "Or did you find a spare lab coat? Come on, you can tell your old mate Feeno."

"Found something even better. A spare penguin."

"Hey, Wainwright's coming back out!" someone yelled, and the stampede began again.

"Who is he?" I asked Feeno.

"Thomas Wainwright, county prosecutor, you jenny. Spokesman for murder and mayhem."

Tall Thin Bald Guy stopped on the steps, Mickey at his side. He held up both hands to stem the questions shouted at him, and waited until the crowd had quieted. I was impressed that they obeyed.

"Approximately ten minutes ago, Mayor Kenneth Whalen died"—murmurs rose up and Wainright again showed us his palms—"as the result of a massive heart attack he suffered last night. As I am sure all of you are already aware, this occurred while he was being pursued for questioning in the death of Gordon de Porres last Thursday. While we cannot give details as to what we learned from Mr. Whalen at this time, the Criminal Investigations Bureau is satisfied that his statement has brought us to a conclusion of this case. More information will be forthcoming shortly. I appreciate your patience. Thank you."

AROUND NOON, I stumbled into the *Moon*, gripping my lunch: a Milky Way and twelve-ounce Styrofoam cup. It was now official:

In the last sixteen hours, I had drunk my entire body weight in coffee.

"Great dress last night," Dovie greeted me. "Fuchsia is really your color." At my confused look, she added, "You were on the 11 o'clock news. On the dock when they were pulling in that mayor's sailboat."

I started to close my eyes, but reconsidered. I might never be able to open them again. "Who else knows I was there?"

"Everybody. Oh, yeah, and Mr. Eaton said to check in with him when he gets back from his meeting with the publisher."

Great. There wasn't enough French Roast in the world to get me through this day.

Slumped at my desk, I thumbed through the city newspapers, yesterday's that I had left unread and today's that I'd picked up at the corner kiosk. Elsewhere in the world, a lot had happened during the past forty-eight hours. President Bush had declared that Democratic candidate Bill Clinton was offering the American people an economic plan of "smoke and mirrors." Unemployment was at an eight-year high. Doctors had finally admitted that the tumor they had removed from Pope John Paul II's colon last week had been malignant. And cocaine kingpin Pablo Escobar had wrested guns from his prison guards as Colombian officials came to transfer him to a military jail, and then escaped as soldiers stormed the ramparts.

Meanwhile, I had impersonated a nun to get into a dying killer's hospital room and eavesdropped on his second-hand confession while I was in the loo.

No point in stalling the inevitable. Pen in hand, I flipped through my notebook. Now that Ken Whalen had been identified as Gordon de Porres' murderer, my interview with Joel was nearly useless. I had plenty of inside dope on Whalen's association with de Porres and the drug smuggling, but how could I justify revealing information I'd overheard from the other side of a bathroom door? More important, I hadn't taped it. No one's word but mine.

Who could I get to confirm it? I knew I couldn't ask Mickey. He'd said he owed me one, but he would probably just arrest me for unlawful trespass instead. And it was only Wednesday, still another day until deadline.

Whom could I talk to? I tapped the ballpoint against my forehead. Who, who, who, who...? The pen clattered onto the desk. Kathleen. The grieving widow.

Just the thought shamed me. Only complete cynics go after the deceased's loved ones, ambush them when they are most vulnerable.

It wouldn't be an ambush, though, I told myself. I would be respectful. I would offer Ken's side of the story, a story about a good man driven to desperate measures. First, his rise as a promising young lawyer and politician undone by all-too-human flaws that kept him from pursuing higher state office. Redeemed by the love of a good woman, he becomes a beloved public figure trying to do right by his community, fighting to give their children a better education, a high school close to home. But he cannot escape his past.

Greed, in the form of Gordon de Porres, threatens his hope of salvation.

Yes, Kathleen would want to set the record straight.

Nice fantasy. But it couldn't hurt to try. It would be an angle our readers would love.

Maybe Joel could help me set up a meeting with her. But where would he be now? No answer at his house. Still in jail? Oh, well. I'd start without Kathleen.

I swiveled to face the computer and, without allowing myself to think too much, began keying in my adventures of the previous night. The story poured out, a foaming, toxic stream of consciousness. "As Mayor Kenneth Francis Xavier Whalen lay below-decks, clutching his chest and gasping for air, the *Bonny Kate* twisted in the wind, the graceful sloop directionless without its captain. Now, justice was closing in by land and sea. Did Whalen use his ever-shortening breaths to beg His Maker for forgiveness or to curse the ill wind that had blown him off course?"

I didn't feel like I was writing so much as channeling some 1930s sob sister. But somewhere in the process it finally hit me what tabloids offer their readers: a graphic lesson in morality. So, in some respects The *Moon* was just a more colorful version of The Catholic National Register.

I hit "Store" just as the phone rang.

"Hey, Andie. It's Pas."

It took me a second to switch mental gears and recognize the voice of Dana Pasquaconiglia. She was my former managing editor on the upstate paper and still a friend.

"I just heard that Lacey Stillwater is retiring from Lifestyles." Dana's Boston accent was music to my ears. "Not exactly the rocket science you're used to, but if you're interested in the spot, I'll bring your name up to Jack. Everybody knows the trouble you had in the city. But, hey, enough time passes..."

It would be a step down, careerwise, but with a chance to rise again. I'd be farther from Cat, but she seemed to be doing okay. And I would be closer to Doug. Maybe a second chance for everything. "You're a pal, Pas."

"It's for purely selfish reasons. I'm in a hive of WASPs up here. None of them appreciates my red sauce. They'd just as soon put ketchup on their macaroni. This keeps up, I'm gonna have to move back to the North End."

"Keep the pot boiling, and maybe I'll see you soon. Thanks again."

I scrolled through the pulsating light gray type on the dusty black background, rereading until the cursor flashed negative-positive on the period of the last sentence: "And now Ken Whalen was dead, the captain of his own fate."

It was hokey. It was hyperbolic. It was the *Moon*. And it would never see print.

With another job on the horizon, I didn't need to feel obligated to this one. No more stakeouts, no more jailhouse interviews. I would soon be editing stuff like "A Dozen Delicious Chicken Dishes" and "Budget-Wise Decorating: Create Curtains from Bed Sheets!" I was almost looking forward to it.

The keyboard blurred. I blinked to clear my eyes, hit "Delete" and headed for the ladies' room.

I splashed water on my face, rooted in my bag for a comb and for something like Spackle to cover up my raccoon eyes. The one good thing: Since I hadn't slept, my clothes didn't look slept in. I could at least look somewhat professional when I went in to face Colin.

Dovie popped her head in. "Mr. Eaton came by your desk again. He wants you in his office right away."

Colin was pacing back and forth, hair raked through, shirttail untucked, a wet spot on the front of his trousers. And I'd been worried about *my* appearance.

"Ah, you. Good, good." He was actually rubbing his hands together. "I see you were right in the thick of things with this new development on the Hartt story. Brilliant. So, what do you have for me?"

"Contempt" would be my knee-jerk answer, and not necessarily true. "Pity" would be more like it.

Instead I said, "Well, I'm still waiting for confirmation on the details from some of my sources." Whomever they might be.

"Yes, but the cover headline and deck? We might as well get that to the composing room. What do you think of 'Emma's Dead Uncle, Captain of His Fate: Drug-smuggling mayor sinks in a sea of sex, greed and murder'? A little wordy perhaps…"

"'Sex'? I don't think sex is involved."

"Sex is always involved."

I did a mental double-take. "Wait—captain of his fate? Drug smuggling? Where did you come up with that?"

"It's in your own bloody story. I saw it on your terminal or monitor or whatever that thingummy is called."

"But I hit Delete. I…" I did, didn't I? I was *soooooo* tired.

"Get confirmation if you have to. You have time."

Unbelievable. The one time Colin actually reads a story off a computer screen, and it's this one. But I couldn't release it, not with all its corny melodrama, not with the possibility of getting another shot at a real newspaper. But I couldn't think straight enough to figure out how to talk Colin into letting me rewrite it into something more conservative. He, of course, loved it the way it was, sensational and sleazy.

My head was pounding and the caffeine wasn't working anymore. I had entered a whole new level of sleep deprivation. When Elise walked by wearing a well-tailored linen suit and a pair of flats, I was sure I was hallucinating.

I told Dovie I was going home.

Ben greeted me with a squeak, a tail wag and a puddle. My fault. I wasn't quick enough with the diaper. I just needed a nap, just a little nap, and then I could deal. I flipped through my CDs and found *Stickin' to My Guns*. Etta James in a black cowboy hat and purple neckerchief, not looking at all like an old cowhand from the Rio Grande, but someone to be reckoned with. Soon she was telling me, *You've got to do what you do/To take care of you/'Cuz it ain't wrong if it makes you feel right/whatever gets you through the night…*

It was dark when I woke up. All I could see was the red light on my answering machine signaling for my attention. Five blinks. Had it been flashing when I'd walked in the door? I couldn't remember. I couldn't even remember walking in the door.

I hit the New Messages button.

10:12 p.m., Tuesday, July 21 came up on the LED.

"Hi, honey, it's Doug!" Excited. "My flight from Seattle is leaving in a half hour. I thought I'd fly into the city first to see you before I head home. I've got some great news!" Concern. "Hope you're not working too hard." *Beep.*

4:37 a.m., Wednesday, July 22.

"Hey, Andie, are you there? Just got into the airport. I didn't want to wake you, but—" Puzzled. "I guess I didn't, huh? I'll try you when I get into the train station." *Beep.*

8:53 a.m., Wednesday, July 22.

"Um, Andrealisa." Hesitant. Full name, no honey. *Uh-oh.* "Sorry I missed you." Pause. "So I just took the train home." Ugh. Guilt grafted onto more guilt. "Listen, um, call me as soon as you, er, get in. We have to talk." *Beep.*

We have to talk. Nothing good ever came of talking.

3: 27 p.m., Wednesday, July 22.

"Yo, Big Sister. I got what you wanted." It was Cat, whispering.

What I wanted? *Oh, no.* I'd forgotten all about asking her for de Porres' autopsy report. Not that *it* mattered now.

"I heard about Ken Whalen this morning, too—it's all over the news. They're saying he killed that other guy and had a heart attack. How convenient. I'm thinking he's faking."

So she hadn't heard about Ken's death yet.

"So I'm printing out the medical records now, then we'll see—*What?*" This last was loud, impatient. "Jesus, Mary and Joseph! I'm just calling my sister, is that a crime? Yeah, it's long distance, so what's your problem? Listen, you want the dime for the call, I'll give you the friggin' dime. I'll give you all the dimes you want, HERE!"

A scream, a crash.

Beep.

• *Chapter 15* •

"I<small>S</small> C<small>ATERINA</small> <small>THERE</small>?" I tried not to worry that it was her room-mate who answered my sister's phone.

"No." Daisy's soft voice was swaddled in sleep.

"Daisy, where could she be at 10:30 at night?" My head hurt.

"She got into a fight at work today," she whispered, as if she didn't want the other voices in her head to hear. "Didn't Miss Ariel call you?"

So, soon after midnight I was back in a hospital. Not Saint Mary's, but Shore Medical. Not intensive care, but the psychiatric unit. It was well past visiting hours, but I'd called the social worker's emergency number and she was waiting for me in the lobby.

"They'll hold her for a few days, for evaluation," she said gently. "You know they have to do that when there's been a complaint."

"What happened?"

To my surprise, she made a goofy face and crossed her eyes. "This dopey clerk in the records office, she's always looking over Cat's shoulder. She was giving her a hard time about something, and Cat threw her purse at her." With regret, "Missed her, though."

"They're going to fire her, aren't they?"

"Well, I'm not sure yet. But she was doing a really good job before—"

"And she's out of the house, too, isn't she?"

She put her hand on my arm. "No, no. I'll take care of that. I'm going to talk to the board. It wasn't really Cat's fault, anyway. They changed one of her meds last week, when her disability insurance wouldn't cover it. I could see the new drug wasn't working as well."

A throbbing began behind my eyes. "I thought Medicaid covered all of her medications."

Ariel looked embarrassed. "Yeah, well. They took away the Medicaid drug benefit too. With her paycheck from the hospital, the agency said she was making $29 too much a month to qualify."

"For a twenty-hour-a-week minimum-wage job?" I was angry now. "This is ridiculous. How much is the other drug?"

"Uh, $364 a month." She held up a hand as I spit out a few swear words. "Don't worry, I'm fighting it." Her face brightened. "This little, uh, confrontation will be good, actually. It proves she needs to be on the Luvox, and then they'll have to pay for it."

To Ariel, all dark clouds had silver linings. How could I get the stuff *she* was on?

She escorted me up to my sister's room. A good thing, too, since the night nurse on that floor nearly jumped me as we walked past her desk. "What are you doing out of bed?" she hissed, dropping her knitting. It took two photo IDs and Ariel's insistence to convince her that I was *not* Cat, just an almost exact replica.

Ariel hugged me good-bye and promised to keep me updated.

Cat's room looked just like the one she had been in last December. Walls painted a soothing blue, dresser and lamp bolted in place, grates on the windows. If they were really afraid someone would leap out, why put the psych unit on the top floor? Just seemed more tempting up here.

Cat was asleep. They'd probably given her a sedative. I pulled the plastic chair up to her bed, leaned my elbows on the mattress and watched her chest rise and fall like a wave cresting, then collapsing, on the beach.

I wished we were there right now. Maybe we'd hit the boardwalk, get some cotton candy or a Kohr's soft-serve, ride the Ferris wheel. It's late, but I'll bet some of the arcades are still open...

A tug on my hair woke me. "I don't remember requesting a roommate." Cat was sitting up. "Why're you here?"

I lifted my head off my arms. A weak gray light oozed through the gaps in the blinds. "I came to hear the end of your message."

"Yeah, I got interrupted."

"Is that a reason to start lobbing handbags at people?"

"The bitch pissed me off. She talks constantly on the phone to her boyfriend, on hospital time, then she accuses *me*. She just wants me out of there. Afraid she'll catch whatever it is I've got."

I smiled. "She should be so lucky."

Cat smiled back, then looked guilty. "But I guess when the psych asked how I was feeling, I shouldn't have said I felt like killing her."

I winced.

"I was just telling the truth! He asked me, and I told him. I didn't say I *would* kill her. I just said I *felt* like it. Jeez. Then why did he ask me about my feelings?"

"Sister Connie was right," I sighed. "You *can't* tell a lie to save your life."

"Let's hope it doesn't come to that." She reached behind her, groping under her pillows.

"What are you looking for?"

"My pocketbook is back there. I hid it. You never know what goes on in your room after they've doped you up."

"I'll get it."

She leaned forward and from out between the bed and the wall I pulled a big canvas shoulder bag. We wouldn't wear matching clothes as kids, but we still had the same taste in accessories.

"Okay, now what do you want with it?"

"You take it."

"I don't know if I should. Won't this be Exhibit A at your trial?" I didn't want to take the bag. A counselor had warned me years ago that by giving in to her paranoia I was only enabling her obsessions.

"I don't want it lying around if I'm going to be here for a while. And the papers are in there."

"The papers?"

"The ones you asked for. The autopsy and—"

"Oh. Sure. Thanks."

I didn't have the heart to tell her I didn't need the autopsy report anymore. *Oh, no.* It hit me that if I hadn't asked her to look for it in the first place, she wouldn't be here now. It was now official: I had maxed out my guilt limit.

I gave Cat a hug.

"Okay then." She pushed me away. "Now go home." A frown. A panicked look. "I just gave you my purse, didn't I?"

"Yes, you did." I slung both bags over one shoulder and patted them for emphasis.

"Keep it with you."

"Okay."

"Repeat it."

"I'm keeping your purse with me."

"Good." A sigh. A smile. "But you'd better come back. You still owe me a lobster dinner at The Beachcomber."

It was 6:30 a.m. when my head hit the pillow. It seemed only a few minutes later that I opened my eyes to a gray muzzle aimed at my face.

It was Ben, head on paws, pleading silently for his breakfast.

Somehow he had climbed up the ladder to the bed loft. A new trick. Good dog.

As he chomped his chow, I took a shower. I was toweling my hair dry when I noticed the answering machine was still blinking, once. The call from yesterday that I had never played back? I hit the button expecting to hear Ariel telling me what I already knew.

4:59 p.m., Wednesday, July 22 appeared on the read-out.

"Hello, I'm calling from Craig Quentin Management. Mr. Quentin wants me to remind you that he will be at your apartment tomorrow morning for the inspection. You do not need to be present. However, if you wish to give him personal access to the premises, he will arrive around nine."

Tomorrow? That would be today.

Nine? It was now 9:15.

My intercom buzzed.

I broke all previous land-speed records in getting dressed. The elevator had been working only a few hours ago, but I prayed that the morning rush had put it out of commission as usual. I didn't want to face this guy today. And it was a little late to worry that pets weren't allowed in the building, but I had to get out of there with Ben. I didn't need to hasten my eviction from the only livable sweatbox in my price range.

I hid Ben's food sack and his bowls under the plastic bag in the kitchen trash bin, grabbed my sandals, scooped Ben into my shoulder bag and shot out the door, closing it softly behind me. I padded up one flight, waiting on the landing above. After a minute, I heard two sets of feet making their way up. An out-of-breath nasally voice: "Sorry. We'll be fixing the elevator once we get some cash in hand." A key clicked in the lock. "This one's small but we should ask for at least $250,000. It's got the river view."

Once the door closed behind them, I made my way to the street and the *Moon*. I was sure that life couldn't get any worse, until I stopped for a chocolate-chip scone at the corner coffee shop, set my bag on the counter and reached inside, Ben nipping playfully at my hand. I pulled out a blue nylon wallet.

It wasn't mine.

I peeled apart the Velcro. A dollar and a hospital I.D. card. Cat's. Pawing through the bag, I found a sheaf of printouts, a pack of cigarettes...and a can of pepper spray. Where did she get *that*? Even more disturbing, there wasn't enough loose change for a scone and coffee.

I got a paper instead, and was scanning the front page as I stepped off the elevator and nearly collided with Colin.

"Ah, there you are," he said. I wondered, not for the first time, if he even knew my name. "That story ready to go?"

My back was to the wall. I couldn't get out of this now. "Er, just about. I need to make one more phone call."

The late-morning edition of the daily paper tied Ken Whalen to Gordon de Porres' death, hinting that they had argued over a local real-estate deal. But nothing tracing their relationship back to any coke deals.

Then I thought over what I'd overheard at the hospital. Mickey said Gina had talked to Whalen on his deathbed. Maybe he'd told her about it and she'd be willing to confirm. Did lawyer-client privilege extend beyond the grave?

She picked up on the first ring. "I've been expecting your call."

"Well, sure you have. But I hope you meant that in a good way."

"Depends on why you're calling. Was that Jesse with you on the dock Tuesday night? You make a nice couple, even squinting in the glare of a Coast Guard searchlight."

"Okay, so now I know you watch Channel 7. Then maybe you can fill me in on more recent developments. I see that Joel is off the hook, but the cops are putting the late Ken Whalen's name down for Gordon's murder. But I don't get it. What reason would he have?" You can get more information from people by playing dumb. At least, I hoped so. "They're saying that Gordon was pressuring Ken to drop the idea of having the town bid for the site of the old auto-parts plant to build a high school."

"'They' who?"

"They who know. I have my sources."

Gina snorted. "Better get yourself some new ones then."

"He wasn't being pressured?"

"Not lately." She hesitated. "Funny, I forgot—well, not funny, considering what happened later—but that nonsense over the land all started the night Emma was murdered."

"New Year's?"

"Yes. We talked about it over dinner. Ken told us the site clean-up had finally been approved by the state and the owner was willing to sell. He had asked Joel to come up with a design for a high school and do a feasibility study for him, what it would cost to put the school there, to present it to the borough council."

"So Gordon knew that Ken was looking into this and that Joel was helping?"

"No, I didn't think so. He seemed surprised and asked all kinds of questions about the property."

"So later he went behind Ken's back, to try to get the land for Hartt Development?"

"No. Joel was content with the projects they had going; he didn't want to overdevelop. Gordon wanted it for himself." Gina sounded embarrassed. "He told me he wanted to create a whole complex, with apartments, shops, health club, day-care center, a marina. He approached the seller himself, and the seller told Ken. Ken went nuts, but Gordon offered Ken a different property in town if he would pull out."

"And Ken wouldn't go for that?"

"The other acreage wasn't on the river. Ken wanted to set up a sailing program for the kids. Gordon tried to convince Ken he was doing everybody a favor, that his project would bring in more tax revenue that would benefit more kids in the long run. But I could see he was just looking to be a bigger player in the eyes of his big-shot friends in the city. That's when I broke it off with Gordon. It's one thing to be ambitious, but this was a stab in the back to Ken and to Joel."

"Did Joel find out?"

"Ken told him. Joel was pissed at Gordon himself, but tried to calm Ken down, said he'd do what he could to talk Gordon out of it. But Ken didn't trust either one of them at that point. He thought Joel had shown Gordon the feasibility study."

"Was Ken mad enough to kill Gordon?"

"Back then maybe, but not now."

"Why not now?"

"Ken already bought the land himself. He was going to make it a gift to the town. He'd worked a deal with the seller, who was an old friend of his. I handled the paperwork."

I thought, *Was this Ken's way of redeeming himself?* But I said, "Where would Ken get that kind of money?"

"I guess he had his sources too. But I know he also sold the sailboat. He was taking it out for the last time when he had his heart attack."

Ironic. Or just tragic. "When did he close on the land?"

"Two weeks ago. Gordon found out last Thursday, the day he died. He came to me, believe it or not, to see if he could file some kind of conflict of interest suit. I couldn't see anything illegal about the transaction, not that I would have taken his case if I could."

"But now it looks like Gordon hadn't given up yet."

"I don't see what he could have done about it at this point. That's why this whole confession sounds fishy. I think Mickey is just pinning it on a dead man. Makes it easier for him."

"What if Gordon had something else on Ken?" I was leading the witness.

"These guys always have something on each other. It's how they do business. But I can't see Ken giving in to blackmail. As a threat to his political career? He would have been out of the game soon. He wasn't planning on running for re-election next year."

I was through being subtle. "You haven't heard anything

related to that old drug case, the one that sent Ray Dougherty to prison all those years ago?"

"What are you talking about?" Gina sounded genuinely puzzled.

"I heard that Ken might have had something to do with that cocaine disappearing. Ken was Ray's lawyer and —"

"Like I said, you need a better class of sources." She was angry now. "Listen, I don't care what anyone says about Ken. He was a good guy. He helped me when I was starting my practice. He wanted the best for this town and he was still trying to get it. If he did kill Gordon..." Even she couldn't go as far as saying "he must have had a good reason."

"Okay, okay." I knew better than to get into a fight with Gina. "At least, you must be relieved that they've dropped all charges against Joel."

"Nothing's official yet, though Joel has been out on bail since yesterday afternoon. But you've got to be kidding if you think there's joy here in Mudville." Gina sighed deeply. "You know, Joel went straight from jail to the hospital to help Kathleen? He's trying to get the county to release Ken's body, so he can start making the funeral arrangements. In the last two years this guy has lost his wife, his daughter, his partner and now his brother-in-law. I don't know how he hasn't lost his mind."

I didn't either. "How are you holding up?"

"I'm thinking of going into another line of work. Maybe air-conditioning and refrigerator repair. I see the ads for the Apex School on TV all the time. Looks like a good field, steady work."

"At least you haven't lost your sense of humor." I heard another voice in the background, then a baby's laugh. "How's Artemis?"

"She said a new word the other day."

"What was it?"

"'Guilty.'"

My CONVERSATION WITH Gina left me unsettled. What she'd said seemed to confirm that it was more than a property dispute between Ken and Gordon. If Gordon had been threatening to expose Ken's involvement with the cocaine switch in order to get the land, it hadn't worked. Ken had bought the land himself. He obviously hadn't cared what the consequences might be.

So did the drug deal still figure in? I couldn't be sure now. But if I didn't break the story, someone else would.

Ken would be the bad guy, no matter what. But Gordon's greed and self-interest had played a big part. I wondered if he had his contacts approach Ken with the idea of the cocaine switch just to have some leverage with him if he ever needed it down the road. That didn't seem so farfetched. He was someone who planned in advance, someone who would go to any lengths...

My thoughts started racing. Would Gordon be willing to sacrifice his goddaughter for his dreams of glory? If Joel had been arrested for her murder, Gordon would have had complete control of the development company and could have done whatever he wanted. Gordon had tucked Emma into bed on New Year's. Was *he* the last one to see her alive?

Maybe Emma was already dead before Evan tried switching the scarf. Maybe Doreen just assumed...

Whoa! That was a plot worthy of a dimestore potboiler, if there were still any dimestores left.

In other words, worthy of the *Moon*.

Now I was scaring myself. If I could spin the story that way, Evan and Joel could rest in peace. Gordon wasn't around to deny it. Even if no one could prove it, if it was in the *Moon*, some people might believe it. Hell, most people would. The trick was to always end the headline in a question mark: *Mogul Murdered Moppet Model?*

Even those who said they didn't believe it would always wonder if it were true. That's the effect of publications like the *Moon*. So why not use this power for good instead of evil? And if that job upstate came through, this could be my last act for the tabloid and for myself. My own bid for redemption.

Would Joel go along with it? He'd already done so much to protect Evan, why not this? I dialed. Eight rings later I was about to hang up, when, "Hello, this is Evan Hartt. Who is this, please?" Joel had brought the boy up well.

"This is Andrealisa Rinaldi, Evan. Is your Dad home?"

"Hi, Andie! No, not yet. He had to go do something for Aunt Katie. My Uncle Ken died, you know. Are you going to come over and bring Ben? You promised I could take his picture."

I guess dogs make a lot more sense to kids than death.

As if he'd heard his name, Ben nuzzled up from the bag at my feet and *yurped*, then yawned. I scratched behind his ear-flaps. "Sure, I could do that. I'll bring him right now." My innocent four-legged excuse for trespassing.

I WAS ABOUT to turn up my old street when I saw a TV station camera van parked at the bottom of the hill. Oh, jeez. Probably waiting to ambush Joel, to get a reaction to the news about his brother-in-law. Other reporters might already be camped out on his doorstep.

I kept driving and made a U turn a few blocks away. I pulled over in front of The Rock Bottom. I didn't see Mickey's car, though it might have sustained too much damage from the fire fallout to be drivable. Not that I expected him to be there at eleven in the morning.

But The Confectionery was open. I counted out the remainder of Cat's change—just enough for a Nestlé's Crunch, the breakfast of champions.

I savored it as I made my way along the dirt path, dropping the crumpled wrapper into my bag rather than add it to the litter collection I was passing.

"Hey, wait up, Miss Carleton!" It was Beth, Jesse's niece, trotting behind me. She had something large and rectangular bundled in brown paper, clutched to her chest.

"Hi, Beth." I felt the need to confess. "Actually, it's not Carleton. Or Amy, for that matter. My name isn't, I mean." I was blathering, embarrassed to have lied to an adolescent, fer gods-sake. "It's Andrealisa Rinaldi. Really."

She giggled. "I know. Uncle Jess told me. *You Can't Go Home Again*, right?"

"Exactly." And in more ways than one. "Heading to Evan's?"

"Uh-huh. He said you were going to bring your dog over. Where is he?"

I opened my bag and pointed to Ben, who was gnawing at the candy wrapper. I pulled the foil-and-paper wad out of his mouth and stuck it in my back pants pocket.

"Wow! He's so tiny! What kind is he?"

"One of a kind, I guess. Part mutt, part Muppet."

"I'd love a dog like that."

"If I ever find another one, I'll let you know."

The path turned down, leading us past the cliff face and to the Hartt wildflower garden. I followed Beth up the stone stairs, catching a harsh whiff of citronella from the brass tiki torches. Evan must have been watching for Beth, for he came out through the back door from the kitchen almost immediately, carrying his photo albums. I wondered if he ever let them out of his sight. Maybe that was his way of keeping his sister close.

"Hey, Evan, I've got it!" Beth bounded up the last steps.

Evan opened one of the albums and brought out an eight-by-ten. Beth unwrapped her package on the patio table. Wordlessly, the two of them worked the photo into the light wood frame, then held up their handiwork.

"It's a picture of my Uncle Ken from the last time we went sailing," Evan explained.

"His Aunt Katie is really sad and we thought this might cheer her up." Beth tucked a blonde wisp behind her ear. "Evan developed it yesterday, and I found the frame. It used to have a picture of New Kids on the Block in it, but I am *so* over them."

My heart ached at their earnestness. "Yes, I'm sure your Aunt Katie will love it."

Evan pulled a magnifying glass out of his pocket and brought it close to the photo. "I don't know. It's a little blurry. I'm just learning how to make bigger prints."

"No, it's great, Evan. Just like these." She flipped open the fairy-tale album and turned to me. "Aren't these great?"

"Yes, they're wonderful." I thought it was sweet of Beth to try so hard to bolster Evan's confidence. "I liked Cinderella the best."

"This is my favorite." Beth stopped at Sleeping Beauty.

He looked over her shoulder. "I wish I could have gotten a picture with the other scarf, though." He may have been only twelve, but Evan was already as self-critical as any professional.

"It's great, Evan. *You're* great," said Beth firmly.

I could suddenly see her, twenty years from now, the eternal muse, stroking the egos of a succession of tortured artist boyfriends.

Evan wasn't listening. "I was afraid I'd get caught, when I was supposed to be in bed. After I took this picture, Emma made a noise. I thought I heard Dad coming down the hall to check on her, so I hid in the closet."

So much for pinning this on Gordon. Emma was definitely still alive after her godfather had tucked her in for the night, and before Evan tried his scarf trick. Well, who would know the truth and who would care?

"Then I heard Emma calling for Mom. I waited until I heard the door close and tried again, but—"

"I told you, she must have been having a dream about your mother." Beth put her hand on his shoulder. "But it's okay. She's with your mom in Heaven now."

Evan nodded, as if Heaven was somewhere just outside of town. It was good, though, that he had been able to talk to Beth about that night, that he had someone he *could* talk to.

Evan closed the album gently. When he lifted his head to me, his face was untroubled. "Where's Ben?"

I scooped the pooch out of my bag and set him on the table.

"Oh, wow!" Evan circled his subject, squinting, as if deciding on camera angles. Ben obliged by offering his profile wherever

Evan went. "My Dad has these books by a guy who takes pictures of his dogs and he dresses them up in people clothes."

"William Wegman?" I asked.

"I guess so. Man Ray and Fay Ray are the dogs."

"That's Wegman."

"Oh, yeah, you showed me once," said Beth. "Ben looks just like Man Ray, only much smaller."

Did I have a toy Weimaraner on my hands? Was there such a thing?

"I just had an idea!" Evan's voice rose, and I heard the crack of impending puberty. "What if I did a whole fairy tale book with Ben? Dressed him up in baby stuff or—"

"Oh, I know! Bo-Peep!" Beth jumped up and down. "I think I might have a doll bonnet, and my brother has a toy lamb from Easter. They're at my Grandma's."

"I'm gonna get my camera." Evan started for the back door.

Beth grabbed his arm. "Evan, I forgot. You left it at my house. I was going to bring it."

"We'll go, and we'll get the other stuff too." Evan looked shyly at me. "Is that okay, if I shoot Ben? Can you stay? Beth's Grandma lives close, and it'll only take a minute."

Caught up in their energy and innocence, I'd almost forgotten why I'd come. Now I felt like a complete idiot. What was I doing here? What did I think I was doing? Would Joel really agree to implicate Gordon in Emma's death? If Joel came back soon, maybe I'd get a two-sentence quote from him about Ken. Maybe Kathleen would be with him and I'd have something to add to the original story. Otherwise, I'd just go with what I had, the hell with trying to play Avenging Angel.

I tapped my watch. "I'll give you an hour, but I'll bring Ben again some other time too. I promise."

"Okay!" The two dashed down the steps and were soon out of sight.

Ben seemed disappointed that he was no longer the center of attention. I set him on the patio and he began exploring, snuffling noisily. Then he lifted his leg against one of the clay pots holding the tiki poles. I pulled him away. That would stain, and I was sure Doreen would trace it to me somehow. I reached into my bag and pulled out the sheaf of papers Cat had risked her job for. At least they might have some use now. I lay the sheets on the ground and plopped Ben on top.

"Okay, fella. Do your business."

Instead, he trotted off his mark and began gnawing a metal table leg.

"No!" I yelled. "You already get enough iron!" I dropped him back in my bag and slung it over the chairback.

As I bent to pick up the papers, a breeze lifted a few out of my reach. I grabbed the batch still on the ground and chased the others. I shuffled the sheets together. Most were from Gordon de Porres' autopsy. A broken neck from a fall, dead before the fire started. Well, that indicated the kill wasn't planned. No assault with a deadly weapon. Whalen could have pled involuntary manslaughter.

One page was Ken's medical stats from his last few hours on earth. Another was a printout of his medical history: appendix removed at age fifteen, mumps at forty-five, his previous heart attack at fifty, when he met Kathleen...

What was this? A sheet headed, "Whalen, Kathleen," with dates and procedures going back several years. Some were fertility treatments. Oh, jeez. In her obsessive-compulsive way, Cat must have printed out anything she found under "Whalen" as well as Gordon's autopsy. Bad enough to invade the privacy of dead men. But if anyone had caught Cat with these papers, not only would she be unemployed, she'd also have been fitted for a stylish orange jumpsuit from the state correctional facility.

Another sheet had drifted onto the table. More of Kathleen's file. I saw the date at the top. Oh, that's nice. A hysterectomy right before Christmas. How jolly. Doreen had said Kathleen had some kind of operation. God, what that whole family has been through this past year.

The page had landed beside Evan's photo of Ken Whalen. I picked the picture up and held it at arm's length. It was an interesting shot. Actually, it would be a great pic to go along with the story for the *Moon*. Whalen's back, in a navy blue windbreaker, was to the camera, though; he probably didn't even know his nephew had taken the picture, snapped as the sailboat skirted the shoreline, near the riverfront. The mast's riggings and boom seemed almost an extension of the lines of the boom cranes and the crosshatch of scaffolding of the construction site on shore. The main sail puffed out above Whalen's thick white hair, which ruffled out from the edge of his captain's hat. Caught in profile, he really looked like an old sea captain, one hand on the helm, the other on the bowl of a pipe stopped midway to his lips.

Whalen's gaze was intense, as if he were seeing a squall at sea ahead. But he was looking left, inland. At the site of the Hartt apartment complex. Before the fire.

Evan had left his magnifying glass on the table. I picked it up to peer at the lefthand corner of the photo. There was the scissor lift, the one I had ridden on with Jesse down to the ground. It had been moved to the river side of the site, its loading platform now level with what was probably the third floor. Two figures were on it, one tall with dark hair, one much shorter. Too short to be Joel Hartt. Obviously not Ken Whalen either.

Stupid, stupid, stupid me. Joel had said Ken promised to take the boy sailing that night, and he had. Ken wouldn't have left Evan on the boat alone while he went off to commit a murder.

"He saw me that night."

At her voice, I jumped and turned almost in one motion. I hadn't heard her come up behind me. I expected her to be upset at finding me here, but she looked like she didn't even see me.

I took a breath to calm my racing heart and stepped backward. "Listen, I'm sorry. I know I shouldn't have come at a time like this, but Evan—"

The way she stood there, hands behind her back, sent a prickle up my neck.

"It's you in that photo, isn't it?" I said. "Evan took it the night Gordon de Porres was killed. You were at the construction site and Ken saw you there with Gordon."

She kept her eyes on me but still unseeing. "That man, he said Ken had set Ray up all those years ago. Ken shouldn't have done that. Ray was his nephew." Her voice was sing-songy, like a child reciting a prayer.

"Ken must have felt guilty about that. He did confess to Gordon's murder to protect you."

"That man, he wanted me to bring Ken a message, to sell that land to him or he would let everyone else know what he knew. He wanted me to take that little car, to remind Ken. I knocked it out of his hand."

"With what? A two-by-four?"

"He told me he saw me that night."

"Huh?" An Etta James song popped into my head. *It Ain't Always What You Do (It's Who You Let See You Do It)*. "You already said Ken saw you."

She seemed confused, and she was confusing me. Maybe she was on something. Her pupils looked huge.

"He saw me in Emma's bedroom. If I didn't convince Ken to sell the land, he would tell what happened."

"Wait—what? Ken saw you in Emma's bedroom?"

"He read your story, what I said about the last time I saw her. 'You are a good Catholic-school girl. I thought good Catholic-school girls never tell lies,' he said. 'And good Catholic-school girls certainly don't break the Sixth Commandment.' You see? He knew."

The Sixth Commandment? Wasn't that "Thou shalt not covet thy neighbor's wife"? I could never remember the order. What did that have to do with this?

"What does that have to do with Emma?"

"I was upset that night. I regretted what I'd done, but it was too late."

"What you did?" I couldn't see where she was going with this.

"He couldn't give me my child. It wasn't my fault, don't you see?" She brought her hands forward then, palms up, in the pleading gesture of the Mary statue in the Holy Mother Church garden. No knife at least.

"Okay, I think I understand." I didn't, but—

"You can't even begin to know!" she shrieked, then lunged toward me.

Oh, God, no. Not again.

She collapsed against me, sobbing. "It was an accident. Can't you see that? I didn't know what I was doing!"

Hadn't I heard that before?

Another weepy scene. I had already been through this once already, with Doreen. I was wearing a silk blouse and now it was going to be tear-stained and—

Instead of wetness, I felt a stinging pain in my left buttock.

"Ow!" I hollered and pushed her away.

She stumbled against the patio table, then rushed toward me again, the needle still in her hand.

Oh, shit. I backed away, realizing that, yet again, I was blocked from the stairs and the house's back door. I had nowhere to go but up, or down, and I hadn't honed my rappelling skills since the last time I was in the same spot.

I sidestepped.

Grabbing her forearm, I twisted it down and cracked it across my knee.

"Fuck," she said.

The syringe clattered to the slate patio and she howled some more, cradling her arm.

Twice in the same century, my *Honey West* move had saved the day.

But not for long. She was now baring her teeth and growling like an enraged animal, and in my fascination with her transformation, I almost forgot she was trying to kill me. Which she still was.

With her one good arm, she pulled a tiki pole out of the nearest clay pot, and flailed. Citronella oil spattered across my shirt-front. Another blouse for the rag bin.

I ducked and ran around the table, hoping she'd follow me far enough to give me a clear shot down the stairs. She swung around wildly, sweeping the photo albums and Ken's picture off the table, and knocking over the metal chair with my shoulder bag draped on the corner.

My purse hit the slate patio. Then my purse started moving.

Ben shot out, squeaking.

"*What the*—!" she yelped as my loyal rat-dog began nipping at her ankles, driving her farther away from me.

I dove for the shoulder bag.

Just then she kicked Ben to the sidelines. That really pissed me off. I came up from my crouch blasting Cat's pepper spray.

"MOTHER OF CHRIST!" Saint Kathleen said before she sailed backward off the cliff edge and landed, groaning, in a bed of black-eyed Susans. Her right leg seemed to be bent in a way that would make it hard for her to kneel in front of the Virgin Mary for quite a while.

Adrenaline was coursing through me. Nauseous and disoriented, I stood panting for a few seconds, then looked around for the syringe. I found it under the table.

It was marked "100 U." But 100 U's of what? Whatever had been in it was gone.

"What did you shoot me up with?" I shouted down at Kathleen.

Her face scrunched in agony, she could only shake her head.

I grabbed Ben, who, though limping, was still skittering along the edge of the patio making his rubber-ducky noises at Kathleen. He was in the bag and I was down the steps in four jumps, trampling through the wildflowers to get to Kathleen. She cried out in pain as I frisked her, but I could care less. In the pocket of her slacks I found the glass vial, with its metal-and-rubber cap. It was labeled in red "Humulin."

I sat back on my heels, sweating and trembling. "Human insulin, right?"

Her words came out in gasps. "It's all your fault. You wrote that the last time I'd seen Emma was when she'd said goodnight in the living room. But Gordon had tucked Emma in. Then he snuck into Joel's study, looking for the plans for the high school. When he came past, he saw me in Emma's room."

"But why would that matter? Unless you..." My eyes could barely focus on her face.

Kathleen was back to the sing-song voice. "I wasn't feeling well. It was like ants were crawling over my skin. I had to go to the bathroom. I walked by her room. She shouldn't wear a scarf to bed. Joel should have been more careful. It could twist in her sleep and.... I had to get it off. I had to take the scarf off. I pulled but it was wrapped around tight. Then she said, 'Mom?' She was half-awake. She was lovely. She could have been my daughter. Everyone thought she looked like me. She said it again. 'Mom?' I don't know how it happened. I had both ends of the scarf...I wasn't feeling well. I thought she'd just gone back to sleep. She was so still. I don't know what happened."

What happened was realizing that no one would ever call you Mom. Maybe Kathleen could get a good defense attorney, blame her hormones, blame the Virgin Mary. But she wasn't going to get off for Gordon. "And Gordon threatened to tell Ken?"

She seemed puzzled. "No, Gordon would tell *you*, then you would write about it and Joel would know, everyone would know. Ken already knew. He still loved me. He knew it was an accident. I told him everything."

More family secrets. They had all protected each other or thought they had. From what? They were already in a living hell.

"But Ken didn't tell *you* everything," I said. "Not about the cocaine deal."

"He told me after he saw me with Gordon. Ken blamed himself for what happened that night. Gordon was threatening me. I hit him. He fell. I didn't mean to kill him."

Another accident. *Right.* I felt a wave of dizziness, as another thought crossed my mind. "You knew Joel thought Evan had killed Emma, didn't you? And you let him keep believing it."

Kathleen looked away. "Evan wasn't his real child."

Whatever sympathy I might have had for her was gone. As I rose shakily to my feet, Kathleen grabbed my wrist. I thought I'd have to jujitsu her other arm, but then she let go.

"God forgive me," she said.

I knew what Mickey would say to that. "You should be more worried about a jury of your peers."

Only a few minutes had passed, but I had already wasted too much time. What did I know about insulin? It's a hormone. It helps cells get energy from glucose, the breakdown of carbohydrates in the body. Sometimes the pancreas doesn't produce enough of its own insulin or cells can't use what's available. Too much glucose, too little insulin leads to diabetes. Uncontrolled diabetes leads to all kinds of problems, including death.

But too much hormone, too little glucose? I wasn't exactly sure what happened when 100 units of insulin were pumped into someone who didn't need it, but I knew it couldn't be good.

What were the symptoms of insulin shock? I wracked my barely functioning brain. The same as an adrenaline rush: trembling, sweating, nausea, dizziness... I had all that in spades. But what came next? Delirium, unconsciousness, coma. How quickly would that happen? Ten minutes? Five?

Now I was afraid to run, afraid that I would only speed the drug into my system. But I kept moving toward the only antidote I knew.

At the bottom of the lane, I passed the TV news van. I stumbled through The Confectionery door, trying to focus on the checkered paper cap that was dancing before my eyes.

Before R.J. could ask, "Can I help you?" I had helped myself, sliding across the glass case to grab a handful of Pixie Stix, ripping the ends off the paper straws and pouring the colorful sugar granules straight down my throat. Glucose in its purest, tastiest form. Ben jumped out of my bag and hopped around, hoping I'd spill some on the floor.

Mickey told me later that, just before I passed out, I had the biggest smile on my face.

• *Chapter 16* •

Wɪᴛʜɪɴ ᴍᴏᴍᴇɴᴛꜱ ᴏꜰ my sugar fix that July day, Joel had come home to find Kathleen crawling along the front walk toward her car, energetically taking The Lord's name in vain. I guess once you've broken the Sixth Commandment—"Thou shalt not kill"—it's easy to toss the Third right out the window. Maybe Kathleen had been planning to work her way through all Ten.

She uttered a few more choice words after Joel had called for an ambulance. Almost immediately one pulled up—with me already in it, and a police car close behind. Even with a fractured wrist and broken leg, Kathleen expressed her displeasure so forcefully that the EMTs radioed for separate transport to the hospital. I was just glad Evan and Beth didn't show up until after they had taken her away. I would hate to have their youthful minds corrupted by such bad language.

I had come around by then and I was equally expressive in my desire to avoid Kathleen as a traveling companion.

Unlike her, I walked out of Saint Mary's hours later with a clean bill of health, a plastic I.D. bracelet and a raging headache.

Mickey was waiting for me, and Ben was with him, snuffling the Elvis-mobile's new tires.

"I'm releasing Ben back into your custody," Mickey said. "But he's an eyewitness to an attempted murder, so he'd better not leave the country before he testifies."

"I'll cancel his vacation to the Canary Islands." I watched Ben squat. "What the heck did you feed him? I've never seen anything like that come out of him before."

"He had the same lunch I had. The Belly's Number 2 sub."

"This makes sense then."

"I thought you two would need a lift back to your car." Mickey opened the passenger door.

Ben jumped into the back. I suggested that Mickey put the convertible top up, so Ben wouldn't blow away, then I slid onto the front seat. The red leather had been cleaned of ash and felt like silk.

"Is this part of your official duties?" I asked once Mickey got the engine purring.

"I'm off the clock now."

"I'm not. I have a big story that goes to bed" — I checked my right wrist — "in no less than four hours." I had dictated my new version of events to Dovie from my hospital room, and I wanted to proofread it before it went to press that night.

"Plenty of time for dinner then. I might even give you a few more good, *exclusive* quotes, if I get enough red meat in me."

I hesitated for all of three seconds. My head was still pounding, probably from low blood sugar. "A girl can't live by Pixy Stix alone," I said.

On the drive, Mickey filled me in on what had happened after he questioned me at St. Mary's. He had gone back to Joel's and, with his permission, confiscated the photo that showed Kathleen with Gordon at the construction site. That and Evan's alibi would clear Ken. The trick would be to find enough circumstantial evidence to charge Kathleen with Gordon's murder.

"And what about Emma's?"

Mickey maneuvered the Caddie to the curb. "That's more of a problem."

"What do you mean? She told me *she* did it, not Evan. That was her real motive in getting rid of Gordon."

He turned off the engine. "We have to talk about that."

"What is there to talk about?"

"Let's eat first."

"But—"

"Eat."

We left Ben napping on the rear-window ledge, like a collapsed bobble-head Chihuahua.

I trailed Mickey through The Rock Bottom's swinging doors and into a wall of people.

"Why is it so busy on a Thursday?" I asked him.

"Karaoke night. A big draw. Everybody and their poodle think they're Madonna or Elvis."

Over the usual bar din, someone was groaning "I Will Survive" as if maybe she wouldn't. I strained to look over the heads of the crowd, but all I could see was Georgie's wiry red hair behind the bar.

Mickey pushed his way through, with me in his wake. Finally in a clearing I glimpsed Grace Kelly, in a skintight shimmery number, following along as the words of the Gloria Gaynor anthem crawled across a TV screen set in front of a small stage. Actually, she wasn't bad. But she shouldn't quit her day job.

Mickey called out to Georgie. When Georgie turned, I saw his nose was in a padded sling that cupped his nostrils, held on by an elastic strap over each ear. Mickey soon had a beer bottle and a club soda in his hands, then chucked his head at me to follow him through to the restaurant.

As I passed Georgie, I gestured at his nose. "Does that help with your sniffles?"

"Nah, it's fixed! I just had the operation!" he shouted above Grace's moaned *Oh, as long as I know how to love I know I'll stay alive.* "But it takes a few days for everything to drain out. Then I'll be free and clear."

I smiled my congratulations.

We were ushered to the only free table in the restaurant. "I guess you have a standing reservation, huh?" I said over my menu.

"Rank has its privileges."

"Must be nice." We gave our orders to the waiter, who saluted Mickey and left. "Do you make them all do that?"

"They *want* to."

I looked around at the happy diners. "A thriving business you have here, plus The Rock Bottom. I thought cops weren't allowed to own bars."

"Who said it's in my name?"

I shook my head. "Still changing the rules to suit yourself. No wonder Doreen thought you bought this place with the cocaine from Ray's arrest."

"Where'd she come up with that?"

"Where'd you come up with the down payment?"

He grinned. "Cards."

"Credit cards?"

"A poker deck. I've been playing high stakes since eighth grade. The one thing my father taught me right. I invested the proceeds and put myself through college on a 'Hoyle's scholarship.' Eventually, I had enough to put down for this place and The Rock."

"Wait. I saw you play cards with Georgie's daughter Megan. I wouldn't have thought you could win enough to buy a half-price beer."

"Gin rummy? You've got to be kidding." He huffed. "Gin is luck. Poker takes skill. So does the stock market. I have quite a few talents you don't know about."

"Juliet told me some of them." I had finished my salad and reached for my club soda. "Maybe the second ex-Mrs. Giamonte can fill me in on the rest."

"I'm sure she'd be happy to. We seem to have settled our differences."

"You're getting back together? That's really great." I was surprised that I didn't mean it.

"No. We've reached a settlement. As soon as she finds a new place, I get the condo back. Of course, she still gets the bird and everything else."

"Sounds amicable."

"Very." He eyed me over a swig from his beer bottle. "And how is it between you and the potential future ex-Mr. Rinaldi?"

"We have to talk, he says."

"Ow. Nothing good ever comes of that."

"My thought exactly."

Mickey sighed. "Love's like being lost in a coal mine—you're always feeling your way around in the dark before the roof caves in. What is it you women want?"

"For now, food. What is it you men want?"

"A good woman, a better car and absolute power. Not necessarily in that order."

"Ambitious."

"I told you I was." He waved a hand. "I hear there's a job opening for mayor. I might have a shot. My stock is pretty high right now."

"Thanks to me."

"Yeah, thanks." Plates were placed before us. "Dinner's on me."

"Good. Because all I have is the six cents left in the bottom of Cat's handbag."

I suddenly realized that I hadn't had a real meal since Tuesday night with Jesse at The Barge. I dived into tonight's special, zuppa de pesce.

"Wow," Mickey said admiringly. "I've seen hyenas take more time with a zebra carcass."

I mopped up the last of the red sauce with a hunk of semolina bread. "Okay, I've eaten." And my headache was gone.

"Now I want to hear what Kathleen had to say about Emma."

"Nothing."

"What!"

"She won't admit to killing her."

"She admitted it to *me*, isn't that enough?"

"We have nothing else to go on. She claims that after her husband died yesterday, her doctor put her on some anti-anxiety drug that she had a bad reaction to. She didn't know what she was saying, didn't know what she was doing. So she admits nothing. And maybe she shouldn't."

"Now you've lost me."

He explained it to me.

"Did you tell Joel about all this?" I asked when he was done.

"No. She confessed to you, not to me. I'll leave it up to you to explain it to Hartt. Let me know how he takes it."

"Thanks. You're a pal. And please note that I'm being sarcastic." I got to my feet. "One more thing. How did you steal that swing set from the Lincoln Elementary playground? You never did tell me."

Mickey stood up, put a generous tip on the table and said, "One piece at a time."

THE NEXT DAY, my story of Kenneth Whalen's last hours and Kathleen McCarrick Whalen's arrest hit the street. No paper but the *Moon* had all the details, since no reporter but me could give an eyewitness account—or get County Chief of Detectives Michelangelo Giamonte to confirm how a thirteen-year-old drug case tied it all together. At least Ray Dougherty was now cleared of masterminding the scheme.

Before driving down the shore that Friday night to check on Cat, I made a detour to talk to Joel. As he sat motionless in his darkening study, I explained to him what Mickey explained to me. That even though Kathleen had confessed to me that she had killed Emma, now that she was in custody, she denied it. That with the death of the only witness and the absence of other proof, it was doubtful she could be charged and convicted. That Joel himself, as well as Doreen, was guilty of compromising a crime scene at the very least. That trying Kathleen for Emma's murder would bring up too many issues that could affect Evan. That Kathleen was already assured a life-long prison term, with one murder and another attempt to her credit.

"You could file a civil suit, but I've already talked to Gina," I finished. "She agrees with Mickey that you'd only hurt yourself and others by pursuing it."

Joel was quiet for so long I thought he'd left the room. Finally, he said, "I'll have to talk to Gina."

"Really, she doesn't think—"

"Kathleen will need a good attorney."

My jaw hit my chest. "You can't be serious. You want Gina to defend her? Why?"

"Kathleen is family."

"Family?"

"Kate said what happened to Emma was an accident, didn't she? Kate wouldn't have done that if she had been in her right mind. She was always good to the kids. And she was devoted to Kristine. She was with Kris night and day before she died."

"Joel, she also tried to kill *me*."

"She'd just lost Ken. She was hysterical. Her doctor had given her tranquilizers."

"She didn't seem too tranquil to me."

"She had a bad reaction to the medication. She wasn't rational."

"*I'll* say."

"Andie, she wasn't herself. I know her. You know her."

Did I? Did anyone? At twelve, Kathleen thought she had a direct line to the Virgin Mary, so her grip on reality hadn't been too firm even back then. A few disappointments—a father who died, a stepfather who abandoned her, a sister who had the baby that should have been hers, a husband who wasn't what he seemed—for a "good girl" like Kathleen, finally realizing that life hadn't given her what she thought she deserved could have pushed her over the edge. Maybe I would have reacted the same way. But probably not.

"I don't get it," I said at last. "How can you want to help her, after all the grief she's caused you?"

"Because I'm tired of the grief. If I can forgive her, I can forgive myself."

"For what?" I couldn't believe what I was hearing.

"For thinking what I did about Evan. And other things."

This whole town was crazy. Or worse. "Are you sure you're not Catholic?" I said.

THE WEEKS AFTER Kathleen's arraignment were a haze. Somewhere in there, my faithful intern Dovie returned to Tennessee and her final year of college. I promised her a glowing recommendation; she promised to send me a box of GooGoo Clusters, a marshmallow-and-chocolate concoction tough to find above the Mason-Dixon Line. I was getting the better deal.

The *Moon* still expected me to churn out breathless accounts of the investigation unfolding across the river, and I did. It was getting easier, especially with my "exclusive" information, which eventually linked Gordon de Porres to several other past and not-so-past drug deals, involving blackmail, two high-profile politicians and one high-living film director.

Then it became easier to suggest that the "victim" may have been involved in the murder of a ten-year-old fashion model on New Year's, in order to take control of his partner's business. It didn't hurt that the good-looking blond police detective on that unsolved case didn't deny the possibility.

Yep, repeat it enough, and rumor soon becomes fact. Those who knew the real story had to live with the consequences. Why should it matter to anyone else?

At the beginning of August, when the mental-health board reviewed the complaints against her, Cat got a thirty-day suspension from her job. She was back on her old medication, and they wanted her to stay at the county facility for observation, but I knew that would only make her worse. With Ariel's help, I wrangled permission to take Cat home, promising to be around to bring her in for any follow-up evaluations. So for now I was making the three-hour weekday commute and spending nights in my old bedroom. Ben was overjoyed to hang out with Cat all day, and Betty Martell kept an eye on both of them when I wasn't around.

One night after deadline, I stopped by my apartment to check my mail and pick up a few things. I saw a familiar figure on my stoop, a cardboard box nearby.

I reached in, grabbed a pizza wedge and sat on the step below.

"Sorry. I got hungry waiting for you," Jesse said, as if he meant something other than pizza. He handed me a napkin and a Yoo-hoo from the paper bag at his feet.

"No apologies necessary." Damn. My fingertips were now tingling. How did he *do* that? "This is a nice surprise."

"Is it? I thought maybe you were avoiding me."

"I was."

"Then at least I'm not paranoid."

"I was going to call you but—"

"I know. No apologies necessary."

"Thanks. And thanks." I waved my slice. "You've been busy too. I noticed that The Mews is taking shape again."

"Sign up now. The rentals should be ready by Christmas. I'm pushing the guys to complete on schedule, so there's one less thing Joel has to worry about. Lots of overtime, everybody's happy."

"Including you?"

"Sure, why wouldn't I be? My sister came home from rehab last week, and Beth went back to live with her at my mom's, so I don't have to worry about leaving her alone so much. Funny thing, I miss having her around." He tossed a crust into the empty box. "Though I won't miss her cooking."

"And you have such fine taste in cuisine. Mushrooms, spinach, extra cheese."

"I heard the way to a woman's heart is through her pizza toppings."

"You heard right."

The slow smile. "So, will you let me in?"

Out of the corner of my eye, I saw the brocade curtain of the ground-floor apartment ripple. The window was open slightly, even though I could hear the air-conditioner humming. Mrs. Pemberton must be interested in my answer, too. "I...I have a few loose ends to tie up."

"Right." Jesse dropped the pizza box over the stair rail and into the trashcan. "You do that." He stood, pulled me up and in close. "Remember, sometimes it's better to just cut 'em clean."

LABOR DAY WEEKEND came hot and still. Sitting on the edge of our bulkhead, I trailed my toes through the water as Cat, Sam and Alex competed to see who could execute the goofiest dives.

I had invited Gina back for another visit, many years belatedly. Now she was sprawled in a lounge chair, cradling a napping Artemis and chatting with Peter Martell.

David Martell had been cornered by Marcus and a very pregnant Paula, probably looking for free tax advice. Uncle Lou had staked out the coolest corner on the back porch, and was making his way through the Sunday papers, trading sections with Don Martell. Aunt Angie was in the kitchen arranging the platters of cold cuts, cheeses and salads she just happened to bring along with her.

Today, that was okay. Today, we had something to celebrate. Tuesday Cat was going back to work, though in a different area of the hospital.

Betty plopped down next to me. "So you're staying at the *Moon*. I thought you were going to accept that job at your old newspaper upstate."

"The money wasn't great, what with Cat's new hospital bills."

"What about that fella you have up there? Don't mind being away from him?"

"Doug got an offer at a research center in Seattle. I got an offer to go with him. But I don't want to be so far from Cat right now. She needs some stability."

"As good an excuse as any." Betty squeezed my shoulder. "But you'll run out of excuses sometime."

"Who says?"

THAT NIGHT, AFTER everyone had left, Cat and I sat on the bulkhead, quiet for a while. The moon was reflected in the black lagoon, and Cat was trying to hit it with a smooth stone, from the handful she'd scooped up from the backyard.

Abruptly she said, "I can't believe Kathleen McCarrick is going to get away with that little girl's death."

"No one said life is fair." I took a stone from Cat, threw it and missed the moon by a mile. "But she's being punished in her own way. I just found out something that didn't make sense to me at the time."

"What's that?"

"She said she regretted what she'd done, that 'he couldn't give me my child.'"

"Kathleen said that? That sounds like Doreen. Like she regretted giving up her child for adoption but Joel wouldn't give her Evan back."

"No, it was Kathleen. What she was regretting was the operation, the hysterectomy she'd had just before Christmas, in the hope that it would cure her endometriosis. She'd had a lot of pain for a lot of years."

"Oh, so she was on estrogen-replacement meds, that's her excuse for why she killed Emma?"

"No, she wasn't. Estrogen can trigger the condition all over again. But that meant no hormones in her system at all. She would have had more ups and downs than the Palisades Amusement Park Cyclone."

"I remember when we rode that coaster, you'd keep your eyes closed the whole time." Cat tossed another stone. "You're saying it *wasn't* her fault."

"Well, she may not have been in her right mind. She also had just found out that her husband had the mumps at the age of forty-five."

Cat stopped in mid-throw. "Huh?"

"Jesse's niece had been sick that New Year's with the mumps, and they started talking about it. Ken said he'd gotten them as an adult. Kathleen hadn't known until then."

"So?"

"Sometimes, mumps can make a male sterile. Kathleen was a nurse. She knew that."

"Now you've lost me."

"All this time, Kathleen had thought that it was *her* fault she couldn't have children, because of her condition. But it might have been *Ken's* problem."

Cat's eyes widened. "And she'd just had a hysterectomy. It was too late."

I nodded. "That was her regret."

She whistled. "How'd you find this out?"

"From Sister Connie. She's been counseling her. It seems Kathleen felt the need to confess *that* to her, though she still hasn't owned up to everything. She also asked Sister if she could still become a nun, even if she was in prison. "

"And Sister Connie shared this information? So much for nun-client confidentiality."

I laughed. "Actually, she told Gina. I also found out from Gina that Sister Connie had a small stroke last year. Since then, she's lost a few of her, er, inhibitions." Not that it was a bad thing. "I'm going to recruit her for the *Moon* if she ever leaves the Order."

Cat was quiet for a while. She looked tired and I was about to suggest turning in when she said, "Weird that she tried to kill you with insulin."

"Well, she was staying at Joel's while he was arranging Ken's funeral. She had the drug with her and some syringes to bring to Doreen's mother that morning. Then she saw me with Evan through the kitchen window and got a better idea."

"Kristine, Kathleen's sister, died of a diabetic coma."

"How did you know that?" I didn't remember telling her.

"Those medical records I printed out. I got a little carried away and pulled up files on the whole family. Didn't you read them?"

"No, I was a little busy that day."

"She had severe gestational diabetes. She was in the hospital to bring it under control."

"Kathleen was her nurse."

Cat nodded. "I saw that on the report. Maybe she'd had some practice giving overdoses."

I looked at Cat.

"Why not? They were only *half*-sisters, after all." My sister smiled. "Don't worry." Cat dropped the rest of the stones from her hand into the water. "You're safe with me."

As the prospect of a trial grew nearer, the media circus expanded to a Barnum & Bailey three-ringer. At the order of the presiding judge, those covering it had to hold a lottery to see who would be the pool reporter. But when my old stakeout pal Feeno Heath growled, "If Andrealisa Rinaldi doesn't get inside, you grunts'll have to answer to me," no one had the guts to challenge an Aussie.

Of course, I had some doubts about the ethics of taking notes on the proceedings while testifying in my own attempted-murder case. But it never came to that.

The case didn't go to trial. Behind closed doors, Gina had somehow convinced the county prosecutor's office that the syringe-wielding psycho who had attacked me had meant no harm. With her medications as a mitigating factor, the charge of attempted murder facing Kathleen was bumped down to aggravated assault. Considering Gordon de Porres' now widely published criminal history, the court also had no trouble accepting her guilty plea for involuntary manslaughter.

On the day of Kathleen's sentencing, I met Juliet for breakfast. Afterward, we went to a pet shop to pick out a new bird for Mickey. Back at her boutique, I lined the bottom of the cage with the latest front page of the *Moon*. I left it all with Mickey's grandmother and added a note: "To hell with the second ex-Mrs. Giamonte. Next time, remember: When this canary stops singing, get out of the coal mine."

At the county courthouse, I saw Joel outside, talking to Gina. A well-dressed young Asian woman stood beside him, her hand protectively on his arm. Kaori Masako? I hoped she was as nice as she looked. Joel needed someone nice.

Then I heard the results of the plea bargain. Kathleen would spend the next fifteen years in prison. Maybe with time off for good behavior.

Man, that Gina was good.

A MONTH LATER Joel asked me to stop by his house after work.

I almost didn't recognize the woman who opened the door. It was Doreen. *Smiling.*

"Andie!" She lunged, and I nearly went into my jujitsu mode again, until I realized she just wanted to hug me. "It's so good to see you!"

"It is?"

"I'm so glad to have a chance to thank you!"

"You are?"

"Joel told me it wasn't Evan who...hurt Emma. It was eating me up, believing he'd done such a thing. I blamed myself for bringing him into the world with such lousy genes. But it's okay. He's fine. He's a good boy, and Joel is a wonderful father. I don't need to keep an eye on him anymore. Now I can go."

"Go?"

"Since Ray's record has been cleared, Joel was able to get him a job with a construction company in Florida. Big building boom down there. The warm weather will be good for Ma's arthritis. Amanda will be away from that crowd she's been running with. Plus the houses are cheaper down there. We'll need a bigger place, now that I'm going to have another baby."

"Baby?"

"Yes, isn't that fantastic?"

It was.

Doreen continued chattering as she led me to Joel's study. Then she gave me another hug and left me at the door.

Joel sat on his leather couch, staring straight ahead at Kristine's portrait, only the light under the painting illuminating the room. He sensed rather saw me.

"I'm sorry about your father," he said.

The reference was so unexpected that I gave him my knee-jerk response, the one I had perfected at fourteen and Evan had learned at twelve. "Not your fault."

Joel laughed hollowly. "In a way, it is."

"You'll have to explain that one to me."

"Prepare yourself. This might take a while."

I didn't move.

"The divorce—my parents'—it was not nice," he began. "Mama wanted to stick Dad where it hurt, and he wanted to be sure she didn't get a dime of the business. So long before the final split, he started siphoning money into an offshore account. But of course, your father noticed, though I don't think he found out the extent of it. He was good man, your dad. I used to wish.... You and Cat always seemed to have so much fun with him." Joel took another deep drink. "Now my father, he wasn't such a good guy. He turned around and accused your dad of skimming. Fired him, of course, to make it look good and not give him a chance to dig around. That's why you moved, did you know that?"

Of course not. Dad had made it seem like we were just off on another of his adventures. We were going to live by the beach all year round. Lucky us.

"Mama found out later about what my father'd done. When

she got sick for the last time, she told me about the rest, about your dad. She felt guilty, I guess. I couldn't...*didn't want to* believe it. I thought she was just trying to turn me against my father, her final act of revenge. It wasn't until my dad died that I found some papers that made me put it all together. Then knowing your dad had so much trouble finding work after my father bad-mouthed him and... Well, everyone in the neighborhood heard what happened after that. People can't help talking."

No, they couldn't help it. Especially not about what happened a year and 171 days after we'd moved. After Aunt Angela claimed she missed her sister who now lived so far away, insisted that we visit for a few days during Christmas break. After Dad said he had a job interview, and stayed home. After Uncle Lou drove us back the day before New Year's and Cat jumped out before the car had even stopped. After Cat saw him first, found Dad in the closed garage, the Barracuda's engine still running.

That is what I had been afraid of, coming back to my hometown. That everybody knew, that I'd have to deal with their questions, their pity. And that they'd ask about Cat too, then more questions, more pity. Caught between a rock and a hard place.

"I am sorry about your father," Joel said again.

It took me a long time to answer him. "Why are you telling me this now?"

"When you showed up here after all those years, I thought maybe I had a chance to make it up to you.... If I helped you, we'd be even. But now I know we'll never be even." Joel faced me, eyes wet. "And maybe you could forgive me."

"Nothing to forgive." I was quicker to answer this time. "Joel, it was *not* your fault."

He started to speak, but hugged me instead. The smell of his skin, of his hair was so familiar to me, as if he had been my own brother, my own child.

After a while, he said, "Before Kristine, you were my only friend. I never forgot you. My daughter's middle name was Andrea. Did I ever tell you that?"

I shook my head.

"I wish you could have met Emma. You'd have liked her. She was a lot less whiney than me." He actually laughed and I glimpsed a Joel I'd never known, someone who might have been happy once and might be happy again. "You saved my life once. Now you've saved it again by giving my son's innocence back to me." His lips brushed my cheek. "I wish I could give you back what *you* lost."

What else could I say? "I wish you could, too."

Is ELECTION DAY an official post office holiday? I checked the mailbox automatically, not expecting anything, but came away with three envelopes. One bore the building management logo and I nearly ripped it up as usual, but caught myself. No point in that now.

The elevator was out again. Seven flights to my apartment, where I batted Ben around for a while, then took my Chinese takeout container over to the TV to watch the election coverage.

Amazing. It looked like we were going to get our first Baby Boomer President. I suddenly felt excited. *Please, Bill, don't embarrass us,* I prayed.

Then "Don't Stop Thinking About Tomorrow" started blasting from the TV speakers and I lost hope. How could you build a bridge to the twenty-first century with Fleetwood Mac?

I switched off the TV and slid a CD into the stereo. While Billie Holiday sang "I Cover the Waterfront," I slit open a square envelope and pulled out a calligraphed card, heavy stock, with a pink fabric baby bootie on the cover.

"Alexis and Samantha Webster joyfully welcomed the arrival of their new sister, Nicole, on November 1, 1992, at 6:36 p.m." Wow. My cousin Paula must have written out the announcements while still in labor.

The next envelope held less of a surprise:

"Dear Tenant: In accordance with the recent notice sent of the sale of properties at this address, and your decline of the purchase option for the premises described in your rental agreement, this apartment must be vacated on or before December 31, 1992."

I picked up the third envelope. No return address. A smudged postmark. Inside, a full-color brochure for "Riverside Mews: Another Project of The Hartt Development Group."

I looked at the envelope again. My address was handwritten in the block capitals that would have made the nuns of Holy Moly proud.

In the margin of the brochure, in the same penmanship: To HELL WITH TOM WOLFE. YOU CAN GO HOME AGAIN.

C. SOLIMINI

• *Acknowledgements* •

Let's get this straight: Many people—especially those mentioned below in more or less alphabetical order—encouraged, educated and/or edited the author throughout a process that was sparked by a dream and begun the day before a nightmare. However, any errors, exaggerations and/or excesses are purely the failings of the author. *Mea culpa, mea culpa, mea maxima culpa.*

Maximum gratitude goes to:

• Debby Buchanan of Deadly Ink Press, for giving me the best news on one of the worst days of my life; and Chris Lupetti for the glorious jacket photo of the George Washington Bridge;

• Byron of Abednego Book Shoppe in Ventura, California, for *not* giving my copy of *The World Almanac & Book of Facts, 1994,* to David Letterman by mistake;

• Susan Druding, tie-dye and textiles queen, and founder of Straw Into Gold/Crystal Palace Yarns (www.straw.com), Richmond, California;

• Jean Linardi Kolder, for serendipitously re-entering my life, sharing her family and memories, and confirming that, even at age 5, I had excellent taste in best friends;

• Linda Konner, my agent and Godmother, who may someday get a return on her investment, and our fellow 15th Street Card Sharks—Laura Langlie, Failey Patrick, Lloyd Schwartz and Allen

Sheinman—for investing their spare change;
- my medical team: Barron H. Lerner, M.D., of the Columbia University College of Physicians & Surgeons, and author of *The Breast Cancer Wars* (Oxford University Press); Doug P. Lyle, M.D., author of books fiction and non-fiction including his latest *Forensics: A Guide For Writers* (Writers Digest Books), who always makes a house call for his fellow members of Mystery Writers of America; and Elliot J. Rayfield, M.D., Manhattan endocrinologist, professor at Mount Sinai School of Medicine and my co-author on *Diabetes: Beating the Odds* (Da Capo);
- legal eagles Thomas J. Pisarri, William F. McEnroe and Frank Careri, Jr., of Pisarri, McEnroe & Careri, and Richard M. Rosa, now with Hartmann, Doherty, Rosa & Berman, in Hackensack, N.J., for responding to my plea for help within 39 seconds—on surely the most law-abiding day in Bergen County history;
- my favorite Men in Blue: dear cousins Ret. Capt. Joseph P. Muti, a 32-year-veteran, and Firefighter Anthony Muti, a 30-year-old veteran, of the Weehawken (N.J.) Police and Fire Departments; and dear cousin's cousin Detective Ed Ring, dear friends and classmates Officer Tom Smith and Captain Joe Klimaszewski, all of the Edgewater (N.J.) Police Department;
- my darling nieces Rachel and Sarah Prindle, who taught me how unalike twins can be;
- Michele Slung, editor *extraordinaire*, who did her best to rein me in and succeeded more often than not;
- the Solimini, DeLauro, Beck and Farawell families—and all the surnames and bloodlines they encompass;
- Kate Stine of *Mystery Scene*, for her advice, support and excuses to talk to the best writers in the field;
- my former *Mary Higgins Clark Mystery* colleagues Kathy Sagan and Mary Higgins Clark, for the conversation that gave shape to the dream; and almost last but certainly not least,
- the Yale Club Irregulars: Roger "The Train Guy" Grannis; Erica "Queen of the First Chapter" Obey and Su "Where's the Sex?" Robotti, who kept me honest and told me to "go, go, go!," while Elderd and Olga kept the turkey burgers coming.

Nothing, real or imagined, would have been possible without my mother, Jaye, who shared her love of reading and mysteries, and my father, Frank, who introduced us all to a certain New Jersey river town three miles long and three blocks wide.

As always, my final thanks and endless love go to Martin.

• *How Sweet It Is!* •
A Boomer Treats Glossary

Almond Joy: Sometimes you feel like a nut...The classic chocolate-dipped almonds-coconut combo was introduced by Peter Paul, now part of the Hershey Company, in 1946; without nuts, it's just a **Mounds** (1921). *www.hersheys.com*

Bazooka: The Topps Co. brought out this distinctive block of bubble-gum after World War II in Brooklyn, New York. Bazooka Joe and his eyepatch (that's what you get for running with scissors, kid!) first came on the comics scene in 1953. *www.topps.com*

Bit-O-Honey: Almond-studded honey-flavored taffy first appeared in 1924, made by the Schutter-Johnson Company of Chicago. The Nestlé Company now continues production. *www.nestleusa.com*

Bonomo's Turkish Taffy: Victor A. Bonomo created the chewy but brittle candy bar after World War II. You saw it advertised on *Wonderama*. In the Fifties and Sixties, 80 million to 100 million smackable, crackable bars were sold a year. Tootsie Roll Industries stopped making it in 1989. *www.tootsieroll.com*

Candy Buttons: Cumberland Valley first rolled out these candy-studded paper strips in 1930. The New England Confectionery Co. (NECCO) has taken over the job since the Eighties. *www.necco.com*

Candy Necklace (Smarties): From a rented New Jersey garage, the Ce De Candy Company started fashioning bite-off-and-chew bling-bling on a string in 1958. In the 1990s ads, Mr. T pitied the fool who wore gold and not a candy necklace. *www.smarties.com*

Chuckles: The jellies hit the market in 1921, but is now produced by

Farley's & Sathers (which also makes Jujubes and Jujufruit). In 1974 the candy went with motorcycle daredevil Evel Knievel in his unsuccessful jump over the Snake River Canyon. *www.farleysandsathers.com*

Fizzies: In 1957 chemists at Emerson Drug Company (the creators of Bromo-Seltzer) perfected a tablet that, when added to water, would create instant soda pop. After fizzling in the late Nineties, Fizzies just made a comeback, thanks to Amerilab Technologies. *www.fizzies.com*

Good & Plenty: The licorice candy, first produced by the Quaker City Confectionery Company of Philadelphia in 1893, is the oldest branded candy in the U.S. Choo-Choo Charlie chugged along in 1950. Now he's an employee of the Hershey Co. *www.hershey.com*

Hershey's: The Pennsylvania company that gave us milk-chocolate bars (1900) with and without almonds, **Kisses** (1907) and **Kit Kats** (1931), then took over making **Fifth Avenue** (1936), **Jolly Rancher** (1949), **Milk Duds** (1928), **PayDay** (1932), **Reese's Peanut Butter Cups** (1920s) and **Zagnut** (1930) — what's not to love? *www.hersheys.com*

Mars: This thoughtful family spawned a family of Boomer classics like **Milky Way** (1923), **M&M's** (1941), **M&M's Peanut** (1954) and **3 Musketeers** (in 1932 it was vanilla, chocolate and strawberry in one bar, then all chocolate by 1945). And they are also why the air over Hackettstown, N.J., smells so sweet. *www.mars.com*

Mary Janes: Made by Charles N. Miller Co. in the Paul Revere House in Boston in 1914, and named after a favorite aunt, the molasses and peanut butter candy in now another NECCO product. *www.necco.com*

Mike and Ike: Thank Just Born, Inc. , for these chewy sweets, born in 1940. The company also makes cinnamony **Hot Tamales** (1950) and, oh, yes, each year releases over 1.2 billion **Marshmallow Peeps**—enough to circle the Earth twice. *www.justborn.com*

Necco Wafers: The New England Confectionery Company (NEECO), the oldest continuously operating multi-line candy company in the U.S., created the lozenge machine that made these wafers possible. In the 1930s Admiral Byrd took more than two tons of Necco Wafers to the South Pole. They have been used as poker chips, for practice before a First Holy Communion and as bull's-eyes at target ranges. NECCO also is also responsible for **Sweethearts Conversation Hearts** and **Candy Cigarettes.** *www.necco.com*

Nestlé Crunch: Following its Swiss-made chocolate (1875), Nestlé lifted the Depression simply by adding some crispy rice in 1938 to bars at its Fulton, N.Y., plant—and set a record, making a 7,000 pound bar in the Eighties. *www.nestlecrunch.com*

Pixy Stix: Poured out by Sunline in 1952, the sugar-filled straws are now made by Willy Wonka, a division of Nestlé.

SweeTarts: In 1963 J. Fish Smith, the owner of Sunline, invented these tangy tablets in response to parents' requests for a less messy candy than the company's Pixy Stix and **Lik-M-Aid.** Yep, Wonka, a.k.a. Nestlé, has gobbled them up too.

Tootsie Rolls: The chewy chocolate made its debut in 1896. **Tootsie Pops** came along in 1931, triggering expansion to a larger plant in Hoboken, N.J. The company then conquered early children's television, sponsoring *Howdy Doody, Rin Tin Tin* and *Rocky & Bullwinkle*. Through acquisitions, Tootsie Roll Industries now also churns out **Mason Dots, Crows, Charm Pops, Dubble Bubble, Andes Mints, Junior Mints, Sugar Daddy, Sugar Babies** and **Charleston Chews,** as well as more than 60 million Tootsie Rolls and 20 million Tootsie Pops each day. Tootsie also makes Wack-O-Wax **Wax Lips and Fangs,** but discontinued **Nik-L-Nip Wax Bottles** in early 2008. *www.tootsie.com*

Yoo-hoo: This chocolate drink, first produced by the Olivieri family of New Jersey, was endorsed by Yogi Berra and his Yankee teammates of the Fifties and Sixties. Yoo-hoo maintains it corporate headquarters and one plant in Carlstadt, N.J. *www.yoo-hoo.com*

What's your favorite Baby Boomer candy?

Printed in the United States
203915BV00010B/5/P

9 780978 744229